Robbers' Roost

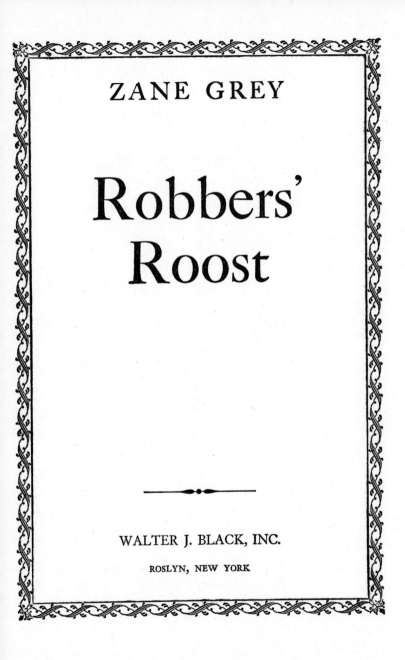

ZANE GREY

Robbers' Roost

WALTER J. BLACK, INC.

ROSLYN, NEW YORK

Robbers' Roost

Chapter One

ONE afternoon in the spring of 1877 a solitary horse-man rode down the long, ghastly desert slant toward the ford at Green River.

He was a young man in years, but he had the hard face and eagle eye of one matured in experience of that wild country. He bestrode a superb bay horse, dusty and travel-worn and a little lame. The rider was no light burden, judging from his height and wide shoulders; moreover, the saddle carried a canteen, a rifle, and a pack. From time to time he looked back over his shoulder at the magnificent, long cliff wall, which resembled a row of colossal books with leaves partly open. It was the steady, watchful gaze of a man who had left events behind him.

At length he rode into a trail and soon came in sight of the wide band of green cottonwood, willow, and arrowweed, and the shining, muddy river, which had evidently broken through the great wall of stone. On the far side, up on the level, stood a green patch and a cluster of houses, strangely lonely in that environment. This was the town of Green River, Utah.

The rider needed to reach that town before dark. His food supply had run out two days ago. But unless there was a boat in which he could row across, he would most likely not make it. His horse was too lame to risk in that heavy, swirling, sand-laden river.

He rode on down the trail to enter the zone of green. In the thick dust he noted fresh horse tracks. Dust rose in clouds from under his animal's hoofs. The arrowweed reached to his saddle and was yellow with it. And when he came to the willows and cottonweeds he found their fresh green similarly powdered. It had not rained for a

1

long time in that section. Yet now the odor of dust appeared to yield to that of fresh, cool water.

Under a cottonwood, some distance ahead, the rider espied a saddled horse, head down, cropping the grass. He proceeded more slowly, his sharp eyes vigilant, and was certain that he saw a man on the river bank before that worthy espied him.

Presently he rode out into an opening from which he could see a place where a ferry touched. A rude cable above his head, attached to a cottonwood, stretched across the river, sagging in the middle. Moored to the opposite bank was the ferryboat.

The rider sat his horse, aware that the man he had observed had stepped behind some willows. Such a move might have been casual. Then the man moved out into plain sight.

"Howdy!" he said, laconically.

"Howdy!" replied the rider. He became aware of a penetrating scrutiny which no doubt resembled his own. Chance meeting at that period was productive of obvious though not offensive curiosity. The rider saw a striking figure of a man, gray with dust, booted and spurred, armed to the teeth. His wide sombrero shadowed a sharp, bold face, the only distinct feature of which was a long, sandy mustache. From the shadow, which resembled a mask, there came a gleam of pale, deep eyes.

"Aimin' to cross?" he queried.

"Yes. I see a ferryboat over there." But on the moment the rider was watching his questioner. Then he swept a long leg over the pommel and slid to the ground, without swerving in the slightest from a direct front. "Lucky for me if I can cross on it. My horse is all in."

"Noticed thet. Fine hoss. Wal, I've been hangin' around for an hour, waitin' to go over. Reckon he'll be along soon."

"Town of Green River, isn't it?"

"That's the handle. You're a stranger hereabouts?"

"I am that."

"Where you hail from?"

"I suppose I might as well say Wyoming as any place," returned the rider, casually.

The other man relaxed with a laugh.

"Shore. One place is good as another. Same as a name. Mine is Hank Hays." He spoke as if he expected it to be recognized, but it caused no reaction in his listener.

"You know this country?" queried the rider, and he too relaxed.

"Tolerable."

"Maybe you can tell me whether I ought to stop or keep on traveling?" inquired the rider, coolly.

"Haw! Haw! I shore can. But thet depends," he said, pushing back his sombrero. The action brought into view a bold visage.

To the rider it was like a printed page, with only the narrow, gray, searching eyes presenting any difficulty.

"Depends on what?" he asked.

"Wal, on you. Have you got any money?"

"About ten dollars."

"Huh! You can't go in the ranch business with thet. Not regular ranchin'. Lots of cattle between here an' the breaks of the Dirty Devil. Henry Mountains, too. Some outfit over there."

"Mormons?"

"About half an' half. This is Utah, but not strong on Mormons over here. Air you a cattleman?"

"No," replied the rider, thoughtfully.

"Wal, thet's straight talk from a stranger," replied Hays, who evidently took the blunt denial as something significant. "Hullo! Another rider. . . . Shore the desert is full of strangers today."

Back up the trail appeared a short, heavy man astride a horse and leading two pack-animals.

"I saw him awhile back. And here comes our ferryman. Looks like a boy."

"Huh! You haven't them eyes for nothin'. Wal, we'll get across now."

The rider, after another glance at the approaching man with the horses, took note of the ferry. The boy had pushed the boat off, and was rowing it into the current. Soon it came gliding across on the pulley. Boat and third traveler arrived at the bank about the same time. Hays appeared interested in the newcomer, and addressed him civilly. He got but a short answer.

Meanwhile the rider led his horse down the sandy bank and on to the big flat boat. It was crudely thrown together, out of rough-hewn planks, but apparently was safe enough. The bay horse appeared nervous.

Hays, after a sharp look at the man with the three horses, led his animal aboard. The ferry-boy grinned all over his freckled face, in recognition of Hays.

"How much is the fare?" queried the newcomer. He was a bearded man under fifty, rather abrupt and authoritative.

"Two bits."

"For man or beast?"

"Well, sir, the regular fare is two bits for each man an' horse. But travelers usually give me more."

Whereupon the stout man threw the packs off his horses and carried them upon the boat.

"Wal now, whatinhell is this fussy old geezer about?" queried Hays, much interested.

It was soon manifest. He tied the halter of his lead pack-horse to the tail of his saddle-horse. The second pack-animal was similarly attached to the first. Then, bridle in hand, he stepped aboard.

"All right, boy. Go ahead."

"But, sir, ain't you fetchin' your hosses on, too?"

"Yes, but I'll swim them over behind the boat. Get a move on now."

The ferry-boy pushed off with his pole, and dropping that for the big oar he worked the boat out into the current, which caught it and moved it across quite readily into the slack water on that side. The rider had to hold his impatient horse to keep him from jumping before the boat was beached.

"Didn't like that, did you, Bay?" the rider said, as he led the animal ashore.

Hays slapped his mount, driving him off the ferry, while he watched the stout man lead his three horses along the gunwale of the boat, until they could touch bottom. Heaving and splashing, they waded out, and their owner followed, carrying one pack.

"Fetch my other pack, boy," he called.

"Johnny, don't do nothin' of the kind," observed Hays.

"I reckon I didn't intend to," said the boy, resentfully.

"Many travelers lately?"

"Nope. First I've had for three days. Then a couple of cowpunchers. We've only had the boat in about two weeks. River too high. Dad reckons Green River will boom this summer."

Puffing hard, the stout man carried his second pack ashore.

"You're not very—obliging," he said, gruffly, as he felt in his pocket for loose change. The ferry-boy came ashore, followed by Hays.

Presently the stout man, grumbling, and evidently annoyed at the necessity of producing a fat pocketbook, took out a one-dollar bill.

"Here. Give me seventy-five cents change."

The boy produced it like a flash, and replied, disgustedly, "I'll bet you don't play thet trick on me if you ever come back."

The rider, amused and interested from his stand on the bank, saw something that made him start. Hays whipped out a gun.

"Hands up!" he ordered.

The stout man stared aghast.

"Throw up your hands!" suddenly yelled Hays, harshly. "I'm not in the habit of sayin' thet twice." And he stuck the gun square into the plump abdomen before him. The stout man, gasping and turning livid of face, hastily complied by lifting hands that shook palpably.

"Wha-at's this? R-robbers!" he gulped.

Hays reached inside the man's coat, for his wallet, and extracted it. Then he stepped back, but still with gun extended.

"Get the hell out of here now," he ordered. And apparently he paid no more heed to his frightened victim. But the rider had his idea that Hays watched him, nevertheless.

"Pretty well heeled, thet old bird," observed the robber, squeezing the fat wallet.

"If there's law in this—country—you'll pay for this," burst out the traveler, working like a beaver to repack his horses.

"Haw! Haw! You ain't lookin' for law, air you, granpaw? . . . Wal, the only law is what you see here in my hand—an' I don't mean your money."

Hays slipped the wallet in his inside vest pocket. Then, with the same hand—and all the while covering the traveler with his gun—he drew a bill from his pocket.

"Thar, Johnny, thet's for all of us," he said.

"But, I— Oh, sir, I oughtn't take so much," faltered the boy, who was somewhat scared himself.

"Shore you ought. It's not his money, you noticed,"

drawled the robber, forcing the bill upon the reluctant youth. Then he addressed the traveler. "Say, Mormon, when you get uptown, or wherever you're goin'—jest say Hank Hays paid you his respects."

"You'll hear from me, you glib-tongued robber," replied the other, furiously, as he rode away.

Hays sheathed his gun. He did not need to turn to face the rider, for, singularly enough, he had not done anything else.

"How'd thet strike you, stranger?"

"Pretty neat. It amused me," replied the rider.

"Is thet all?"

"I guess so. The stingy old skinflint deserved to be touched. Wasn't that a slick way to beat the boy here out of six bits?"

"It shore was. An' thet's what r'iled me. Reckon, though, if he hadn't flashed the wallet I'd been a little more circumspect."

"Is there a sheriff at Green River?"

"I never seen him, if there is. Wal, I'll be ridin' along. Air you comin' with me, stranger?"

"Might as well," returned the other. "But if you don't mind, I'll walk."

"It's only a little way. Good lodgin's, though I never do nothin' but eat an' drink in town."

"That'll suit me for more than one reason."

"Stranger, what'd you say your name was?"

"I didn't say."

"Ex-cuse me. I'm not curious. But it's more agreeable, you know, when a fellar has a handle."

"Call me Wall—Jim Wall," rejoined the rider, presently.

"Wall?—Wal, thet's enough fer me. Kinda hard to get over. Haw! Haw!"

They went up the slow-ascending, sandy lane between

the cottonwoods toward the town, while the ferry-boy watched.

Hays' nonchalance reassured Wall as to the status of Green River. They came, at length, into a wide space, which was more of a square than a street, upon the far side of which stood several low, wide buildings, some of which sought the dignity of height with false, wooden fronts rising above their single story. The hitching rails and posts were vacant. There was not a vehicle in sight, and only a few men, lounging in doorways. Above and beyond this town of Green River stood the great cliff wall, not close, by any means, and now red in the sunset flare, except for the mantle of snow on the top.

"Any dance-hall in this burg?" asked Wall.

"Nary dance-hall, worse luck. Any weakness for such?"

"Can't say it's a weakness, but the last two I bumped into make me want to steer clear of more."

"Women?" queried the robber, with a leer.

"It wasn't any fault of mine."

"Haw! Haw! Reckon you might take the eye of women, at thet. Wal, you're out of luck here, 'cause the only women in Green River air old hags an' a couple of young wives thet you can't git within a mile of."

"Not out of luck for me. But you talk as if you regretted it."

"Wal, women ruined me," returned Hays, sententiously.

"You don't look it."

"Men never look what they air."

"Don't agree with you, Hays. I can always tell what men are by their looks."

"How'd you figure me?" demanded Hays, a little more gruffly than humorously.

"I don't want to flatter you on such short acquaintance."

"Humph!—Wal, here we air," replied the robber, halting before a red stone building.

"What do you suppose became of the fat fellow you relieved of cash?" inquired Wall, who kept this personage in mind.

"I reckon he's gone on his way to Moab," replied Hays. "Thet's a Mormon settlement down on the Green. An' there's a Mormon ranch out here a ways. We won't run into thet geezer here, I'll gamble."

"Quiet town," murmured Wall, as if talking to himself.

A red-bewhiskered man appeared in the doorway that led into a saloon and lodging-house. A rude sign in letters, faded and indistinct, attested to this.

"Howdy, Red!"

"Howdy, Hank!"

"See anythin' of a fat party, sort of puffy in the face? He was ridin' a roan an' leadin' two packs."

"Oh, him? Sure. He rode through town yellin' he'd been robbed," returned the man called Red, grinning.

"Hell he did? Who was he, Red?"

"I dunno. Mormon, most likely. Leastways thet's what Happy said. He was standin' out here, an' when the feller stopped bellerin' thet he wanted the sheriff 'cause he'd been robbed, why, Happy up an' says, 'Hey, my Latter Day friend, did he leave anythin' on you?' Then the feller up an' rode off to beat hell."

It was this pregnant speech of Red's that decided several things for Jim Wall.

"I want to look after my horse," was all he said.

"Take him round back to the barn. If Jake ain't there, you can find water, feed, an' beddin' yourself."

Hays dismounted laboriously, indicating that he had ridden far that day.

"Wal, I'm dog-tired. Send thet lazy Jake after my hoss."

This edifice was the last one on the street. Wall made note of the grove of cottonwoods just down the slope a few hundred yards. The barn mentioned was some distance back, at the end of a pole fence. Upon turning a corner to enter the corral he encountered a loose-jointed young man.

"Say, are you Jake?" he asked.

"You bet. Want your hoss looked after?" returned the other. His protruding teeth were his salient feature.

"Yes. But I'll take care of him. There's a man out in front who calls himself Hank Hays. He wants you to come get his horse. Do you know him?"

The stable-boy's reply to that was to rush off, his boots thudding.

"Enough said," muttered Wall to himself as he looked round the place for what he required. "Mr. Hays stands well in Green River, as far as *this* outfit is concerned."

Wall's mind was active while he ministered to his horse. It had long been a familiar thing for him to ride into a strange camp or town; and judging men quickly had become a matter of habit, if not self-preservation. Utah, however, was far west and a wilder country than that he had roamed for years. He liked the looks of it, the long reaches of wasteland, the vast bulge and heave of the ranges, the colored walls of stone, the buttes standing alone, and the red and black mystery of the mountains.

"Bay, old boy, you haven't had a stall for a coon's age," he said to his horse. "Enjoy it while you can, for it may not be long."

When Wall sauntered back the whole west was one magnificent blaze of red and gold. He would have enjoyed being high up on the cliffs behind, just to gaze out toward those Henry Mountains he had seen all day. But the houses and trees blocked that view. Eastward across the river he could discern the speckled slope of yellow that climbed up to the book-cliff wall, now fading in the dusk.

Jim Wall never turned street corners without knowing what was ahead of him. So that before Hank Hays and the two individuals with whom he was talking were aware of his presence he had seen them. They turned at his slow clinking step. Neither of the two with Hays was the man called Red.

"Hullo! here you air," spoke up Hays. "I was speakin' of you. Meet Happy Jack an' Brad Lincoln. . . . Fellers, this stranger to Green River answers to the handle Jim Wall."

Greetings were exchanged, but not one of the three offered a hand. Their glances meant infinitely more than the casual few words. To Wall the man called Happy Jack fitted his name. The only contradictory feature lay in his guns, which it was not possible to overlook. Like Hank Hays, he packed two. This, however, signified little to Wall. The other, Lincoln, was some one to look at twice—a swarthy, dark, restless-eyed man, who, like Hays and his companion, had nothing of the cowboy stripe in his make-up.

"Let's have a drink," suggested Hays.

"Don't care if I do," responded Wall. "But I haven't had anything to eat for two days."

"Red's havin' supper cooked for us," said Hays, pushing open the door.

The interior, bright with lamplight, proved to be more pretentious than the outside of the saloon. It had a flagstone floor, a bar with garish display of mirrors, paintings of nude women, bottles and glasses. Several roughly clad men were drinking, and ceased talking as Hays and his companion approached. In the back of the big room three cowboys lounged before an open fireplace where some fagots burned. There were several tables, unoccupied except for a man who lay face down on one. From an open door came the savory odor of fried bacon.

The men lined up at the bar, to be served drinks by Red, who was evidently bartender as well as proprietor. Wall missed nothing. Hays took his whisky straight and at a gulp; Happy Jack said, "Here's lookin' at you," and Lincoln sipped lingeringly. Whisky was not one of Wall's weaknesses; in fact, he could not afford to have any weakness. But he drank on politic occasions, of which this was more than usually one.

"Cow-puncher?" queried Lincoln, who stood next to Wall.

"Yes. But I've not ridden the range much of late years," replied Wall.

"You've the cut of it. Where you from?"

"Wyoming."

"Long ways. Don't know thet country. Where you aimin' for?"

"No place in particular," replied Wall, guardedly. "Might try riding here, if I can get on some outfit."

"On the dodge?" queried Lincoln, after a pause.

Wall set down his glass and turned to his interrogator. Their glances locked.

"Are you getting personal?" returned Wall, coldly.

"Not at all. I ain't curious, neither. Just askin' you."

"Ahuh. Well, what might you mean by 'on the dodge'?"

"Anybody particular lookin' for you?"

"I dare say. More than one man."

"Are you movin' along, dodgin' them?"

"Not them," retorted Wall, contemptuously.

"So I thought. Friend, you have the cut, the eye, the

movement, the hand of a gun-fighter. I happen to know the brand."

"Yes? Well, if that's so, I hope it isn't against me in Utah."

Here Hays, who had heard this bit of dialogue, interposed both with personal speech.

"Wall, thet's ag'in' a man anywhere in the West, generally. So many damn fools wantin' to try you out! But I reckon it's a ticket for my outfit."

"Your outfit," declared, rather than questioned Wall, as if to corroborate the robber's direct statement of something definite.

"Shore. Don't mind Brad. He's a curious, blunt sort of cuss. Let's go an' eat. . . . Fellars, we'll see you later."

Wall followed Hays into a back room, where a buxom woman greeted them heartily and waved them to seats at a table.

"Red's woman, an' she shore can cook," said Hays. "Wal, fall to."

No more was said during the meal. At its conclusion Jim Wall had to guard himself against the feeling of well-being, resulting from a full stomach.

"Have a cigar?" offered Hays. "They shore come high and scarce out here."

"Don't care if I do."

"Wal, let's go out an' talk before we join the other fellars," suggested Hays. They returned to the big room. It was empty except for Red, who was filling a lamp.

"They've all gone down to meet the stage. It's overdue now."

"Stage!—From where?"

"West, so set easy," laughed Hays. "Thet one from East won't git in till—wal, now, let me see what day this is."

"Saturday."

"Wal, so it is. *Then next Wednesday.* By thet time you won't be here."

"No? Where will I be, since you seem to know?"

"You may be in the Garden of Eden, eatin' peaches," retorted Hays. "See here, Wall, you're a testy cuss. Any reason why you can't be a good fellar?"

"Come to think of thet, yes, there is," returned Wall, thoughtfully.

"All right. Thanks for thet much. I reckon I understand you better. An' I don't want to know why," he said, with deliberation. He kicked the smoldering fire, and picking up a chip, he lighted his cigar, puffing clouds of smoke. "Aahh! Makes me think of a store I used to run in West Virginia, years ago. . . . What were you, Wall, once upon a time?"

Wall laughed musingly. "A country-school teacher once, for a while, before I was twenty."

"Wal, I'll be dog-goned! You ain't serious?" ejaculated Hays, incredulously.

"Yes, I am. It's funny. I wouldn't have remembered that before supper."

"It do beat hell what a man can be, at different times in his life. But I'm concerned with now. An' I'd like to ask you some questions."

"Fire away."

"You didn't hold it ag'in' me thet I held up the old geezer at the ferry?"

"No. He was about the stingiest man I ever ran across."

"All right. Would you have done thet yourself?"

"Possibly."

"All right. I'd have done it without provocation. Does thet make any particular difference to you?"

"Not any—in particular. It's none of my business."

"Wal, make it your business."

"Hays, you're beating around the bush," returned Wall, deliberately. "Come clean with it."

"I reckoned so," mused Hays, eying his cigar and flicking off the ashes with a slow finger. Then he veered his gaze to the brightening embers in the fire.

Wall felt that this was the first really unguarded moment Hays had shown, although he had appeared nothing if not sincere. It somehow defined his status, if not his caliber.

"You said you was broke?" Hays began again.

"I will be when I pay for this night's lodging."

"Thet's on me. I'll stake you to some money. You'll want to set in the game with us?"

"Any strings on a loan?"

"Hardly thet. With me, it's come easy, go easy."

"Thanks then. I'll take fifty dollars. That'll do me until I can get located."

"Wal, friend, the string is thet I want to locate you."

Chapter Two

"**B**END over here, so I can get your ear," went on Hays, confidentially, and when Wall had complied he said: "I run true to form today when I held up thet Mormon. But it was a blunder, considerin' the iron I have in the fire. If he wasn't a Mormon, I'd feel uncomfortable about thet. . . . Now listen. Lately I've got in with a rancher over here in the Henry Mountains. He's an Englishman with more money than sense. Fact is, he's rich an' crazy as a bedbug. It's beautiful country an' he got stuck on it. Bought ten thousand head of cattle an' a lot of hosses. There's some tough cowboy outfits over there, an' more'n one real rustler outfit. Wal, this Englishman—his name is Herrick—got the idee of hirin' all the hands available, cow-punchers, range-riders, guntoters, an' plain out-an'-out bad men. An' to throw this select outfit ag'in' the whole country. What do you think of thet idee?"

"Original, to say the least. But not practical, unless he can reform bad men," replied Wall, much interested.

"Wal, exactly. But I'm not concerned with the practicability of it. Herrick took a shine to me, made me what he calls his superintendent, an' sent me off all over, lookin' for hard-shootin', hard-ridin' men. An' thet's how you happened to run into me. I call it good luck for us both."

"You've taken me for one of the hard-shooting, hard-riding kind, eh?"

"Shore. I only need to clap eyes on a man. . . . An' don't overlook, Wall, thet I'm not askin' questions."

"I haven't missed that. Go on."

"Wal, I want you in my outfit," resumed Hays. "Brad didn't cotton to you, I seen first off. But he's a gunthrower himself, a suspicious, jealous, queer sort, as most of them fellars air. He's done for I don't know

16

how many ambitious-to-be killers. All the same he's in my
outfit an' I reckon you might get along. It's Heeseman
who sticks in my craw."

"Heeseman? Who's he?"

"You'll take this as confidence, in case you don't want
to throw in with me?" queried Hays, earnestly.

"Yes. I'll regard it all that way."

"Wal, Heeseman is the rustler of Dragon Canyon.
None of the ranchers even round here know thet, but *I*
know it. He's got a small outfit, but shore enough bad.
An' in some way he got wind of Herrick's scheme. Damn
me if he didn't pack over to the Henrys with his outfit
an' start ridin' fer Herrick."

"Heeseman saw the same opportunity as you?" queried
Wall, quietly.

"Wal, yes, I was comin' to thet," resumed Hays,
gruffly. "I got the upper hand, though, an' I'll be the
boss. Thet'll lead to friction, shore as hell. There'll be
two factions sooner or later, an' the sooner thet fight
comes off the better."

"I see. Less of a division of spoils."

"Wall, I'm no rustler," snapped Hays, annoyed.

"Excuse me. If it isn't impertinent, may I ask just
what you are?"

"Ever hear of Henry Plummer?"

"Can't remember if I did."

"Wall, Plummer flourished some ten an' more years
ago, first in Montana an' later in Idaho. He was the greatest robber the West ever developed. Educated man of
good family, born in the East. But the gold fever called
an' he was not the kind of a man to dig. He operated
on the placer mines. Was an officer of the law while he
was head of the biggest robber gang the frontier ever
knew. From Bannock to Lewiston he kept the miners, the
stages, the Wells-Fargo in terror for years. . . . Wal, I

seen Plummer hanged. I was one of his gang, a young man then in years."

"Thanks for the confidence, Hays," returned Wall, in surprise. "You must have strong interest in me to tell that."

"Shore I have. But I don't care to be classed as a rustler."

"Too low down, eh— Well, then, what's your plan with Herrick?"

"It certainly ain't any two-bit cattle-stealin'. . . . However, thet's not the point between you an' me. What I want to know is, will you take a job in my outfit?"

"That depends, Hays," returned Wall, ponderingly.

"Any scruples about it? Remember, I come clean with you."

"No. I broke jail in Cheyenne."

"What was you in for?"

"Shot a man. They were goin' to hang me."

"Ahuh. Was thet square?"

"I didn't think so. . . . Had to kill the jailer to get out."

"When was all this, Wall?"

"Some years ago."

"An' since then?"

"Been shooting my way out of one jam after another. I just couldn't steer clear. So I've come far out West where no one ever heard of me."

"Much obliged," replied Hays. "I feel better, now you've returned the compliment. I've a hunch you haven't sunk to stealin'. Am I right?"

"Not yet. But I've been on the verge often," replied Wall, bitterly.

"Wal, you're a hunted man. You're broke. It's about where you cross the divide."

"One more question. What about this Herrick's family?"

"Wal, he ain't got any," rejoined Hays. "We heard somethin' about a sister comin' out, but she never turned up."

"Sister? It'd be a hell of a note if she did."

"Wal, this shore ain't no country fer women."

It seemed to Jim Wall that this sally completed a definite conscious feeling in his mind toward the self-confessed robber. If it had not been dislike and disgust before, it certainly fixed at that now. Wall sensed a gathering interest in the situation he had happened upon. A thirst for adventure had played no small part in the event which had started him on his rolling-stone career.

Hays called for drinks and insisted on a handshake, which he executed solemnly, as if it were a compact which implied honor even among thieves. Shortly afterward the saloon gradually began to fill with loud-voiced, heavily-booted men.

Among them were Happy Jack, Lincoln, and a giant of a man with a russet beard, whom Hays introduced as Montana. He might have been a miner once, but his hand, which he offered agreeably, was too soft to have been lately associated with hard labor.

By tacit acceptance of a situation not vague to Wall, these men kept off to themselves, and were quiet and observing. Brad Lincoln had the hawk eyes of a man who was not going to be surprised.

Jim Wall sat back with interest and a certain enjoyment long unfamiliar. Saloons and gambling-halls were well known to him, from the notorious Dodge City to Kalispel, but he had not seen any like this of Green River, Utah. There was not a typical black-frock-coated gambler present, nor a half-naked dance-hall girl, nor a long-haired four-flush gunman, looking for an easy mark to add another notch to his gun.

Cowboys were conspicuous by their absence, although before supper Wall had seen three. Teamsters, prospectors, cattlemen were there to the number of a dozen, and the others, making a score in all, had to remain problematical to Wall's keen observance. Then a man, undoubtedly a trapper, entered. He wore buckskin and seemed out of place in that crowd. The bartender, Red, did a thriving business, selling only whisky, at four bits a glass.

"Seems to be no lack of money," observed Wall to the watchful Hays. "Where do they get it?"

"Wal, you're surprised, I see. So was I. This burg here is a stage stop for points in Utah an' west. Lots of travel. But there's big cattle ranges off toward the Henrys. South is most Mormons."

"I see. But at that bar there are half a dozen men who are not travelers or ranchers or riders."

"Wal, fer thet matter, all men in these diggin's have got to be riders. It's a long way from one waterin'-place to another. But you hit into things at thet. There's four or five fellars I never seen before."

"Who's the tall one, with his hat pulled down, so you can only see his black, pointed beard?"

"Thet's Morley. Claims to be a rancher. But if he ain't the boss of the Black Dragon outfit, I'll eat him."

"And the loud fellow—the one with the plaid vest. He's got guns inside that vest, one in each pocket, with the butts pointing out."

"Hell you say! I hadn't noticed. His name is Stud somethin' or other. Seen him before an' ain't crazy about him."

At this juncture the door slammed open, propelled by a vigorous hand, and a stout woman entered with a fierce mien. She had a red shawl tied round her head, and she tramped like a man in heavy boots.

"Sam Butler, you come out of this," she shouted, peremptorily, to a man in the front rank of drinkers. He detached himself with alacrity from his fellows, and amid their boisterous bantering he sheepishly followed the woman out.

"Now thet's the kind of a wife I oughta had," observed Hays, admiringly.

"Let's play poker."

"Shore, but not just among ourselves."

"Got any money, Hank?" asked Happy Jack.

"Did you ever see me broke? Brad, go dig up some suckers. But not thet hombre they call Stud. He didn't get thet name playin' solitaire."

There were only two large gaming-tables, one of which was in use. Lincoln went among the men to solicit players, returning with Morley and the russet-bearded giant, Montana. There was no formality or greeting between Hays and these men. It was dog eat dog, Wall grasped.

"Make it six-handed. Come an' set in, Wall," said Hays. "Friendly little game of draw. Sky limit."

Wall laughed. "I couldn't play penny ante."

"Wal, I'll stake you."

"No thanks. Some other time. I'd rather watch."

"Excuse me, sir, but we don't care for watchers," interposed Morley, curtly.

No sooner had they seated themselves than the man Hays had called Stud strode up. He was a little fellow, but forceful, not one who would be good to meet in a narrow, dangerous place.

"Am I bein' left out of this on purpose?" he demanded, and evidently he addressed Hays.

"Lincoln got up the game," replied Hays, coolly, returning glance for glance.

"You ask my friends to set in, an' not me."

"Wal, if you're so damn keen about it, why, set in with us," went on Hays, fingering a deck of cards. "But if you want to know bad, I'm not stuck on playin' with you."

"Mean thet to insult me?" Stud queried, sharply, his right hand rising to the lapel of his open vest. If Wall had not observed the bulge of two guns inside this vest he would have divined from Stud's action that there was one at least. Probably this fellow was a surly, cross-grained type whom contact with the bottle made unreasonable.

"Not atall," replied Hays, leaning back in his chair. That significant movement of Stud's had not been lost upon him. A little cold glint appeared in his pale eyes. "Reckon you're too slick a poker-player for Hank Hays. I want a run fer my money."

"Slick, eh? Wal, I don't mind bein' called thet. It's a compliment. I've yet to see the gambler who wouldn't be slick if he could. But when you ask my pards to play, an' not me—thet's different."

"Set in, Stud," rejoined Hays, civilly, as he began to shuffle the cards. "I feel lucky tonight. Last time you had it all your way."

The game began then with Happy Jack and Wall looking on. Morley made rather a pointed move and remark anent Wall's standing behind him.

"Shore I'll change seats with you," replied Hays, obligingly, but it was plain he felt irritated.

"Never mind, Hays," interposed Wall, deliberately. "The gentleman evidently fears I'll tip off his cards. So I'll stand behind you, if I may."

From the very first deal Hays was lucky. Morley stayed about even. Brad Lincoln lost more than he won. The giant Montana was a close, wary gambler, playing only when he had good cards. Stud was undoubtedly a player who required the stimulation and zest of opposition. But he could not wait for luck to change. He had to be in every hand. Moreover, he was not adept enough with the cards to deal himself a good hand when his turn came. He grew so sullen that Wall left off watching and returned to the fireside.

But presently he had cause to attend more keenly than ever to this card game. The drift of conversation, if it could be called that, and especially from the gambler, Stud, wore toward an inevitable fight. These men were vicious characters. Wall knew that life out here was raw. There was no law except that of the six-shooter. Back in Wyoming and Montana, where it was tough enough, Wall thought, there were certain restraints bound to affect any man. There were sheriffs, courts, jails, and something wonderfully calculated to check outlaws, desperadoes and cowboys run amuck—and that was the noose. Wall had seen many a man strung up to the limb of a cottonwood.

While he bent a more penetrating gaze upon Stud, to whom his attention gravitated, Wall saw him perform a trick with the cards that was pretty clever, and could not have been discerned except from Wall's position.

Nevertheless, fickle fortune most certainly had picked on Stud. He bet this hand to the limit of his cash, and then, such was his confidence, he borrowed from Morley. Still he could not force Hays to call. He fell from elation to consternation, then to doubt, from doubt to dismay, and from this to a gathering impotent rage, all of which proved how poor a gambler he was. When at last he rasped out: "Wal—I call! Here's mine."

He slammed down an ace full. Hays had drawn three cards.

"Stud, I hate to show you this hand," drawled Hays.

"Yes, you do! Lay it down. I called you."

Whereupon Hays gently spread out four ten spots, and then with greedy hands raked in the stakes.

Stud stared with burning eyes. "Three card draw! . . . You come in with a pair of tens?"

"Nope. I held up one ten an' the ace," replied Hays, nonchalantly. "I had a hunch, Stud."

"You'd steal coppers off a dead nigger's eyelids!"

"Haw! Haw!" bawled the victorious gamester. But he was the only one of the six players who seemed to see anything funny in the situation. That dawned upon him. "Stud, I was takin' thet crack of yours humorous."

"Was you?" snapped Stud.

"Shore I was," returned Hays, with congealing voice. His pales eyes took on a greenish cast.

"Wal, I didn't mean it humorous."

"Ahuh. Come to look at you, I see you ain't feelin' gay. Suppose you say just what you did mean."

"I meant what I said."

"Shore. I'm not so awful thick. But apply thet crack to this here card game an' my playin'."

"Hays, you palmed them three ten spots," declared Stud, hotly.

Then there was quick action and the rasp of scraping chairs, and the tumbling over of a box seat. Stud and Hays were left alone at the table.

"You're a — — — — — — of a liar!" hissed Hays, suddenly black in the face.

Here Jim Wall thought it was time to intervene. He read the glint in Stud's eyes. Hays was at a disadvantage, so far as drawing a gun was concerned. And Wall saw that Stud could and would kill him.

"Hold on there!" called Wall, in a voice that made both men freeze. He stepped clear of the chimney, against which he had been leaning.

Hays did not turn to Wall, but he spoke: "Pard, lay off. I can handle this fellar."

"Take care, stranger," warned Stud, who appeared to be able to watch both Hays and Wall at once. They were, however, almost in line. "This ain't any of your mix."

"I just wanted to tell Hays I saw you slip an ace from the bottom of the deck," said Wall. He might as well have told something of Hays' irregularities.

"Wot! He filled his ace full thet way?" roared Hays.

"He most certainly did."

"All right, let it go at thet," replied Stud, deadly cold. "If you can say honest thet you haven't pulled any tricks go for your gun. Otherwise keep your shirt on."

That unexpected sally exemplified the peculiar conception of honor among thieves. It silenced Hays. The little gambler knew his man and shifted his deadly intent to a more doubtful issue. Such fascination of uncertainty had been the death of untold Westerners.

"Jim Wall, eh?" he queried, insolently.

"At your service," retorted Wall. He divined the workings of the little gambler's mind. Stud needed to have more time, for the thing that made decision hard to reach was the quality of this stranger. His motive was more deadly than his will or his power to execute. All this Jim Wall knew. It was the difference between the two men.

"I'm admittin' I cheated," said Stud, harshly. "But I ain't standin' to be tipped off by a stranger."

"Well, what're you going to do about it?" asked Wall. The moment had long passed in which there had been need of caution.

Stud did not know what he was going to do. And just as plain was the fact that he wanted to annihilate. On the other hand, Wall had no desire to kill this testy, loudmouthed little gambler. These things were manifest. They were Wall's strength and Stud's weakness. The spectators of the drama almost held their breaths.

Wall's deliberate query ended Stud's vacillation. His body shrank ever so slightly. His lean, dark, little hands lifted quiveringly from the table.

"Don't draw!" yelled Wall. "The man doesn't live who can sit at a table and beat me to a gun."

"Hell—you say!" panted Stud. But that ringing taunt had cut the force of his purpose. There were beads of sweat on his face.

"You've got a gun in each inside vest pocket," said Wall, contemptuously. "Men of your stripe don't live long in my country."

The gambler let his nervous, clawlike hands relax and slide off the table. Then the tension of all broke.

"Come on, Stud," spoke up Morley. "Let's get out of here."

Stud shuffled to his feet, malignant, and beaten for the moment.

"Hays, you an' me are even," he said, gruffly. "But I'll meet your new pard some other time."

"Shore, Stud. No hard feelin's on my side," drawled Hays.

The little gambler stalked to the bar, followed by Morley and the russet-bearded giant. "Buy me a drink," said Stud, hoarsely. "I'm cleaned out." They drank and left the saloon.

Not until then did Hank Hays turn round, and when he did it was distinctly noticeable that he was pale.

"Jim, thet —— did have two guns inside his vest. I never saw them till you gave it away. The —— —— —— —— would have killed me."

"I think he would, Hays," returned Wall, seriously

"You were sitting bad for action. You ought to have got to your feet before starting that argument."

"Ahuh!" ejaculated Hays, huskily. He wiped his face, then regarded Wall with new eyes. Happy Jack and Brad Lincoln rejoined Hays at the table. Lincoln's gaze was more expressive than any words could have been.

"Brad, where was you when it come off?" queried Hays.

"I was lookin' out fer myself."

"I seen thet, all right. . . . Jim, I'm much obliged to you. I'd have hated shufflin' off at this particular time. You can gamble I won't forget it. . . . I'd like to know somethin'."

"What's that?"

"Did you bluff him?"

"Hardly. I had him figured. It was a pretty good bet he wouldn't try to draw. But if he had made a move ——"

"Ahuh. It'd been all day with him. . . . This gambler, Stud, has a name out here for bein' swift on the draw. He's killed ——"

"Bah!" cut in Wall, good-humoredly. "Men who can handle guns don't pack them that way."

"Wal, he's the first I ever seen out here, at thet," replied Hays. "You see, when I called him I had my eyes on his hands, which was flat on the table. I thought I could shoot him easy enough an' was a mind to do it. But, hell's fire, how easy he could have bored me!"

"No, he couldn't, with me standing here. . . . Let's go to bed, Hays. I'm sleepy."

"Good idee. We'll all go. Have a drink on me."

They lined up at the bar.

"Jim," said Hays, poising his glass, "funny how a man figgers another. Not only you figgerin' Stud, but down at the ferry, when I met you, I had sort of a hunch you'd be a fellar to tie to. Here's lookin' at you!"

Presently they bade Red goodnight and went outside. The night was dark, windy, cold. Dust whisked along the road, rustling, seeping. The stars blinked white. Black and grim the cliff wall stood up, seemingly to tower over the town.

"Where you sleepin'?" asked Hays.

"Left my pack in the stall out back with my horse."

"You don't call thet pack a bed, do you? Come sleep in a real bed."

"I'll make out all right. What do we do tomorrow?"

"I was thinkin' of thet. We'll shake the dust of Green River. It might not be healthy for us, seein' this is Morley's hangout. Besides, I'm flush with money. I'd only lose it. So I reckon tomorrow we'd better stock up on everythin' an' hit the trail for the Henrys."

"Suits me," replied Wall.

"How about you, Brad?"

"I'll go, Hank, but it's only because nothin' else offers. This new deal of yours, as I size it up, will come to the awfulest mess ever."

"Ahuh. An' you, Happy?"

"Sounds turrible good to me, Hank," replied Jack, with the enthusiasm to be expected from one with his nickname.

"Wal then, good night. Breakfast here early," concluded Hays.

They parted. Jim Wall bent his cautious steps back to the barn. Presently his eyes became used to the darkness and he made better progress. But he was not passing any trees or bushes or corners, nor did he enter the barnyard by the gate. Nothing intervened to occasion more caution. He found his pack where he had left it, and carrying it out into the open he made his bed and lay down in it, after removing only his gun belt.

Then he reviewed the events of the day and evening

That brief occupation afforded him no pleasure. Nevertheless, he decided that he was glad he had fallen in with Hank Hays and his cronies. He had been a lone wolf for so long that the society of any class of men would have been relief. Well he knew, however, that soon he would be on the go again. He could not stay in one locality long, though there had been several places where he would have liked to spend the rest of his life. At least he was not indifferent to beautiful and peaceful country. The rub was that no place could long remain peaceful for Jim Wall. It would be so here in Utah. Sometimes, rarely, however, his thoughts impinged upon the distant past when for him there had been zest and thrill of adventure. He had grown callous. It so happened that tonight he seemed on the threshold of another and extraordinary experience, even for him, and it kept him thought-provokingly awake, with only resentment and disillusion as reward.

Chapter Three

A RED sunrise greeted Wall upon his awakening. He rolled his bed and carried it back to the corral. There was a thin skim of ice on the water in the trough. As it had not been broken, he believed that he was the first up. Bay whinnied to him from the stall.

When, a little later, he presented himself at the back of Red's house for breakfast, he was to find Hays, Happy Jack, and Brad Lincoln ahead of him.

"Mornin'!" said Hays cheerily. "Do you smell spring in the air?"

"Howdy, everybody!" replied Wall. "I guess I like this country."

"Only bad thing about this end of Utah is thet you hate to leave," observed the robber. "Usually we winter here an' go somewhere else in summer. It's hotter'n hell here in July an' August. But I always want to come back. Gets hold of a feller. An' thet's bad."

They had breakfast. "Brad, you fetch your pack-hosses round back," ordered the leader, when they got outside. "Happy, you get yourself a hoss. Then meet us at the store quick as you can get there. . . . Jim, you come with me."

"Hays, I'm in need of some things," said Wall.

Hays drew out a handful of bills and pressed them upon Wall without any interest in how much or little was there.

"Shore. Buy what outfit you need an' don't forget a lot of shells," replied Hays. "If I don't miss my guess, we'll have a smoky summer. Haw, Haw! . . . Here's the store. Run by Josh Sneed, friendly to Mormons. I've a sneakin' hunch he's one himself. Hasn't any use for us. But he'll take our money, you bet, an' skin the pants off us, if we let him "

The store proved to be similar to most Western stores dependent upon the stage line for their supplies. It consisted of the whole floor of a stone-walled building, and general merchandise littered it so that moving around was not easy.

A bright young fellow, who looked to be the son of the proprietor, took charge of Wall. A new saddle blanket was Wall's first choice, after which he bought horseshoes and nails, a hammer and file, articles he had long needed, and the lack of which had made Bay lame. After that he selected a complete new outfit of wearing apparel, a new tarpaulin, a blanket, rope, and wound up with a goodly supply of shells for his .45 Colt, bearing in mind the cardinal necessity of constant practice, a habit neglected of late, for the very good reason that he had no funds. Likewise he got some boxes of .44 Winchester shells for his rifle.

After this stocking-up he was surprised to find that he had considerable money left. Hays had been generous. Whereupon Wall went in for some luxuries, such as a silk scarf, razor and brushes and comb, towels and soap, and finally, amused at himself, some boxes of nuts and candy.

All these purchases he rolled in the tarpaulin, which he threw over his shoulder. Starting out, he passed Hays, who was buying food supplies.

"I'll need a pack-horse," said Wall.

"Ha! I should smile you will!" replied the other, with a grin. "Take your pick. We got five or six extra hosses. . . . Did you buy saddle-bags an' a canvas water-bag?"

"No. I didn't think of them."

"Wal, I'll fetch them things round for you. Rustle Happy an' Brad over here, will you? An' throw the pack-saddles on. We want to be hittin' the trail."

Wall met the two men on the way to the store.

"Hays wants you to rustle," he said.

"We're mozyin' along. You've a fust-rate pack-hoss, Wall," returned the genial Happy Jack.

Jim thought so himself by the time he had reached the corral. He was glad he no longer needed to make a pack-animal of Bay. There were six or eight horses in the corral several of which took Jim's eye. Still, they could not compare with Bay.

Spreading out his possessions, he packed them in one small and two large bundles. This he performed with care, having in mind a long journey over bad trails. By the time he had finished Happy Jack and Lincoln arrived, staggering under burdens. While they rested Hays came along, and the pack he carried attested to the fact that he was no shirker.

"Hank, you look like a thundercloud," observed Brad Lincoln, chuckling.

"Wal, I feel like one. What do you think, fellers? Thet fox-faced Sneed always did make me pay cash, but this time I had to produce beforehand."

"These Mormons are slick business men," said Happy Jack.

"Hank, it ain't only your credit thet's bad here in Green River," added Lincoln, satirically.

"Wal, I'll tell you what," growled Hays. "If we didn't have this Star Ranch deal on we'd take every damn thing Sneed has."

"Let's do it, anyhow."

"Nope. At least not now. Mebbe this fall . . . I'd like to have a shot at Sneed's sharp nose. . . . Rustle an' pack now, fellers. We're behind."

Half an hour later the four men, driving five packed horses and two unpacked, rode off behind the town across the flat toward the west. Coming to a road, Hays led on that for a mile or so, and then branched off on a seldom-used trail which appeared to parallel the wonderful, gray-cliffed mountain wall that zigzagged on to the purple-hazed distance.

They went down a long hill of bare clay earth dotted with rocks and scant brush, at the bottom of which ran a deep, wide, dry wash. Green River with its cottonwoods dropped behind the hill, to be seen no more.

Gradually the pack-horses settled into single file on the trail and required little driving. The riders straggled along behind. Jim Wall brought up the rear. If he was ever contented it was when he was on horseback with open, unknown country ahead. This for him was familiar action. Once he caught himself looking back over his shoulder, and he laughed. It was an instinct, a habit.

When the opposite, endless, slow-rising slope had been surmounted, Wall saw all around country that wrenched a tribute from him. Texas, Kansas, Colorado, Wyoming, Montana left much to be desired in comparison with Utah. Jim had not ridden over Arizona, so could not judge. But Utah was stunning.

To his right ran the crooked rim-rock, gray and yellow, with its speckled slides, its jagged peaks, its rough wildness increasing on and on. Ahead a vast rolling plain, bare in the foreground, stark and ghastly in patches, and in the distance rolling from monotonous gray to faint green. Above the horizon towered the black Henry Mountains, far away, dim and strange, with white peaks in the blue.

But it was the region to the left and south of the Henrys that fascinated Jim Wall.

Beyond the bulge of the plain, buttes stood up here and there, lofty and sentinel-like, isolated, hinting of rough country. More, toward Wall's left, the plain dropped off, allowing him to see boundlessly in that direction. A shiny, wandering line of river, bordered with green, disappeared in a chaotic wilderness of bare rock, carved and broken into every conceivable shape.

The thought came to Wall that a rider down in there would have little to fear from pursuers. He would be alone. He could sleep. He could idle for hours, with never a need to hurry or think or watch. But how could he live? It looked formidable and forbidding.

These impressions of Wall's did not materially change as the miles passed by, except to augment. The trail grew sandy, though not dragging. Thin, bleached grass, with a little touch of green, began to show on the desert. Wall watched for some evidence of wild creatures. What a bleak, inhospitable land! Hours passed before he sighted a track, and that had been made by an antelope. Patches of sunflower stalks, beginning to green, showed in the sandy swales. There were no birds, no lizards, no hawks, no rabbits, nothing but endless rolling plain tinged with green. But the hours did not drag. They never dragged for Wall on a ride like this, when he could forget all that he had turned his back upon and could look ahead to the calling horizons.

Toward sunset they drew down to the center of a vast swale, where the green intensified, and the eye of the range-rider could see the influence of water. Gradually the Henrys sank behind the rim of this bowl, and the zigzag wall, growing crimson, appeared to lose its lofty height. Only one of the buttes showed its blunt crown of gold and red. For the rest, all was sunset flare, a blazing sky of rose and salmon, with gold clouds on the west. And the huge, circular swale was bathed in an ethereal violet light.

Hays halted for camp at a swampy sedge plot where water oozed out and grass was thick enough to hold the horses.

"Aha! Good to be out again, boys," said Hays, heartily. "Throw saddles an' packs. Turn the hosses loose. Happy, you're elected cook. Rest of us rustle somethin' to burn, which is shore one hell of a job."

Jim rambled far afield to collect an armload of dead stalks of cactus, greasewood, sunflower; and dusk was mantling the desert when he got back to camp. Happy Jack was whistling about a little fire; Hays knelt before a pan of dough, which he was kneading; Lincoln was busy at some camp chore.

"Wal, I don't give a damn for store bread," Hays was saying. "Give me sour-dough biscuits. . . . How about you, Jim?"

"Me too. And I'd like some cake," replied Jim, dropping his load.

"Cake!—Wal, listen to our new hand. Jack, can you bake cake?"

"Sure. We got flour an' sugar an' milk. Did you fetch some eggs?"

"Haw! Haw! . . . Thet reminds me, though. We'll get eggs over at Star Ranch. None of you ever seen such a ranch. Why, fellers, Herrick's bought every durn hoss, burro, cow, steer, chicken in the whole country."

"So you said before," returned Lincoln. "I'm sure curious to see this Englisher. Must have more money than brains."

"Hell yes! He hasn't got any sense, accordin' to us Westerners. But, Lordy! the money he's spent!"

Jim sat down to rest and listen. These riders had accepted him and they were out in the open now, where one might expect frankness.

"Rummy deal—a rich Englishman hirin' men like us to run his outfit," pondered Lincoln, in a puzzled tone. "I don't understand it."

"Wal, who does? I can't, thet's shore. But it's an honest God's fact, an' we're goin' to be so rich pronto thet we'll jest about kill each other."

"More truth than fun in thet, Hank, old boy, an' don't you forget it," rejoined Lincoln. "How do you aim to get rich?"

"Shore, I've no idee. Thet'll all come. I've got the step on Heeseman an' his pards."

"He'll be aimin' at precisely the same deal as you."

"Shore. We'll have to kill Heeseman an' Progar, sooner or later. I'd like it sooner."

"Humph! Thet ain't goin' to be so easy, Hank."

"Wal, Brad, don't jump your ditches before you come to them," advised Hays, philosophically.

"I don't like the deal," concluded Lincoln, forcibly.

Presently they sat to their meal, and ate almost in silence. Darkness settled down; the staccato cry of coyotes came on the night wind; the little fire burned down to red coals. Lincoln essayed to replenish it with fresh fuel, but Hays made him desist. One by one they sought their beds, and Wall was the last. He did not lie awake long.

Dawn found them up and doing. Wall fetched in some of the horses; Lincoln the others. By sunrise they were on the trail.

It turned out to be a windy day, cold, almost raw, with only a pale sun. Blowing dust and sand shrouded distant landmarks. About noon they passed close to one of the buttes, a huge disintegrated rock, the color of chocolate, and so weathered that it resembled a colossal pipe organ. Not long afterward another loomed up through the dust—a mound with the shape of an elephant. Thereafter outcropping ledges of rock and buttes grew increasingly more abundant, as did the washes and shallow, stony defiles.

The gray, winding wall sheered off more to the north. About mid-afternoon the trail led down through high gravel banks to a wide stream-bed, dry except in the middle of the sandy waste, where a tiny ribbon of water meandered. It was a mile across this flat to the line of green brush.

"This here's the Muddy," announced Hays, for Jim's benefit. "Bad enough when the water's up. But nothin' to the Dirty Devil. Nothin' atall!"

"What's the Dirty Devil?" asked Jim.

"It's a river an' it's well named, you can gamble on thet. We'll cross it tomorrow sometime."

Next camp was on higher ground above the Muddy, and as it was a protected spot, in the lee of rocks, the riders were not sorry to halt. Wood was fairly plentiful, but there was an entire absence of grass and water. The horses, however, would not suffer, as they had drunk their fill at the river. They were tied up for the night and fed grain.

Hays and Lincoln renewed their argument about the Herrick ranch deal. It proved what Wall had divined— this Brad Lincoln was shrewd, cold, doubtful, and aggressive. Hays was not distinguished for any cleverness. He was merely an honest, unscrupulous robber. These men were going to clash. That was inevitable, Jim calculated; and for that matter he had never ridden with an outfit of hunters or cowboys some of whom did not clash. It was the way of men in the open. Jim remembered a posse with which he had once ridden, in pursuit of rustlers, whose members had argued and fought so much among themselves that they failed to catch their quarry. And certainly it was common knowledge to Westerners that gangs of robbers were continually at strife. Hank Hays was evidently a robber of some degree, though scarcely an outlaw yet. It was difficult to define an outlaw in a country where there was no law.

Early the next day Jim Wall had reason to be curious about the Dirty Devil River, for the descent into the defiles of desert to reach it was a most remarkable one. The trail, now only a few dim old hoof tracks, wound tortuously down and down into canyons of gray, yellow, brown, violet, black earth where stone appeared conspicuous for its absence.

At midday the sun poured down into this colorful hole so hotly that horses and men sweat tremendously, and suffered from thirst and choked with acrid dust. The tracks Hays was following failed and he got lost in a labyrinthine maze of deep washes impossible to climb and seemingly impossible to escape from. Their situation became serious, and they halted for a conference.

"Hell hole!" gasped Happy Jack.

"How much more of this, Hays?" asked Wall, seriously.

"I wish I was shore. If we get off down into the brakes proper it's all up with us. For this ain't nothin' to the seventy miles between here an' the canyon country. I've heared of men bein' chased down in there, an' of prospectors goin' in thet nothin' was ever known of them again."

"We've walked round and round a good many miles," said Wall.

Lincoln got off his horse and went down the canyon, evidently searching for a place to climb to the rim above. But he did not find it. Nevertheless, he returned in an assertive manner, and mounting, called for the others to follow.

"No. Thet's the wrong way," shouted Hays. "Thet's south an' if we keep on we'll never get out."

"Wal, I hear the river an' I'm makin' for it," returned Lincoln.

Jim had heard a faint, low murmur which had puzzled him, and which he had not recognized because he did not dismount. They all followed Lincoln, who halted at the mouth of every intersecting gorge to step away from his horse and listen. Eventually he led them into a narrow, high-walled canyon where ran the Dirty Devil. The water was muddy, the current mean, the sandbar treacherous, but as it was shallow the riders, by driving the pack-animals on a rim, and plunging after themselves, forded it without more mishap than a wetting. The great trouble with the horses was that they were so thirsty they would have mired down had they not been forced on. At last a gravelly bar afforded solid enough footing for the animals to drink, and the men to fill their water-bags.

Still they were lost. There was nothing to do, however, but work up a side canyon, which fortunately did not break up into innumerable smaller canyons, as had those on the other side of the river. Eventually they got out, when Hays at once located himself and soon led them to a camp-site that never could have been expected there.

"Fellers, I'll bet you somethin'," he said, thoughtfully, before dismounting. "There's a roost down in thet country where never in Gawd's world could anybody find us."

"Ha! An' when they did it'd be only our bleached bones," scoffed Lincoln.

"Wal, mebbe you won't need such a place," returned Hays, curtly. "Jim, what do you think?"

"I never saw such a place in all my riding. Nothing would surprise me," replied Wall. "When will we get up high where we can see?"

"Tomorrow. Just before we reach the foothills. Wonderfulest country I ever seen, an' different. Thet's what fetched the Englishman. He's plumb crazy over the view. Wal, it's grand, shore as shootin'."

"Hank, you always had the same weakness."

"Ahuh. A man has to have weaknesses, hasn't he? Yours is whisky, hard feelin', an' greediness," returned Hays, deliberately.

That sally did not set well with Lincoln, though it effectually silenced him. There never had been any love lost between these two men, Jim conjectured.

A good camp-site left the men more leisure, except Happy Jack, who evidently liked to work as well as talk and laugh. He was capable, too. After supper Jim strolled away from camp, down to where the canyon opened upon a nothingness of space and blackness and depth. The hour hung suspended between dusk and night. He felt an overpowering sense of the immensity of this region of mountain, gorge, plain, and butte into which he was traveling.

He heard running water over rocks, a welcome, soothing sound. Coyotes had raised their hue and cry; now and then a shrill whistle of a nighthawk rent the air; cracking of weathered rock and rustling of brush indicated the presence of nocturnal animals. Hays had led up out of the barren network of canyons to the edge of a zone of life. The wind had a whisk, a tone, an icy touch of the mountain heights. While Jim Wall meditated there in the gathering darkness he was visited by an inexplicable reluctance to go on with this adventure. A blank, impondering fate seemed to stand up, vague, indefinable, yet more bitter than a fugitive life. He could not laugh it away. It needed daylight, and clear view of this calling wilderness, to dispel unrealities. He had had presentiments before, all of which had turned out incredibly true, but this clamped his soul somehow. He seemed to catch a glimpse of that soul, in the shape of a naked man, driven to and

fro across the sand and the rock, tormented by horrors
that were not physical, tortured by a spirit within.

Jim ponderingly retraced his steps. He could make but
little of such a visitation, and that little had to do with
his youth, his home, his sister, his mother, all of whom
were but ghosts of a dim past. Every man, even these
brutalized robbers, had some caverns of memory, into
which sleep or unsolicited turn of consciousness thrust
them momentarily. It was singular that the instant he
caught sight of Hays and Lincoln lying prone on the
ground, dark, still, betraying faces turned up to the starlight, this strange feeling left him. It never returned.
But Jim Wall went to bed with a feeling that right then
he should have found his horse and ridden off into the
unknown.

Next morning he remembered something like a distorted dream, but he could not recall details. He had
smoked too much these several days, and the strong drink
Hays had brought along was not conducive to quiet
nerves. Jim found himself confronted by a choice of drift-
ing on in the ways of these men or returning to the lone-
wolf character which had long been his. For the time
being he chose the former.

Despite the abundance of water and feed thereabouts,
some of the horses had strayed. Lincoln came in with the
last few and he was disgruntled. Hays cursed him
roundly. They got a late start. Nevertheless, Hays assured Jim that they would reach Star Ranch toward
evening.

The trail led up a wide, shallow, gravelly canyon full
of green growths. Like a black cloud the mountains
loomed ahead and above. Jim was glad to ride up at last
out of that interminable canyon into another zone—the
slope of the foothills. At last the cedars! Was there ever
a rider who did not love the cedars—sight of their rich,

green foliage and purple berries, their sheathed bark hanging in strips, their dead snags, their protection from wind and cold, their dry, sweet fragrance?

But upon looking back Jim forgot the foreground. Had he ridden out of that awful gulf of colors and streaks? Hays caught up with him. "Come on, Jim. This here ain't nothin'. Wait till we get around an' up a bit. Then I'll show you somethin'."

They rode on side by side. The trail led into a wider one, coming around from the northeast. Jim did not miss fresh hoof tracks, and Hays was not far behind in discovering them.

"Woods full of riders," he muttered, curiously.

"How long have you been gone, Hays?" inquired Jim.

"From Star Ranch? Let's see. Must be a couple of weeks. Too long, by gosh! Herrick sent me to Grand Junction. An' on the way back I circled. Thet's how I happened to make Green River."

"Did you expect to meet Happy Jack and Lincoln there?"

"Shore. An' some more of my outfit. But I guess you'll more'n make up for the other fellers."

"Hope I don't disappoint you," said Jim, dryly.

"Wal, you haven't so far. Only I'd feel better, Jim, if you'd come clean with who you air an' what you air."

"Hays, I didn't ask you to take me on."

"Shore, you're right. Reckon I figgered everybody knew Hank Hays. Why there's a town down here named after me—Hankville."

"A town? No one would think it."

"Wal, it ain't much to brag on. A few cabins, the first of which I threw up with my father years ago. In his later years he was a prospector—before thet a Mormon. I never had no Mormon in me. We lived there for years. I trapped fur up here in the mountains. In fact I got to know the whole country except thet Black Dragon Canyon, an' thet hell hole of the Dirty Devil. . . . My old man was shot by rustlers."

"I gathered you'd no use for rustlers. . . . Well then, Hays, how'd you fall into your present line of business?"

"Haw! Haw! Present line. Thet's a good one. Now, Jim, what do you reckon thet line is?"

"You seem to be versatile, Hays. But if I was to judge from our meeting with the fat Mormon at the ferry, I'd say you relieved people of surplus cash."

"Very nice put, Jim. I'd hate to be a low-down thief. . . . Jim, I was an honest man once, not so long ago. It was a woman who made me what I am, today. Thet's why I'm cold on women."

"Were you ever married?" went on Jim, stirred a little by the other's crude pathos.

"Thet was the hell of it," replied Hays, and he seemed to lose desire to confide further.

Jim revolved in mind a story to tell this robber, if only to please him and establish some kind of background.

"Well, Hank, my story isn't anything to excite pity, like yours. And sure not friendship."

"Ahuh. I had you figgered, Jim," replied Hays, wagging his head. "Shore Jim Wall ain't your right handle. Wal, any handle will do out here. . . . Don't be afraid to tell me about yourself, now or some other time."

"Thanks, Hank. A man gets to be cautious. A rolling stone gathers no moss."

"Wal, I'd rather train with enemies than alone. I can't stand bein' alone much."

"That accounts for Lincoln. He rubs you the wrong way, Hank."

"Brad's a cross-grained cuss, but he has his good points. They don't show in times like this."

Jim had to make conjecture about the times that did

bring out a desirable side of Brad Lincoln. And he had his doubts about it. The trail narrowed into rough going, which necessitated single file, and gradual separation of the riders. The morning was bright, cool, beautiful, with air full of sweet smells of sage, which soft gray growth had come down to meet them. Blue jays squalled, mocking-birds sang melodiously; ring-tailed hawks sailed low over the slopes. Deer loped away among the cedars. As there were three riders ahead of Jim, none of whom got off to shoot, it appeared no time for him to do so, either. Star Ranch probably abounded with game. Jim wondered about this new ranch. It would not last long.

They rode into the zone of the foothills, with ever-increasing evidence of fertility. The blue, cloudy color of the still pools of water in rocky beds gave proof of melting snow. But Jim's view had been restricted for several hours, permitting only occasional glimpses up the gray-black slopes of the Henrys and none at all of the low country.

Therefore Jim was scarcely prepared to come round a corner and out into the open. Stunned by the magnificence of the scene, he would have halted Bay on the spot, but he espied Hays waiting for him ahead, while the others and the pack-animals disappeared round a gray rock-wall bend.

"Wal, pard, this here is Utah," said Hays, as Jim came up, and his voice held a note of pride. "Now let me set you straight. . . . You see how the foothills step down to the yellow an' gray. Wal, thet green speck down there is Hankville. It's about forty miles by trail, closer as a crow flies. An' thet striped messy pot of hash beyond is the brakes of the Dirty Devil. Reckon a diameter of seventy miles across thet circle wouldn't be far wrong. Thet's the country nobody knows. My father told me of a hole

in there I'd shore like to see. Wal, where the green begins
to climb to them red buttes—there you're gettin' out of
hell. An' beyond lays grassy plain after grassy plain,
almost to Green River."

Jim's silence was eulogy enough. In fact, he could not
think of adequate expression.

"Now shift an' look across the canyon country," went
on Hays, stretching a long arm. "There's two hundred
miles of wind an' water-worn rock. You see them windin'
threads, sort of black in the gray. Wal, them's rivers. The
Green runs into the Grand to make the Colorado, less'n
sixty miles from where you're sittin' your hoss. An'
look at the threads meetin' the Colorado. Canyons! I've
looked down into Escalante, San Juan, Noki, Piute. But
thet was when I rode with my father. I couldn't take you
to one of them places. We heard of great stone bridges
spannin' the canyons, but only the Injuns know of them.
. . . Thet round-top mountain way across there is
Navajo. An' now, look, Jim. See thet high, sharp, black
line thet makes a horizon, level as a floor. Thet's Wild
Hoss Mesa. It's seventy-five miles long, not countin' the
slant down from the Henrys. An' only a few miles across.
Canyons on each side. It reaches right out into thet canyon
country, which makes our Dirty Devil here look like a
Mormon ranch full of irrigation ditches. Nobody knows
that country, Jim. Think of thet. My father said only
a few Mormons ever got on top of Wild Hoss Mesa.
. . . What you think of it?"

"Grand. . . . That's all, Hank."

"Ahuh. I'm glad you ain't like Lincoln. We'll get somewhere together, Jim. . . . An' now, comin' nearer home,
there's the Black Buttes, sometimes called Bears Ears,
an' here's Gray Bluff—thet wall thet dances toward us
from the gray out there. . . . An' this mess of rocks

across the valley is Red Rocks. An' so on, as you'll come to know. Round the corner here you can see Herrick's valley an' ranch. It's a bit of rich land thirty miles long an' half as wide, narrowin' like a wedge. Now let's ride on, Jim, an' have a look at it."

But Jim elected to stay behind, trying to realize what it was that caused him to stare blankly, to feel his temples throb. Had he ridden half across the wild West to be made to feel like this?

Jim tried to grasp the spectacle that his eyes beheld. But a moment's sight seemed greater than a thousand years of man's comprehension. It would take time and intimacy to make this Utah his own. But on the moment he trembled, as if on the verge of something from which he could never retrace his steps. His sensations were not his to control.

Across the mouth of Herrick's gray-green valley, which opened under the escarpment from which Jim gazed, extended vast level green and black lines of range, one above the other, each projecting farther out into that blue abyss, until Wild Horse Mesa, sublime and isolated in its noonday austerity, formed the last horizon. Its reach seemed incredible, unreal—its call one of exceeding allurement. Where did it point? What lay on the other side? How could its height be attained?

Nearer, and to the left, there showed a colossal space of rock cleavage, walls and cliffs, vague and dim as the blank walls of dreams, until, still closer, they began to take on reality of color, and substance of curve and point. Mesas of red stood up in the sunlight, unscalable, sentinels of that sepulcher of erosion and decay. Wavy benches and terraces, faintly colorful, speckled with black and gray, ran out into the void, to break at the dark threads of river canyons.

All that lay beyond the brakes of the Dirty Devil.

Here was a dropping away of the green-covered mountain foothills and slopes to the ragged, wild rock and clay world, beginning with scarfs of gray wash and rims of gorge and gateways of blue canyons, and augmenting to a region that showed Nature at her most awful, grim and ghastly, tortuous in line, rending in curve, twisting in upheaval, a naked spider-web of the earth, cut and washed into innumerable ridges of monotonous colors, gray, drab, brown, mauve, and intricate passageways of darker colors, mostly purple, mysterious and repelling. Down in there dwelt death for plant, animal, and man. For miles not one green speck! And then far across that havoc of the elements which led on to a boundless region of color—white jagged rents through miles of hummocky ground, and streaked by washes of gray and red and yellow, on to vast green levels, meadowlike at such a distance, which stretched away to the obstructing zigzag wall of stone, the meandering White Bluffs along the base of which Jim had ridden for many days.

"Down in there somewhere this Hank Hays will find his robbers' roost," soliloquized Jim, and turned his horse again into the trail.

Before late afternoon of that day Jim Wall had seen as many cattle dotting a verdant, grassy, watered valley as ever he had viewed in the great herds driven up from Texas to Abilene and Dodge, or on the Wind River Range of Wyoming. A rough estimate exceeded ten thousand head. He had taken Hays with a grain of salt. But here was an incomparable range and here were the cattle. No doubt, beyond the timbered bluff across the valley lay another depression like this one, and perhaps there were many extending like spokes of a wheel down from the great hub of the Henry Mountains. But where was the market for this unparalleled range?

Herrick had selected as a site for his home what was undoubtedly the most picturesque point in the valley, if not one that had the most utility for the conducting of a ranch business. Ten miles down from the apex of the valley a pine-wooded bench, almost reaching the dignity of a promontory, projected from the great slope of the mountain. Here, where the pines straggled down, stood the long, low cabin of peeled logs, yellow in the sunlight. Below, on the flat, extended the numerous barns, sheds, corrals. A stream poured off the mountain, white in exposed places, and ran along under the bench, and out to join the main brook of the valley.

Somewhat apart from both the corrals and outbuildings on the flat stood a new log cabin, hurriedly built, with chinks still unfilled. The roof extended out on three sides over wide porches, where Wall observed three or four beds, a number of saddles, and other riders' paraphernalia. The rear of the cabin backed against the rocks. Jim understood that Hays had thrown up this abode, rather than dwell too close to the other employees of Herrick. From the front porch one could drop a stone into the brook, or fish for trout. The pines trooped down to the edge of the brook.

Naturally, no single place in all that valley could have been utterly devoid of the charm and beauty nature had lavished there, but this situation was ideal for riders. Hays even had a private corral. As Jim rode up to this habitation his quick eye caught sight of curious, still-eyed men on the porch. Also he observed that there was a store of cut wood stowed away under the porch.

"Wal, here we air," announced Hays. "An' if you don't like it you're shore hard to please. Finest of water, beef,

lamb, venison, bear meat. Butter for our biscuits. An'
milk! An' best of all—not very much work. Haw! Haw!"

"Where do we bunk?" asked Jim, presently.

"On the porch. I took to the attic, myself."

"If you don't mind I'll keep my pack inside, but sleep
out under the pines," responded Wall.

When at length Jim carried his effects up on the porch
Hays spoke up: "Jim, here's the rest of my outfit. . . .
Fellers, scrape acquaintance with Jim Wall, late of Wy-
oming."

That was all the introduction Hays volunteered. Jim
replied: "Howdy" and left a return of their hard scrutiny
until some other time.

Hays went at once into low-voiced conference with
these four men. Happy Jack hauled up the supplies. Brad
Lincoln occupied himself with his pack. Jim brought his
own outfit to a far corner of the porch. Then he strolled
among the pines, seeking a satisfactory nook to unroll his
bed. Jim, from long habit, generated by a decided need of
vigilance, preferred to sleep in coverts like a rabbit, or
any other animal that required protection. He was not
likely to depart from such a habit, certainly not while in
the company of Hank Hays and comrades. His swift
glance at the four members new to him had not been
comprehensive, but it had left a sharply defined impression. Any rancher who would hire this quartet of lean,
dark-faced, hard-lipped, border-hawks for cowboys was
certainly vastly ignorant, if not mentally deranged. Jim
was most curious to meet the English rancher.

At length he found a suitable niche between two rocks,
one of which was shelving, where pine needles furnished
a soft mat underneath, and the murmur of the brook just
faintly reached him. Jim would not throw his bed where
the noise of rushing water, or anything else, might pre-
clude the service of his keen ears. There was no step on

his trail now, but he instinctively distrusted Lincoln, and would undoubtedly distrust one or more of these other men. Hays exemplified the fact of honor among thieves. Jim had come to that conviction. This robber might turn out big in some ways.

Chapter Four

NOT until the following morning did Jim Wall get a satisfactory scrutiny of the four members of Hays' outfit.

His first impression was that not one of them had ever been a cowman, which gave their presence there such incongruity. Nor would any of them ever see their thirtieth year again.

Before breakfast, at the table, and afterward, out on the porch, it was give and take between Wall and this quartet. His lot had never been cast with just such men, but he knew how to meet them.

The eldest, who answered to the name of Mac, was a cadaverous-faced man, with a clammy skin and eyes like a ghoul. He was always twisting and squeezing his hands, lean, sinewy, strong members.

"Whar you from?" he had asked Wall.

"Wyoming last," replied Jim, agreeably.

"An' before thet, Texas, I'll gamble."

"Funny how I'm taken for a Texan, for I'm not. I never was in that state."

"Not funny atall," replied the other, with a laugh. "Leastaways not to Smoky hyar. Haw! Haw! You shore have the look of a Texan."

"Hope that's not against me here in Utah."

"Jest contrary, I'd say," rejoined Mac.

Jeff Bridges, a sturdy, tow-headed man of forty or thereabouts, probably once had been a farmer or a villager. He had a bluff, hearty manner, and seemed not to pry under the surface.

"Glad Hank took you on," he said. "We need one cattleman in this outfit, an' that's no joke."

Sparrowhawk Latimer, the third of the four, greatly resembled a horse thief Wall had once seen hanged—

the same beaked nose, the same small sleek head, the same gimlet eyes of steel.

"Jim Wall, eh, from the Wind River country," he said. "Been through thar, years ago. Must be populated now. It wasn't a healthy place then."

"Lots of ranchers, riders—and sheriffs," returned Jim, easily. "That's why I rode on."

"Wal, them articles is scarce hyar. Utah is wild yet, except over east in the Mormon valleys."

Hays had said to Slocum, the fourth member of this quartet, "Smoky, you an' Wall shore ought to make a pair to draw to."

"You mean a pair to draw *on*," retorted the other. He was slight, wiry, freckled of face and hands, with a cast in one of his light, cold-blue eyes.

"Hell, no!" snorted the robber, in a way to fetch a laugh from his men. "Not *on*! . . . Smoky, do you recollect thet gambler, Stud Smith, who works the stage towns an' is somethin' of a gunslinger?"

"I ain't forgot him."

"Wal, we set in a poker game with him one night. I was lucky. Stud took his losin' to heart, an' he shore tried to pick a fight. First he was goin' to draw on me, then shifted to Jim. An' damn if Jim didn't bluff him out of throwin' a gun."

"How?"

"Jim just said for Stud not to draw, as there wasn't a man livin' who could set at a table an' beat him to a gun."

"Most obligin' an' kind of you, Wall," remarked Smoky, with sarcasm, as he looked Jim over with unsatisfied eyes. "If you was so all-fired certain of thet, why'd you tip him off?"

"I never shoot a man just because the chance offers," rejoined Jim, coldly.

There was a subtle intimation in this, probably not lost upon Slocum. The greatest of gunmen were quiet, soft-spoken, sober individuals who never sought quarrels. They were few in number, compared with the various types of would-be killers met with on the ranges and in the border towns. Jim knew that his reply would make an enemy, even if Slocum were not instinctively one on sight. There was no help for these things, and self-preservation lay solely in being able to instil doubt and fear. Respect could scarcely be felt by men like Slocum. Like a weasel he sniffed around Jim.

"You don't, eh?" he queried. "Wal, I work on the opposite principle. Reckon I'll live longer. . . . Wall, you strike me unfavorable."

"Thanks for being honest, if not complimentary," returned Jim. "I can't strike everybody favorably, that's sure."

Hays swore at his lieutenant. "Unfavorable, huh? Now why the hell do you have to pop up with a dislike for him?"

"I didn't say it was dislike. Just unfavorable. No offense meant."

"Aw, buffalo chips!" ejaculated Hays, in disgust. "You can't be pards with a man who strikes you unfavorable."

"I have been, up to the limit."

"Smoky, I won't have no grudges in this outfit. I've got the biggest deal on I ever worked out. There's got to be harmony among us."

"Hank, you're in your dotage. Harmony among a bunch of grown men, all hard, bitter, defeated outlaws? Bah!"

"Smoky, because you're an outlaw doesn't make me one, or Happy or Brad or Mac or any other of us, unless Jim here. He hasn't confided in me yet."

"I'm no outlaw," declared Jim, coolly.

"It's a little matter thet'll soon be corrected. This Englishman has money enough to fetch the law out on this border. There's your mistake, Hank. I've been ag'in' this deal an' I'll stay ag'in' it."

"Same here," interposed Lincoln.

"Wal, we don't agree," said Hays, calmly. "An' thet's nothin'. But Smoky bobbin' up ag'in' my new man— thet's serious. Now let's lay the cards on the table. . . . Jim, do you want to declare yourself?"

"I'm willing to answer questions—unless they get nasty," replied Jim, frankly. He had anticipated some such circumstance as this, and really welcomed it.

"Will you tell the truth?" queried Slocum, bluntly.

"I'll agree to—if I answer at all," rejoined Jim, slowly.

"How do you size up Hank an' his outfit?" went on Slocum.

"Well, that was easy, as far as Hank is concerned," replied Wall, leisurely. "We met at the ferry on Green River. A third party came over with us. Stingy Mormon who swam his horses to save two bits. Hank held him up."

"Wal, I'll be jiggered!" ejaculated Slocum. "Right thar in town? An' a Mormon, too!"

"Smoky, it was a fool thing to do, but I just couldn't help it," declared Hays, in exasperation.

"We'll be huntin' a roost in the canyons before long," declared Slocum, derisively. And then he addressed Wall again: "Thet puts another complexion on your showin' up with Hank. All the same, since we started this, I'd like to ask a couple more questions."

"Shoot away, Smoky," rejoined Jim, good-humoredly, as he sensed now less danger of a split.

"You got run out of Wyomin'?"

"No. But if I'd stayed on I'd probably stretched hemp."

"Rustlin'?"

"No."

"Hoss-stealin'? Thet hoss of yours is worth stealin'."

"No."

"Hold up a stage or somebody?"

"No. Once I helped hold up a bank. That was years ago."

"Bank robber! You're out of our class, Jim."

"Hardly that. It was my first and only crack at a bank. Two of us got away. Then we held up a train—blew open the safe in the express car."

"What'd you get?" queried Slocum, with an intense interest which was reflected in the faces of his comrades.

"Not much. Only sixty thousand dollars in gold. It was hard to pack away."

Smoky's low whistle attested to his admiration, if no more. The others stood spellbound. Mac rubbed his suggestive hands together.

Jim turned to them: "That, gentlemen, is the extent of my experience as a robber. I was never caught, but the thing dogged. Still, I don't want to give the impression I left Wyoming on that account. As a matter of fact, both deals were pulled off in Iowa. Something personal made Wyoming too hot for me."

"Women!" grinned Hays, his face lighting.

"No."

"Guns?" flashed Slocum, penetratingly.

Jim laughed. "One gun, anyhow."

They all laughed. The tension seemed released.

"Smoky, I call it square of Wall," spoke up Hays. "He shore didn't need to come clean as thet."

"It's all right," agreed Slocum, as if forced to fair judgment. Yet he was not completely satisfied, and perhaps that was with himself.

Hays plumped off the porch rail with boots ringing his relief and satisfaction. "Now, fellers, we can get to work."

"Work! My Gawd! man, we've been druv to skin an' bones since you left," complained Mac.

"What doin'?" asked Hays, in surprise.

"Doin'? Diggin' ditches an' post-holes, cuttin' an' snakin' poles, mixin' mortar, packin' rocks, killin' beeves. Say, fellers, what ain't we been doin'?"

"Wal, you're cowboys now," returned Hays, face-tiously. "An' thet reminds me. Herrick puts a lot of things up to me. I ain't no cattleman. Jim, do you know the cattle game?"

"From A to Z," smiled Wall.

"Say, but I'm in luck. We'll run the ranch now. Who's been boss since I left?"

"Herrick. An' thet shore made Heeseman an' his outfit sore. There's trouble brewin' with him, Hank. We got to get rid of him an' his pards before we can pull any deals."

"Listen, I've only one deal in mind," replied Hays, powerfully. "Thet'll take time."

"How much time?" queried Lincoln.

"I don't know. Ought to have a couple of months. . . . Shore Heeseman sticks in my craw. We'll have a pow-wow tonight. I'll go see the boss. Rest of you get to work. Haw! Haw!"

"What'll I do, Hank?" asked Jim.

"Wal, you look the whole diggin's over."

Jim lost no time in complying with his first order from the superintendent of Star Ranch. What a monstrous and incredible hoax was being perpetrated upon some for-eigner! Jim had no sympathy for him. He was just curious.

Evidently there had been ranchers here in this valley before Herrick. Old log cabins and corrals adjoining the new ones attested to this. The barns, the pastures, the pens teemed with ranch life. Jim did not recall ever hav-ing heard so much of a clamor. Burros were braying all

over the place; horses whistled and neighed; turkeys gob-
bled; pigs squealed; roosters crowed; sheep baaed. It
was certainly a farm scene, and despite the overcrowding,
the disproportion to the natural effects of a normal ranch,
was colorful, bustling, thrilling in the extreme.

He would have been willing to wager something that
no Westerner had ever seen a barn like the one newly
erected. Jim did not know whether to proclaim it a mon-
strosity or a wonderfully new and utilitarian structure.
Probably it was English in design. If Herrick did not
mind expense, this sort of improvement was all right.
There were fences new and puzzling to Jim, as in fact
were all the peeled-log constructions.

Jim passed cowboys with only a word or a nod. He
could get along with that breed, whether here or anywhere, because he had developed his own range life with
them. He made unobtrusive effort to espy ranch hands
of another type—that which was giving Hays concern.
He talked with a stable-boy who proved easy to make
friends with, and to an old man who said he had owned
a homestead across the valley, one of those Herrick had
gathered in. Jim gleaned information from this rancher.
Herrick had bought out all the cattlemen in the valley,
and on round the foothill line to Limestone Springs,
where the big X Bar outfit began. Riders for these small
ranches had gone to work for Herrick. They were Mormons. Jim concluded this was a desirable state of affairs,
because it might account for the natural antagonism sure
to arise between the real cowboys and the older employees
of uncertain vocation. He was told, presently, that Heeseman, with ten men, was out on the range.

Presently Jim encountered Hays, accompanied by a
tall, floridly blond man, garbed as no Westerner had ever
been. This, of course, must be the Englishman. He was
young, hardly over thirty, and handsome in a fleshy way.

"Mr. Herrick, this is my new hand I was tellin' you about," announced Hays, glibly. He was absolutely shining of eye and face. "Jim Wall, late of Wyomin'. . . . Jim, meet the boss."

"How do you do, Mr. Wall," returned Herrick, extending his hand, which Jim took with a bow and a word of acknowledgement. "Hays has been ringing your praises. I understand you've had wide experience on ranches?"

"Yes, sir. I've been riding the range since I was a boy," replied Jim, aware of being taken in by intelligent blue eyes.

"Hays has suggested making you his foreman."

"That is satisfactory to me."

"Are you a Mormon?"

"No, sir."

"To what church do you belong?"

"My parents were Methodists," replied Jim.

"Married?"

"No, sir."

"You are better educated than these other men. It will be part of your duties to keep my books. I'm in a bloody mess as to figures."

"Mr. Herrick, if you haven't kept track of purchases, cattle, supplies, wages—all that sort of thing—it won't be easy to straighten it all out. I've tackled that job before."

"So I was tellin' the boss," interposed Hays. "But I'm shore, Jim, you're equal to thet."

"As I understand ranching," went on Herrick, "a foreman handles the riders. Now as this ranching game is strange to me, I'm glad to have a foreman of experience. I was advised in Salt Lake City and at Grand Junction not to go in for cattle-raising out in this section. The claim was that the Henry Mountains was a rendezvous for several bands of steer thieves. That fact has been verified here by the ranchers from whom I bought land and cattle. My idea, then, was to hire some gunmen along with the cowboys. Hay's name was given me at Grand Junction as the hardest nut in eastern Utah. Not so flattering to Mr. Hays, by Jove! but eminently satisfactory to me. So eventually my offer reached Hays and he consented to work for me, in the capacity, you understand, as a buffer between me and these cow-stealers. It got noised about, I presume, for other men with reputations calculated to intimidate thieves applied to me. I took on Heeseman and his friends. . . . Would you be good enough to give me your opinion, Wall?"

"It's not an original idea at all, Mr. Herrick," responded Jim, frankly, seeing the impression he was making on the Englishman. "That has been done before, in some cases, even to the setting of a thief to catch a thief. Its value lies in the fact that it works. But you really did not need to go to the expense—and risk, I might add —of hiring Heeseman's outfit."

"Expense is no object. Risk, however—what do you mean by risk?"

"Between ourselves I strongly suspect that Heeseman is a rustler and head of the biggest Mount Henry gang."

"By Jove! You don't say? This is ripping. Heeseman said the identical thing about Hays."

Jim was on the lookout for that very thing.

"Hays will kill Heeseman for that," retorted Jim, curtly. "But of course not while he's in your employ. . . . It seems important, Mr. Herrick, for you to understand something of Western ways. There is a difference between hard-riding, hard-gambling, hard-shooting Westerners and rustlers, although a rustler can be that, too. But rustling is low-down. Hank Hays' father was a Mormon prospector. Hank never grew up with cattle. But with horses. He has been a horse-trader ever since

I knew him. If you go over to Green River, to Moab, and towns to the east you will hear that Hays is absolutely not a rustler."

"I took Hays at his word," replied the Englishman. "Heeseman did not impress me. It's rather a muddle."

"Wal, Mr. Herrick, don't you worry none," interposed Hays, suavely. "Shore I don't take kind to what Heeseman called me to your face, but I can overlook it for the present. Just let Heeseman ride on till he piles up. Then it won't be our fault, an' whatever blood-spillin' comes of it can't be laid to you. Besides, so long as you hire his outfit you'll be savin' money. Jim had it figgered wrong about expense. You see, if Heeseman is workin' for you he can't rustle as many cattle as if he wasn't."

"Meanwhile we will be learning the ropes," put in Jim. "Such a big outfit as this needs adjustment. You oughtn't sell a steer this summer."

"Sell? I'm buying cattle now."

"That makes our job easier," returned Hays, with veracity. "Anythin' come of thet deal you had on with thet Grand Junction outfit?"

"Yes. I received their reply the other day," rejoined Herrick. "We'll have to send a letter to Grand Junction to close the transaction. . . . By Jove! that reminds me. I had word from my sister Helen. It came from St. Louis. She is coming through Denver and will arrive at Grand Junction about the fifteenth."

"Aw yes, I recollect—a sister comin' out," replied Hays, constrainedly.

"Young girl—if I may ask?" added Jim, haltingly.

"Young woman. Helen is twenty-two."

"Comin' for a little visit?" asked Hays.

"By Jove! it bids fair to be a life-long one," declared Herrick, as if pleased. "She wants to make Star Ranch her home. Friends of ours ranching it in Colorado were instrumental in my traveling out here. Helen and I are alone—except for distant relatives. We are devoted to each other. If she can stick it out in this bush I'll be jolly glad."

"Ahuh," replied Hays, without his former radiance. "Utah ain't so good a place for a young woman."

"How so? By Jove! she will love it!"

"Rough livin'. Rough men. No women atall. An' Mormons! . . . Excoose me, Mr. Herrick, but is this here sister a healthy girl?"

"All English girls are healthy. She's strong and rides like a Tartar. It's conceivable that she'll turn Star Ranch on end."

"I reckon any good-lookin' girl would do thet, Mr. Herrick," said Hays, resignedly. "But, Jim an' me, here —we only guarantee to handle rustlers."

"By Jove! you'll have to handle these Mormon cowboys, too," laughed Herrick. "Can you drive from Grand Junction in one day?"

"Shore. Easy with buckboard an' good team," replied Hays.

Jim Wall sustained his first slight reaction of dismay.

Their colloquy was interrupted by cowboys driving a string of heifers through the yard before the stable. And when they had passed Herrick resumed his walk with Hays, leaving Jim to his own devices.

Jim strolled around the corrals, the sheds, down the lane between the pastures, out to the open range, where for miles the gray was spotted with cattle, and back to the blacksmith shop. Here he scraped acquaintance with the smith, who proved to be a genial fellow named Crocker. He was another of the homesteaders Herrick had bought out, but he was not a Mormon. Manifestly he and his farming associates had been bewildered by the onslaught of the Englishman upon their peaceful valley and were frankly far the richer for it.

From the smithy Jim gravitated up the winding road to the top of the bench, where the rambling, yellow ranch-house, so new he smelled the rosin from the peeled logs, and the stately pines, and especially the view down the valley, wrought from him a feeling he seldom experienced—envy. How inconceivably good to own such a place—to have a home—to be able to gaze down the trails without keen eyes alert for riders inimical to life, and to revel in the far-flung curves and spurs and deeps of the desert! It was something Jim Wall could never know. His lot did not lie in the pleasant lanes of life.

This Englishman's sister—this Helen Herrick—she would be coming to a remote, wild, and beautiful valley that any healthy-minded girl would love. But whatever the joy of reunion with her brother and the thrill of such unfettered life in the West, such a visit could only end in tragedy. Jim did not like the idea. A woman, especially a handsome one, always made trouble for men, though on the moment Jim was thinking only of her. What queer people the English! He remembered a gambler at Abi-line, an immaculate, black-frocked, white-vested English-man who frequented the dives of that frontier cattle town. He had been the coldest, nerviest proposition Jim had stacked up against. This Herrick had something of the same look, only one of pride and position instead of disgrace and ruin. What would the girl be like? Twenty-two years old, strong, a horsewoman, and handsome—very likely blond, as was her brother! And Jim made a mental calculation of the ruffians in Herrick's employ. Eighteen! More, for including himself there were nine-teen.

He seemed to feel disgust at the prospect of his being party to the misfortune of a young woman. But here, as in so many instances of recent years, he found discontent in the very things he might have avoided. Why rail at circumstance? Hank Hays had befriended him, even if his aim was selfish. Beggars could not be choosers. A robber should not be squeamish, and he, for one, could not be treacherous. Still ——

He strode on and let action change the current of his thought. Avoiding another long gaze at the vast expanse half a hundred miles below, yet exquisitely clear in the rarefied atmosphere, he found a precipitous path down to the level, whence he made his way back to Hays' cabin, satisfied yet dissatisfied with the morning.

Chapter Five

JIM passed the afternoon astride his horse, familiarizing himself with the valley adjacent to the ranch-house.

Riding through the sage was a pleasure to which he had not treated himself for a long while. It added to his growing conception of Star Ranch.

On the way in he passed Heeseman's camp, a group of soiled tents and a chuck-wagon, situated on the opposite side of the bench from that of Hays', and farther back. The bench was stony there and unscalable. A road passed the camp, heading straight for the notch in the valley, and the pass between these two spurs of the Henrys. This was the main road to Grand Junction, a long fifty miles distant.

Jim halted to pass the time of day with the cook, a burly fellow busy at the shelf end of his wagon.

"Howdy! Is this Heeseman's outfit!" asked Jim, civilly.

"Howdy yourself! Git down an' come in," replied the man, taking stock of Jim. "The boss hasn't rid in yet."

"Then I won't wait. About grub-time over at Hays' cabin. Will you tell Heeseman I left my respects? Jim Wall, late of Wyoming."

"Jim Wall, huh? Sure I'll tell him. It's more'n any other of Hays' outfit has done," replied the cook, gruffly.

"They're an unsociable bunch. We're not that way in Wyoming."

Jim rode on back through the barnyards, meeting lean-faced riders, mere boys in years, who eyed him askance and whispered among themselves. Upon arriving at the corral near Hays' cabin he unsaddled and turned Bay loose with the other horses there. He left his saddle, too, but took his Winchester.

Hays greeted him from the porch bench, where he sat among several of his men.

"Where you been, Jim? Gettin' the lay of the land?"

"Just taking 'heap look' round, as an Indian would say. Stopped to say hello to Heeseman, but he wasn't in camp."

"Wal, there's nothin' wrong with your nerve, Jim. I've just been tellin' Brad an' Sparrowhawk here how favorable you hit the boss."

"Come an' get it before I throw it out for the other hawgs," yelled Happy Jack, cheerfully, from within.

There ensued a scramble. Jim did not rush. Entering last, he came upon Smoky Slocum just in the act of sitting down on a box seat, at the end of the long table. Jim kicked the box, which moved away just the instant Smoky stooped and sank. He thudded heavily to the floor with most ridiculously clumsy action. A howl of glee ran from that end of the table up to the head, when Hays, standing aside to see, suddenly roared.

Smoky slowly got up, feeling of his rear and glowering at Jim.

"Can't you see where you goin'?" he growled. "Accidents like that have cost damn fools their lives before this."

"Slocum—I can't lie—about it," laughed Jim. "It wasn't an accident."

"You dumped me on purpose?" bellowed the little man.

"I kicked the box. . . . Just couldn't help it. You'd have done the same to me."

"Wal, I'll be —— —!" ejaculated Smoky, suddenly animated. "So we've got a trick-player in camp. If you'd lied about thet, Mr. Wyomin' Wall, I reckon I'd burned you where you set down. . . . Laugh, all you durned jackasses! But it ain't funny. It jarred my teeth loose."

Hays laughed longest, evidently taking the incident

as another clever move of Jim's, upon whom he beamed. Then he led the assault upon Happy Jack's ample dinner. At the conclusion of the meal he said:

"Fellers, we've a pow-wow on hand. Clear the table. Fetch another lamp. We'll lay out the cards an' some coin, so we can pretend to be settin' in a little game, if anybody happens along. But the game we're really settin' in is the biggest ever dealt in Utah."

So it came to pass that Jim Wall sat down with a crew of robbers to plot the ruin of a rich and eccentric rancher.

"Talk low, everybody," instructed Hays. "An' one of you step out on the porch now an' then. Heeseman might be slick enough to send a scout over here. 'Cause we're goin' to do thet little thing to him. . . . Happy, dig up thet box of cigars I've been savin'.'"

"Cigars!" ejaculated Smoky Slocum.

"Hank, trot out some champagne," jeered Brad Lincoln.

"Nothin' to drink, fellers," returned Hays. "We're a sober outfit. No gamblin' for real money. No arguin' or fightin'. . . . Any of you who doesn't like thet can walk out now."

They were impressed by his cool force, as well as by the potency of the future. Certainly not one of them moved.

"All right. Wal an' good. We're set," he went on. "Today I changed my mind about goin' slow with this job. Never mind why."

Jim Wall had a flash of divination as to this sudden right-about-face. Hays was deeper than he had appeared at first.

"Herrick reckons there are upwards of ten thousand head of stock on the range. Some of these Mormons he bought out sold without a count. I bought half a dozen herds for Herrick. An' I underestimated say rough calculatin' around two thousand head. So there's twelve thousand good. Thet's a herd, fellers. Can it be drove?"

"Are we a lot of cowboys?" queried Lincoln, scornfully.

"No, an' neither air we a lot of rustlers," resumed Hays, just as sarcastically. "If you can't help me figger, why, just keep still. . . . Air there any of you who wouldn't care to play a game for twelve thousand head of cattle at forty dollars per?"

There did not appear to be a single one.

"Ahuh. Wal, thet's okay. Now can we drive such a big herd?" Hays this time directed his query at Jim.

"How far?" asked Jim.

"Fifty miles. Fair to middlin' road. We can meet buyers there who'll pay an' no questions asked. No stiff count."

"Yes. With eight riders well mounted it can be done in three days—provided they don't have to fight."

"Aha!" said Smoky puffing a cloud of smoke.

"Wal, we'd have to fight shore as hell. An' Heeseman's outfit is bigger than ours."

"No sense in stealin' stock for some other outfit," added Brad Lincoln.

"Agree with you," returned Hays, promptly. "I didn't like the idee. But it's so damn easy!"

"Boss, listen to this idee," spoke up Smoky. "Most of these Star cattle range down the valley twenty miles below here. How'd it do for say five of us to quit Herrick an' hide below somewhere? Meanwhile you go to Grand Junction an' arrange to have your buyers expect a bunch of cattle every week. A thousand to two thousand head. We'd make the drives an' keep it up as long as it worked.

You're boss, an' Wall here is foreman. You could keep the cowboys close to the ranch."

"Smoky, it's shore a big idee," declared Hays, enthusiastically. "But what about Heeseman?"

"Wal, we couldn't keep it from him."

"Not very long, anyway."

"Heeseman's the rub. We gotta do away with him."

"Let's clean out his bunch."

Hays shook his shaggy head over these various replies.

"Fellers, if we pick a fight with thet outfit, some of us will get killed an' others crippled. Then we couldn't pull the deal. A better idee is for one of us to kill Heeseman."

"Reckon it would. Thet'd bust the outfit."

"Who'd you pick on to do thet, Hank?"

Jeff Bridges boomed out: "Why, Smoky, of course, or Brad."

"Nope," said Hays, shaking his head. "With all thet's due Smoky an' Brad I wouldn't choose either. Jim, here, is the man for thet job."

"An' why?" demanded Smoky, in the queerest of tones.

Whether he was insulted or jealous would have been difficult to say.

"Wal, for two reasons. Jim has it on any of us handlin' a gun, an' second —— ——"

"How do you know thet?" interposed Lincoln, acidly.

"Hell's fire!" burst out Hays, suddenly ablaze. "There you go, you — — —! I suppose you think I ought to let you try Jim out? Wal, you can gamble on this. If I did we'd be two men out."

His fiery intensity silenced them. Jim personally was relieved to see this little by-play. It showed Hays was a strong leader and it gave a line on the testy Slocum and the taciturn Lincoln.

"Go on, boss. I'm shore we figger you have the best

for all of us at heart," spoke up Mac, for the first time. "You never played no favorites."

"Jim, it'd be murder for you to throw a gun on Heeseman," said Hays, spreading wide his hands.

"I'm like Brad. How do you know that?" rejoined Jim, coolly.

"Wal, Heeseman's gifts don't lie thet way. He's killed a couple of men thet I know of. But I'll bet I can go pick a quarrel with him an' do it myself. To be dead certain, though, we'd better sic Jim on him. Besides, Heeseman doesn't know Jim."

"If you ask me, I say the better plan is to waylay Heeseman an' his outfit," said Lincoln. "Do for him sure an' all or most of his men. There's a couple of rattle-snakes among them."

"Waylay them, huh," mused Hays, scratching his unshaven chin. "Sort of low-down for *us*."

"We're playin' for big stakes."

"Mebbe we could drive off six or eight thousand head of stock before Heeseman ever found out," put in Smoky. "What's the sense of fightin' it out till we have to. Let's don't cross any Dirty Devils till we come to them."

The suggestion found instant favor on all sides.

"But we don't want Heeseman trailin' us," expostulated Hays.

"You mean after we pull the deal?" queried Brad, incredulously.

"Shore I mean after."

"Wal, what in thunderation do we give a damn for him, when we've got the coin an' on our way to thet roost we're due to find?"

"I don't just like the idee, fellers," replied Hays, evasively.

Jim Wall, studying the robber leader closely, imagined that Hays was not exposing all the details of his plot.

"Aw, to hell with Heeseman, before or after!" exclaimed Smoky. "Let's put my idee to a vote."

When this suggestion was solemnly complied with, making use of the deck of cards, it was found that Slocum had won.

"So far so good," said Hays, as if relieved. "Now let's see. . . . Smoky, tomorrow you take your gang, includin' Brad, an' quit. Pack a slue of grub an' grain, an' hide out below. Cache what you don't need. I'll go to Grand Junction for new hands. See? But all I'll come back with will be instructions for you to follow. Then you can go drivin'."

"Good! An' how about the cash?"

"Wal, them buyers won't pay me in advance, you can gamble on thet. But they'll pay you. Just divide with your outfit an' save our share."

"Short an' sweet. I like it more all the time," declared Smoky. The trust imposed upon him sat lightly. Jim had no doubt of his honesty with his leader and comrades. Herein lay another reason for the loyalty to Hays. The robber began to loom to Jim.

"We'll want to know where your camp is," went on Hays. "Reckon I'd better ride out with you tomorrow."

"No. You rustle for Grand Junction. We'll see thet Happy an' Jim know where to find our camp."

Jim thought of something. "Men, has it occurred to you that you can't drive cattle up this road and through the ranch?"

"Shore. No need. It'd be a seventy-mile drive if we came this way. But we'll drive round by Limestone, an' up the other valley road. About the same distance to Grand."

"Air we forgettin' anythin'?" muttered the leader, his big eyes staring into space.

"Nothin' but Heeseman," croaked Lincoln.

"Wal, there are a couple of more things, but we needn't go into them now," responded the leader. He slid several cigars into his vest pocket, and throwing the box upon the table he said: "Divide 'em even. An' I hope it won't be your last dollar smoke."

The conference ended. Hays turned to the open fire, and seeking a seat in the shadow by the chimney, he pondered. It was Jim's opinion that the chief had vastly more on his mind than he had divulged. Lincoln gave him a suspicious stare. The others seemed eminently pleased with the outlook, though no more was said in Jim's hearing. They joked and smoked.

"Let's play noseys," suggested Happy Jack.

A howl of protest and derision went up from half those present.

"I'd play for two-bits a card, but not just to have my beak all red," said, Smoky.

"What kind of a game is noseys?" asked Jim, curiously.

"Set in with Happy an' see."

"What's it like, Happy?"

"Wal, it's better'n poker, any day," replied Happy Jack. "Takes as good playin'. A hell of a lot more guts. An' doesn't lose you much money. . . . You deal three cards around. First feller left of dealer leads. You have to follow suit. If you can't you draw off the deck till you can. High card, of course, takes trick. When the decks all drawn you have to eat the card led. Thet is you take it up an'. . . . But come an' let me show you."

"Not me. I want to know where the noseys come in."

"Wal, whoever gets left with any cards, even one, is the loser. An' everybody gets three whacks at his nose with three cards only. Also he has to pay two-bits to every player for each card he's left with."

"Fine game for this outfit," laughed Jim.

"Shore there air a lot of big beaks to beat. It's the fightenest game you ever seen."

Jim bade them good-night and went out. His last glimpse of Hays was thought-provoking. Lighting another cigar, which he vowed would be the last of his smoking for a while, Jim strolled up and down the porch, revolving in mind the conference.

It was a spring night, starry, with an edge on the mountain air that meant frost in the morning. Coyotes were barking. And there came another sound which never failed to rend—the peeping of spring frogs. Plaintive, sweet, they probed the deeps of memory. Jim did not like the night so well as the day. And although he had crossed the Rubicon, had involved his word and meant to see this deal through, he liked it less and less. Was it possible that this lantern-eyed robber had evil intentions toward Herrick's sister? Jim scouted the suspicion. Certainly, if the man was susceptible to women, he would react normally under favorable conditions. But to plot more than he had expressed, to involve his men in something vastly worse than the mere stealing of a herd of cattle, to betray them with murder and abduction—No! this Hank Hays was too big a man for that. He had the loyalty of his band. And yet ——

"Damn the girl part of it, anyhow," he muttered, flinging his half-smoked cigar out into the noisy brook. Why did a woman have to come along to upset the best-laid plans of men?

Jim went to his comfortable bed up under the dark pines, and lay awake in the shadows, listening to the whispers about him. The very rocks seemed to have voices. Nature had endowed Jim with sensitiveness and life had dealt him iron. The harder he grew the more this secret, deeply-hidden faculty of feeling had to be resisted.

The next morning brought sombre faces and action. Five of Hays' outfit rode away with six of the pack horses and most of the supplies. Hays watched them until they disappeared among the cedars.

"Wal, now I'll brace the boss," he said.

"What excuse will you give him?"

"Anythin' would do to tell Herrick. But Heeseman will see through me, I'm afeared."

"Very well. You tell Herrick that your outfit split over me."

"Over you—? dog-gone! That ain't so poor. But why?"

"Both Slocum and Lincoln are sort of touchy about gun-throwing, aren't they? Well, tell him how queer that brand of gunmen is—how he instinctively hates the real gunman. And that Slocum and Lincoln made you choose between them and me. You chose me and they rode off with their pards."

"Ahuh. Sort of so the idea will get to Heeseman's ears that in a pinch with guns I'd rather have you backin' me than them?"

"Exactly. Only elaborate it. Herrick won't understand, so the more mysterious you make it the better."

Not long afterward Hays returned to the cabin jubilant. "You'd never guess, Jim. That Englisher laughed like the very devil. An' he ordered me to ride off after some desperadoes who're not afraid of Jim Wall."

"Ha! Ha! But Heeseman won't get a laugh out of it."

"See here. Don't fetch things to a ruction with him."

"I'll steer clear, Hays. But if Heeseman should happen to brace me ——"

"Shoot the lights out of him," interrupted Hays,

fiercely. "Wal, I'm off for Grand. Happy, pack me a snack of grub."

"How long will it take you to ride over?"

"Eight hours, I reckon. An' I'll be back tomorrow night."

"Won't take you long, then, to make connection with your buyers?"

"Wal, I should smile not."

"Excuse my curiosity, boss, but I can't help wondering how you can establish connection so quickly, since you claim you are not a rustler."

"Thet's my affair, Jim. But I'll tell you some day."

"Certainly these buyers will know you're selling stolen cattle?"

"Oh, shore."

After Hays had gone Jim settled himself to pass the hours away.

"Mebbe it won't be so tedious," observed Happy Jack, dryly. "We've got three rifles an' a sack of shells right handy. So let 'em come."

Jim half expected a visit from Herrick, but the morning dragged by without any sign of anyone. About mid-afternoon, however, six riders appeared coming down the lane along the bench. The sight made Jim start. How often had he seen the like—a compact little company of riders, dark-garbed, riding dark horses! It was tremendously suggestive to a man of his experience.

"Come here, Jack," called Jim. "Take a squint down the road."

Happy Jack looked. "Wal, they're comin' shore enough. Reckon I'd better have a peep at our supper. It might burn."

Jim reached inside the door and, drawing out his rifle, he advanced to the front of the porch, where he leaned carelessly against a post. When the group of riders reached the point where the lane crossed the brook, just out of pistol range, they halted, and one, evidently the leader, came on to the bridge.

"Hi, thar!" he yelled, reining his horse.

"Hi, yourself!" shouted back Jim.

"Is this your day fer visitors?"

"We're at home every day and Sundays."

The man, whom, of course, Jim took to be Heeseman, walked his horse half the intervening distance and stopped again. Jim's swift eye ascertained that the caller's rifle-sheath was empty, a significant fact. It was still too far away to see what he looked like, but he had stature, and the figure of a man used to the saddle.

At this juncture Happy Jack emerged from the cabin and carelessly propped a rifle against the wall.

"Who's callin'?" he boomed.

"I don't know," replied Jim.

"I'm Bill Heeseman, an' I come over to talk," called the visitor.

"Friendly talk?" queried Jim.

"Wal, if it ain't you'll be to blame."

"Come right over."

The five men left behind over the brook puffed their cigarettes and turned dark faces to watch their leader dismount and walk unconcernedly along the path.

Jim leaned his rifle against the rail and stood aside. Heeseman did not look up as he mounted the steps. He took off an old sombrero to disclose the tanned, clear-skinned face of a man under forty, with narrow blue eyes reddened by wind and dust. It was a more open visage than Jim had expected to see. Certainly Heeseman was a more prepossessing man, at first sight, than Hays.

"Mind if I set down?" he asked.

"Make yourself at home," replied Jim, and while the other sat down Jim took a less suspicious posture.

"Air you Wall?"

"Yes, that's my name. And this is Happy Jack, another of Hays' outfit."

Heeseman nodded to Jack, who replied with a civil, "Howdy!" and went back into the cabin. Then Heeseman leaned against the wall and treated Jim to a frank, shrewd gaze, which yet was not unmixed with steely speculation. Jim did not feel any revulsion toward the man, but he knew the cold, curious glint of that look.

"You're Hays' right-hand man, just late from Wyomin'?"

"Last is correct, anyhow."

"Old pards? Hays has roamed around a good bit."

"Not so old."

"Do you *know* him?" queried Heeseman, in lower voice.

"Perhaps not so well as you," replied Jim, who suddenly reminded himself that he knew Hays but slightly.

"I'm goin' to tell you somethin'."

"Heeseman, you'll only waste your breath," declared Jim, impatiently. That was the thing to say, but he was impatient with himself.

"Wal, I don't waste much of thet," drawled the other. "But if you wasn't new to Utah I'd save myself this trouble. An' you're goin' to believe what I tell you."

"Why will I?"

"Because it's true."

No argument could gainsay that; moreover, the man had truth in his blue slits of eyes, in his voice, especially in the slight unevenness, which hinted of resentment or justice.

"Did Hays tell you I was a rustler?"

"I think he mentioned it."

"Did he tell you we was pards once? . . . That he double-crossed me?"

"No."

"Can you swear honest thet what I say doesn't make you think?"

"I couldn't swear that honestly," returned Jim, intensely interested despite the antagonism he had determined upon.

"Wal, I'll let it go at thet," returned Heeseman, coolly. "Much obliged for lettin' me come up. An' if you get curious, just ride over to see me."

He rose, stretched his long length, and walked off the porch to mount his horse, leaving Jim about as surprised as he had ever been. Happy Jack came out in time to see him join his comrades and ride back with them toward the corrals.

"Short visit. Glad it was. What'd he want?"

"Darn if I savvy, altogether. Didn't you hear any of our talk?"

"No. I reckoned the less I heard the better. Then Hank couldn't razz me. But I had a hunch of what he was up to."

Jim did not press the question. He carried his rifle back into the cabin, rather ashamed of his over-haste and feeling already curious enough to call on Heeseman. Later, Happy Jack went hunting in the hope of packing in a haunch of venison. Jim had the place to himself until sunset, when the cook returned, staggering under his load.

"Like shootin' cows," he said, depositing his load. "Got a nice fat buck. I skinned out a ham an' hung up the rest. We'll take a hoss tomorrow an' pack it down."

They had supper, after which Jack smoked and talked, while Jim listened. Evidently Happy Jack had taken a liking to him. Jim went to bed early, not because he was sleepy, but to keep from calling on that fellow, Heeseman.

How many nights Jim Wall had lain down under the

dark trees to wakefulness, to the thronging thoughts that must mock the rest of any man who had strayed from the straight and narrow path! It tormented him at certain times. But that never kept the old concentrated pondering over tomorrow from gaining control of his consciousness. Men of his type made a complexity of self-preservation.

There had been no hesitation about Hank Hays declaring himself in regard to Heeseman. Callous, contemptuous, Hays had indicated the desirability of ridding the range of Heeseman. But Heeseman had been subtle.

Unquestionably his motive had been to undermine Hays in Jim's regard. And a few questions, and an assertion or two, had had their effect. Jim made the reservation that he had not accepted Hays on anything but face value. Still, the robber had gradually built up a character of intent force, cunning, and strength. These had crashed, though there was no good reason for that. Jim had not accepted Hays' word for anything.

Reduced to finalities, Jim found that Heeseman's last suggestive statement was at the bottom of the trouble. Not that Hays had been a rustler partner of Heeseman, not that he had been or was still a Mormon, but that he was not a square partner! This stuck in Jim's craw.

Why this seemed true puzzled Jim. He knew nothing about Mormons. And now he guessed they were secretive. Heeseman had simply verified a forming but still disputed suspicion in Jim's mind—that Hank Hays had evil designs upon Herrick's sister. Heeseman and Hays had probably known for weeks that this English girl was expected to arrive.

Suppose he had! What business was that of Jim's? None, except that he now formed one of Hays' band and as such had a right to question activities. Rustling cattle,

at least in a moderate way, was almost a legitimate business. Ranchers back to the early days of the cattle drives
from Texas had accepted their common losses. It had
been only big steals that roused them to ire and action,
to make outlaws out of rustlers. Nevertheless, it was ex-
tremely doubtful, out here in the wilds of Utah, that even
a wholesale steal would be agitating. To abduct a girl,
however, might throw Western interest upon the perpe-
trators. Hays' object assuredly was to collect ransom. In
that case he would be pretty much of a hog.

Still, that had not been Heeseman's intimation, nor
had it been Jim's original suspicion. He gave it up in
disgust. Time would tell. But he did not feel further inclined to call upon Heeseman. He would stick to Hays,
awaiting developments.

The ensuing day passed uneventfully. No one of
Smoky's outfit showed up, nor did Hays return. Jim
waited for Herrick to give him orders, which were not
forthcoming. The rancher was chasing jack rabbits and
coyotes with the hounds.

Next morning Jim made it a point to ride over to the
barns. The rancher came down in a queer costume. The
red coat took Jim's eye. A motley pack of hounds and
sheep-dogs was new to Jim, as he had not seen or heard
any dogs about the ranch. Jim was invited to ride along
with Herrick and the several cowboys. They went by
Heeseman's camp, which was vacant. Jim was to learn
that the rancher had put the Heeseman outfit to work on
the cutting and peeling of logs up on the slope, pre-
paratory to the erection of a new barn.

Jack rabbits were as thick as bees. The cowboys led
the dogs, which soon became unmanageable and bolted.
Then the race was on. Where the ground was level and
unobstructed by brush or cut up by washes Herrick did
fairly well as to horsemanship, but in rough going he

could not keep to the English saddle. He would put his horse at anything and he' had two falls, one pretty jarring.

"Boss, shore as the Lord made little apples you'll kill yourself with thet pancake," said one of the long-legged cowboys, most solicitously.

"You are alluding to my saddle?" queried Herrick, standing to be brushed off.

"Thet's no saddle. It's a pancake," was the reply.

Then ensued a most interesting argument which Herrick, despite his persistence, certainly lost. He appealed to Jim.

"Mr. Herrick, in this rough country you want a cow-saddle," replied Jim. "You see, aside from heavy cinches and stirrups, and room to tie your rope, canteen, rifle-sheath, saddle-bags, and slicker, or even a pack, you want something to stick on. For so much of the riding is up and down steep hills."

Notwithstanding this, Herrick finished out the hunt. He was funny and queer, but he was game, and Jim liked him. On the way back Jim amused the Englishman by shooting running jack rabbits with his Colt. He managed to kill three out of five, to Herrick's infinite astonishment and admiration.

"By Jove! I never saw such marksmanship," he ejaculated.

"That was really poor shooting."

"Indeed! What would you call good shooting, may I ask?"

"Well, riding by a post and putting five bullets into it. Or splitting the edge of a card at twenty feet."

"Let me see your gun?"

Jim Wall broke his rule when he handed it over, butt first.

Herrick looked at it with mingled feelings. "Why, there's no trigger!" he exclaimed, in utter astonishment.

"I do not use a trigger."

"Thunderation, man! How do you make the pistol go off?"

"Look here. Let me show you," said Jim, taking the gun. "I thumb the hammer . . . like that."

"By Jove! But please explain."

"Mr. Herrick, the cocking of a gun and pulling the trigger require twice as much time as thumbing. For example, supposing the eyesight and the draw of two men are equal, the one who thumbs his hammer will kill the other."

"Ah!—Er—Yes, I see. Most extraordinary. Your American West is quite bewildering. Is this thumbing a common practice among you desperadoes?"

"Very uncommon. So uncommon that I'll be obliged if you will keep it to yourself."

"Oh! Yes, by Jove! I see. Ha! Ha! Ha! I grasp the point. . . . Wall, you're a comforting fellow to have round the place."

Herrick was evidently a free, careless, impressive man who had been used to fulfilling his desires. His eccentricity was not apparent, except in the fact of his presence there in wild Utah. He liked horses, dogs, guns, the outdoors, physical effort. But he had no conception whatever of his remarkable situation in this unsettled country.

When they arrived at the barn he asked Jim to ride up to the house, where they would have a brandy and soda and look over some English guns.

The big living-room had three windowed sides and was bizarre and strange to Jim, though attractive. Herrick had brought with him a quantity of rugs, skins, pictures, weapons, and less easily named articles, which, along with Western furniture and blankets, an elk head and a bear skin, made the room unique.

"I've sworn off drinking," said Jim, lifting his glass. "But one more, Mr. Herrick. To your good luck!"

The heavy English guns earned Jim's solemn shake of head. "No good at all here, Mr. Herrick. Not even for grizzly. Get a forty-four Winchester."

"Thank you. I shall do so. I'm fond of the chase."

Herrick had his desk near a window, and upon it, standing out in relief from books, papers, ornaments, was a framed picture of a beautiful, fair-haired, young woman. The cast of her features resembled Herrick's. That was a portrait of his sister.

Jim carried a vision of it in his mind as he rode back down the bench. He cursed the damned fool Englishman who was idiot enough to bring such a girl out to Utah. This was not Africa, where a white woman was safe among cannibals and negroes, so Jim had read. Then he cursed Hays. And lastly he cursed, not himself, but the predicament into which he had allowed himself to become inveigled.

"I'll have to stick it out," he muttered, that fair face and shining hair before his inward eye. "I might have chucked this outfit."

Chapter Six

"WAL, I run into Smoky's outfit over the divide," announced Hays, complacently. "Damme if they wasn't drivin' over two thousand head."

Jim had nothing to say, though there were strong queries on his lips. Hays' plans were carrying through. The robber had a peculiar radiance.

"Dumplin's! Dog-gone, Happy, but I'm a hawg. Gimme some more."

"I'll have to hoof it up to see the boss tonight," he said, after finishing the late supper. "Put me wise to what's come off in my absence."

"We've had no sign of Smoky's outfit. So we don't know where his camp is."

"I do. It's not more'n a mile from where I showed you the brakes of the Dirty Devil."

"Up or down?"

"Up. Back up in a canyon. Good place an' out of sight. I gave Smoky orders to pack supplies back from Grand Junction every trip."

"Hank, reckon you're figger'n on a long hole-up somewheres," said Happy Jack, with a grin.

"Have you run into Heeseman?" went on Hays, ignoring Jack's hint.

"Yes. He called on us," replied Jim, casually.

"*What?*"

"I told you, Hank. Heeseman came down to see us."

"Hell you say!" ejaculated Hays, certainly astounded. "Tryin' to pick a fight?"

"Not at all. I think he was curious to look me over."

"Wal! What satisfaction did he get?"

"He's pretty shrewd, Hank. He sized me up. If that is why he called, he got satisfaction all right."

"Did he say anythin' about me?" demanded Hays, sullen fire lighting his eyes.

"That was the funny part of it," replied Jim, frankly lying. "He never mentioned you."

"Humph! I don't savvy that dodge. It's no good. Heeseman is the slickest customer in Utah. Just tryin' to scrape acquaintance, eh?"

"I think so. It struck me that he might be wanting to throw his outfit with yours."

"Ahuh. I had thet hunch. It might wal be," replied Hays, meditatively. "Won't hurt for us to lay low, lettin' him make advances. Heeseman's a slow cuss. But he's as sure as a rattler."

"Herrick put Heeseman's outfit to cutting and peeling logs. He wants more horses, and a barn for them."

"Thet's good. It'll keep that outfit from ridin' down Limestone way. An' the cowboys—where have they been?"

"Plenty of work around, but little riding, except after the hounds. I had a chase after jack rabbits with the boss."

"Hounds an' jacks! What next? However, it's not so bad. Anythin' for us but regular ranchin'. Haw! Haw!"

"Herrick took me up to see his guns," went on Jim, easily, with furtive eyes on Hays. "Have you seen them?"

"Shore. Cannons, I'd say. Worse than the old buffalo needle-gun."

"I'd hate to be bored by that five-hundred express, I think he called it."

"Humph! If I gotta be bored, the bigger the bullet the better."

"That's a beautiful living-room of Herrick's. Have you been in there?"

"Yes. He makes that his office. Funny lot of knick-knacks. There's one thing I'm a-goin' to own, though."

Jim laughed. He did not need to ask any more. Suddenly then a tigerish sensation shot through his vitals. It was like an unexpected attack.

"I'd like to own all that stuff," he said, carelessly. "Well, what's on the cards now? You're back. Smoky's outfit is on the job. Heeseman is stalled, I think, though I'll not swear to that."

"We'll aim to keep everybody workin' hard around this neck of the woods. An' we'll pitch in ourselves. That's all on the cards for the present."

Three days of genuine labor around the ranch, more especially in construction of the new barn, left Jim so happily tired each night that he would have liked it to go on indefinitely. Work was good. Jim could handle tools, and that soon became manifest. But on the fourth day, toward the close, Herrick approached Jim.

"Wall, I want you to go to Grand Junction tomorrow after my sister," he said. "Take the cowboy Barnes with you. His home is in Grand Junction. Have him hitch the black team to the buckboard and start early. My sister will not arrive until the following day or the next. Usually that stage gets into Grand Junction before ten o'clock. Start back at once and come speedily."

"Yes, sir," replied Wall, resuming his work. But out of the tail of his eye he saw Hays.

"Boss, I reckon I'll go along with Wall," he said, coolly.

"Hays, I did not ask your services," returned Herrick. "You are needed here." His tone as much as his words settled the matter.

Jim purposely delayed his hour of quitting, in order to avoid Hays. His state, not improbably, was identical with Hays', but Jim did not care to have the robber know that. By the time he had arrived at their cabin, however, he had himself well in hand, though still perplexed and vaguely startled that he had been chosen by Herrick. He sustained some other feeling, too; and if it were not a crowing over Hays he failed to interpret what it was.

Dusk was falling. The day had been warm for April. The spring frogs were shrilly peeping. Jim stopped a moment on the porch to gaze out over the darkening ranch. Cattle were lowing. This feeling he had now was evasive, but he sustained it long enough to realize regret. He liked ranch work. For years he had missed it. Sighing, he went on to the washbench.

Inside the cabin Hays appeared in a brown study, but he had nothing to say upon Jim's entrance. At Jack's cheery call they took their seats.

Hays did not eat as heartily as usual. And at table, when he took a moment to speak, he was jolly. After the meal ended he lighted his pipe, and without facing Jim he said:

"Jim, had the boss mentioned this here trip before?"

"No. I was as surprised as you."

"Wal, suppose you make some excuse an' let me go instead?"

"What?" exclaimed Jim, blankly.

"I could use a couple of hours in Grand Junction," rejoined Hays. "There was one buyer I didn't see. So this offers a good chance."

"But Herrick won't like that, Hays," protested Jim. "He turned down your proposal cold."

"Shore, he did. Damn funny, I take thet, too. But if you wouldn't or couldn't go, I'd be next choice."

"He'd think it strange," said Jim, sharply, trying to pierce through the back of Hays' head.

"What'n'hell do I care what Herrick thinks?" retorted Hays, losing patience. "If you'll do what I say I'll get to go."

"Hays, you surprise me. Here you are on the eve of

a big deal—the biggest of your life. And you risk anger-
ing Herrick at this stage. Man, can't you think? It would
be a bad move. A mistake. For Heaven's sake, why are
you so keen on going to Grand Junction? What for?"

"I told you," snapped Hays, taking refuge in anger.

"Hays, I refuse," declared Jim, shortly. He must keep
up his pretence of cautiousness for all their sakes, but he
wanted to flash out stingingly with the truth. "Herrick
ordered me to go. And I'm going."

Hays puffed his pipe. He was beaten. And now he must
save his face.

Jim turned to the surprised cook.

"Happy, I'll want breakfast at daylight tomorrow."

"Any time, Jim."

Finally Hays veered around heavily, with traces of
anger vanishing. "Wal, I reckon mebbe you're right,
Jim," he said, honestly. "Only it didn't seem so."

By sunrise next day Jim Wall was on his way to Grand
Junction. Young Barnes, the cowboy, had his hands full
with the spirited team.

Frost sparkled on the sage and rocks; the iron-shod
hoofs rang on the hard road; the swift pace engendered
a stinging wind; deer bounded ahead to disappear in the
brush on the slope; bold coyotes stood and gazed.

"Are the horses gun-shy?" asked Jim, his lips near the
driver's ear.

"No. But they're feelin' their oats an' I reckon you
hadn't better shoot yet, leastways fer nothin'."

Jim had to wrap the robe about him, and then he felt
uncomfortably cold, until a rising grade slowed down
the team and the sun began to warm his back. Then he
applied himself to a twofold task—that of winning the
driver's confidence and gaining what information was
available.

He asked numberless questions about the country, in fact whatever popped into his mind. Trails, waterholes, ranchers, riders, the pass they were climbing, timber and game in the mountains—all these claimed their share of Jim's interest, but he did not yet touch on any other than casual things.

The pass was long, of gradual ascent, and afforded little view. Once over, however, the scene ahead was superb, a great valley ending in a long red and black range. Jim kept sharp watch for a road coming in on the left. He was not greatly concerned about cattle tracks, however, because there were plenty under the wheels of the buckboard. And it was a hard, white gravel-and-limestone road, on which it was difficult to judge tracks.

"I like the country powerful well," said Jim, frankly. "But I'm not so crazy about my job."

"Bet you was a cowboy once," replied Barnes, with a grin.

"You bet. And sure wish I was still. But I got to going wrong, and first thing I shot a man. . . . Heigho! I wasn't any older than you."

"What's yer job hyar?" asked the boy, emboldened by Jim's confidence.

"Say, didn't you know why Herrick hired Hays and Heeseman?"

"All us fellers had idears."

"Well, I think Herrick wanted some hard-shooting riders as a sort of protection."

"You ain't long in Utah."

"You're right there. So I don't know the ropes."

"Wal, Mr. Jim, I'll say this. It was a good idear of Herrick's if you fellers play square. This neck of Utah is bigger'n all outdoors, an' it's overrun with varmints, two-legged as wal as four-legged."

"Barnes, you've hit the thing plumb center," replied Jim, soberly. "Thanks for speaking right out."

"Nobody much in Utah knows who's a rustler an' who ain't," went on Barnes. "Your neighbor might be one, an' your boss might be the boss of a rustlin' outfit. Thet's the hell of it."

"How about Heeseman?" asked Jim. "Don't talk against your good sense, Barnes. I'm just asking. I don't know anything about this game up here, as you can see. And what you choose to tell me I'll keep to myself."

"I had a hunch thet way. . . . Wal, some people says Heeseman's outfit rustles, an' some don't believe it. He has a brand, H bar, an' a range over back of Monticello."

"That's straight talk. How about Hank Hays?"

"I'd be up a stump if the boss asked me thet. I'd shore have to lie. Everybody between the Green an' the Grand knows Hank Hays, an' what he is. But nobody ever whispers it."

"Ahuh. Darned interesting. I sort of liked Hank, first off. Rustler, then? Or just plain robber?"

"I ain't sayin', Mr. Wall."

"You can call me Jim," returned Jim, thinking it time to change the subject. "Let me drive a little."

He fell silent for a while. Curiosity might prompt him further, but he really did not need to know any more about Hank Hays. A dawning and impatient antagonism to the robber began to gain strength. It presaged events.

About noon they halted at a wayside stream, and while resting the horses they ate the lunch Happy Jack had provided.

Beyond this point cattle began to show on the valley floor, and green notches in the slopes across bore traces of homesteaders. Ten miles from Grand Junction, according to Jim's informant, was the Utah Cattle Company, a big outfit from Salt Lake.

Presently Jim's ever-watchful eyes caught dust far ahead, and dots of riders getting off the road into the cedar thickets. They would be Smoky's outfit, Jim calculated, and gave them credit for seeing the buckboard first. They did not appear again, and Jim knew they were hiding on their way back to Star Ranch to make another raid.

The country appeared to be flattening out, greener and more cultivated in the open places, though the red cedar-dotted bluffs stood up here and there, and far off white-tipped mountains loomed. At four o'clock they drove into Grand Junction, which was considerably larger and busier than Green River. Like all Western hamlets, it had a single, wide street, lined by stone and frame buildings.

"Barnes, here we are," said Jim. "This is a metropolis, compared with Green River."

"Fust I've been home fer long," rejoined Barnes. "I'll take care of the team at my Paw's. An' say, Mr. Wall— Jim—will you come home an' stay with us or hyar at the hotel."

"Thanks, but I'll stay here. Is this the hotel?"

"Yeh. It ain't much on looks, but the grub's good an' beds clean."

"Fine. Now, Barnes, you and I are getting along. Do you give me any hunch on how to conduct myself?"

"Haw! Haw! Jim, you'll be looked over a heap, but nobody won't ask no questions. See you later."

Barnes drove off down the road, and Jim leisurely entered the lodging-house, which, it turned out, was run by a buxom woman, who made herself agreeable and certainly was not above making eyes at him. As far as any curiosity on her part was concerned, he might as well have lived there always. She was loquacious, and very shortly Jim gained the surprising information that no cattle herds had passed through Grand Junction this week.

After supper Jim strolled out to see the town. It was
still daylight. The street appeared to be practically deserted. He went down one side and up the other, and
crossing to the overland stage office he found the door
locked. There was a sign, "Wells Fargo and Co.," on the
front. Evidently this town was on the stage line from
Denver to Salt Lake. The big store on the corner was
open, however, and Jim went in. He bought some things
and incidentally corroborated Herrick's statement as to
the arrival of the stage next morning. Finally Jim wandered into a saloon.

To his surprise it was a large place, in which fully a
score of men lounged at the bar or sat around as if waiting for something. Jim fitted this atmosphere. He felt
at home in it and knew he gave that impression. And he
had not been in there very long before he realized that
well-armed strangers were really not strangers to that
place and community. There were no drinking, hair-rais-
ing cowboys or any flashy gamblers or any drunkards.
Some of those present had shifty eyes. A few were idle,
tattered louts. For the most part, however, the occupants
were dusty-booted men who did not radiate either civility
or hostility. That suited Jim. He had expected just such
a town.

He read an old newspaper that he found, and after he
had exhausted its contents, he watched a card game, but
at a respectable distance with other onlookers, and passed
a quiet evening without learning anything.

That night he slept in a bed, the first time for so long
he could not recall the last occasion, and the softness of
it, or his nearing closer and closer to tomorrow's adventure, kept him awake till late. All this while he heard a
roulette wheel, but he could not tell whence the sound
came. Probably there was a gambling-hall above the
saloon.

Awakening early, he got up and leisurely shaved and dressed, paying more than usual attention to his appearance. This occasioned him a bitter smile. Jim Wall, erstwhile cowboy, bank bandit, train-robber! What was he now? He could not define it. But he was there to escort an English girl fifty miles across the wilderness to Star Ranch. One thing he was sure of, and that was that it would be vastly better for Miss Herrick than, if Hank Hays had been sent. Suddenly this fact struck Jim as singular. Was he any better than Hank Hays? He conceded that he was. Still, there had never been a time since his wild cowboy days that sight of a pretty girl or a handsome woman had not made his heart leap. But for long years he had avoided women, not because he was not hungry for them, but because he seldom saw one that did not rouse his disgust.

After breakfast he went out and found a boy to shine his high top-boots and brush his dark, worn suit and his black sombrero. Presently, then, he encountered Barnes.

"Howdy, boy! Did you have a nice time home?"

"Gee, I did!" grinned the cowboy. "I was with my gurl last night an' she wouldn't let me off."

"Right she was. You sure look bright this morning."

"Wal, you look kinda spick an' span yourself, Jim," drawled Barnes. "Funny how the idear of a gurl gets a feller."

"Funny? You mean terrible, my friend. A woman is as terrible as an army with banners."

"Gosh! who'd ever dreamed you had been inside a Bible?" exclaimed the cowboy.

"It's funny, though, how I happened to remember that. Now, Barnes, listen. This Miss Herrick might take me for an honest, decent fellow like you. But if I let that

pass I'd be sailing under false colors. I don't do that. And
as I can't very well tell her myself, you must."

"Tell her what?" queried Barnes, with a puzzled grin.

"You know . . . the kind of a man I am."

"I sort of like you myself. So if you want me to tell
her anythin' you must say what."

"Well then, tell her about Herrick hiring all the des-
perados in Utah, and that I'm one of them. Make me
out worse than Hays and Heeseman thrown together."

"Shore. That's easy. But what's the idear, Jim?"

"I wasn't always an outcast. . . . And I think it'd
hurt me less if this girl was scared and repelled. If she
took me for a real Westerner, you know, and talked and
laughed—well, I'd go get powerfully drunk and probably
shoot up Star Ranch. So you fix it for me, will you,
Barnes?"

"Shore, I'll fix it," replied Barnes, with a sly glance
at Jim. "You jest give me a chanst when the stage rolls
up. She's due now. I'll run down an' drive the buckboard
up."

But the stage did not show up for an hour—a long,
nervous, dragging one for Jim Wall. Grand Junction was
no different from other Western points remote from
civilization—everybody turned out to see the stage come
in. It was a gala occasion for the youngsters, of whom
there was a surprising number. The women onlookers,
Jim observed, rather hung in the background.

The four-horse stage came rolling up in a cloud of
dust. The driver, a grizzled old frontiersman, brought it
to a stop with a fine flourish, and he bawled out: "Grand
Junction! Half hour fer lunch."

There were six passengers, two of them feminine. The
last to leave the stage was a tall, veiled young woman,
her lithe and erect figure incased in a long linen coat.

She carried a small satchel. Expectantly she looked around. Jim stepped before her, baring his head.

"Are you Miss Herrick?"

"Oh! Yes," she exclaimed, in relief.

"Your brother sent us to meet you," went on Jim, indicating Barnes, who stood to one side.

"He did not come!" The full, rich voice, with its foreign intonation, struck pleasantly upon Jim's ear.

"No. There's much work at Star Ranch. But it's perfectly all right, Miss Herrick. We will drive you safely over before dark."

Jim could not see clearly through the tan veil, but he discerned well enough that big eyes studied him.

"Didn't he send a letter or anything? How am I to know you men are employed by my brother?"

"I'm afraid you'll have to take my word," replied Jim, gravely. "But, Barnes, here, he can prove his identity. He lives in Grand Junction, and of course there are responsible people who will vouch for him."

"Miss, the boss did send word," spoke up Barnes, touching his hat, and stepping closer, he added in a lower tone, "He told me last night you was to fetch what come by Wells Fargo."

"Then it is all right," she replied, apparently relieved. "My luggage is inside, on top, and tied on behind. The name is on every piece. Helen Herrick."

"I'll attend to the baggage, Miss Herrick," rejoined Jim. "Meanwhile Barnes will show you where to eat. It might rest you to walk a little. We have an eight-hour drive."

"Thank you. I've been riding steadily for two weeks and I'm stiff."

Whereupon Jim set about collecting the pieces of baggage marked "Herrick." It appeared that the stage had been loaded down with them. Nineteen in all! Manifestly

Miss Herrick had come to stay. To find room for all of them in the buckboard was going to be a task. He set about this methodically, his mind at once busy and absent. By packing carefully under the seats, and on them, too, Jim got the bags all in. He went to the store and bought rope to tie some of them on securely. Wonder what she looks like, he thought! He had felt vaguely uncomfortable when she looked him over through that veil. His task completed, Jim stood beside the restless horses, waiting. And it seemed he was waiting for he knew not what.

Presently Barnes returned, wearing an excited grin. His eyes were important.

"Jim, I fixed it. I shore gave her an earful," he said.

"Did you? Much obliged, cowboy."

"She took off thet coat an' veil. Lordy! . . . Utah never seen the likes of her. Red lips, pink cheeks, hair like gold, an' eyes like violets! Jim, for a minnit I went plumb back on my gurl! But, shucks! thet's crazy! She asked me to set at table. I did. She's just as nice an' free as Herrick. It was while we was eatin' thet I had the chanst to tell her about the nootorious Jim Wall. Mebbe I didn't spread it on. An' she looked— Gee! such eyes! She said, 'So Bernie Herrick sent a desperado to be my escort? How perfectly rippin'!' Honest, Jim, thet's what she said. So I shet up pronto. . . . When I jest come away she said she'd walk a little in the orchard an' after goin' into the Wells Fargo office she'd be ready."

"Have you double-crossed me?" queried Jim, suspicious of this boy. "You were to make me out low-down."

"Jim, honest to Gawd, if thet gurl ain't scared to death of you she's a new one on me," declared Barnes. But there was fun and evasion in his keen hazel eyes. Somehow he had failed to follow instructions.

"I'll go in the Chink's here and get a bite to eat. You watch the horses."

Upon his return Jim espied Miss Herrick emerging from the yard of Mrs. Bowe's lodging-house. She carried the linen coat on her arm, and without it did not appear so tall. She had a wonderful step, a free, swinging, graceful stride, expressive of health and vitality. She did not look slender, as in the long ulster, but superb, broad of shoulder. She wore a half-length coat over her brown dress. It had a collar of dark fur which presented vivid contrast to her exquisite complexion. The veil was tucked back and now permitted sight of a wave of shining golden hair. At a little distance her eyes looked like great, dark holes set in white. But as she approached Jim saw they were violet in hue, warm, beautiful, fearless.

"Are we ready to go?" she asked, gayly.

"Yes, if you have seen the Fargo people," replied Jim.

"I have it in my satchel," she returned, indicating the half-hidden receptacle under her linen coat.

Jim tried to interest himself in that satchel because he was in league with robbers, but it did not work. Suddenly he had a murderous desire to kill Hays. This girl—for she appeared a girl in vivid freshness of youth—seemed not in the least frightened, absolutely free from revulsion. Indeed, she was regarding him with undisguised interest and delight.

"Mr. Jim Wall, you're not in the least what my brother's letters have led me to believe," she said.

"Letters! Why, Herrick has not had time to write about me," exclaimed Jim, incredulously. "It takes long for a stage letter to go. . . . I've been at Star Ranch only a few days."

"Oh, he did not write about *you*, individually," she laughed. "But from his letters about bandits and desperadoes I had evolved a rather frightful conception."

"Thank you, Miss Herrick," he replied, gravely. "Don't

trust appearances on our Western border. . . . Will you get up? We must be going."

And he attempted to assist her inside the back seat of the buckboard.

"If you are going to drive, I want to sit in front," she said, frankly.

With a bow he helped her up the high step, cursing inwardly at Hank Hays and Herrick and the inscrutable fate that had brought this about. For some way or other he was lost. He almost forgot to wait for Barnes, who was saying good-by to a red-cheeked, wide-eyed girl in the crowd. Barnes came running to leap into the buckboard, and then Jim got in. Owing to the way he had packed the baggage, there was not a great deal of room in the front seat. His heavy gun and sheath bumped against Miss Herrick.

"Rather tight quarters, with that gun there," he remarked, and swung the sheath round in his lap.

"Do you sleep in it?" she asked, quizzically.

"Yes. And never am dressed in the daytime till it's buckled on."

"What startling folk, you Western Americans!"

"Some of us are indeed startling. I hope you won't find us unpleasantly so," he replied and, loosening the reins, let the spirited team go. In a few moments the noise, dust, heat, and the staring populace of Grand Junction were far behind, and the red and black ranges lifted above the meadows and sage.

"Oh, glorious!" she cried, and gazed raptly ahead as the curving road brought into view a wonderful sweep of Utah.

Jim was hard put to it to keep the blacks from breaking out of a brisk trot. He thought grimly that he would have liked to let the team run off and kill them both. Far better that might be! Miss Herrick's photograph on her brother's desk fell infinitely short of doing her justice. It failed to give any hint of her color, of the vivid lips, of the glory and gleam of her hair, of the dancing, laughing violet eyes, of her pulsing vitality. Jim Wall felt the abundant life of this girl. It flowed out of her. It got into his veins. It heated his blood.

"The wind makes me cry," she said, merrily. "Or maybe it's because I'm so happy. You say we'll get to Star Ranch before dark?"

"Surely."

"Oh, it's been such a long, slow, dusty, cramped journey," she exclaimed. "But now I want to see, to smell, to feel, to gloat."

"Miss Herrick, this is fine country. But tame compared with that all about the Henrys. You will see them when we top the next hill. I've seen most of the West. And the canyon desert below Star Ranch is the wildest and most sublime of all the West, probably of the whole world."

"Indeed! You speak strongly, not to say surprisingly. It never occurred to me that a gunman—that is what you are, is it not?—could have any appreciation of the wonder and beauty of nature."

"A common mistake, Miss Herrick," rejoined Jim. "Nature develops the men who spend their lonely, hard, bloody lives with her. Mostly she makes them into boasts, with self-preservation the only instinct, but it is conceivable that one now and then might develop the opposite way."

"You interest me," she replied, simply. "Tell me of this canyon desert and such men."

Jim talked for a full hour, inspired by her unflagging interest. He described the magnificent reaches and escarpments ending in Wild Horse Mesa, and the unknown canyoned abyss between it and Navajo Mountain, and lastly the weird, ghastly brakes of the Dirty Devil.

"Ugh! how you make me shiver!" she ejaculated. "But it's wonderful. I'm sick of people, of fog, rain, dirt, cold, noise. I'd like to get lost down in those red canyons."

Chapter Seven

THEY came to a long level valley where the white road was like a floor, and the horses went like the wind. Wall's letting them out was unconscious: it was a release of his vagrant and startling imagination.

Here the English lady could not catch breath enough to talk. The tan veil was flying and so were some strands of her hair. She appeared to be a beautiful thing of porcelain and gold, animated by throbbing life.

What was going to be the effect of this extraordinary female upon the fierce men of this lonely region? Upon that swarthy Hank Hays! Once in a long time, perhaps, his pale eyes alighted upon a fresh, red-cheeked, buxom girl, but for the most part, Jim knew, Hays never saw any but flat-chested, lanky-limbed, big-footed, and hard-handed women, whose faces were dark, coarse, weathered with skin dried in the wind. They wore overalls and boots, as often as feminine garments, and they were always married. Utah was still so wild and unsettled that the hags and camp-followers common to Wyoming had not arrived.

At last the horses had to be held in at the base of the longest ascent on the journey. Miss Herrick tucked her disheveled hair with the ends of the veil under her bonnet.

"What a run! I'm used to horses—but not tearing along —with a vehicle like this," she said, breathlessly.

"Wait till one of these old drivers get a chance at you. I'm really no teamster."

"Are you a cowboy?"

"I used to be. And I still ride after cattle occasionally. But now I'm only a—a range-rider."

"What's the difference?"

"Well, a range-rider just travels from camp to camp."

"It must be a wonderful life. Like a gypsy's. I have

been among the gypsies in Spain. But that can scarcely be the nature of your position on my brother's ranch."

"Didn't young Barnes tell you who and what I am?" queried Jim, turning to her.

"He talked like—like that babbling brook we just passed," returned the lady, with a musical laugh. "Much of it was Greek to me. But I grasped that you were a stranger to Utah—that you were from Wyoming, where you had killed many bad men, and that your mere reputation was enough out here to keep rustlers and desperadoes away from Star Ranch. Mr. Wall, you certainly are a hero in his eyes."

It did not take great perspicuity to grasp that Jim was not far from that in her eyes. He groaned in spirit.

"Miss Herrick, this young fellow is an awful liar," said Jim.

"How so? He seemed very frank and sincere to me. And he has such honest eyes. I don't know Westerners, as they call you folk, but what of that?"

"You are in for a terrible disillusion."

"Mr. Wall, you cannot quell my enthusiasm. I know I am going to love this wild, glorious country. I've lived in London most of my life. I got to hate the crowded streets, the mud, the clamor, the dark, cold rooms where you had to have a light at midday, and the endless, ever-hurrying throngs of people. There's a strain of primitive blood in me. One of my ancestors was a viking. I think another must have been an American Indian." Here her rich laughter rang out. "At any rate, I am going to indulge my wild strain. The red gods have always whispered to me. Even as a child I knew I was intended for something big, strange, extraordinary."

"I hardly understand you, Miss Herrick," returned Jim, in perplexity. "My education has been limited, except out in the open. I had some schooling, and I taught a country school before I was twenty. But I never saw anyone like you. So if I appear ignorant, please excuse it."

"On the contrary, Mr. Wall, you have impressed me as far above the average Westerner," the girl returned, kindly, but without a trace of condescension. "I've met numberless people on the way out. Pioneers, farmers, ranchers, drivers, cowboys, and a good few that I couldn't place or learn from. But I talked with all of them. You certainly do not need to apologize for yourself. . . . And you have been a school-teacher! That is something that I would never have attributed to you. And what else have you been?"

On the moment Jim was too stricken to take advantage of the opportunity to repel her once and for all. The astounding idea flashed over him that he did not want to repel her.

"A little of everything—Western I guess," he floundered. He felt her gaze.

"I see that you will not tell me about yourself," she went on. "Pardon my inquisitiveness. But I must inform you that I expect to go into the ranching business with my brother. You will be working for me, then, as well."

"I hope you don't, Miss Herrick," he burst out, impulsively. "Somebody must tell you. It oughtn't come from a—a—rider like me. But this Utah is no place for such a girl as you."

"What do you mean, Mr. Wall? That hardly seems a compliment to me. I can work, and I want to. I shall adore this wild country. I tried to explain why. I can milk cows, bake bread, take care of horses. It doesn't follow just because I have money that I do not want to work."

"Miss Herrick, you didn't get my meaning," replied Jim, hastily, with strong feeling. "It is not you who couldn't fit in. You've convinced me you could. And that is the biggest compliment I could pay you. . . . I meant that you will not be able to live, and work, too, in Utah the way you want to. You absolutely cannot indulge that primitive strain you spoke of—not out here. You dare not ride around—or even leave the house. Even that ——"

"For mercy's sake, why not?" she demanded, in astonishment.

"Because, young woman, you are too new, too strange, too lovely to risk yourself in sight of these Utah men. . . . Not all of them, nor a tenth of them. But *some* of them. And they are the men you would meet at Star Ranch."

His sudden intensity, perhaps as much as the content of his words, made her realize his sincerity, and that there was something amiss which her brother had failed to tell her.

"You cannot be serious."

"I swear it, Miss Herrick."

"But what of the vaunted chivalry of Westerners! England rings with the daring, the gallantry, of Americans on the frontier. I've read of Frémont, Kit Carson, Crook, and many others. And of the thousands who are unsung."

"That is true," he replied, his voice husky. "Thank God, I can say so. But you won't find *that* at Star Ranch."

"You say I am too new, strange—too, too lovely to risk—I understand you, of course. I must doubt it, despite your evident strong feeling. You may be playing a Western joke on me."

"I wish I was."

"My brother will know if there is anything in what you say."

"No! No!" burst out Jim, passionately. He was at the limit of patience with her and himself. What possessed him to talk this way? "Herrick doesn't know. He *never*

will know. He is English. He can't see through a mill-
stone with a hole in it.—Oh, don't misunderstand me.
Herrick is a fine chap, generous, friendly, not the least
stuck-up. But Utah is no place for an English gentleman
and sportsman, any more than it is a fit place for his
sister."

"That is for us to decide," she returned, coldly. "It is
less disturbing than what you say against me having my
fling. I shall ride, anywhere and everywhere. I've always
ridden. I'd go mad not to get on a horse in this glorious
country."

"I've done my best. I've told you," he said, curtly, as
if he were also addressing his conscience.

"I thank you, Mr. Wall," she said, quick to catch the
change in him. "No doubt you Western folk regard
Bernie as eccentric. And I'm bound to admit his ranching
idea—ripping as it is to us—must appear new and strange
to you. So I'll compromise. If it's really dangerous for
me to ride about alone, I will take you with me. Not,
however, that I'd be afraid to go alone. Then I would be
perfectly safe, would I not?"

Wall flicked the reins.

"Look, Miss Herrick. We're on top at last. There's
your country. The black snow-capped mountains are the
Henrys. We go through that gap—a pass—to Star Ranch.
That purple space to the left—with the lines and streaks
—that's the desert. Magnify its everything by ten thousand."

"Ah-h-h!" she had cried out, breathlessly.

Jim halted the horses and gazed himself, trying to see
with this stranger's eyes. Her silence, after that one out-
break, was amply eloquent. But he got no satisfaction out
of his own gazing. He had an instinctive desire to get on
a horse and ride off alone into this wilderness. He had
more—a presagement that it would not be long until the

open wasteland claimed him again. For him the bursting
of one of the Henry peaks in volcanic eruption would be
no more startling than what would accrue from the
advent of this white-faced, golden-haired woman.

Jim anticipated, presently, an outburst from Miss Herrick, but it was not forthcoming. He drove down the
hill, and again put the blacks to keen gait on a level
road, this time a straight white line across a longer valley. The warm sun had begun its descent from the zenith.
Jim calculated that he would beat the time he had declared, and reach Star Ranch before sundown. Only one
more hill to climb and that the Pass, which was comparatively short on this side. He wished he could fly. The sister of Bernie Herrick had an unaccountable effect upon
Jim. Bernie! The name suited Herrick, as that of Helen
suited this girl. It was a fatal name for a pearly-skinned,
blue-eyed, golden-haired beauty. Vague legend stirred in
Jim Wall's memory.

Fast as he drove, it was yet not fast enough to escape
from himself. Then when the wind tore off Miss Herrick's bonnet, he had to stop the iron-jawed blacks—
no slight task—and get out and walk back. But the
change seemed to soothe him somehow. He strode back
with the flimsy headgear. Far from prepared was he,
however, for sight of Miss Herrick bareheaded.

"Thank you," she said. "Too bad to make you get out
and walk. But you drove so terribly fast. It's a wonder
my clothes didn't follow my hat."

Jim made a light reply, he knew not what. To him
the wonder was—flashing like a flame from the darkness
of his mind—that he did not turn the team off the road
and drive down into the wilderness, never to let the gaze
of another man rest upon this destroying woman.

In an hour more he had crossed the valley and again
addressed a slope, where the slow gait of the horses gave

Miss Herrick further opportunity to talk. He both dreaded and longed to hear that rich voice, so different from the few women's voices he recalled. But she surprised him again, this time by silence. She had been overpoweringly struck by the two hours' riding toward that gorgeous region of color and upheaval. Not until they got to the top of the Pass, when Jim pointed down the Star Ranch Valley, did she awaken out of her trance. Then during the hour and a half it took to reach the ranch Jim answered queries and explained what this and that was which caught her eye. Such wholly objective conversation was easy for Jim, and the time flew by.

When he drove past Heeseman's camp all that worthy outfit were at supper. The road passed within fifty feet of their chuck-wagon.

"What a ruffianly crew!" murmured Miss Herrick. "Who, pray, are these men?"

"Part of the outfit your brother hired to protect his cattle from rustlers," replied Jim. "Funny thing about that is they are rustlers themselves."

"Deliciously funny, though hardly so for Bernie. Does he know it?"

"Not to my knowledge. Heeseman—the leader of that gang—came on his own recommendation and got the job."

"I'll have the fun of telling Bernie. . . . Oh, what's that? . . . What an enormous barn! All yellow. And a new one going up. Logs and logs. . . . Look at the horses! I want to stop."

"No, Miss Herrick," he replied, grimly. "I'll drive you home safely or die in the attempt. . . . Don't look at this tall man we're coming to."

"Which?" she asked, laughingly.

"The one standing fartherest out," replied Jim. "He's

got on a black sombrero. . . . Don't look at him. That's Hank Hays. . . . Miss Herrick, drop your veil."

She obeyed, unobtrusively, though her silvery laugh pealed out. "You are teasing, of course. But I must reward your effort to entertain me."

Jim drove by Hays, who stood apart from a group of cowboys. He had the stiff, alert posture of a watching jack rabbit that imagined itself unseen. If he noticed Jim at all, it was totally oblivious to Jim. But Wall's glance, never so strained, pierced the shadow under Hays' dark sombrero rim to the strange eyes below. They were not pale now. Jim's hand clenched tight on the reins. He became preoccupied with the nucleus of the first deadly thought toward Hays.

"Hank Hays. Who is he?" Miss Herrick was saying.

"Another of your brother's vigilantes."

"Uh!—How he stared! But it wasn't that which struck me most. In India I've seen cobras rise and poise, ready to strike. And your Mr. Hays looked for all the world like a giant ring cobra with a black sombrero on its head. Wasn't that silly of me?"

"Not silly. An instinct. Self-preservation," returned Jim, sternly.

She passed that by, but only perhaps because she caught sight of the ranch-house up the slope. Here her enthusiasm was unbounded. Herrick stood on the porch steps with his dogs. He wore high boots and a red coat. He waved.

Presently Jim reined in the sweating horses before the steps. He was most curious to see the meeting between brother and sister. She stood up.

"Bernie, old top, here I am," she said, gaily.

"Yes, here you are, Helen," he replied, and stepped out to help her alight. "Did you have a nice trip?"

"Ripping—from Grand Junction in."

They did not embrace or even shake hands. Jim decided that when it came to intimate feelings, these English either did not have them or else they hid them. Jim, coming to himself, leaped out and began removing the bags. Barnes, whom he had totally forgotten, jumped out on the other side.

"Barnes, carry the bags in. Jim, hurry the blacks down. They're hot. You must have pushed them."

"Yes, sir. Stage was late, but we made up for it."

"Helen, where's that Wells Fargo package?" queried Herrick.

"Here in my satchel. Oh, Bernie, it's good to get home —if this can be home."

"Come in and take off that veil," he said, and with his arm in hers led her upon the porch.

Jim let Barnes take the team, while he crossed the bench and made his way down the steep, rocky declivity to Hays' cabin. Happy Jack was whistling about the fire, knocking pans and otherwise indicating the proximity of supper.

"Howdy, Jack! What's tricks for today?" asked Jim.

"Glad you're back, Jim," declared the cook, cordially. "Anyone'd have thunk you was goin' to dish the outfit— judgin' from Hays. He's been like a hound on a leash. Smoky rode in today full of ginger, news an' a roll of long green that'd have choked a cow. But even that didn't ease the boss."

"What ailed him, Jack?" inquired Jim, not without impatience.

"Dinged if I know. It had to do with your goin' to Grand, a darned sight more than Smoky's."

Heavy footfalls outside attested to the return of Hays. Without more comment Jim stood up and away from the table, to face the door. Hays entered, not the genial Hays of other days, yet it was hard to define the change, unless it consisted in a gloomy, restless force behind his stride. Smoky followed him in, agreeable by contrast.

"Hullo! Here you air. I waited at the barn," said Hays, gruffly.

"Howdy, boss! I took a short cut down," replied Jim, with a nod to Smoky.

"I seen Barnes an' had a word with him. So your trip come off all right? You shore made them blacks step."

"It wasn't as pleasant a drive as you'd imagine," returned Jim, darkly.

"Haw!—You must be one of them woman-haters. . . . Outside of thet side of it, what happened to jar you?"

"Nothing to concern you or your outfit. Smoky saw me yesterday before I got a line on him. He ducked off the road. At Grand Junction nobody paid any more attention to me than I'd expect."

"Ahuh. Thet's good," replied Hays, and going over to the pack beside his bed he rummaged about to return with a packet, which he slapped down upon the table.

"There you air, Jim. On our first deal."

The packet unrolled and spread out—greenbacks of large denomination.

"What's this for?" queried Jim, blankly.

"Quick action. Thet's how we work. Your share. Smoky fetched it."

Jim did not care to give the impression that he was unused to this sort of thing. Straddling the bench, he sat down to run through the bills.

"Five thousand six hundred," he said, as if to himself, and he slipped the money inside his pocket. "Much obliged, Smoky. Now I'll be able to sit in in a little game of draw."

"Jim, ain't you got any news atall?" inquired Hays, searchingly. "A feller with your ears an' eyes shore would pick up somethin'."

"Miss Herrick fetched a Wells Fargo package to her brother," rejoined Jim, slowly yielding to what he felt was due himself as an ally of this robber.

"Then it's come," said Hays, cracking his hands. "Herrick was expectin' money last stage."

"Yes," returned Jim, indifferently.

"Boys, set down an' fall in," called out Happy Jack.

As usual, supper was not a conversational matter. Hays' outfit always ate as if they were facing starvation. It was a habit of riders, engendered by the fact of being always on the move. After supper Smoky was the first to break silence.

"Boss, now Wall is back, you can make up your mind about what I'd like to do."

"Jim, listen to this. Smoky an' the other fellers, except Brad, want to make a clean sweep with this next drive. What you think?"

"Clean Herrick out?" asked Jim.

"Thet's the idee."

Jim pondered a moment. His mind answered that in a flash, but he considered it wise not to be precipitous.

"It'd be harder work, but save time, and perhaps our bacon as well. These cowboys are going to find out pretty soon that the cattle have thinned out. If Smoky drives a couple thousand more it'll be sure to be found out, sooner or later."

"See thar, boss. Wall see's it just as I do. There's plenty of water along the road an' feed enough. Let's make it one big drive."

"Meanin' for me an' Jim an' Happy to fall in with you?" queried Hays, tersely.

"Shore, unless you think thet ain't so good."

"Wal, it'd mean leavin' Star Ranch sudden," cogitated the robber chief.

"Shore. An' thet's good."

"But I don't want to pull out of here sudden," declared Hays.

"Why not, if we git away with ten thousand head?" queried Smoky, astounded.

"Thet ten thousand won't close the deal I'm on."

"What've you up your sleeve, Hank?"

"Thet's my business. Yours is drivin' cattle."

"You mean to rob the Englisher? Fer Gawd's sake, Hank, don't be a hawg!"

"Hays, if you'll excuse me I'm thinking Smoky talks sense," interposed Jim, quietly.

"Wal, I'm listenin', but I reckon you can't change me," returned Hays.

"If we put it to a vote, Hank, you wouldn't be nowhere. I don't want to buck ag'in' you. But you're way off on this. . . . Listen. I had the gall to tip Hadley off thet he'd better run up to Salt Lake an' get a big lot of cash. He took the hunch. Said he'd go an' thet he'd guarantee buyin' us out, every damn hoof."

"Thet's all right. It's good figgerin'. Only I see no call for rush."

"But we do. We're all on edge fer it. Brad thinks it wise. He doesn't like this English deal, anyway. An' now Jim Wall backs us up."

Hays knocked the bowl of his unsmoked pipe on the table, and he arose, gaunt and virile, to stalk up and down the room, plainly a victim of conflicting tides of feeling. But indecision did not last long. His gesture, abrupt and passionate, not only indicated the men who opposed him, but infinitely more.

"My mind's made up. We'll stick to our first idee. You fellers make drive after drive, goin' slow. . . . Thet'll give me time ——"

"Ahuh. So you'll risk goin' ag'in' the whole outfit," interrupted Smoky, with a curious gaze at his superior.

"Wal, hell, yes, if you put it thet way," replied Hays, and he stalked out.

"No help fer it, men," said Smoky, presently. "Somethin's got into the boss. Reckon I'll hit the trail fer camp. Didn't intend to leave till mornin'. But it's jest as well. Jim, don't you want to come along?"

"I'd like to, at that. But how'd Hays take it?"

"He'd swear you was double-crossin' him. I hope to Gawd he doesn't do the double-crossin'."

"Smoky, will you start that second drive tomorrow?" asked Wall.

"I'll lay it up to my outfit. Wal, so long. See you soon, one way or another."

He went out. Jim heard a few sharp words pass between Smoky and Hays, and then silence. Happy Jack looked at Jim, shaking his head dubiously. Jim waited awhile, hoping that Hays would return, but as he did not, Jim went to bed. For once he hated to be alone in the dark and quiet. In his inmost heart he realized that he was tremendously upset by the advent of this Herrick girl.

Next day he went back to work on the new barn. A subtle change in Hank Hays augmented his suspicion of that individual. Jim let him alone. He did not require much more to satisfy himself about Hank Hays.

While Jim worked with the cowboys he watched, and he had the eyes of a hawk. Herrick was around as usual, interested in every detail of the building. Hays had gone off with the cowboys across the valley to put them upon some job there, which no doubt was a ruse to keep them away from Limestone Springs, where most of the stock grazed. He did not see Hays until supper. And the day had ended without one glimpse of Helen Herrick. Jim measured the incredible fact of his desire to see her by the poignancy of his disappointment. Then he cursed himself for a fool. His mood changed as subtly as had Hays', with the result that he and the moody leader made poor company.

This night Jim deliberately set himself to study the robber near at hand and to watch him from a distance. At table and round the fire Hays apparently made some effort to be his former self. But the effort betrayed constraint. And out in the dark, when Hays imagined no one saw his actions, he seemed a hounded man. What was on his mind? What further plot was he hatching? Could it be possible that intent to rob Herrick of money, and any valuables procurable, could obsess him to this extent? After all, Jim did not know Hays well. He had to give him the benefit of a doubt.

At breakfast the following morning Hays surprised Jim.

"Was the Herrick girl out yesterday?" he inquired.

"Didn't see her," replied Jim, setting down his cup.

"You didn't say what kind of a looker she was. An' the other night she had her face hid by some contraption. Might as wal wore a mask. I seen her hair, though. Like sunflower! An' she shore has a shape."

"Oh, that!" laughed Jim. "I forgot or didn't think you were interested. She's a washed-out, pink-and-white thing. No blood. Consumptive or anemic, I reckon."

"Consumptive! With thet breast?" rejoined Hays, scornfully. "Wal, I'd like to see her once before our deal's off here."

"Are you thinking better of Smoky's idea?"

"Not of thet. But I'm worryin' about him."

Hays had his wish fulfilled next day. He was at work on the new barn, on the far side from where Jim was occupied, when Miss Herrick came down with her brother. Jim stared as if his eyes deceived him. An English riding-habit was known to him only from pictures. She looked queenly. Jim did not look at her face. Besides, he wanted most to see the effect upon Hank Hays. That worthy's hawk-like head was erect, but Jim could not see the tell-tale eyes. Hays stood transfixed, then suddenly, in strange gesture, as of finality, he flung down the tool he had been using. Was that his satisfaction at having seen this wonderful girl? Was it hail and farewell to such beauty as might once only come under the gaze of a man of his class? Most certainly it was repudiation of something.

Herrick and his sister walked toward Jim's side of the barn. They talked. Jim heard that laugh again. He seemed to be bewitched. Then she approached.

"Good morning," she said. "So you are a carpenter as well as a vigilante?"

Jim doffed his sombrero and stood up straight. His gun struck the scantling with a perceptible little thud. She could not help noticing that and it gave her pause.

"I'm not at my best with *this* kind of a hammer," replied Jim, with a smile, after greeting them.

"Apropos of that, Bernie told me how you shoot bob —no, jack rabbits from the saddle," she said, admiringly. "I want to see you do that. And I want to learn how. Will you show me?"

"I'd be pleased, Miss Herrick," he returned. "But I can't guarantee you'll hit any of them."

"I may surprise you. Tomorrow, then, you will ride with me?"

"I'm at your service," replied Jim, hearing his voice as something far off.

"Wall, you'll oblige me by riding with my sister when it suits her," said Herrick. "By Jove! I can't live on the back of a horse, and I don't want her to ride alone."

"Yes, sir," returned Jim, gazing across at the statue-like Hays.

The couple moved off toward the open yard where mounted cowboys were leading out saddled horses. Presently Jim heard them ride away with the barking dogs. He looked up, however, when Hays accosted him, at his elbow.

"I seen her, Jim," he said, as if the event were epic. "She walked right by me. I smelled her."

"Oh, hello! You startled me," replied Jim, essaying a laugh. "What if you did, Hank?"

"Nothin'. Only you gave me a wrong idee. Pink-an'-white washed-out thing, you said. My Gawd!"

"Hank, I've no use for blond women," replied Jim, testily, tired of the deception.

"Hell! you needn't bite my head off," said Hays. "I'll bet you haven't any use fer any color women. . . . What was she sayin' to you?"

"It seems Herrick told her about my shooting jacks from my horse, and she wants to see it done."

"Wal, I'll be jiggered! You're goin' ridin' with her? . . . The luck of some men!"

"Hank, I'd a darn sight rather they'd asked you," declared Jim, and then a keen idea struck him, which would, if Hays was not wary, clear up a knotty question. "Shall I tell Herrick you'll go in my stead?"

"Nix, much as I'd like to. I can't hit jumpin' rabbits. An' I wouldn't want to be showed up bad."

"Like as not I'll be rattled and miss a lot," returned Jim, lowering his eyes lest the thought in them might be read. Then he went back to work. Hays hung around the barn, mostly idle, watching the valley, until the Herricks returned to ride up the hill toward the house. The cowboys brought the horses down. Whereupon Hays abruptly left. And he did not come back. From that hour he became an elusive man. Jim, preoccupied with his own troubles, barely noticed this circumstance until that night.

That day ended Jim Wall's carpentry. On the next he was summoned, early after breakfast, to ride with the Herricks. He went. And it would have been idle for him to deny that the event was enthralling. These English people were thoroughbred. Not improbably, in their minds unconsciously, the abyss between them and him was so wide and deep, that it was not thought of at all. That accounted for things. He divined vaguely, however, that for him the abyss did not exist.

Under the stimulation of this girl's inspiring presence Jim gave an exhibition of swift and accurate shooting that surpassed any he had ever accomplished.

"Marvelous!" she exclaimed, with dark-flashing, admiring eyes on Jim. "It would be suicide for men to oppose you. . . . But poor little jack rabbits! What a pity they are destructive around the ranch!"

"Helen, he's a bally good shot," declared Herrick.

That night Hank Hays evinced slight but unmistakable symptoms of jealousy, occasioned, perhaps, by Jim's report of killing thirteen out of fifteen bounding jack rabbits. Happy Jack, wide-eyed and loud-voiced, acclaimed Jim's feat as one in a thousand.

"Air you thet good frontin' a man who you know is swift?" drawled the robber chief.

Jim stared, coming out of his natural gratification. "Hank, I'm not so good then," he replied, slowly.

"Wal, somebody'll try you out one of these days," added Hays, without significance.

"I dare say," he rejoined, coolly, and sought his seclusion. He refused to let that linger in his mind. Something else haunted him. His slumber was troubled.

Next day Herrick did not accompany his sister on the

daily ride, a circumstance which, if anything, gave freer
rein to her spirit. Jim had concern for her safety. He could
not judge well of her horsewomanship, because of the
side-saddle she rode. Bluntly he disapproved of the atro-
cious thing and said it was worse than the "pancake" her
brother rode. But she rode after the hounds just the
same, and held her own until she was thrown.

If she had alighted upon rocks or even hard ground
she would have been seriously injured, if not killed out-
right. But when the horse stumbled she hurtled over his
head and hit in the sand. Jim was off almost the instant
she struck, and he yelled for the cowboys.

Kneeling, he lifted her around and held her head up.
She appeared to have been stunned. Her face was gray
with sand.

"Water, Barnes!" he called, as the cowboy dashed up.

"There ain't none close," replied Barnes.

"I'm all—right," spoke up Miss Herrick, weakly. "I
came—a cropper—didn't I?"

She sat up, evidently not hurt, though she clung to
Jim's arm. With his scarf he wiped the sand from her
face, aware that his hand was not steady. If he had had
to rely upon a gun then! The stiff hat she wore with
this riding-habit had rolled yards away. Barnes got it.
Her hair had come partly loose, to fall in a golden mass
on her shoulder. She rearranged it and put on her hat,
deftly despite gloved fingers.

"Help me up, please," she said.

Jim placed a strong arm under hers and lifted her to
her feet. She appeared able to stand alone, so he released
her. However, she still clung to him.

"Deuced clumsy of me," she said, flexing her right
knee.

"Miss Herrick, are you sure you're not hurt?" asked
Jim, solicitously. "It was a nasty spill."

"I'm not really hurt," and letting go of Jim she essayed a few steps to prove it.

Then something cold and tight within Jim let go, and his reaction was to take refuge in anger. "Miss Herrick, I told you that saddle was no good. It's a wonder you were not killed."

"Oh, don't exaggerate. I've come many croppers cross-country riding at home."

"Barnes, back me up in this," appealed Jim to the cowboy.

"Miss, he's tellin' you true," said Barnes, earnestly. "You was ridin' fast. If this hyar had been stony ground, like it is lots of places, you'd never knowed what hit you."

"I believe I did strike pretty hard," she admitted, ruefully.

"You want a cow-saddle with a double cinch, and overalls," concluded Jim.

"Overalls!" she exclaimed, and she blushed rosy red. "You mean like these blue—trousers Barnes has on?"

"Yes. Then you can ride. This is the West, Miss Herrick. You like to run a horse. It's dangerous. I shall have to speak to your brother."

"Don't. I've never ridden astride, but I'll do it, since you are so very fearful about me. . . . Please help me up."

That experience left Jim shaky, probably a good deal shakier than it had left Miss Herrick. But it was not fear for her. Jim reveled in the torturing sensations engendered by contact with this beautiful girl. He shook like a leaf at the staggering realization that when she lay on the ground with her arms spread wide, her hair gold against the sand, he longed to snatch her to his breast. A natural impulse, under the circumstances, but for him—idiotic!

Hays was not present that night at supper. This omission in no wise concerned Jim. He was too preoccupied to care or think about the chief. Days passed by, heady or blank, according to whether or not he rode with Miss Herrick.

She took to the Western saddle like a duck to water. She could ride. Moreover, that spirit of which she had hinted certainly overtook her. More than once she ran off alone, riding like the wind, and upon one of these occasions it took the cowboys till dark to find her. That with Hank Hays and Heeseman there to see her gallop away unescorted! Herrick did not seem to mind.

As far as Jim Wall was concerned, however, these rides with her centered him upon the love which had come to consume him; and the several she took alone were more torturing because they roused fear of Hank Hays. It could not be ascertained whether or not Hays followed her, but when the day came that Jim discovered Hays had been riding the trails frequented by Miss Herrick, then it seemed time to act.

This placed Jim in a worse quandary. To act, for a man of his training, at such a time and place, was to do only one thing. But how could he kill his leader upon mere suspicion of sinister intent to kidnap the girl? It was a damnable predicament for a man who had always played fair, alike to honest friend and crooked ally.

Jim paced under his dark sheltering trees, in the dead of night, when he should have been sleeping. Days had passed without his once seeking to avoid disaster; and he had not sought because he knew it was of no use. To wish to be with this blond girl seemed irresistible. More than once he had caught himself in the spell of a daring impulse—to tell Miss Herrick that he loved her. The idea was sheer madness. Yet the thought persisted, and when he tried to shake it the result was it grew stronger in a haunting, maddening way.

His manhood cast this aside. The love of the male,

especially a lonely one of the wilds, expressed itself in many thoughts that Jim realized were the heritage of barbarism. They occurred in strange, vague, distorted dreams. They were strong in a man in whom the primitive instincts prevailed. But seldom did they gain ascendency. Jim remembered his mother and sister; and then he thrust away from him any possibility of distress coming to this Herrick girl from him.

That was how he met temptation. Then he was to be confronted by the fact that making love to her was insignificant to what Hank Hays might do. Whereupon the battle was fought all over again. He won as before, though with dark doubts in his mind. What could come of this tangled circumstance but disaster?

At breakfast next morning Hays raved about the fact that Smoky had not been there for over two weeks.

"Things air comin' to a head," he concluded, gloomily.

"Reckon they ought to have made two drives by now," rejoined Happy Jack. "I rid down the valley yestiddy eight or ten miles. Cattle thinned out, boss. Any cowboy with eyes in the back of his head would be on to us by now."

"Shore. Haven't I kept them workin' up here? But I've no control over this —— hossback-ridin' after hounds. Pretty soon Herrick will be chasin' down Limestone way. Then the fire'll be out."

"Hank, he wouldn't know the difference," interposed Jim.

"Aw, I don't give a damn," replied Hays, harshly, and that finality intimated much. "Wait till Smoky's outfit shows up!"

Every morning when Jim rode down to the corrals he fell back under the spell of something sweeter than wine. The sunny hours with the sage flat ahead, the fragrant pines, the baying hounds, and always out in front this bright-haired girl, were vastly different from the dark hours when the day was done. Nothing could be truer than that this utterly incongruous and bitterly sweet situation could not last. In moments of humility, engendered by the higher emotions this girl aroused, Jim clasped to his breast the fact that he was protecting her from worse men.

Barnes and another of the cowboys had taken the horses for the Herricks up to the house. To Jim's honest dismay he espied Helen riding ahead, with the cowboys behind, leading her brother's mount. Herrick was not coming. The hounds bounded and cavorted about her, keen for the chase.

Miss Herrick looked far less proud and unattainable in the boy's riding-garb she had adopted. Moreover, it had transformed her, yet her femininity appeared more provokingly manifest than ever.

Barnes turned Herrick's horse over to a stable-boy, and with his companion fell in behind Miss Herrick, who rode out upon the valley. Jim joined them, and they trotted their horses together.

"Why didn't Herrick come?" asked Jim.

"He was rowin' with Heeseman," replied Barnes, soberly.

"You don't say! What about?"

"Reckon I don't know. They shet up as I come along," returned the cowboy. "But I seen enough to calkilate somethin's wrong. They was on the porch. Herrick looked sort of peevish. He didn't want his sister to go huntin' today, I heard thet. An' she said right pert she was goin'."

"How did Heeseman look?" went on Jim, ponderingly. Something was up. For two days Heeseman's outfit had been through hauling timber.

"Dead serious, like he was tryin' to persuade the boss to somethin'."

Jim lapsed into silence. What turn would affairs take next? It was getting warm around Star Ranch.

Each day the hunters had to ride farther afield to find game. Jack-rabbit chasing had grown too tame for Miss Herrick; besides, the rabbits had run off down the valley.

Three or four miles out the hounds jumped a coyote from a clump of sagebrush, and the chase was on. At first the hounds gained, but after a mile or so the coyote kept the distance even between them. At what was only fifty feet the chase was noisy, fast, and exciting. The coyote led toward the low, wooded slope to the west and gained it, where the chase slowed up as far as the riders were concerned.

The cowboys took the lead, then came Miss Herrick, while Jim brought up the rear. It was a long, gradual ascent up to an open ridge, where pine trees alternated with clumps of chaparral; very fragrant and picturesque country.

Here the hounds jumped a herd of deer. Despite the yelling of the cowboys, they dashed up the ridge with a chorus of wild yelps and barks. Barnes and his companion rider gave pursuit, trying to call them off. They all passed out of hearing.

Jim caught up with Miss Herrick, who waited in an open spot among the pines. Flushed and disheveled, with her sombrero on the pommel, panting from the arduous ride, she made a distracting picture.

"Hunt's off for us, Miss Herrick," said Jim. "The cowboys will be hours catching that pack."

"Too bad! But wasn't—it fun—while it—lasted," she replied, gaily. "I'm glad the coyote—got away. I had designs on—his brushy tail."

"Shall we ride down?" went on Jim, uneasily. He had been alone with this girl on a couple of brief occasions, just long enough to realize the danger of such a fateful accident as this.

"Let us rest the horses. I'm out of breath myself. . . . Listen. Don't I hear the hounds? They might fetch those deer back. Oh, I love to see deer bound on their springy legs."

Jim turned his ear to the wind. First he heard the beating of his blood, like a muffled drum, and then the swish of the tree-tops.

"No. It's not the hounds you hear. Only the wind in the pines."

"How mournful and sweet!" she murmured.

Jim dismounted to tighten his saddle-cinches. He felt queerly helpless, and impatient to be on the move.

"Wall, take a look at my cinches," she said.

"May I ask you not to call me Wall?" he queried, with unreasonable resentment. He hated the way she addressed him occasionally. "I must remind you I'm no butler."

"Pray pardon me," she rejoined, in surprise. "I presume I should address you as Mister Wall?"

"Yes, if you're too stuck up to call me Jim," he said, rudely.

She lifted her chin and deigned no reply. And that infuriated him.

"While I'm at it I'll tell you this, too," he went on, doggedly. "You must not ride around alone again. I've had no chance to speak with you. But I told your brother. He laughed in my face. He is a damned fool."

"Mr. Wall, I will not listen to such talk," she spoke up, spiritedly.

"Oh, yes, you will!" he flashed, striding over to her horse. "You're not in an English drawing-room now, confronted by a disrespectful butler. You're in Utah, girl. And I am Jim Wall."

"That last is obvious, to my regret," she returned,

coldly. "Will you please be so kind as to tighten my cinches? It will be the last service I shall require of you."

"Thank the Lord!" ejaculated Jim, in grim heartiness. "All the same, I'll tell you. If you were an American tenderfoot, it wouldn't be hard to make you understand. If you were Western, you would not need to be told. But as an English lady of quality, who thinks class, *her* class will protect her anywhere, you need to be jarred. . . . It's wrong for you to ride around alone on this range like any wild tomboy."

"Why? You intimated this on our way from Grand Junction. But you do not give me any concrete reasons why it is wrong."

"Some of these men might kidnap you for ransom."

"Nonsense!" she retorted, contemptuously.

"Or one of them might waylay you with worse intention."

"Mr. Wall, I still believe *your* intention is good, but you grossly exaggerate the dangers out here, if there are any. Bernie asked Heeseman about this and was assured that you, being from Wyoming, maligned Utah."

"Ha! Ha! Ha!" laughed Jim, at himself as much as at that information. "What do you say, Miss Herrick, when I tell you that Hank Hays has been watching you from the ridges, riding the lonely trails, biding his chance to waylay you?"

She paled at that, or at his piercing look and change of tone.

"I don't believe it," she said, presently. "For some reason you are over-zealous on my behalf. It is becoming absurd."

"You think I lie?"

"Mr. Wall, I didn't call you a liar," she returned, in annoyance. "I did say ——"

"And you'll go on riding alone when it suits your royal fancy?" he queried, witheringly.

"That is no longer any concern of yours," she replied, at last stung. "But I certainly shall ride when and how I please."

"Then you're as big a damn fool as your nincompoop brother," declared Jim, hotly. "Here I am, the only man in this Star outfit with honesty enough and guts enough to tell you the truth. And I get insulted and fired for my pains."

She sat her horse, mute. Jim laid a strong hand on her pommel and shook it.

"Your saddle's loose. Will you oblige me by getting off?"

"I can ride it back," she rejoined, icily.

"But your blanket will slip out. The saddle might turn with you. . . . At that it might be a good thing for you to fall off and hit your head on a rock."

She removed her boot from the stirrup. "Tighten the cinches then—and hurry."

Jim complied expeditiously enough, but in doing so he accidentally touched her. Something like fire shot through him at the contact. Under its stimulus he looked up to say a few more words to her, words to mitigate his offense and protest his sincerity. But they were never uttered. She had bent over to fasten a lace of her boot, and when Jim raised his head it was to find his face scarcely a foot from her red lips. Without a thought, in a flash, he kissed them, and then drew back stricken.

With startled movement she jerked erect, her face flushing scarlet.

"How dare you!" she cried, in incredulous amaze and anger.

"My God! I didn't mean that!" ejaculated Jim. "It just happened. I—I don't know ——"

She swung her leather quirt and struck him across the mouth. The blood spurted. The leap of Jim's fury was as swift. He half intercepted a second blow, which stung his neck, and snatching the squirt from her hand he flung it away. Then his iron clutch fastened in her blouse. One lunge dropped her out of the saddle. He wrapped his other arm around her and bent her back so quickly that when she began a furious struggle it was too late.

His mouth hard pressed on hers stilled any but smothered cries. There was a moment's fierce wrestling. She was no weakling, but she was in the arms of a maddened giant. Repeatedly he kissed her lips, long, hard, passionate kisses. Suddenly she collapsed, heavily in his arms. The shock of that—its meaning—pierced Wall with something infinitely more imperious and staggering than bitter wrath. He let go of her. Reeling away from him to collide with the pine tree, she sank against it, slid to her knees, and thrust out with repelling gesture of hands spread toward him.

"There—my English lady—maybe that will convince you!" he panted, hoarsely. His chin quivered and there was terrific commotion in his breast. "If you weren't a —pink-and-white-faced—washed-out—ninny of an aristocrat . . . if you had any—blood in you—I'd *prove*—by God!—what men are in Utah! . . . But I wouldn't lay —another hand on you—to save my life. . . . Now get up."

She obeyed him, slowly, with one hand clutching nervelessly at the bark of the pine, the other at her breast. There was blood on her lips and cheeks; otherwise her face was like alabaster.

"I think I must have been in love with you—and wanted to protect you—from men worse than myself," he went on, huskily. "I hope to God this will be a lesson to you. . . . Keep your beautiful face and body from sight of Hank Hays—or any of these robbers. Their thirst for gold is nothing compared to that for a woman. They are starved. They would almost eat you alive. It's criminal carelessness for you to go about as you do, brazenly, as if it were your due to let the sun shine on your head for men to see. Your brother was crazy to come to Utah—crazier to let you come. Go home! Go before it's too late. Make him go. He will be ruined shortly."

She wiped the blood from her cheeks, and then, shudderingly, from her lips.

"You—outraged me that way—to frighten me?" she presently whispered, in horror, yet as if fascinated by something looming.

"Get on your horse and ride ahead of me," he ordered, curtly. "Now, Miss Helen Herrick, one last word. Don't tell your brother what I did to you till after I'm gone. . . . If you do, I'll kill him!"

She left a glove lying on the ground. Jim made no effort to recover it. His horse had grazed a few paces away, and when he had reached him and mounted, Miss Herrick was in her saddle. Jim let her get a few rods in advance before he followed.

The excess of his emotion wore off, leaving him composed, and sternly glad the issue had developed as it had. The situation had become intolerable for him. It mocked him that he had actually desired to appear well in the eyes of this girl. How ridiculous that one of a robber gang should be vain! But he was not conscious that being a thief made any difference in a man's feeling about women. He knew that he could not command respect or love; but that in no wise inhibited his own feelings. Strange to realize, he had indeed fallen in love with Helen Herrick.

She rode on slowly down the ridge without looking to

right or left. Her gaze appeared to be lowered. The droop of her head and of her shoulders indicated shame and dejection. Outraged by a few kisses taken by force! She would remember them—the brutal kisses of a hard man. Jim would remember forever that first kiss, surprised on sweet, full lips.

The ranch-house came in sight, not far down now, standing out yellow against the green and gray. Miss Herrick saw it and halted a moment as if that had been the last thing in her mind. It recalled perhaps that she must face her brother presently. Jim had nearly caught up with her when she rode on again, bracing in her saddle. The next time he looked she had recovered the old poise and grace.

When they got down to the level bench at a point where the road curved up from below, Miss Herrick waited for Jim to come up abreast of her.

She gazed straight ahead, her face coldly pure against the green.

"Can you be gentleman enough to tell me the truth?" she asked.

"I have not lied to you," replied Jim, in weary amaze. Who could make anything of a woman?

"That—that first time you kissed me—was it honestly unpremeditated?"

"Miss Herrick, I don't know what to swear by—having no God or honor or anything. But, yes I have. My mother! I swear by memory of her that I never dreamed of insulting you. . . . I looked up. There your face was close. Your lips red! And I kissed them."

They went on for perhaps ten paces, as far as the road, before she spoke again. "I believe you," she said, without a tremor of the rich, low voice, though it was evident her emotion was deeply stirred. "Your action was inexcusable, unforgivable. But I should not have struck you with the whip. . . . That, and your passion to frighten me, perhaps justified your brutality. . . . I shall not tell. . . . Don't leave Star Ranch."

For an instant Jim felt as if he were upon the verge of a precipice. That was the crowning shock of this unnatural experience. What she meant no wit of Jim's could fathom; he could only take her literally. But her change from revulsion to inscrutable generosity called to all that was good within him.

"Miss Herrick, I'm sorry, but I must leave," he replied, sadly. "I'm only a wandering rider—a gun-slinger and—a member of a gang of robbers. And I was mad enough to fall in love with you. . . . Forget it. . . . Go home to England. But if you won't do that—never ride out alone again."

He spurred his horse and galloped down the road, by the barns and across the court, into the lane that led along the brook. Suddenly he espied a compact group of mounted riders coming down the road beyond Hays' cabin. They bestrode bays and blacks, and there was that about them which drew Jim sharply up with a fiery thrill. Smoky's outfit!

Chapter Eight

HAYS stood out in front of the cabin, bareheaded, his legs spread apart as if to anchor himself solidly, his hands at his hips, his sandy hair standing up ruffled like a mane.

"Huh! The boss isn't mad. Oh no!" soliloquized Jim. "Not at all! I'll bet his teeth are grinding thunder. . . . Small wonder. Smoky's outfit has busted loose or is going to. . . . Well, now, I've a hunch there's luck in this for me."

Jim turned off into the corral, and took his time unsaddling. He did not wish to appear in a hurry to know what was up. He fed Bay grain and did not turn him into the pasture. Moreover, he left his rifle in its saddle-sheath. If he did not miss his calculation he would be riding away from Star Ranch that night, a thought that afforded relief even while it stabbed.

Above the babble of the brook he heard the angry voice of the robber leader. Jim made for the bridge then, and crossing, looked up to see the horses of Smoky's outfit standing, bridles down, and the riders up on the porch. Jim mounted the steps.

Hank Hays sat upon the bench, his shaggy head against the wall, his pale eyes blazing hell at the row of men leaning on the porch rail. Hays' long legs stuck out, with his spurs digging into the porch. He looked an infuriated, beaten man, and his twitching lips attested to impotent speech.

Smoky was lighting a cigarette, not in the least perturbed, but his eyes had a hard, steely gleam. Brad Lincoln sat back on the rail, eying the chief with a sardonic grin. Mac appeared more than usually ghoulish; Bridges and Sparrowhawk Latimer betrayed extreme nervousness.

"Howdy, Jim!" spoke up Smoky.

"Hello men! What's the mix? Am I in or out?" returned Jim, sharply.

"I reckon you're in," replied Slocum. "Hank is the only one thet's out. . . . Hyar, Jim, ketch this." He drew a dark-green bundle from a bulging pocket and tossed it to Jim, so quickly that it struck Jim in the chest. But he caught it on the rebound—a large heavy roll of greenbacks tied with a buckskin thong.

"Yours on the divvy, Jim," went on Smoky. "Don't count it now. There's a heap of small bills inside, an' if you untie them hyar there'll be a mess. But it's a square divvy to the last dollar."

The denomination of the bill on the outside was one hundred. The roll would not go inside his vest or hip pocket, and it took force to put it in his side pocket.

"That's a hefty roll, Smoky, for a man to get for nothing," observed Jim, dubiously. "But the boss doesn't look particularly happy about it."

Jim then noticed that a roll of bills, identical with the one he had just received, lay on the floor.

"— — — —! You double-crossed me!" burst out Hays, at length.

"Wal, thet's accordin' to how you look at it," retorted Slocum. "You wasn't with us when you ought to 'ave been. We couldn't ride forty miles every day to talk with you. Things came up at Grand Junction. We seen some of Heeseman's outfit. Shore as hell they're onto us, or will be pronto. So we jest took a vote, an' every damn one of us stood for one big drive instead of small drives. An' we made it. We was ten days drivin' thet bunch of stock, in the saddle night an' day, half starved to death. Your buyers swore they was short of money an' would pay twelve dollars a head. Talk about robbers! Wal, I took thet an' said I liked it. . . . Now, boss, there're the cards face down, an' you can like them or lump them."

"I'm lumpin' them, Smoky Slocum. . . . An' I've shot a man for less!"

"Shore. But I can't see you shootin' me. I wasn't to blame, I tell you. We took a vote."

"Hell! You disobeyed orders."

"Put it up to Jim, hyar. He's most a stranger to us an' he won't play no pards. . . . What do you say, Jim?"

Thus appealed to, Jim made a serious matter of it and addressed Hays point-blank.

"Smoky's right. If you meant to clean out Herrick, that was the way to do it."

"Aw—shore, you'd side with them."

"I wouldn't do anything of the kind, if I thought they were wrong," retorted Jim, angrily. Here was a chance to inflame Hays that he jumped at. If the robber could be drawn into a fight, when his own men were against him, the situation for the Herricks could be made easier for the present.

"I make my own deals," snapped the robber.

"Yes, and this one here at Star Ranch is a damn poor one, whatever it is."

"Wal, thet's none of your bizness, Jim Wall," declared Hays, more sharply.

"But it is. What do you think I am? A sucker? If I'm in this outfit, anything you plan and all you plan is my business, same as it's Smoky's and the rest of the outfit."

"You'd better shet up."

"I won't shut up, Hays. Some one has to have the guts to tell you. And I'm that fellow. There's no hand-out against you in this outfit. I never saw an outfit as loyal to a man as this one is to you. Never heard of a bunch of riders who'd work like dogs while the boss was twiddling his thumbs and talking mysterious."

Hays glared like a mad bull. He dragged his feet up under him and guardedly rose.

"Take care, boss," spoke up Smoky.

"Who's runnin' this outfit?" he hissed.

"Nobody jest now. I tried to talk sense to you. An' Jim shore *is* talkin' sense. Thet guy can talk, Hank. An' you gotta get it in your thick head thet he's talkin' for all of us."

"Who's thet thick skulled? But I'm sorer'n hell. I ain't ready to leave Star Ranch, an' now, by Gawd! I'll have to!"

"Why ain't you ready?" queried Smoky, curiously. "Our work's all done. We've cleaned out the ranch, except for a few thousand head. We've got the long green. You ought to be tickled to death."

"I'm not through here," replied the robber, righting himself.

"Wal, you ought to be. Thet Heeseman outfit will be after us. What's the sense of fightin' fer nothin'? This rancher, Herrick, likely has some cash around the house. He pays cash. But, hell; Hank, you can't rob the man of his spare change. We've done awful good an' we're heeled as never before."

Hays appeared gradually to relax under the cool persuasive arguments of his lieutenant. Jim saw his coveted chance glimmering.

"Smoky, why don't you ask Hays what this mysterious deal is?" queried Jim, sarcastically.

From a cornered lion Hays degenerated into a cornered rat. Jim sank a little in his boots while his upper muscles corded.

"Hank, what'n hell's got into you?" queried Smoky.

high-voiced. "Glarin' at Jim like a trapped coyote. An' me too!"

"Smoky, the boss is up a tree," said Jim, caustically. "He means to rob Herrick, all right. But that's only a blind. It's the girl!"

"Thet gold-headed gurl we seen you drivin' hyar?"

"Yes. Herrick's sister."

"Wal, for Gawd's sake! Haw! Haw! Haw! So thet's what's eatin' you, Hank?"

Hays had reached his limit and probably, but for Smoky's mirth, would have started hostilities. He hesitated, but there was a deadly flare in the eyes he had fixed on Wall.

Smoky got between them. "See hyar, Hank. So thet's the deal? An' you'd do fer pore Jim hyar jest because he's onto you? . . . Wal, if you're so damn keen as thet to draw on somebody, why, make it me. I started this. I dragged Jim into it. An' I'll be ―― if you're goin' to take it out on him."

There was an instant when a touch to the flint would have precipitated fire. Then Hank came back to himself.

"I weaken. Jim's right. Smoky, you're right," he declared, hoarsely. "I'm bull-headed. . . . An' I lost my bull-head over Herrick's sister and the money I could make out of her."

"There. Spoke up like a man," declared Smoky, heartily relieved. "Why didn't you come thet clean long ago? Neither Jim nor me nor any of us blame you fer admirin' thet gurl. She's a bloomin' rose, Hank. But, hell! air you gettin' dotty in your old age? An' if you'd gone crazy, like you did once, an' dragged her away into the brakes with us, by Gawd! we'd quit you cold."

Hays bent to pick up the roll of bills, which he tossed up and caught as if it were a ball. To Jim Wall's penetrating eye the chief had capitulated for the moment, but he was far from vanquished.

"Happy, how about grub-time?" he called through the door.

" 'Most ready, boss."

"Fall to, men. I've got to do some tall thinkin'," he said.

Before they were half finished with their supper Hays entered and sailed his sombrero into a corner. His face was a dark mask.

"We're shakin' the dust of Star Ranch tonight," he said, deliberately. "Pack up an' leave at once. I'll come later. If I don't meet you at Smoky's camp at sunup, I'll meet you shore at midday in thet cedar grove above the head of Red Canyon."

"Good!" ejaculated Smoky.

"Wal, it was about time," added Brad Lincoln. "You'll aim to roost up somewheres till this blows over?"

"Thet's the idee. Smoky, did you remember to pack out them extra supplies I told you to?"

"Yep. We could hole up six months an' not get scurvy."

No one asked any more questions or made any more comments. Whatever they thought about Hays' peculiar way of leading his band they kept to themselves. Jim Wall was not greatly relieved; still, he concluded that Hays must abandon any plot he might have concocted toward Herrick's sister. To be sure, he would take the bull by the horns this last night, and attempt to rob Herrick. But that latter possibility did not worry Jim particularly. The young woman had just had a valuable lesson. She would not be easy to surprise or take advantage of. At any rate, whatever was in Hays' mind, Jim could not further risk alienating him or his men. Jim would have to ride out with them. If he stayed behind to spy upon Hays or frustrate any attempt he might make to call upon the Herricks, he would have to kill Hays. He did not mind that in the least, but he did not care to go riding it alone in this unknown country, with Smoky and the others hunting for him.

"Pack up fer me, somebody," said Hays. "I'll keep watch outside. We shore don't want to be surprised by Heeseman the last minit."

Dusk was mantling the valley when Jim went out. Under the bench the shadows were dark. From the shelter of the pines he looked for Hays, expecting to find him standing guard. But the robber was not on the porch. He was stalking to and fro along the brook, and he was no more watching for Heeseman than was Jim. His bent form, his stride, his turning at the end of his beat, his hands folded behind his back—all attested to the mood of a gloomy, abstracted, passion-driven man.

Jim cursed under his breath. Here was a situation where, if he gave way to suspicions that might be overdrawn, prompted by his own jealousy rather than facts, he would certainly outlaw himself from Hays' band. Almost he yielded to them. Almost he distrusted his own fears. But he was in love with Miss Herrick and that had biased him. Hank Hays was blackguard enough to do anything to make money out of a woman, but he would scarcely betray his faithful followers. Hays was as loyal to them as they were to him. Honor among robbers! Still, in the case of a magnificent creature like Helen Herrick ——

Jim wrenched himself out of sight of the stalking robber. He was not superhuman. He had to make a choice, and he made it, on the assumption that his fears for Helen, surrounded by servants and with her brother, were actually far-fetched, if not ridiculous.

Whereupon Jim repaired to his covert, rolled his bed and made a pack of his other belongings. What to do with the two packages of bills, this last of which was large and clumsy for his pockets, was a puzzle. By dividing the two into four packets he solved it. Then he carried his effects down to the cabin. All was cheery bustle there. The men were glad to get away from Star Ranch. They talked of the robbers' roost Hays had always promised them, of idle days to eat and drink and gamble, of the long months in hiding.

"Wal, you all ready?" queried Hays, appearing in the doorway.

"Yep, an' bustin' to go."

"On second thought I'd like one of you to stay with me. How about you, Latimer?"

"All right," declared Sparrowhawk.

"This all right with you, Smoky?"

"Suits us fine. If you ask me, I'd say you'd better keep Jim an' me, too, with you."

"I would if there was any chance of a fight. . . . Take Sparrow's pack-hoss, an' mine, too."

In a few more minutes all the men leaving were mounted. The pack-animals, with packs gray against the darkness, straggled up the trail. Jim tried hard to get a look at Hays' face, but the lights were out and gloom hung thick everywhere.

"Wait at your camp till sunup," said Hays, conclusively. "An' if I'm not there I'll meet you about noon shore at head of Red Canyon."

Without more words or ado Smoky led off behind the pack-horses, and the five riders followed. Once across the brook, all horses took to a brisk trot. Jim Wall looked back. The cabin faded in the gloom under the bench. Not for a mile or more did Jim glance over his shoulder again. Then he saw a bright light on the bench. That was from Herrick's house. He and his sister would be sitting in the living-room, reading or talking. After all, how easy for Hank Hays to corner them there! Jim's reluctance, his uneasiness, would not down. An unfamiliar sensation, like a weight of cold lead in his breast, baffled Jim. He knew he was glad that he would never see Helen Herrick again.

The spring night waxed cold as the hours wore on and the riders took to the slope. When they got up above the valley, out of the gray mists and shadows, the stars shone bright and white. A steady clip-clop of hoofs broke the silence. The riders proceeded in single file and seldom was a word spoken, except to a lagging pack-horse.

About midnight Smoky turned the pack-animals up the slope into the woods, and after a mile of rough going emerged into an open canyon head. Water splashed somewhere down over rocks.

"Hyar we air," said Smoky, making leather creak as he wearily slid off. "Throw things an' git to sleep. I'll stand first guard."

Evidently the horses were not to be turned loose. Nevertheless, Jim put hobbles on Bay. The men spoke in subdued voices while they unsaddled and threw the packs. Jim overheard Brad Lincoln offer to bet that Hays would not show up at sunrise. Gradually they quieted down, one by one. Jim unrolled his bed beside a rock and, pulling off his boots and unbuckling his gun-belt, he crawled under the blanket. He was neither tired nor sleepy. White stars blinked down pitilessly and mockingly. Would he ever lie down again without the face of Helen Herrick before him, without the lingering fragrance and softness of her lips on his? But that was something different to remember. He welcomed it. And he lived over everything leading up to that kiss, and after it that fierce attack he had made upon her lips. Lastly came her amazing request to him not to leave Star Ranch, and this abode with him until he fell asleep.

Crack of ax and Happy Jack's voice pierced his slumber both recognized before he opened his eyes. The sun was topping the eastern range. Jim sat up, stretched, and reaching for his boots he gazed around. The camp was an open draw, with level floor narrowing to a timber belt below. Behind rose shrubby limestone walls, in a crack of which poured a gush of water. The men were stirring, two around the camp fire and others among the horses. Happy Jack fetched an armload of wood; Bridges was slicing bacon. Jim smelled a mixture of wood smoke and coffee.

"Wal, long past sunup," said Slocum as he approached the fire. "Who was it bet Brad thet Hank wouldn't show up?"

"Nobody," replied Lincoln.

"Jim, suppose you take your rifle an' sneak down an' knock over a deer," suggested Smoky. "I see a buck an' three does a minnit ago. If you get one, gut it an' leave it lay. We'll throw it on a hoss as we go down. We're gonna need fresh meat. But shore step out of the woods first an' see if Hank's comin', or anybody."

Three hundred yards down the slope Jim emerged into the open. Such a wonderful blaze of sun! The valley burned purple and red. There were no riders on the winding, white trail. Jim took a long look at the lilachazed, canyoned abyss to his left. It was a sight to make even a hardened rider gasp. It was enough to make Westerners love their wilderness. There seemed to be no reality in the endless black line of Wild Horse Mesa.

Stealthily working back into the timber, he soon espied two deer about sixty paces distant, long ears erect. He killed the buck standing, and sent a quick shot after the bounding doe, but missed.

Upon his return to camp, Smoky greeted him with a grin. "I jest bet Brad thet you busted two."

"Sorry; you lose. I missed the doe. Buck's big and fat, though."

"Fine. We got two extra pack-horses. Wal, Jim, gobble some grub. We're on the prod."

"How far to Red Canyon?" asked Jim.

"I don't know. About fifteen miles—Utah miles, haw! haw! Don't you remember thet heavy grove of cedars leadin' down into a red hole?"

"Reckon I do. If Hays joins us there, it'll mean he comes by another trail, doesn't it?"

"If! So you figger he might not?—course he'd come around the mountain, or mebbe over another pass. He shore knows trails thet we don't."

"Aw, Hank'll show up on time."

"Wonder if he stayed back to plug Heeseman? He hates thet rustler."

In less than hour the riders were on the move down the mountain. Packing on the deer Jim had slain occasioned a little delay for all, because Smoky kept them close together. At the edge of the timber belt he halted them again while he peeped out to reconnoiter. Then he called, "Come hyar, a couple of you long-sighted fellers."

They all rode out to join him, where he sat his horse, pointing to a faint blur on the purple valley floor. "Is thet dust?"

Most of the riders inclined to the opinion that it was just haze.

"Ten miles or more back and hard to make out," spoke up Jim. "If this was my range, I'd say it wasn't haze or smoke."

"Wish I had Hank's glasses. My eyes are no good any more fer long shots. Wal, let's mozy. At thet distance we don't give a damn what it is."

Nevertheless, Jim noted that Smoky led to the left, across the ravine, along the edge of the timber belt over a ridge, and then down to the trail. Soon they turned a yellow corner of wall to come out at the point where Hays had described the expanse to Jim. It had been wonderful enough then, at noonday, when all was pale and dim in the white, solemn light, but now, just after sunrise, it seemed a dazzling world of rainbow wheels, glorious to the gaze. So different was it that Jim could not recognize any particular point Hays had designated. There were now a thousand striking landmarks rising out of the colorful chaos.

To Jim's regret, however, this spectacle soon dropped behind gray foothills.

Smoky pushed the pack-horses at a trot. They wound in and out of the brushy hills, at length to leave them for the long slant of greasewood and gravel which led down into the brakes. Here on the left the great bulk of the black white-tipped Henrys towered majestically, lost in perpetual clouds. Once Jim caught sight of the winding serrated wall of rock across the ghastly barrens, and it was a brilliant purple, except at the far-distant end, where it paled to lavender. Far ahead a black fringe of cedars thickened to a grove above a red jagged line which was the canyon head where the riders had a rendezvous with Hays.

When they reached another turn from which it was possible to look back for five miles or more, Smoky halted while the others caught up.

"Jeff, you hang right hyar," he said, "an' keep your eyes peeled on the back trail. I ain't so shore thet gray patch back on the valley was haze. It sort of moved to me. An' there wasn't a lick of wind. Wal, from round this corner you can easy see the cedar grove where we'll hang up fer the boss. An' if you ketch sight of any more'n a couple riders on the back stretch, you come ridin' hell-bent fer election. Don't stay long after noon."

Perhaps another five miles down the slope lay their objective to which they headed. The gait was slowed a little, if anything, yet in somewhat over an hour the riders arrived at the cedars. Jim recalled the place, but it was not, as he had imagined, the point where Hays had led up out of the brakes of the Dirty Devil.

The hour was still some time before noon. Smoky scanned the slope to the south and east. It would not have been possible to see riders at any distance, as the rocks, brush, ridges, and washes intervened profusely.

"What'll we do, Smoky? Throw the packs or not?" queried one of the riders.

"Dog-gone if I know," replied Slocum, peevishly. "It's a rummy deal. Hot as hell now an' gettin' hotter. I forgot to ask Hank. Reckon you'd better herd the hosses an' we'll wait. I'll keep a lookout fer the boss."

Jim tied his horse in the shade of a cedar, and climbed a jumble of rocks so he could command a better view. Almost at once he sighted riders coming down a wash about a mile away, and he had opened his mouth to shout the good tidings, when something checked him so abruptly that he bit his tongue.

He rubbed his eyes and looked again. Three riders! Assuming that two of them were Hays and Latimer, who could the third be? They disappeared behind a corner of bank. Jim sank down in a cold sweat. Perhaps these men were Indians, or strangers from Hankville, or prospectors. But he had not seen any pack-animals.

After a long, anxious watch he saw the three reappear in the wash, considerably closer. The one in the middle rode a gray horse and otherwise contrasted sharply with the dark mounts and dark clothes of the other two. A second time the trio disappeared. Smoky was peering about in a desultory manner, but he was too low down to sight the riders. Jim was now shaking. An awful premonition attacked him. He had met it and most overcome it as another unaccountable attack of nerves when the foremost horseman emerged from behind a bank. He recognized the stalwart figure, the wide, black sombrero, the poise in the saddle. That man was Hank Hays.

Jim scarcely dared shift his gaze back to the second rider, but he was irresistibly forced to. A slighter figure in tan, drooping in the saddle!

"So help me God!" he whispered, and sank down on the stone. That center rider was Helen Herrick. For a moment a hell rioted in Jim Wall's breast. How he cursed himself for a vacillating idiot! His intuition had been right. He had seen through this robber leader's behavior at Star Ranch. But like a fool he had not trusted himself. That trick spelled death for Hank Hays. Jim grew cold to his very marrow. Yet his intelligence did not wholly succumb to his fury. He strove to think. This blackhearted hound had gotten Helen, just how, it was useless to conjecture. But to kill him then, right on the spot? That gave Jim Wall pause. Hays' men would roar at this deal, involving them in the abduction of a woman; still, they would hardly go so far as to resist him with arms. He would be cocky, radiant, conciliatory now. Jim crushed down his deadly impulse. He would wait. He would hear what the others had to say. He would bide his time.

Well indeed had it been for Jim to espy this trio long before they reached him. He had time to recover, to think what was best. If Hank Hays had come upon Jim suddenly, it would have been to his doom.

One of the pack-animals neighed shrilly and then all the horses stuck up their ears.

"Say, I heerd a hossshoe ring on a stone," called Mac, who had ears as keen as a horse.

"What's thet?" queried Smoky, sharply. He leaped up.

"Look! Riders comin'," exclaimed Brad Lincoln.

"Can't be nobody but Hank."

Jim leaped off the rock, crashing down behind the watching men, startling them. "Smoky, it's Hays. I saw him a mile off."

"Why'n hell didn't you say somethin', then?" retorted Slocum, gruffly.

"I was too flabbergasted," replied Jim, coolly, as he joined them.

"It's Hank, all right," said Mac.

"Shore, I see him now. Thet's Hank."

"Jim, what flabbergasted you?" demanded Slocum.

"*Three riders!*" flashed Jim.

"Wal! . . . So I see. What you make of thet?" ejaculated Slocum.

The three emerged clearly from behind the cedars. A blank silence ensued. Jim at last got the tigerish nerves under control. His thoughts were whirling.

"Humph! Little rider in between," commented Lincoln.

"Thet's Sparrowhawk behind."

"Who's the third party?"

"Hank shore is a queer duck, takin' up with strangers like he does."

"Somebody with a mask on!"

"An' a long slicker."

"Fellers," rasped out Slocum, "thet's a woman with a veil!"

Jim thought the moment had come. "Men, Hank has doublecrossed us. He's stolen Herrick's sister!"

"The — — — — — —!" cursed Slocum.

No more was said after that profane outburst. It probably voiced the unity of the watchers. Hank Hays led his two followers to within a few feet of the cluster

of riders, when he leaped off and checked the gray horse.
Sparrowhawk came right on. Jim's lightning-swift
glance took the three in, their dust-caked horses, and
flashed back to fasten upon Miss Herrick. Her features
were not visible through the veil. The linen coat showed
the wear and tear of contact with brush. To Jim's incredulous amaze, she had on riding-boots and overalls.
She sat free in the saddle, with neither hands nor feet
bound. The gray horse carried a long pack folded over
the cantle.

"Wal, you're all here but Jeff," began Hays. He had a
bold front, a piercing eye. Fear of man or beast or God
did not abide in him them.

"Jeff'll be comin' by now," replied Smoky.

"We ain't got a hell of a lot of time to wait," said Hays.
"Whar you aimin' fer?"

"Brakes of the Dirty Devil."

"But we was goin' around an' head thet hot hell hole."

"No time."

Brad Lincoln thrust himself forward, black of face,
hitching his gun-belt. "Who's the third party?"

"Wal, you can guess," leered Hays.

"I take it you've fetched Herrick's sister."

"You're a bright boy. Go to the head of the class."

"Hank Hays, after all you double-crossed us," roared
Smoky.

"Wal, if I did—turn about is fair play."

"Fair play—hell! You're a liar. You're a cheat. You're
a ——. You think you can drag us in on a deal like this.
I thought you acted powerful queer. So it was this
double-breasted gurl you tricked us fer? . . . You
— — —!"

Jim Wall strode forward and aside, his swift action
menacingly significant.

"Hays, your jig's up. She goes back!" he thundered.

"You can all go to Hell," the robber replied, stridently. "Stick or quit, if you want. But if you give me a word edgeways I'll say somethin'. I fetched this gurl fer ransom. She come willin', 'cause if she hadn't I'd killed Herrick. He'll pay twenty-five mebbe fifty thousand for her. Is thet to be sneezed at?"

"So thet was your deal?" queried Slocum.

"Thet, an' nothin' else. Now what're you goin' to do about it?"

"Hank, on the face of it thet's different. All the same you double-crossed us."

"Same as you did me. I swore to get even with you."

Jim interposed again. "Hays, you're a dirty liar. You didn't steal this girl for ransom," he called out fiercely.

"Well, I can allow fer you all bein' riled. But I can't stand names like thet forever."

Jim turned to the dejected figure on the gray horse. "Miss Herrick, is he telling the truth?"

"Yes, he stole me for ransom," she replied, with emotion. "They broke into my room—one through the window—the other at the door. They threatened me with guns. . . . If I screamed they'd kill me! If I didn't come with them they'd kill my brother! . . . I agreed. I had to dress before them—the beasts! They forced me to dress for riding. . . . And I've been on this horse since midnight."

"What'd they do to Herrick?"

"Oh, I didn't see. I don't know whether they told the truth or lied."

"Jim, if you're so damn pert to know everythin', I'll waste more time by tellin' you," interposed Hays. "We tied Herrick up before we got the gurl. An' after, we made him promise to pay handsome. An' ——"

"That's enough," snapped Jim. "Give me a man or two. We'll take her back and get the money."

"Hold on. Thet was somethin' I had in mind," drawled Hays. "But it didn't work. I had to kill Progar. An' ——"

"Who's Progar?"

"Wal, he's Heeseman's right-hand man. Now it happened thet foxy Heeseman was plannin' the same trick I pulled. Progar an' another feller ketched us takin' the gurl out. The other feller got away."

"—— —! Thet's wuss then ever," screamed Smoky. "Heeseman will find out."

"Huh! I should smile in perticular thet he will. We seen his outfit on your trail!"

"Shet up! Hosses comin'!"

"Grab your rifles an' dig fer cover!"

The ensuing rush was quelled by Smoky's ringing order. "Hold on! It's Jeff!"

"Lordy! Look at him come! No wonder he sounded like a stampede."

An opening in the grove showed Bridges plunging upon them. Wild-eyed and snorting smoke, his big charger threw gravel all over them.

"Heeseman's outfit trailin' us," he announced. "Back about five miles when I left my post."

Smoky turned in cold fury upon their leader. "Now —— — you! See what you've got us up ag'in'!"

Chapter Nine

FROM that speech, Jim calculated, dated the beginning of a definite breach between Hank Hays and his lieutenant, Slocum.

"Wal, it's no time to cuss me," snarled the robber leader.

"By Gawd! I wish I had some," replied Slocum, bitterly. "Fellers, grab your rifles an' take to cover."

"There ain't no cover, Smoky," asserted Brad Lincoln.

"This place won't do," interposed Jim, sharply. "Miss Herrick might be hit. We'd better make for a canyon."

"No sense in a fight, anyhow," rejoined Hays.

"But, man, we'll have to fight," rasped out Slocum. "Heeseman's ridin' light. We've got this pack outfit. He'll ketch us shore. An' I say let's hide behind these trees an' wait fer him."

There was no gainsaying the little rider's wisdom, and Jim would have backed him up but for the girl. If she fell into Heeseman's power she would be as badly off, if not worse.

"Jeff, air they comin'?" queried Hays of Bridges, who was standing in his saddle, peering back.

"Nope. But I see dust over the ridge, an' I reckon thet's him."

Hays made a dive for his horse, and mounting, he leaned over to take up a rope halter round the neck of the horse Miss Herrick was riding.

"You lied—to me!" she cried, angrily. "You assured me that if I'd come without resistance you'd soon arrange for my freedom. Here we are miles from Star Ranch."

Hays paid not the slightest attention to her, but started off, leading her horse.

"Jim Wall, are you going to permit this outrage?" She turned in her saddle to entreat him.

"I'm powerless, Miss Herrick," he replied, hurriedly. "I'm only one of Hays' band. We are being tracked. If Heeseman catches us you'll be worse off."

"Oh, how dreadful! I will not be dragged down into that ghastly hole."

"Drive the pack-horses behind me an' keep 'em movin'," yelled Hays. "Once we reach the river I can give them the slip."

"Aw, you're crazy," derided Smoky. "Heeseman knows this country as well as you."

The leader did not answer that taunt. He headed down the slope, dragging Miss Herrick's horse. Sparrowhawk Latimer fell in with them. Jim could hear the girl's protestations. The other riders made haste to line the pack-horses. Smoky brought up the rear.

The wash that Hays had come down was the one which led into the Red Canyon. It was shallow, dusty, hot. The dry stream-bed afforded easy progress. Jim could not see any sign of a trail or even of an old hoof track. No doubt about Hays knowing his way! He rode as one familiar with this red-clay and gray-gravel canyon. Soon it merged with another coming in from the left, and then all features were magnified. It began to drop, the stream-bed grew rough, the walls higher. All landmarks above were lost sight of; even the Henry Mountains disappeared. The pack-horses kicked up a dust like a red cloud; the riders pulled their scarfs up over mouths and noses. Their yells and curses sounded muffled.

Jim kept unobtrusively working ahead until there were only three pack-horses in front of him and he could see Hays and the girl at intervals. Latimer hung close to them. The canyon deepened. No more places occurred where it might have been possible to lead a horse up. And not long after that the walls became so steep that a man could not have climbed them.

The direction of this canyon appeared to be swinging toward the north, but how much Jim could not estimate. As it twisted, the sun was often in front, then to the right, and again almost behind. Short patches of shade were exceedingly welcome. The horses began to be covered with a lather of dust, sweat, and froth. Jim looked back. Brad Lincoln, his face uncovered, red and wet, rode close behind the last pack-horse. Then followed Jeff, Mac, Happy Jack, and lastly Slocum, dark harsh figures, their very attitudes expressing resentment at this unexpected flight. Slocum was the only one who betrayed any sign of their being tracked, and he kept looking back and up at the ragged rims.

Gradually the sand and rocks and holes slowed the pack-horses to a walk. Hays yelled back for his riders to hurry. He pointed to the left wall as if any moment their pursuers might appear there. Jim thought if they did that, it was all up with Hank Hays' outfit. What to do kept harassing Jim, until that problem, combined with the heat and dust, wrought him far from his usual coolness of mind.

From the first moment that he espied the girl in Hays' power he had conceived the idea of rescuing her. But how, when, where? He could only go on and await developments. The immediate necessity was flight, until some safe retreat had been found.

An hour or more of this travel, the first half of which had been rapid, the last slow, brought them to a comparatively long stretch of canyon with a turn. This was too open and unsafe to suit Jim. And evidently it increased Smoky's concern, for he bawled out to push the pack-horses harder.

The next sign from Smoky was a rifle-shot. It bellowed

out from wall to wall. Jim wheeled to see that he was
throwing in another shell, both gun and face pointed back
and up toward the right wall.

"What you shootin' at?" yelled Brad, jerking out his
rifle. The other riders shouted hoarse queries.

Jim espied something flash along the rim, high up and
far back, out of range, if it were a pursuer.

"Rustle!" shrilled Smoky. "I seen riders. They ducked
back. They'll aim to head us off."

Hays bawled back an order and pointed aloft. Jim,
from his point, could not see the very evident danger.
Halfway down this long stretch, on the right side,
opened a deep canyon. That would surely block pursuers,
at least until they had headed it, which might require
miles of travel. At any rate, it relieved Jim.

He, with the riders behind, had the pack-horses loping,
a risky thing, because if a pack slipped thereby stopping
the horse, it would have to be abandoned. And to these
fugitives, going down into this hole, packs were incalculably precious.

Suddenly riders popped into view back on the point of
the intersecting canyon. Hays and Latimer opened fire
with their side-arms, the .45 Colts, the heavy bullets of
which fell short, puffing yellow dust on the sloping point.
The riders began to return the fire with rifles. Jim saw
Latimer knocked off his horse, but he leaped up and
mounted again, apparently not badly injured. He raced
ahead after Hays, who rode fast, dragging the girl's
horse, and at the same time shooting at the riders until
he passed around a corner of the canyon. Latimer soon
disappeared after him. Then the riders above turned their
attention to the rest of Hays' outfit.

"Come on!" yelled Jim to those behind. "Run for it!
Our only chance!" And charging after the galloping pack-

horses ahead, he let Bay find the way and threw up his rifle.

The distance to the pursuing horsemen above, who were riding up and down, yelling, shooting, dismounting to run out, was close to four hundred yards—a long shot with the .44 Winchester from a horse. Heeseman's outfit had the upper hand. They could stand or kneel and shoot. Apparently they saw their advantage, for they did not take to cover. Jim heard their piercing yells, as well as the bellowing replies of the riders behind him.

He had a quarter of a mile to ride to pass the corner ahead to safety. The pack-horses were scattered, tearing up the canyon. Jim gained on them. Then he began to shoot, aiming as best he could at that swift pace. Suddenly the canyon awoke to an infernal din. The reports banging from wall to wall magnified a hundredfold, until there was a continuous roar.

One of Jim's first shots hit a horse, and his seventh connected with a rider, who plunged like a crippled rabbit back out of sight. The others of Heeseman's outfit took alarm, dodged here and there to hide, or ran back. Jim emptied the magazine of his rifle just before he passed round into the zone of safety. Neither Hays nor the two with him were visible, but the canyon ahead had another sharp turn.

Jim hauled Bay to a halt, and soon the pack-horses galloped by, every pack riding well. From below came the slackening bellow of guns. Lincoln dashed into sight first, closely followed by Mac, Happy Jack, and Jeff, all with guns smoking. And lastly came Slocum, hatless, blood on his face, to rein his mount among them.

"Smoky, did they—git you?" queried Lincoln, in alarm.

"Jest barked," panted Slocum, spitting fire. "— —

— —! If we could only—fight it out! . . . Looks all right ahead. Load yer guns—an' ride on!"

Around the next turn they came upon Hays and his two riders. The pack-horses had slowed down behind them. With another big intersecting canyon on the right it looked as if their pursuers were held up.

"Fellers, Heeseman will have to go back," declared Lincoln. "Thet'll take hours. I reckon Hank knowed what he was about."

"Wal, thet was a hell of a close shave," replied Smoky. "Bullet hit my rifle an' glanced—skinnin' me over the ear."

"Latimer," replied Jim. "I saw him knocked off his horse. But he was up, like a cat, and on again."

"Ahuh. Luck's with us. Say, it's hot. If we don't come to thet river soon we're cooked."

"Must be close now."

That last hopeful assertion, however, was wrong. The Dirty Devil, expected at every winding corner, failed to show up. Deeper and deeper grew the canyon, until its ragged, crumbling, colored walls as denuded as the dry floor, rose three hundred feet, and everywhere slides and shelves of soil hung ready for an avalanche.

Mid-afternoon found the fugitives entering a less con-stricted area, where sunlight and open ahead attested to the vicinity of a wider canyon, surely the Dirty Devil. And so it proved. Mud-holes appeared in the stream-bed, and at last pools of clear water, from which the thirsty horses could scarcely be dragged.

Then Red Canyon joined that of the Dirty Devil, a union which was startling in its nakedness. All was drab gray, yellow, and red, with the sullen river running shal-lowly over sandbars.

Hays waited for his riders and the pack-animals to reach him.

"Cinch up an' look to the packs," he ordered. "We've hell ahead, but nothin' no more behind."

"No! Haven't we, though?" queried Lincoln. "Don't you fool yourself about Heeseman not follerin' us."

"Wal, he'll track us this fer, an' thet'll be his limit," declared the robber. "There ain't no man in Utah who can foller me into the brakes of the Dirty Devil."

"Hank, air you aimin' for thet roost you always give us a hunch about but never produced?" asked Slocum.

"I've saved it up, Smoky, fer jest some such deal as this. . . . Pile off now. Once we hit the quicksand we cain't stop fer nothin' or nobody. Look to saddles an' packs."

The riders complied. Jim, over the back of his horse, watched Miss Herrick when Hays made her get off. The long coat fell below her knees. She walked as if the use of her legs was almost gone. He saw her bend over stiffly, to rub them, and then lift her veil to let the gentle breeze blow upon her face. But presently, when Hays harshly called her to come back, she replaced the veil again. She was tiring and her head drooped.

"Fellers, listen," began Hays. "The river's low. I was feared it might be up. It ought to be, 'cause by now the snow must be meltin'. Luck shore is with us. Wal, jest foller me. Drive the pack-hosses fast as they'll go. Don't stop for nothin'."

"Ahuh. All right. But Sparrowhawk looks pale an' weak," replied Slocum.

"He'll make it. We cain't stop now to doctor him up."

"Sparrow, I ain't trustin' the boss so damn much. How bad air you hurt?"

"Not so bad, Smoky," replied Latimer. "I was hit in the back, high up. The bullet's in there. Hurts like hell."

"Ain't you spittin' blood?"

"Shore, a little. I reckon my lung got nicked. But not bad; I can ride. Don't worry about me, Smoky."

Hays laid a rude hand on Miss Herrick. "Git on, an' don't let me hear any more squawks out of you."

The robber took up her halter and straddling his horse he spurred into the muddy stream. The going looked worse than it was. There was quicksand, but it had a stiff crust; it bent but broke only as the hoofs of the horses were being withdrawn. The pack-animals bunched on the shore; then one led, and the others followed. Jim was alongside the foremost. Bay feared quicksand, yet trusted his rider.

Hays led into the middle of the river and then turned downstream. He was never in difficulties and the gray horse carrying the girl got along still better. The water was scarcely six inches deep and this fact no doubt rendered traveling easy at that point.

Soon the whole cavalcade was splashing down the river, the riders behind and on each side of the pack-horses. They left no trace of their tracks now. Washes and gorges and canyons opened into the Dirty Devil on both sides. Half a mile down, the river made a sharp bend and the canyon narrowed again to a dark, forbidding, many-hued crack. Hays kept on, getting into swifter and deeper water, where he plunged his horse and dragged the gray. He passed one wide intersecting gorge from which a slender, muddy stream emerged. That, thought Jim, should have been a good place to go up. But this robber knew where he was heading. He had a goal in mind. Nothing but death could have stopped him.

The pack-horses floundered in places. Some of them stuck, only to be beaten to violent exertion, when they freed themselves to go on. Jim's sight covered all the surroundings from moment to moment, always to be drawn back to that tan-clad form on the gray horse. Time and again water splashed all over her; her horse staggered, sank one hoof and then another, plunged to free himself, and got out; she swayed in the saddle; often she looked back, and no doubt, through her veil, could see Jim never far from her. Jim took it that she realized this was no accident.

Hays passed other gorges breaking in from the left wall, and ever the way grew more forbidding. At last he turned into a crack that could not be seen a hundred yards back, and when Jim reached it he was amazed to see the robber leading up another narrow gorge, down which ran another swift, narrow stream. Jim appreciated that a man would have had to know where this entrance was, or he could never have found it. The opening was hidden by a point of wall which curved out and around. It opened down the river, and against the dark shade there was not visible from the opposite side of the canyon or from upriver any line of demarkation to show this secret gateway, which undoubtedly led into the wildest part of the brakes.

This gash wound like a snake into the bowels of the colored, overhanging earth; and part of the time Jim could not see Hays ahead nor more than a few of the pack-horses behind. When, however, the water began to lose something of its muddy nature, Jim concluded that the loamy soil of this canyon changed, or else it was not long.

The former proved to be the case. The canyon widened and the walls lowered; grass and shrubs made their appearance upon banks and shelves; a heavy, gravel bottom gave the stream a rippling murmur; huge rocks and caverned cliffs made their appearance. Still the volume of the stream did not diminish.

By sunset Jim calculated the horses had traveled seven or eight miles without stepping once out of the water. The

heat and dust had vanished. Twilight thickened between
the cliffs. And at last, at a point where the walls were
scarcely a hundred feet high the canyon forked. Hays
took the left fork, which was dry. And darkness soon
hid from Jim any distinct features. Seldom did he see
a gleam of Miss Herrick's gray horse. The rims grew
black; stars burned in the strip of sky above; the weary
hoofs cracked on stone.

Two long hours later Hays led up out of the boxing
canyon. A hummocky, lonely, black-and-gray landscape
rolled away on every side to the horizon of stars. Up
and down, on through grass and weeds, across flats and
ridges, the robber led for two or more hours longer,
until Jim began to wonder how much more the pack-
horses could stand. Then abruptly they began to descend
into a black, round hole the dimensions of which were
vague. Presently they reached a bottom from which
weird, black, bold walls stood up, ragged of rim against
the sky. Jim felt thick grass under his feet. He smelled
damp earth; he heard a rustle of cottonwood leaves.

"Hyar we air," called out Hays. "Throw saddles an'
packs. Let the hosses go. No fear of hosses ever leavin'
this place."

Jim alone heard the chief, and he passed the word back
to his nearest follower, and presently the pack-horses
stood drooping, gray-backed in the gloom. The riders
were not too weary to express themselves after that
grueling trip.

"Where'n hell air we?"

"Smells good."

"Dawg-gone! I cain't eat, but I shore can sleep."

"Sparrow, how air you?"

"Alive yet an' not bleedin'."

In the gloom Jim's night-owl eyes discerned Hays lifting Miss Herrick off her horse and half carrying her off

toward the rustling cottonwoods. Jim, making pretense of leading his horse, followed until Hays stopped at the border of what appeared a round grove of cottonwoods impenetrable to the sight. He heard the tinkle of water near and a musical flow farther away and down.

"Oh, for God's sake—let *go* of me!" gasped the girl, and sank down on the grass.

"You may as wal get used to *thet*," replied Hays, in low voice. "Do you want anythin' to eat?"

"Water—only water. I'm—choking."

"I'll fetch some an' a bed for you."

Little did Hays realize, as he strode back to the horses, that Jim stood there in the gloom, a clutching hand on his gun and mad lust for blood in his heart. Jim knew he meant to kill Hays. Why not now? But as before, he had the sagacity and the will to resist a terrible craving.

With nerveless hands he unpacked his outfit and turned the wet, raw-shouldered pack-animal free with the others. Then he sat down upon his bed-roll, exhausted by the physical and mental excess of the last twenty-four hours.

Above him a few rods the men were unpacking, their relief voiced in low talk. Hays passed with a bed-roll on his shoulder. Jim heard it thud to the soft turf close by in the shadow.

"Any wood around this bloomin' hole?" Happy Jack shouted. "It's midnight, but I'll hatch up a snack of grub an' coffee if we can start a fire."

"Darker'n hell," growled Smoky. "An' I shore got a headache. I'd like to meet the hombre who bounced thet bullet offn my head."

Hays returned. He was full of energy and his voice vibrated.

"Plenty firewood," he said, cheerfully. "I'll pack some up, Happy. Tomorrow you'll see the greatest roost fer robbers in all Utah."

"It needs to be," growled Lincoln.

Jim listened, while he gazed around. He appeared to be down in a round hole, the circular walls of which stood up a hundred or more feet above him. Only a couple of notches, one V-shaped and large, to the west, and another small and shallow to the north, broke the level rim of the insulating walls. The stars turned very white in a dark blue sky. The low voices of the men and rattle of packs and the cutting sound of horses grazing seemed only to make the deep silence more permeating. The place fascinated. An owl hooted down somewhere in a canyon, and far away a wolf bayed blood-thirstily.

Soon a crackle of fire turned Jim to see a growing light, and dark forms of men. Happy Jack was whistling. His cheerfulness was irritating. Could nothing upset him, tire him? Jim waited until he saw Hays pass in the shadow, back to the camp fire, and then he, too, joined the men.

"Boss, any guard tonight?" asked Lincoln.

"Nope. We won't stand guard except in daytime," replied the robber. "Tomorrow I'll show you the lay of the land."

"What kind of a roost is it, Hank? Anythin' like thet Dragon Canyon?"

"No indeed. I seen thet place once. It's a cave high up—forty feet mebbe, from the canyon bed. You have to go up on a pole with steps cut in. But I was never up. Only one outlet to that burrow, an' thet's by the same way you come. This roost has four. We could never be ketched in a hundred years."

"Ahuh. How about the hosses?"

"Wal, you-all know that hosses will travel from barren country. They'll stick here. We'll never even have to go up on top to find them. Best of pure water—no alkali—an' grass till you can't believe your eyes. I haven't been here fer ten years, but I know it'd never change."

"Any game?"

"Antelope an' rabits in flocks."

"Jest where air we?"

"I'll show you in the mornin' when we can see."

"Hank, how'd the lady stand the ride?"

"She's all in."

"Gosh! no wonder! Thet was a job fer men."

"Reckon I'll put up the little tent fer my lady guest."

"Say, Hank, do you aim to sleep in thet tent with her?" queried Smoky, who had not spoken before. His tone was peculiar.

"No, if it's any of your mix," returned Hays, after a considerable pause.

"Ahuh. Much obliged. I was jest curious."

"Hank, how'n hell air you goin' to collect thet ransom now?" inquired Lincoln.

"Damn if I know. Heeseman shore spoiled my plan. But I'll make another, an' after we lay low awhile I can work it."

"Keepin' thet gurl hyar all the time?" queried Smoky.

"What else can I do, man? I meant to hang out over on the other side till I got the money for her. But now thet's no good."

"It never was no good, boss. An' if it hadn't been fer Heeseman hot on our trail, I'd never stood fer this."

"Wal, you'll have to stand fer it now, whether you like it or not."

"Ump-umm!" muttered Smoky, as if to himself.

That concluded the conversation for the moment. Happy Jack gave each one a cup of coffee, a slice of cold meat, and a biscuit.

"Wal, thet's better," said Hays, presently. "Now, Sparrow, I'm a-goin' to look after your gunshot."

"Wait till daylight, boss. I'm restin' tolerable comfortable," replied Latimer.

"You know thet's bad. When blood-poisonin' sets in it does it quick. I'll go get my salve an' some clean linen. Stir up the fire, Jack, an' have me two pans of hot water, one of them boilin' hot."

Jim watched the robber chief minister to his wounded comrade. Latimer cursed, and stuck out his boots to dig his spurs in the ground.

"Thet bullet will have to come out, or your name is cold cabbage. Tomorrow, mebbe, I can find it. A lot depends on thet, Sparrow. Bullets in fleshy parts ain't so bad. I've got one in me somewheres. But if this forty-four chunk of lead in you ranged down instead of up, I'm thinkin' you'll cash.

He was cold-blooded and methodical, but his earnestness and solicitude were not to be questioned. While he was bandaging the wound Jim stole away in the darkness toward where the chief had left his prisoner. He did not run great risk of detection because he could see all within the camp fire circle of light, while it would be impossible for any one from there to discern him out in the blackness.

Chapter Ten

I T WAS dark as pitch toward the grove of cottonwoods, which were shadowed by the bluff, here very
close. The rustling of the leaves and the tinkle of water
guided Jim. There was also a first tiny peeping of spring
frogs.

At length Jim located gray objects against the black
grass. He stole closer.

"Where are you, Miss Herrick?" he called in a tense
whisper. "It's Jim Wall."

He heard a sound made by boots scraping on canvas.
Peering sharply, he finally located her sitting up on a half
unrolled bed, and he dropped on one knee. Her eyes appeared unnaturally large and black in her white face.

"Oh, you must be careful! He said he'd shoot any
man who came near me," she whispered.

"He would—if he could. But he'll never kill me!" Jim
whispered back. "I want to tell you I'll get you out of this
some way or other. Keep up your courage. Fight him—
if ——"

"I felt you'd—save me," she interrupted, her soft
voice breaking. "Oh, if I had only listened to you! But I
wasn't afraid. I left both my door and windows open.
That's how they got in. I ordered them out. But he
made that Sparrow man point a gun at me. He jerked
me out of bed—tearing my nightgown all but off—throwing me on the floor. I was half stunned. Then he ordered
me to dress to ride. I ran in my closet. But he kept the
door open. . . . He—he watched me—the unspeakable
beast!"

"I saw him pawing you," said Jim, under his breath.

"Yes—yes. He never loses an opportunity. I—I'm sick.
I begin to fear this talk of ransom is only a blind. If he
robbed me—which he did—certainly he would rob Ber-

nie. And it takes weeks for money to come by stage. Meanwhile ——"

"I tell you to keep your nerve," interposed Jim, with a backward glance toward the camp fire. "But I'll not deceive you. Hank Hays is capable of anything. His men are loyal. Except me. I'm with them, though I don't belong to the outfit. I could kill him any time, but I'd have to fight the rest. The odds are too great. I'd never save you that way. You must help me play for time—till opportunity offers."

"I trust you—I'll do as you say. . . . Oh, thank you."

"You said he robbed you?" went on Jim, with another look back at camp. Hays was standing erect.

"Yes. I had four thousand pounds in American currency. It was hidden on the top of my trunk, which they broke open and searched. The Sparrowhawk man found it—also my jewelry. . . . Another thing which worries me now—he made me pack a bundle of clothes, my toilet articles ——"

"Ahuh. But where was Herrick all this while?"

"They said they had tied him up in the living-room,' she went on hurriedly. "I remember now that I heard considerable noise and loud voices. But it didn't alarm me. What a complacent imbecile I was! Oh, I should never, never have come to Utah!"

"How much money did Herrick have on hand?"

"I don't know, but considerable."

"Where did he keep it?"

"I have no idea. We Herricks are careless with money."

"It is a good bet he robbed your brother, too. That'd make this ransom deal look fishy, even if there were nothing else. Hank Hays is the kind of robber who burns bridges behind him."

"Oh, what am I to do?" she moaned. "I'm utterly at his mercy."

"It's hell, Miss Herrick. But you were warned. Now you must take your medicine, as we say out here. If life means so much to you, I can save that, sooner or later. Even that depends on my playing along with Hays and his men until something turns up. Heeseman's outfit is after us, as you certainly know. They may find us. I hope they do. . . . But for the rest—your—your womanhood. . . .

"My God! . . . But you could kill me!"

"I couldn't—I simply couldn't. . . . I love you myself. . . ."

"There! He is coming. Go—go! You are my only hope."

Without a look Jim rose to glide away along the grove. He made no sound. The darkness cloaked him. Once it nearly proved his undoing, for only in the nick of time did he sense that he was on the verge of a gully. This proved to be behind the grove and between it and the wall. He heard water down there. Hays' deep voice floated to him from the other direction. Circling to the left, he got on higher ground from which he saw the camp fire again. The horses were grazing near.

Jim paced to and fro. This was not the thing for him to do. Suppose Hays or Smoky should discover him! If they concluded that he was thinking too much they would be right. Jim sought his bed and crawled into it.

He had committed himself. He had sworn to save this girl from Hank Hays. He loved the fair-skinned, golden-haired girl, but in any case he would have saved her. Once or twice at Star Ranch he had answered to old memories and instincts; he had beaten down in their very inception the promptings of his longing to make love to her. But Miss Herrick at home, with her brother, and in the light of her position and class, was a tremendously different person from a girl captive, in the hands of a robber, out in the wilderness.

Jim Wall realized, as he lay under the pitiless white watching stars, that if Miss Herrick were kept there by force for a week or a month, subject to the jest and scrutiny of these robbers, she would surely suffer mentally and physically from such an ordeal.

Every day to see her shining hair, her white face and wonderful eyes—that could never lose their beauty! Every night, perhaps, in the dead silence of this weirdly insulated place, to fear to hear her cry. It would be too much.

Moreover, Jim realized, through his association with lonely men of the open, that when Hank Hays stole this girl from her home he had broken the law of his band, he had betrayed them, he had doomed himself. No matter what loyalty, what comradeship they felt for Hays, the woman would change it. Her presence alone meant disintegration, disruption, and death.

At length sleep came to Jim. Morning disclosed as remarkable a place as Jim had ever seen. The air was fresh fragrant, and not at all cold. Mockingbirds, blackbirds, and meadow larks were mingling their melodies, more wildly sweet for this solitude. The new leaves of the cottonwoods were turning a thousand, shining faces to the sun.

Jim gazed around, and then got up to see if the place was real or only a dream. But it magnified reality. Below him the little gray tent Hays had raised for his captive had been pitched against the grove of cottonwoods, which occupied a terrace and was composed of perhaps fifty trees, none of them old or even matured. One-half of the trees stood considerably higher than the other, which fact indicated rather a steep bank running through the middle of the grove. The luxuriant jungle of vines, ferns, flowers, moss, and grass on that bank was eloquent of water.

This grove was a point that was separated from the wall on each side by a deep gully. But these gullies ended abruptly where the point spread into the oval floor of the hole. Also both gullies opened into a canyon below, dark-walled, rugged, and deep, winding out of sight. Looking the other way, Jim saw some of the men at the camp fire, among them Hays. Beyond them rose a wall of white, gray, and reddish stone, worn by erosion into fantastic shapes. This cliff, on the other side, was red and gray, more precipitous, with shelves and benches covered with moss and cactus and flowers. Farther up a gorge split the cliff, and Jim was reminded of what Hays had said about outlets to their burrow. There was also, on the other side, the steep entrance down which Hays had come to get into this fascinating place.

The inclosed oval contained perhaps twenty-five acres of level sward, as grassy as any pasture; and at the far end the walls slanted down to a wide gateway, through which a long brush-dotted valley led to gray, speckled slopes. The walls all around were veined with ledges.

Evidently the horses had grazed on out of this hole, which fact spoke volumes for the grass farther on. Jim made the discovery that the middle of the oasis contained a knoll, considerably higher than its margins. Aside from the features that made this retreat ideal for robbers, and which they naturally would give prominence in calculations, it was amazing in its fertility, in its protected isolation, and in the brilliance of its many colors.

Jim strode over to the camp fire to wash. "Good morning, men. Wonderful place this is of Hank's. I don't care how long we stay here."

"Hell gettin' in, but shore good now," replied some one.

"How's Sparrowhawk?" asked Jim.

"Stopped bleedin'." It was Hays who answered this time. "If fever don't set in he'll pull through. But I gotta dig out thet bullet an' I'm plumb feared I can't."

"Let it be awhile. How's our prisoner?"

"Say, all you fellers askin' me thet! Fact is, I don't know. She was dead to the world last night."

"Let her sleep, poor girl. That was an awful ride."

"After grub we'll climb up an' look our roost over," announced Hays, presently. "You can't appreciate it down here. Thet gully below is one way out an' I reckon the best. There's a waterfall about fifty feet high an' it looks impassable. But it ain't, as I found out by accident. There's a slant thet you can slide a hoss down. It's slippery an' mossy under the water an' takes nerve to put a hoss to it. I reckon any one foller'n' us could do the same, if they saw our tracks. Thet gully heads into the one we took up from the Dirty Devil. Shore we could go back by the canyon we come up last night. A third way out is up the draw, an' thet peters out on the uplands. An' there's a fourth way out, by thet north gap. But if we took it I reckon we'd get lost in the canyons."

"It certainly is a great robber's roost," agreed Jim, wiping his face. "If we get surprised we'll simply go out on the other side."

"Wal, we jest can't be surprised," said Hays, complacently. "One lookout with a glass can watch all the approaches, an' long before anybody could get close we'd be on our hosses an' gone."

"But, Hank, you fetched us hyar in the dark," said Smoky.

"Shore, but it wasn't easy. I was lost a dozen times. An' I knowed the way."

"Ahuh. Did any other men know this place?"

"Yes, but they're dead."

"Dead men don't track nobody, thet's shore," said Smoky. "But, Hank, I wouldn't swear nobody atall could never track us in hyar. What you think, Brad?"

"It would take a lot of nerve to tackle thet Dirty Devil," replied Lincoln.

"What d'you say, Jim?"

"If I was Heeseman and had seen you, as he sure saw us, I'd find you in three days," returned Jim, deliberately. "Provided, of course, I had pack-horses and supplies."

"Wal, I'll bet you two to one thet you can't even git out of here," declared Hays.

"Why, man, you just told us all how to get out."

"Down the gully, yes. But you've never seen it an' you'd shore be stuck. . . . Wal, we'll keep watch durin' daylight. What's your idee about keepin' watch? One man's enough. Two hours on an' ten off? Or four on, an' every other day."

"I'd like the four-hour watch better," replied Jim.

"Me too."

"Reckon thet'd suit."

"Wal, four hours on it'll be, then," asserted Hays. "An', Jim, seein' as you spoke up so keen, you can have first watch. There absolutely ain't no need of any watch before breakfast."

"Hays, don't forget thet *you* got here after nightfall, an' some other man might," said the pessimistic Lincoln.

At breakfast Hays departed from his habit of silence and he talked, betraying to the thoughtful Jim the presence of excitement. He repeated himself about the security of the place and sought to allay any doubts in the minds of his men.

"It'll be hotter'n blazes down here in summer," he said. "An' it rains. Say, but it rains! Course you-all got a hunch of thet from the cut-up canyons we come through. An' never be ketched in any of them when it rains hard. . . .

I'll build some kind of a shack, an' we'll need a shelter to eat an' gamble under, an' as fer sleepin' dry, there's some shelvin' cliffs thet air as good as cabins. So after eatin', I'll show you the lay of the land from up on top. We'll leave Jim on guard, and start to work."

It chanced that during the part of this speech referring to shelter, Jim happened to see Smoky and Brad Lincoln look at each other in a peculiar way. They did not change glances. They merely had the same thought in mind, and Jim wagered he had caught it.

"Fellers," Hays said at the end of the meal, and his impressiveness was marked, "I forgot to tell you thet we took a little money from Herrick. I'll make a divvy on thet today."

This news was received with manifest satisfaction.

"How much, about, Hank?" asked Bridges, eagerly.

"Not much. I didn't count. Reckon a couple thousand each."

"Whew! Thet added to what I've got will make me flush. An' I'm gonna keep it."

"Hank, as there's no deal in sight all summer, an' mebbe not then, we can gamble, huh?"

"Gamble yourselves black in the face, provided there's no fightin'. It's good we haven't any likker."

"Boss, I forgot to tell you thet I bought a couple of jugs at the junction," spoke up Smoky, contritely.

"Wal, no matter, only it 'pears we're all forgettin' things," said the leader, somewhat testily.

"It shore do," rejoined Lincoln. "Hank, when're you aimin' to collect ransom fer the girl?"

"Not while thet hard-shootin' outfit is campin' on our trail, an' don't you fergit it."

"Brad, so long's the boss had honest intentions we can't kick about how the deal's worked out," said Jim, thinking it wise not to be always silent.

"No—so long's he had," admitted Smoky, casually. But Lincoln did not reply.

Later Jim caught Smoky aside, digging into his pack, and approached him to whisper:

"Smoky, I wish we had time to talk. But I'll say this right from the shoulder. It's up to you and me to see no harm comes to this girl."

"Why you an' *me*, Jim?" returned Smoky, his penetrating eyes on Wall's.

"That's why I wish I had time to talk. But you've got to take me straight. If I wasn't here you'd do your best for her—that's my hunch. . . . Shoot now, quick! Hays is suspicious as hell."

"Wal, yore a sharp cuss, Jim," returned Smoky, going back to his pack. "I'm with you. One of us has always got to be heah in camp, day an' night. Do you savvy?"

"Yes. . . . Thanks, Smoky. Somehow I'd have sworn by you," replied Jim, hurriedly, and retraced his steps to the fire.

After breakfast Hays led his men, except Latimer, up through the west outlet, from which they climbed to the highest point in the vicinity. It was to the top of a bluff fully five hundred feet above the draw. It afforded a magnificent view of this baffling country. Every point of the green hole was in plain sight. Every approach to it, even that down the dark gully, lay exposed; and a sharp-eyed scout with a field-glass could have detected pursuers miles away, and have caught their dust long before they came in sight.

"No use talkin'," was Smoky's comment.

Others were loud in their encomiums.

Brad Lincoln said, sarcastically: "So you been savin' this roost for your old age?"

They all laughed, then Jim put in his quiet opinion:

"A band of men could hang out here for twenty years—unless they fought among themselves."

"Ha!" Slocum let out a single sharp exclamation, impossible to designate as containing mirth or censure, yet which was certainly corroborative.

"Wal, I never give it no name," concluded Hays. "An' we'll let the future do thet. I'll gamble every dollar I got thet *some* outfit will last hyar twenty years. If Heeseman does for us, then Morley will do fer him. An' so it'll go. None of us will ever live to see cowboy posses ride into these brakes."

They left Jim on the bluff to keep the first watch.

"I'd like this job every day," he replied to jocular remarks.

"Shore you would, an' git out of real work. So would I. Haw! Haw!"

Jim was well pleased to be left alone. The die was cast now. Hays had made his bed and must lie in it—no doubt to a last long bloody sleep. He had betrayed his loyal allies, not only in the matter of making way with the girl, but in regard to honest division of stolen gains. Jim had Miss Herrick's word as to the amount taken from her. It was a certainty that Hays had also robbed her brother. But he had not reported the truth as to amount; and this was another singular proof of the disintegration of the chief's character. Only by strict, fair dealings could he ever have gained the confidence and loyalty of that hardened crew.

In all likelihood Sparrowhawk Latimer was aware of this omission on the chief's part, for men of his type were not easily fooled. Probably he had been bribed to keep his mouth shut. Jim resolved to lose no time being kind and thoughtful to the wounded man. Whatever there was to learn, Jim meant to learn. Latimer was seriously ill.

Presently the outfit would begin to gamble and then for them the hours would pass as moments.

There was a round depression on the mound-like eminence of the bluff, and it made a comfortable seat. It would be very hot here in midsummer, but a sunshade of some sort could be erected. Today the sun felt good.

He could see the men with his naked eye, and with the field-glass he could almost read their thoughts. How much more jealously and savagely could he now watch Hays than if he were below! It was an unique situation, but devastating. Jim had nothing to hide up there.

Notwithstanding the cue he had for passion, he did not neglect exercising the requirements of a good scout. And presently he applied himself to a careful study of his surroundings. The horses grazed in the valley below, between him and the camp, and in all probability they would stay there indefinitely. As summer advanced with warm rains, the valley would grow more and more luxuriant. Horses used to the barrens would have to be dragged away. That disposed of the all-important necessity of having the animals close.

To the north and west the whorls of red rock dominated the scene, but there were many grassy plots and meadows and valleys down in between. The main canyon, an extension of Hays' retreat, ran for miles, to widen and grade out on the western horizon. Jim espied innumerable rabbits, some coyotes, and many antelopes. That country to the west must be a paradise for the fleet-footed, white-rumped deer of the plains. There was no evidence of water in that direction.

To the south and east spread the brakes, and it was one white slash, red slash, gray slash, yellow slash after another, clear to the dark slopes that formed the base of the mighty Henrys, black and deceiving, their peaks lost in the clouds. Only a blue, faintly streaked gulf marked the zone of the canyon country, of which the Dirty Devil brakes were merely the stepping-off point. Jim remembered the great, dim cliffs glancing down from Wild Horse Mesa. They would be thousands of feet in depth and all sheer rock; the walls of the brakes were mostly clay, loam, gravel, and only hundreds of feet at their deepest. Still they were forbidding, and inaccessible except to the most desperate and resourceful of men.

What would Heeseman's persistent pursuit of Hays mean, provided it were persistent? That chase and attack of the other day did not amount to much. Riders without pack-animals could easily have made that. But if Heeseman made a long pursuit of it his motive would be either revenge or money, very likely both. Jim had divined in Heeseman a strong antipathy for Hays, something born far back in the past. Jim rather inclined to Lincoln's skepticism and looked for further dealings with Heeseman.

While Jim's thoughts ran in this fashion, skipping from one aspect to another, his keen manipulation of the field-glass followed suit. He would study the white-ridged draw by which Hays had entered the hole, and try to follow its devious wanderings till he lost it in the brakes. He would bend his magnified sight upon the dark seamed gorge heading under the terrace of cottonwoods. And the two other exits to that rendezvous came in for their share of attention. In this way he gradually became acquainted with them. And after each survey he would shift the glass back to the oval bowl where the robbers were at work.

Some were carrying water, brush, stones, while others were digging post-holes. Hays was apparently a mason, for at once he began to lay a square fireplace of flat stones. The stone, sand, water were fetched to him, but he did the building himself. An hour or so after the start, the square grate appeared to be completed, and the chimney was going up. Four cottonwoods formed the four corner posts of the shack. Poles of the same wood were laid across for beams. Probably Hays would construct a roof of brush, and give it pitch enough so that the rain water would run off.

That growing structure became fascinating to Jim Wall. What was going to happen in it? Three times Hays left off work to walk across the green to the tent where Miss Herrick kept herself. No doubt the robber called to her. The third time he peeped in.

"Go in, you —— scurvy bloodhound!" ejaculated Jim, fiercely. There was a hot joy at the ring of his words in his ears. He need not even deceive himself. He could roar like a bull if he wished.

But Hays did not attempt to enter the tent. Certain it was, however, that he glanced back to see if any of his men were watching him. They were, though perhaps to his estimate not at all obtrusively. Jim, however, with the strong field-glass, could actually catch the expression on their faces. Smoky spoke to Lincoln, and with a suggestive jerk of his head toward Hays and the tent added a volume of meaning. Then Hays retraced his steps back to the job.

The sun grew hot, and when it reached the zenith Hays and his gang suspended their labors for a while. The others gathered at the shelter, evidently eating and drinking. Presently Latimer appeared, coming out of the cottonwoods, and he walked unsteadily across to the group. One of them came out to help him. They spent an hour, perhaps, under Happy Jack's shelter. All this morning no sign of life from the tent!

Long after noonday, and when Jim had spent at least six hours on watch, Jeff Bridges detached himself from his comrades and laboriously made his way out the west entrance and up the long, gray-green slope to the red bluff, upon the top of which Jim was stationed.

Jeff was a heavy man, not used to climbing on foot. His red face was wet with sweat. "Jim, we 'most forgot you," he panted, good-naturedly. "The boss had us— a-goin'. He's shore—enthusiastic over makin' a roost of thet hole!"

Jim relinquished the glass and his seat to Bridges. "I don't mind," he said. "Sort of like it up here." He left and made his way leisurely down off the smooth red ledges to the slope, and eventually to the valley floor. Cottontail rabbits scurried out from under his feet, to crouch in the grass or under a bush not far off. Jim drew his gun, and selecting a favorable shot he put out the eye of a rabbit; and presently he repeated the performance. With the rabbits dangling, one from each hand, he turned into the oval, amused to find not a single man in sight. They had heard his shots and had taken to cover.

As he approached, one by one they reappeared, out of the earth it looked to Jim, and when he reached Happy's camp-site they were all back.

"Huh! You scared the very hell out of us," declared Hays, forcibly. "How'n hell could we know you was shootin' rabbits."

"Young rabbit for supper won't go bad," rejoined Jim.

"They shore won't," agreed Smoky. "Lemme see, Jim." He took the rabbits and examined them. "Look ahyar, Brad. He shot the eye out of both of them."

"Durned if he didn't," said Brad, enthusiastically. "How fer away, Jim?"

"I didn't step it off. Reckon one was about twenty paces and the other farther," returned Jim, stretching the truth a little. He knew such men, how their morbid minds centered about certain things.

"Ahuh. You're a poor shot," declared Lincoln.

"Hank, fer Gawd's sake don't let's give Jim a chanct to shoot at us!" ejaculated Smoky, with a loud laugh.

The robber chieftain did not see any levity in the circumstance.

"Hell, no. We don't want Jim shootin' at us any more'n he wants us shootin' at him." That was a distinction with a difference. But Smoky was sincere, Lincoln was dubious, and Hays was deceitful.

"Fellows, make all the fun you want out of my perfectly good intention of supplying meat for supper," he said, genially. "But don't joke about my shooting. I'm sensitive."

"Can you hit a bottle in the air?" queried Smoky.

"I wouldn't if it was full."

"Aw, no foolin'. Can you, Jim?"

"Whenever you want to bet, come on."

"Hey, save your ammunition, you cowboys," interrupted Hays, gruffly. "We'll git all the shootin' you want, mebbe. . . . Jim, take a snack of grub, an' then come to work with us."

Chapter Eleven

WHILE they were at it Smoky suggested they erect a sun and rain shelter for the prisoner, and Jim casually seconded the proposition. Hays consented with a bad grace. So before dark they built one for Miss Herrick that would add materially to her comfort.

"Reckon this cottonwood grove is her private grounds, fellers," added Smoky.

In the main they were kindly disposed and amenable. Lincoln's bitterness toward the chief, however, rather augmented, if anything. He said, "I got it figgered thet Hank reckoned this grove was *his* private grounds."

"Wal, he figgered wrong, then," snapped Smoky. "It ain't no fault of ourn if this gurl is hyar. But since she is, we'll see she gets treated like a lady."

That was strong speech, yet passed over by Hays. He had resourcefulness, after he had accomplished his design in getting the girl there.

The shelter extended from the edge of the grove, where her tent stood, out far enough to permit of other conveniences. A tiny stream ran out from under the trees. Jim banked it up with clean red rocks, forming a fine little pool of clear cold water. Smoky, who had skill and artistry, deftly fashioned a rude armchair, which, when covered with saddle-blankets, made an acceptable chair. Hays, not to be wholly outdone, cut and carried a great armload of ferns.

"Come out, miss," he called into the tent. "We're makin' you comfortable. An' heah's some ferns to put under your bed."

Helen emerged quickly enough, her eyes suspiciously red, but that did not mar the flash of them. Jim tried to turn away, only he could not. Hays carried the bundle of ferns inside and spread them out.

"I'll make my bed, please," she called, impatiently, whereupon the robber chief crawled from the tent.

"Hays, am I to gather from this kindly service that my enforced stay here with you will be indefinite?" she queried.

"Wal, it looks like thet. But what else can I do?" returned Hays, avoiding her gaze.

"You can send Jim Wall and another of your men back to Star Ranch. I'll write a letter to my brother to pay and ask no questions nor make any moves."

"Shore I reckon Jim would go. It's easy to see thet. But none of my regular men would risk it," returned Hays.

"There's a better way, Hank," spoke up Smoky. "Send Jim an' me back with the girl. If she'll promise 't we'll get the money."

"I give my word," swiftly agreed Miss Herrick.

"It ain't to be thought of," returned the robber, dryly.

Jim watched his opportunity to give Helen a warning look when Hays could not see. She had forgotten his cautioning her. And that halted whatever retort she had on her lips. Smoky, however, was making good Jim's estimate of him—that he was deep, and would answer unexpectedly to any situation.

"Hell you say, Hank. It *is* to be thought of," he rejoined, coolly. "You nor nobody else can think my thoughts."

"Wal, I mean *I'm* not thinkin' that way, an' as I'm boss of this outfit, what I say goes. Do you savvy?"

"Shore. Thet's short an' sweet."

"Wal then, let's have no more to say. When it suits me—which is when it's safe to send fer thet ransom money—I'll do it, an' not before."

He stalked away toward the cook shelter, evidently to secure a bucket and basin for Miss Herrick. Happy Jack loudly disclaimed any intention of letting go any of his few and precious utensils. Jim heard the chief say: "Wal, at thet she don't need a bucket. Them two lady-killers dammed up the brook for her. I'll take a basin an' call it square."

During this interval Helen had appealed to Jim with eyes so eloquent of fear and hope that he almost threw up his hands in despair.

"You—what's your name?" she asked, turning to Smoky.

"Wal, you can call me Smoky," drawled that worthy, with an inscrutable smile. But something in her, beauty or purity or spirit, had reached his depths.

"Jim has made you a friend—to help me?"

"I reckon so, but fer Gawd's sake don't talk so loud. Try to savvy this deal an' what's your part in it." Smoky wheeled to his task as Hays strode back into earshot.

Miss Herrick entered her tent, where Jim heard her spreading blankets upon the ferns. After that little more was spoken between the men, and presently, at Hays' suggestion, they quit for the day.

"Whar you bunkin', Smoky?" inquired Hays.

"Under the cliff with Sparrow. Thet poor devil needs nursin'."

"Sorry aboot him. But we could have got in a hell of a jam over ther. Figger it out, if we'd been a quarter hour later."

"Wal, thet'd been the end of Hank Hays an' outfit," remarked Smoky, caustically.

"An inch is as good as a mile. . . . Jim, whar you sleepin'?"

"There's my bed and pack and saddle," replied Wall, pointing. "I'll leave them there till it rains."

Hays made no comment. They repaired to Happy Jack's shelter and to their evening meal. Later by the light of the camp fire Jim saw Helen come out of her tent to walk up and down in the dusk. And she got nearly as far as where Jim's things lay in the lea of a low shelf. He wondered if she was keen enough to calculate that he would be nearest to her and that he was the lightest of sleepers.

Darkness soon settled down, and with it the robbers, worn out with their labors. Jim stayed up long enough to see Hays stretch in his blankets under Happy's shelter. So far so good! A heavy breath of oppression eased off Jim's chest. It could have been far worse. His impulse to appeal to Smoky had been an inspiration. Still, he had intuition. Smoky was probably as great a rogue as any unhanged, yet he had subtle qualities that men like Jim felt in extremities. Before this game was far spent Smoky would loom splendidly, of that Jim was certain. He went to bed, and for a long hour kept himself awake with poignant thoughts, while he listened and watched.

The next day came, and was like the preceding, with its camp tasks and improvements, the guard duty, attendance upon Sparrow, and the universal if covert observance of Miss Herrick. To do her credit, she kept out of her tent, ate, exercised, and watched with great anxious eyes that haunted Jim.

After that, day after day, full of watching and suspense for Jim, wore on. Every morning dawned with a sense of something about to happen. And he divined that suspense would go on and on. Yet it could not last forever. In the clear light of day, during his watches up on the bluff, he had gone sternly and finally over the situation. He could not attempt anything radical until something happened. And he would adhere to that.

Meanwhile he and Smoky had assumed all the care of Latimer, who had improved for a few days, and then had a relapse. Hays, in his growing absorption, had gladly relinquished the work to Jim. And then Smoky had shared it. Between them they did all that was humanely possible for Sparrowhawk, but he went from bad to worse. Often in lucid moments he asked about Hays and the girl.

"Dog-gone it, Jim," complained Smoky during a moment when they were alone, "Sparrow's conscience is hurtin' him."

"Yes, and I think he feels Hays' neglect."

"Ahuh. He's been longest with Hays. What's your idee about somethin' stickin' in his craw?"

"Sorry he had a hand in stealing the girl, maybe," offered Jim.

"Nope. Thet wouldn't phase Sparrow," declared Smoky, with decision.

"Well, he killed Progar, you know, and that put Heeseman on our trail. Hays admitted it."

"Ump-umm. You don't know Latimer. He'd never think twice about killin' a man. It's somethin' else an' closer to home."

That gave Jim an idea, which he was careful to keep to himself. Latimer surely knew that his chief had not divided the last Herrick money fairly. It might be this. Anyway, Jim, though he could not have been any kinder to the wounded man, spent more time with him.

The seventh day, during the heat of the afternoon, while some of the men were asleep and others absent, and Jim was on the lookout from the bluff with his field-glass, Hays began carrying things from the grove to the shack he had built. It had been set some distance away, on a level gravel flat, just out from a notch in the south wall. A deep wash separated it from the camp.

Jim's field-glass brought things close—too close for his peace of mind. Hays' first bundle was his own pack. which he took into the cabin. Jim cursed. On the second trip Hays fetched his bed-roll. Like a hawk Jim watched. It was certain that cold sweat broke out all over Jim.

His hour was about up, and leaving the lookout he ran down the slope and into the oval, slowing up when near camp. He came upon some of the men arguing.

"Hell, no!" ejaculated Smoky, as Jim arrived.

"Hell, yes!" returned Lincoln.

"Fellers, it'd be too low-down," went on Smoky, with passion. "We're a lot of bad eggs, but Hank ain't thet bad. . . . Collect the ransom an' send her home to her brother after degradin' her!"

"Smoky, you're a faithful cuss," rejoined Lincoln, admiringly. "When air your eyes goin' to open?"

"They're open, all right," replied Smoky, doggedly.

"Cheese it. Hyar comes Hays now."

Jim was satisfied with the slow wearing away of their faith.

"Fellows, I heard you, and I'm agreeing with Lincoln," he said, hurriedly. "Looks as if Hank is bent on dragging Miss Herrick over to his shack."

There was an intense silence.

"I've been watching through the field-glass," added Jim.

"Wal, by Gawd!" burst out Smoky, convinced against his will. "I been hopin' we was hard on Hank. But, hell, let's give the man a chance. . . . Jim, if he does fer me, you take it up."

"Let me face him first," demanded Jim, harshly.

"What the hell, Smoky!" ejaculated Lincoln.

"Shet up! Hyar he comes. Keep out of it now."

When the chief reached the shelter he would have passed on without noting them, so great was his abstraction.

"Hays, come hyar," called Smoky, ringingly, as he stepped out. The robber swerved off his course, startled.

"We been arguin' aboot you. Wal, you know me. I'm askin' you damn straight. Do you mean bad by this Herrick woman?"

"Bad!" echoed Hays, his face changing from red to white.

"Thet's what I ast," retorted Smoky.

"Wal, an' suppose I say I do?" demanded Hays, "if it's any of your damn bizness!"

"Then you can shoot it out with *me*, right hyar an' now!"

"Smoky!" gasped the chief, incredulous.

"An' if you do fer me you've got Jim to take on," snapped Smoky.

"More double-crossin'!" bellowed Hays, suddenly wild.

"Shore. More from you, Hank."

The leader spat in his fury; and then it was remarkable to see him pull himself together.

"I jest wanted to know how fer you fellers would go," he declared. "An' you've shore give me a cud to chew. . . . As fer thet gurl, I've no more bad feelin's toward her than any one or all of you. Savvy? An' let me say if I heah any more sich talk I'll be bustin' up this outfit."

"It's busted now, Hank," replied Smoky, betraying the bitterness of the disillusioned.

Jim sought seclusion until sunset, dragging through one of the most horrible hours he had ever lived. Hays would not fight. Jim's hands were tied until further complications untied them. Even an overmastering love could not change his creed, and his creed was similar to that of Smoky Slocum. And he was not so sure but that there were others in Hays' gang who lived up to the honor of thieves. It looked as if Hank Hays had at last broken upon the rock of woman's lure.

Smoky espied Jim returning, and came to meet him.

"Sparrow's askin' fer you," he said, moodily. "I'm afeared he's wuss."

When Jim bent over the wasted Latimer it was indeed to feel a cold apprehension.

"What is it, Sparrow? I've been on watch," said Jim, taking the other's thin hand.

"Am I a-goin' to croak?" queried Latimer, calmly, and the look accompanying the words was something to stir Jim.

"You've a fighting chance, Sparrow. While there's life there's hope."

"Wal, I've been shot before. But I never had this queer feelin'. . . . Now, Jim, if I git to sinkin', don't keep me from knowin'. If I'm dyin' I want to tell you and Smoky somethin' thet I'd keep if I lived. Savvy?"

Smoky, kneeling at Latimer's other side, nodded sadly.

"Sparrow, I couldn't honestly ask for that confession yet," replied Jim. "You might pull through. But I promise you, and I'm shaking your hand on it."

"Good. Thet eases my mind. Gimme a drink of cold, fresh water."

Smoky took up the dipper and strode down to fetch it.

"Jim, I like you—a heap," said Latimer.

"Thanks, Sparrow. I'm sure I return it," replied Jim.

"Fellers like me can only expect to die this way. I always knowed. . . . But it's different—now it's hyar. . . . Jim, did you ever think it'd be better to go—back to honest livin'?"

"Not lately," replied Jim, gloomily.

"Wal, you're younger'n most of us."

Smoky returned with the water, and the two men helped Latimer to drink.

"Sparrow, you can't gain strength on water," complained Smoky, earnestly. "I'm gonna fetch you somethin'."

On the walk across the oval Smoky said, very seriously: "Jim, I reckon we better have Sparrow tell us tomorrer—whatever he has on his chest. That is, *if* we want to know it. Do you?"

"I sure do, Smoky."

"Wal, I ain't so damn keen about it myself," rejoined Slocum, darkly.

"But, Smoky, if it's something Latimer *must* confess, it's something we *ought* to know."

"You think so, even if it splits the outfit?"

"If there's anything that can do that—you bet your life we ought to know," rejoined Jim, forcibly.

"Not so loud, man. These hyar walls have ears. We'll see tomorrer."

That night Jim took his time at supper, and afterwards he lingered around the camp fire, and long after Hays had stalked off into the gloom with a significant parting speech: "Good night all. I'm turnin' in."

"Reckon Hank's tired of layin' awake nights listenin' to thet gurl cry," said Mac.

"Looks like thet."

"Thet's what it 'pears to me," replied the cook. "I fixed up her supper before callin' you-all. Hank took it over. He was late comin' fer his own supper, as you saw."

"Wal, it's decent of him."

Jim moved his bed closer to the grove, farther from the camp fire, and it commanded a view of the rise of ground where any one passing could be detected above the horizon. And he sat on his bed watching until he was too tired to sit up any longer. But even after he had crawled under his blankets he watched. There was an overhanging shelf of rock, black as coal, then a strip of velvet blue sky, studded with stars, and last the dark, uneven rise of ground. A coyote passing along that near horizon would have seemed as large as a horse.

But nothing passed. The hours wore on until the utter loneliness of the deep pit weighed heavily upon Jim's oppressed breast. Even the crickets ceased to chirp. The wind failed. He might have been lying in a stone sepulcher. He was fixed in a solitude that seemed to be working upon him. But Jim Wall did not believe in ghosts, and always he had scoffed the few intimations of spirit that had whispered to him from nature. Bent unalterably upon dealing death to the robber who had befriended him, he did not listen to still, small, inward voices.

He fell asleep and dreamed that he was riding a gigantic, black horse with eyes of fire, and that there was a white flower growing out from a precipice, and in a strange, reckless desire to pluck it he fell into the abyss. Down, down he plunged into blackness. And suddenly a piercing, terrible cry rose from the depths.

He was sitting upright in bed, his brow clammy with sweat, his heart clamped as in a cold vise. What had awakened him? The night was silent, melancholy, fateful. He swore that a soul-wrecking cry had broken his slumber. Then he remembered the dream. How absurd that he should dream of plucking a white flower and plunging to hell! Nevertheless, it disturbed him. There were things hard to explain. He was not subject to dreams. The rest of the night he dozed at intervals, haunted by he knew not what.

One by one the members of the gang appeared at Happy Jack's calls to breakfast. With no work to do, no horses to find or rides to make, the robbers were lazy.

Jim was the last to arrive, except Hays, who had not yet appeared.

"Darn good thing we ain't in an Injun country," observed Mac.

"Humph! Fer a feller who lays ten hours in bed I sleep damn little," rejoined Smoky, moodily. "I hear things an' I'm always waitin' fer somethin'."

"Yell fer the boss. My voice is gone," said Happy Jack.

Nobody took the trouble to comply with this request. The men fell to eating. Brad Lincoln had not spoken, and he kept his eyes lowered. But Lincoln was always morose in the mornings. After the meal, Jim, as was his custom, hurried toward the shelf where Latimer lay. He had gotten about halfway when Slocum caught up with him.

"Jim, you look like the wrath of Gawd this mornin'."

"Smoky, I didn't sleep well. I'm cross, and I reckon I need a shave."

"Wal, if thet's all. . . . Say, Jim, did you hear the gurl scream last night?"

"Scream! . . . Did she?"

"Huh. If she didn't, I've shore got the jimjams. . . . My Gawd! look at pore Latimer!"

Their patient had wrestled off his bed out into the grass. They rushed to lift him back and make him comfortable. He appeared to be burning up with fever and alarmingly bright-eyed, but he was conscious and asked for water. Jim hurried to fetch some.

"How'n hell I rolled out there I don't know," said Latimer, after he had drunk thirstily.

"Reckon you was delirious, Sparrow," replied Smoky.

"No, sir. I was scared."

"Scared!— You? Thet's funny," rejoined Smoky, looking across at Jim.

"What scared you, old man?" queried Jim, bathing Latimer's hot face with a wet scarf.

"It was after I got my sleep. Must have been late, fer I always am dead to the world fer five or six hours. I was wide awake. It was shore a lonesome, still night. Mebbe my sins weighed on me. . . . But all of a sudden I heard a cry. It scared me so I jumped right off my bed. Hurt me, too, an' I didn't try to get back."

"Maybe it was a coyote right by close," returned Jim.

"Fellers, I'll bet you'll find thet gurl dead. . . . Murdered!" concluded Latimer, hoarsely.

"Wal, I'll be ——!" ejaculated Smoky.

"Sparrow, you don't look flighty," replied Jim, gravely. "But your talk is. Else you've a reason to think it."

"Shore I have," rejoined Latimer, lowering his voice to a whisper. "Hays beat an' robbed Herrick! . . . Thet's part I wanted to tell you, if I was goin' to croak. But I gotta tell it anyhow. An' I ask you both, as pards, to keep what I tell you secret till I'm dead."

"I swear, Sparrow," said Smoky, huskily.

"You can trust me, too," added Jim.

"Wal, thet's why I feel Hank must have done fer the gurl, too."

"Robbed Herrick!" exclaimed Slocum, incredulously. "Was there a fight?"

"Yes. But Hank might have avoided it. He drove the man crazy."

"Fellers, Hays'd steal coppers off a dead nigger's eyes —shore. But what he said he wanted was the gurl fer ransom. Yet he picked a fight with Herrick an' beat him with a gun."

"Sparrow, how come you didn't tell us before?" asked Smoky, sternly.

"I'm beholdin' to Hank. But I will say thet if I'd knowed his game, I'd never have gone with him. After it was too late—wal, I stuck. An' I'd kept it secret. But

I feel in my bones I'm done fer. So I'm squealin', an'
I'm doin' it because Hays double-crossed you all."

"Reckon I'd have done the same, if Hank had a hold
on me," conceded Smoky, generously. "Suppose you take
a nip of whisky an' tell us what happened."

"I'm hot enough without liquor. But I'll tell you. . . .
Gimme some more water."

After a moment Latimer drew a long breath and resumed: "Hank picked me because he had a hold on me.
. . . After you fellers left thet night Hank went out
an' got another hoss. He had a saddle hid somewhere.
We took them hosses up the bench back of the house
an' tied them. Then we went down toward the house."

"Ahuh. He'd had this deal in mind all the time," said
Smoky, nodding his head.

"Yes. Before we got to the house he told me he meant
to hold Herrick up fer what money he had on hand—
then steal the gurl fer ransom. I opened my trap to kick
ag'in' the gurl part of it, anyway, but he cussed me somethin' fierce. I seen then he was blood-set on it, so I shet
up. . . . Herrick was in the livin'-room. We walked
round the house, an' Hank showed me the gurl's winder,
which was open. . . . Wal, we went back, an' up on the
porch, an' into the livin'-room. When Herrick looked
up Hank threw a gun on him. 'Keep quiet an' shell out
your money,' Hank ordered. Thet didn't phase the Englishman. He jumped up, thunderin' mad. Hank hit him
over the head, cuttin' a gash. Thet didn't knock Herrick
out, but it made him fight till Hank got him good an'
hard. Then he opened his desk and threw out some
packages of greenbacks. After that he slid to the floor.
Next Hank ordered me to go out an' round to the gurl's
winder. It was bright moonlight, but I didn't locate thet
winder quick. An' at thet I was guided to it by the gurl's
voice. . . . Gimme another drink."

Latimer quenched his inordinate thirst again, while Jim and Smoky exchanged thoughtful glances over him.

"Wal, where was I? . . . When I straddled thet winder-sill I seen the gurl sittin' up in bed, white as the sheets about her. Hank had a gun pointed at her head, an' he was sayin' if she yelled he'd shoot. Then he told me to look around fer money an' jewels. I started thet, keepin' an eye on them. The room was as moon-light as outdoors. Hank told her to git up an' dress fer ridin'. She refused, an' he yanked her clean out of bed, splittin' her night-gown half off. 'Gurl,' he said, 'yore brother is hawg-tied down in the livin'-room, an' if you don't do as I tell you, I'll kill him. . . . I'm takin' you away fer ransom, an' when he pays up you can come home. So long's you're quiet we won't hurt you.' . . . At thet she got up an' ran into a closet. I heerd her sobbin'. He made her put on ridin'-clothes an' pack what else she wanted. Meanwhile I found a heap of gold things an' diamonds, an' a package of money, still with the Wells Fargo paper on it. These I stuffed in my pockets, an' I shore—was a walkin' gold-mine."

"How much was there?" asked Smoky, curiously, when Latimer paused to catch his breath.

"I'll come to thet. . . . We went out the winder, an' Hank hustled her into the woods, with me follerin'. Soon we come to the hosses, an' Hank put the gurl up on the gray. He blindfolded her an' told me to see she didn't git away. Then he run back down the hill. The gurl talked a blue streak, but she wasn't so damn scared, except when we heard a shot, then some one runnin' on hard ground. Hank come back pronto, pantin' like a lassoed bull. He said he'd run plump into Progar an' another of Heeseman's outfit."

" 'Miss Herrick,' he says, 'them fellers—was bent on robbin' your brother—mebbe killin' him. I shot—Progar, but the—other—got away.' . . . He tied the bundle on his hoss, an' leadin' the gurl's hoss, he rode up the mountain. We rode the rest of the night, stoppin' to rest at daylight. Hyar I turned the money an' trinkets over to Hank. He counted the money Herrick had turned over —somethin' more'n sixteen thousand—but he never opened the Wells Fargo package I'd found in the gurl's trunk. . . . Thet's all, fellers. We rode till noon, meetin' you as agreed in the cedars."

"What was in thet Wells Fargo package?" asked Smoky, after a long pause.

"Money. Hundred dollar bills. I tore a corner of the paper off. It was a thick an' heavy package."

"Ahuh. So Hank went south with thet an' the jewelry?"

"Yes. When he made the divvy hyar he give me his share of thet sixteen thousand. It's hyar in my coat. You an' Jim air welcome to it. Cause where I'm goin'—I won't need any."

"Sparrow, it was a long story fer a sick man—an' hard to tell," said Smoky, feelingly. "Jim an' me will respect your confidence. An' if you pull through—as I hope to Gawd you do—we'll never squeak. . . . But, pard, don't be surprised at what comes off."

Chapter Twelve

FIVE days later Sparrowhawk Latimer died during the night, after a short interval of improvement which gave his comrades renewed hope. He passed away alone, evidently in agony to judge from his distorted face. When Slocum found his body in the morning it was stiff and cold.

"Wal, I don't know but thet Sparrow's better off," remarked Smoky, with pathos. "This hyar game ain't hardly wuth playin'."

They buried him in his tarpaulin on the spot, and divided his effects among them by drawing lots.

"What'd you do with the money you found on him?" queried Hays.

"We didn't find none. Sparrow gave it to me an' Jim some days ago," replied Smoky.

"Reckon you better divide it."

"Ump-um," rejoined Smoky, nonchalantly, his beady little eyes on the chief.

"Why not?"

"Wal, Sparrow wanted us to have it, not, I reckon, because we took care of him when *you* forgot him, but jest because he cottoned to us."

"Smoky, tell Hays the other reason," spoke up Jim.

"Thet'll wait, Jim. No hurry. An' I'm not so shore Sparrow wanted us to tell."

Hank Hays turned livid of face and the gaze he flashed upon his two cool subordinates held nothing if not the lightnings of a desperate soul.

"Ahuh. Mebbe you'd both be wise to stay shet up," he said, and left.

Brad Lincoln was the first of the others to voice intense curiosity.

"What's all this gab?" he demanded.

"Keep your shirt on, Brad," returned Smoky, provokingly.

"Fellers," continued Lincoln, turning to the others, "I've had a hunch all along there was a stink in this deal. Air you with me in demandin' a show-down from Smoky an' Jim?"

"We shore air," rejoined Bridges, and Mac and Happy Jack expressed like loyalty.

"Smoky, you're square. If there's anythin', we want to know."

"Wal, there's a hell of a lot. It's due you. Jim an' me have no mind to keep silent, now Latimer's gone. But we're stuck hyar in this hole, an' we don't want to fight among ourselves."

"Right you air. But no matter," snapped Lincoln.

"It'll bust up the poker game, Brad. You're behind, an' so long as there's a chanct to win Hays' roll, why not take it?"

Lincoln made a passionate gesture. Smoky had hit his weakness. He was the top gambler of the outfit. They were all gamblers when they had money and leisure, but Lincoln had the distinction of winning most.

"Smoky, you're sluggin' me one below the belt. You know damned well I'd pass up anythin' to beat Hank. I'm game. Keep your mouth shet till it's gotta come out. An' you can bet your life if it's as serious as you hint, there'll be a hell of a row."

"Mebbe we can slick it over," replied Smoky, smoothly. "If we win all the boss's money—an' he'll shore be easy now with thet gurl on his mind—I reckon there won't be any sense in tellin' at all. Eh, Jim?"

"I don't make any rash promises, Smoky," returned Jim. "I admire you a lot, Slocum, but I'm thinking you run this into the ground. In all justice these men ought to be told something."

"Damn you, Wall!" flashed Smoky, but he was not venomous.

Lincoln leaped up and hissed like a snake. His rage was confirmation of suspicions. Smoky laid a restraining hand on him.

"It sorter r'iled me, Brad. But take my word for it, it's a case of choosin' between the cards an' bein' told."

"I say cards. You fellers can't keep it forever," rejoined Lincoln, darkly.

From that hour dated the grim and passionate gambling in which they all participated. With one man on lookout duty, the others spent most of the daylight hours sitting at Happy Jack's table of cottonwood poles. Hays was a gambler by nature; he gambled with everything, particularly life and death.

Jim had separated his money into two parts—one consisting of the bills of large denomination, and the other of small. The former was very much in excess of the latter. While on guard up on the bluff Jim sewed this considerable sum in the lining of his coat and vest. He had a premonition that he would need it some day. The other he kept out for gambling, intending to quit when it was lost.

But fortune was fickle. He did not lose it. Instead, he won steadily. There was no hope of his getting out of the game so long as he was ahead. He wanted to watch, think, plan. Luck changed eventually, and he lost all he had won. Then he seesawed for a day, before he struck another streak of losing, and lost everything.

"I'm cleaned," he said, rising. "But, by gosh! I gave you a run."

"Jim, you shore had rotten cards lately," replied Hays. "But you can't be clean busted."

"No. I've saved out a little, and I'm going to hang on to it."

"I'm way ahead. I'll lend you some," offered Hays, generously.

"No, thanks. I'm glad to get off this well. I'll go up to the rock and send Mac down. From now on I'll do most of the lookout work. I like it."

"Thet's civil of you, Jim. . . . How many cards, Jeff? . . . Say, Smoky, don't you ever talk no more? I can't read your mind."

"Hell of a good thing you can't," replied Slocum, glumly. Gambling roused the worst in him, as indeed in all of them. Hays was loud, merry, derisive when he won, and the reverse when he lost.

Jim was glad this phase of his connection with the outfit was past. He had played for days, won and lost, all in the interest of the scheme fermenting in his mind. He wanted to be alone. If nothing else intervened, this gambling would lead to the inevitable quarrel. Whether Hays won all the money or lost what he had, there would be a fight. Daily the stakes had grown higher, the betting more reckless, the bitterness or elation more pronounced. There was too much cash in the possession of these robbers. It had been begotten in evil and only in evil could it end.

Mac was so glad to be relieved of his lonely duty in the hot sun that he ran like an overgrown boy down the slope and back to camp.

But Jim welcomed the change. The sun had no terrors for him. Nevertheless, he had packed up a bundle of thick brush and three long trimmed poles, with which he essayed to erect a shelter. This proved not an easy job, for the reason that there was no place to stick the poles. However, by carrying up stones he finally accomplished his design, and took his well-earned seat in the shade.

And at once a restless, baffled, hurried condition of

mind seemed to leave him. To face those men hour after hour, day after day, hiding his thoughts, had engendered irritation. Happy Jack was an agreeable and likable man, who really had no business among these robbers. He had no force. He veered like the wind, and the person who last had his ear convinced him. Smoky Slocum was the salt of the earth, if such tribute could be paid one of Hank Hays' band. The others, however, had palled upon Jim. When the split came and the shooting began Jim wanted to be around. He would help it along considerably.

He plied the glasses as diligently as before, sweeping all the hazy distances, the purple canyons, the white washes and valleys of green from which heat veils rose like smoke, and the mounds and ridges of red stone. Then he would watch the gamblers for a while. Often he would take a long look at the tent shelter where the girl spent her weary days. Savage as Jim was to precipitate eruption and catastrophe, here he had the sagacity and stamina to wait. Time was a conspirator with him. As surely as the sun shone blazingly down upon Robbers' Roost by day and the stars pitilessly by night, just as surely would tragedy decimate the gang. Every day brought that hour closer.

The season of storms arrived and showers of rain fell almost every day. Dust cleared out of the air; the heat diminished; and flowers and grass sprang up out of the earth.

Jim kept his slicker at the lookout, in expectation of a long, drenching rain, but seldom did he put it on. Often he stood out from under the brush shelter to let the rain beat upon him. He loved the smell of the hot stone, the sand, the dust after they had been wet. In the mornings the sky would be clear and azure blue, except round the peaks of the Henrys, where the storms formed. About noonday or later the white clouds would sail up on all sides, and they would darken and swell and gloom. Then streaky curtains of rain, gray as steel, would wind down from the clouds and move across the desert. Here would be sunshine, and here shadow, and in between, rainbows of gorgeous vividness, of transparent, ethereal delicacy, or dark, sinister, ruddy hue, and of every shape that was possible for a curve.

One day in midsummer when Jim was returning to camp somewhat before sunset he heard a shot. It startled him. Gunshots, except his own while hunting rabbits and antelope, had been marked by their absence. And this one either had a spiteful ring or so it sounded to Jim's sensitive ears. He listened for others. None came.

The moment he entered the oval to see Hays striding for the cabin, his hair standing up, and his men grouped outside of the camp shelter, Jim knew that there had been trouble. It had been long in coming, but it had arrived. Jim hoped Hays had not shot Smoky or Happy Jack. Any one of the others would be one less.

Presently Smoky detached himself from the group and came to meet Jim. He walked slowly, his head down. They met at the rise of ground opposite the little cove where Hays had erected the cabin.

"What now, Smoky?"

"Hank did fer Brad."

"How? Why? . . . You don't mean Hays beat Lincoln to a gun?"

"He did, Jim. By Gawd he did!" ejaculated Slocum, his eyes gleaming strangely. "But Hank was at the end of the table an' had a free throw. You know thet bench Jack fixed on the side next to the fire? Wal, Brad was sittin' on it an' his gun bumped the table. Thet gave Hank the edge. He bored Brad. I was the only feller who seen it. The rest was duckin' to beat hell."

"What was it about, Smoky?"

"Wal, Brad has been gittin' sorer every day, an' today we cleaned him. Hank had a bad run, too. But you know he was way ahead, an' most on Brad's money. Brad opened up on Hank, no doubt meanin' to call him fer fair. But Brad didn't git goin' good before Hank hissed an' went fer his gun."

"Smoky, he had his mind made up," declared Jim, tensely.

"Shore. That's the queer part of it. Hank was not goin' to let Brad spit out much. . . . An', friend Jim, that's a hunch fer us."

"You and me?"

"So I take it."

"Hays can't beat me to a gun," rejoined Jim, with a cold ring in his voice.

"Nor me, either. Thet's a safe bet."

"Does Hays *know* that?"

"Wal, he orter know it, leastways about me," replied Smoky, in perplexity. "But he's grown so cocky lately thet mebbe he's damn fool enough not to believe it."

"Shall I call him out?"

"Hell, no!" flashed Smoky, with a passionate gesture. "After all, Brad was to blame. . . . But, Jim, I jest can't advise you no more. We both gotta paddle our own canoes."

"Well, I'm not so squeamish," declared Jim, with meaning. "I like you, Smoky. I reckon you're the one real, square man in this bunch. And if you want my advice you're welcome to it."

"Jim, I've sorta cottoned to you," admitted Smoky. "But honest to Gawd I'm afeared to ask you anythin'."

"What're you afraid of, Smoky?"

"I don't know. Mebbe it's a queer hunch Hank has busted us over this gurl."

They reached the camp. Lincoln lay face down over

the table, his right arm hanging low, and his gun lying
near his hand.

"Fellers, if I'm gonna cook your supper, you'll hold
obsesquees fer our departed pard," observed Jack.

"Wonder who'll go next?" queried Mac, gloomily,
twisting his lean hands.

"Lend a hand, some of you," ordered Slocum, peremptorily.

They carried Lincoln, face down, across the oval to
the lower side of the cottonwood grove, where he had
his bed and pack.

"I'll search him," said Slocum. "Mac, you go through
his pack. Jim, fetch the ax an' anythin' we can dig with."

In half an hour Lincoln had been consigned to the
earth, and his possessions divided among the men who
buried him.

"Grave number two?" speculated Smoky. "Fellers, it
runs in my mind thet Robbers' Roost in these next twenty
years will be sprinkled all over with graves."

"How so, when nobody has any idee where it is?"

"Heeseman will find it, an' Morley, an' after them
many more," concluded Slocum, prophetically.

"Let's rustle out of the damned hole," suggested
Bridges.

It was dark by the time Happy Jack called them to
supper. Jim carried over an armload of brush to make a
bright fire. By its flare Hays was seen approaching, and
when he drew near he said, "Jim, did they tell you straight
how I come to draw on Brad?"

"Reckon they did," replied Jim, coldly.

"Anythin' to say?"

"No. I don't see how you could have acted any dif-
ferently."

"Wal, you've coppered it with the ace. The second
Brad jumped me I seen in his eyes he meant to egg me

on to draw. So I did it quick. . . . Jack, what you got fer supper?"

By tacit consent and without a single word the men avoided Happy Jack's table that night and ate around the camp fire. Hays stood up, Smoky sat on a stone, Jim knelt on one knee, and the others adopted characteristic poses reminiscent of the trail.

"Cool after the rain," remarked Hays, after he had finished. And he took up a blazing fagot of wood. "Reckon I'll make a little fire fer my lady prisoner."

He stalked away, waving the fagot to keep it ablaze.

"I call thet nervy," declared Smoky. "What you think, Jim?"

"Just a bluff. Watch him."

"Hank's gone dotty," snorted Happy Jack, for once affronted. "Thet gurl hates his very guts."

"Men, what this Herrick girl thinks or feels is noth-ing to Hays," chimed in Jim, ringingly.

"I seen her last night when he called me to fetch her supper," said Jack. "Fust time I'd had a peek at her face lately. Seemed a ghost of thet other gurl."

"Yes, and you fellows saw only a ghost of the money Hays got from the Herricks," retorted Jim, divining the moment for revelation had come.

An angry roar arose. Smoky threw up his hands and left the camp fire. Then Jim, in brief, cold terms, exposed the machinations of their chief. After the first outburst they accepted the disclosure in astounded and ominous silence. Jim left the poison to brew and paced off into the darkness.

The fire Hays had built in front of the shelter cast a bright light, showing the girl walking to and fro. Jim kept in the shadow of the cliff and stole within a couple of hundred feet, then sat down on the grassy bench. If the girl spoke, when Hays brought her food, it was too low to hear. Jim quivered when she faced in his direction and at the end of her short walk gazed across at the camp fire. It was too long a gaze to be casual.

Jim had a feeling that he could not much longer stay his hand. Right then if he had seen Hays as much as touch the girl he would have shot him and risked having it out with the men. But the chief sat there, a fading figure in the dusk. Finally Helen went into her tent. Jim grasped at that break in the tension of the hour and stole away to his bed. Tomorrow! He could wait through tomorrow. There would be a row and anything might happen. Hays was in no mood to tolerate inquiry or criticism. Most of them all, he had answered to a vitriolic devastation of character through crime. He wanted that money, that which he had kept, and all of theirs. He wanted it for more than gambling. Robbers' Roost was a hiding-place only; Utah had grown too small for him. So Jim Wall's divining mind whirled on, until slumber claimed him.

Sometime during the night Jim was awakened. He opened his eyes. Above him arched an opal starry sky. The moon had gone down, yet its radiance still dominated that of the stars. Pearly tints crowned the high bluffs. The hour was late and wolves were mourning in the distance. Perhaps they had roused him. Still, there was something mysterious and melancholy in the moment, as if he had been under the influence of a dream.

As he closed his eyes again a soft hand touched his cheek and a whisper brought him wide awake, transfixed and thrilling.

"Jim! . . . Wake up. It is I."

Helen knelt beside him. Jim sat up with a violent start. "*You!* . . . What is it?— Has that devil——"

"Hush! Not so loud. Nothing has happened. . . . But

I couldn't sleep—and I must talk to you—or go out of my mind."

In the starlight her face had the same pearl-white tint as the clouds, and her eyes were like great black gulfs peering down upon him. After a moment he could see more clearly.

"All—right. Talk—but it's risky," he whispered huskily. His hand rested upon the blanket. She put hers on it, as if in her earnestness to assure him of her presence and her feeling.

She bent lower, so that her face was closer, and she could whisper very softly.

"First I want to tell you how cruelly it has come home to me—my ignorance, my failure to believe and trust you, even after you—so—so rudely insulted me that day up on the mountain trail. If I had only had faith in you then! It's too late. But I want you to know I have the faith *now*."

"Thanks. I'm glad, though I didn't kiss you—handle you that day—just to frighten you. I fell!"

"I don't believe that altogether. No matter. If I had listened to you I would not now be in this terrible predicament. The fear—the suspense are wearing me out."

"But you are well—all right still? . . . He has not harmed you? *Helen!*"

"No he has not harmed me, and I am not ill. I'm losing flesh because I can't eat. But that's nothing. . . . Lately I don't sleep because I'm horribly afraid he will come—and—smother me—or choke me—so I can't cry out. I've slept some in the daytime. . . . Jim the thing is I—can't stand it much longer." Jim smothered a violent curse. "He has not tried—lately," she went on. "I swore I would jump over the cliff. I think I frightened him. But I can see—I can feel— Oh! Jim, for God's sake, do something to end—this horror ——"

She leaned or fell forward in the weakness of the moment, her head against him. He stroked it gently, his reaction as far from that passionate and mocking embrace at Star Ranch as could have been possible.

"Helen, don't—give up," he replied. "You have been brave. And it has gone—better than we could hope. . . . Only a little while longer!"

"We might steal away—now."

"Yes. I've thought of that. But only to get lost and starve—or die of thirst in these brakes."

"That almost—would be better—for me."

"If you can't stick it out we'll plan and go—say tomorrow night. We must have food, horses. . . . It's only honest, though, to tell you the chances are a hundred to one against us. . . . We've got an even break if we wait."

"How can you—think that?"

"This gang is about ready to go up in smoke. There'll be a terrible fight. Hays surely will be killed. And just as surely, more than he. That will leave a proposition I can handle without risk to you."

"Even then—we still have to find a way out of this awful place."

"Yes, but I'd have time, and I could pack water and food. . . . Helen, trust me, it's the best plan."

"If you take me back to my brother, I'll give you the ransom."

"Don't insult me," he replied, bitterly.

At that she drew up suddenly, and threw her hair back from her face. "Forgive me. . . . You see I have lost my mind. That never occurred to me before. But I'll reward you in some way."

"To have saved you will be all the reward I ask—and more than I deserve. . . . You've forgotten that I love you."

"Yes—I had," she whispered. Her great eyes studied him in the starlight, as if the fact had a vastly different significance here than it had had at Star Ranch.

"The proof of it is that I'm one of this robber gang— yet ready to betray them—kill their chief and any or all of them. Except Smoky. I've worked on him so that he's our friend. He is a real man, as you'll see when the break comes. . . . If you were American, you'd be human enough to grasp the situation and help me through with it."

"I am human and I—I've as much courage as any American girl," she flashed, stung by his caustic words. "You—you talk of love as freely as you Westerners talk of horses—guns—death. . . . But surely you don't mean that it's because you love me you'll save me?"

"I'm afraid it is."

"I cannot believe you. . . . I never accepted you as a desperado."

"Miss Herrick, all that doesn't matter," he rejoined, almost coldly. "We are wasting time—risking much ——"

"I don't care. That is *why* I had to come to you. I knelt here for moments before awakening you. It helped me somehow—and it is easing my nerves to talk."

"Well, talk then. But make it low. . . . You must have crept very softly to my side. I sleep with one eye open."

"Indeed you don't. Both yours were tight shut. And your lips were stern. A strange thought came to me. I wondered if you had not had a good mother, and sister perhaps."

"I had," whispered Jim, feelingly.

"That accounts."

"It did not keep me from ——"

Suddenly she stiffened, no doubt at the slight sound

that had checked Jim's speech. She put a hand over his lips and stared at him with wide, vague eyes.

Over her shoulder Jim's eye was arrested by a glint of starlight upon a bright object on the ground. Above and behind it a shape, darker than the dark background, gradually took the outline of a man on hands and knees. Cold terror assailed Jim Wall, despite his iron nerve. That was Hays crawling upon them with a gun in his hand. A bursting tide of blood through Jim's veins paralleled the lightning flash of his thoughts. Death for both of them was terribly close. His gun was under his pillow. Helen knelt between him and the robber. A move of even the slightest kind would be fatal. Cunning must take precedence of action. He swerved his rigid gaze from the humped black form to Helen's face. It was white as marble in moonlight. Her eyes showed the tremendous strain under which she labored. In that instant she could almost read his very thoughts. Her fingers still crossed his lips and they had begun to tremble.

"*It's Hays,*" he whispered, scarcely audibly. "*Follow me—now.*" Then, exerting all his will to speak naturally, he said aloud: "No, Miss Herrick, I'm sorry, but I can't oblige you. I don't approve of Hays' kidnapping you, but it's done. And I'm a member of his band. I would not think of going against him, let alone trying to run off with you."

There was a tense silence, fraught with much apprehension for Jim. Would she be able to play up to him? There was just a chance that Hays had not heard any of their whispers, in which case it was possible to deceive him. Helen comprehended. It was Jim Wall's privilege then to see the reaction of a woman at a perilous moment.

"I'll give you the ransom money," she said, quite clearly, and certainly most persuasively. "My brother will reward you otherwise."

"You can't bribe me," he rejoined. "And I wouldn't advise you to try it on Smoky or any of the others."

"Hays may have had only money in his mind at first, but now ——"

"*Don't move, Jim!*" came a low hard voice from the shadow.

Helen gave a little gasp and sagged on her knees. Jim waited a moment.

"I won't, Hank," he replied.

Then Hays' tall form loomed black above the rise of ground. He strode forward. If he had sheathed his gun, Jim would have made short work of that interview. But he held it half leveled, glancing darkly in the star-light.

The robber chief gazed down upon Jim and Helen. His features were indistinguishable, but the poise of his head was expressive enough. Still, Jim sensed that he had been misled.

"You cat!" he declared, roughly. "If I ketch you again —tryin' to bribe any of my outfit—I'll treat you so you won't want to go back to your baby-faced brother. . . . Now you git to your tent!"

Helen rose unsteadily and vanished in the gloom.

"Jim Wall, you ain't been with me long, an' I don't know you, but I'm takin' this deal to heart," Hays said, slowly. "I'm much obliged. I reckon you're the only man in the outfit who could of withstood thet woman."

"No, you're wrong, Hank. Smoky wouldn't have lis-tened to her. And I'm sure the others would have stood pat."

"My faith was damn near gone."

"That's in you, Hank. You've no call to lose it. You've about split your gang over this woman."

"Wal, I'm not askin' judgments from you or any of

the outfit," growled the chief, gloomily. "You'll all be good an' glad to git your share of the ransom."

"The thing is—boss—will we get it?" queried Jim, significantly.

Hays made a violent move, like a striking snake. "What you mean by thet?"

"I'm askin' you."

"Air you insinuatin' you mightn't git yours?" demanded Hays. And Jim, used for years to sense peril, divined he was not far from death then. He had not moved a hand since Hays' arrival. If he had had his gun within reach he would have ended that argument. But the chances were too greatly in Hays' favor. Wit and cunning must see him through. He could feel how intensely the chief wanted to know what Jim knew.

"No. You might say I was askin' for all of us," replied Jim, curtly.

"Wal, I'll git the outfit together an' do some askin', myself."

"It's a good idea. It *might* prevent the split—provided you divide the money you stole from Herrick."

"I'll wring thet white cat's neck," hissed the robber.

"You're wrong, boss. She didn't tell me. She doesn't know you robbed her brother. Sparrow confessed before he died."

Hays swore a mighty oath. ". . . An' he squealed?"

"Yes. To Smoky an' me. We kept it secret until we had to tell. They *knew* somethin' was wrong."

"All the time you knowed!" There was something pathetic in the fallen chieftain's shame and amaze. By this he seemed to realize his crime.

"You see, Hank, how your outfit has stood by you, even in your guilt."

"Ahuh! . . . If it ain't too late—I'll make amends," he rejoined, hoarsely, and stalked away in the darkness.

Jim lay back on his blankets with a weight of oppression removed. He had saved himself for the hour, but what would the outcome be? After deliberation it seemed he had put Hays in a corner from which there could be no retreat.

Chapter Thirteen

NEXT morning Jim, who slept ill the rest of that night, was building a fire when Happy Jack, who had his bed under the shack, heard him and rolled out with his merry whistle.

"Thet's downright good of you, Jim," he drawled. "I like cookin', but I shore hate to rustle firewood an' chop. When I was a kid I 'most cut off my big toe."

"Happy, you're a card," replied Jim. "How in the hell can you whistle and smile when you know this outfit is primed to blow up?"

"Wal, Jim, show me the sense of bein' sore an' unhappy, no matter what's comin' off," rejoined Jack, philosophically. "As a feller grows older his mind sets one way or another. Look at Brad. Gamblin' got to be breath of life to him an' he lost thet breath. Look at Hays. Love of robbin' lost him wife, family, ranch, respect. An' look at you, Jim. Lone wolf, your hand always itchin' wuss to throw your gun."

"So you figure me that way!" exclaimed Jim, in genuine surprise.

"Reckon I see through a lot I don't git credit for."

"You see through me wrong, Jack. I don't ride around looking for trouble. But I can't help being worked on by other men and conditions."

"Wal, I'm admittin' Hays eased us into a rotten deal."

Jim had breakfast before the other men were up. It still wanted half an hour till sunrise. This was the beautiful time of day. All was balmy, sweet, fresh, fragrant. Mockingbirds were bursting their throats. To Jim their melody was indeed a mockery, not of other birds, but of men and life and nature. The dawn, the air, the sky, the birds, the cliffs—nothing that was there in Jim's sight held any intimation of the hell about to break in Rob-

209

bers' Roost, nor of that captive imperiled woman! Jim hurried away on scout duty before Hays and his accusers had assembled at the camp fire.

With rifle in hand Jim headed toward the western exit. Not until he was out in the valley did he realize that he carried his rifle. The fact surprised him. There was plenty of fresh meat in camp. He had no idea of hunting. That act had been instinctive and it puzzled him. But there was a release of a clamped tension within. This day would see events, and he felt almost elated.

Perhaps that had something to do with a singular sense of the mounting beauty of the morning, of the magnified solitude, of the rarefied atmosphere that gave the buttes and mountains a most deceiving nearness. The outside world of Utah seemed to be encroaching upon this wil. derness of canyon brakes.

The sun was still beneath the rim of the escarpments in the east, but its approach was heralded by a magnificent glory of red and gold, of flushed peaks and rose-shrouded mesas, of burning faces of the zigzag walls along distant ramparts.

Jim had never before been up high here at such an early hour. Any man would have been struck by the spectacle. He felt that if he were to die that day he would be leaving earth without having fully realized its sublimity, its mystery, its solemn warning, its inscrutable promise. And there ran through his mind a thought of how Miss Herrick would have reveled in this glorious scene.

"Well, I *am* loco," he soliloquized, blankly, suddenly brought up sharply by the absurd reflection. Excitement and emotion had reacted so powerfully upon him that he was not himself. Right then he made the stern decision that when he started back to camp, to face Hays again, he would be a thousand times his old self.

The sun-shelter he had erected had once before toppled over, and this morning he found it again flat, except one of the poles. Jim gathered up the dry brush and made a seat and back-rest of it. He did not examine into his premonition that the shelter had served its turn. Then he sat down to watch.

It was as if he had never seen a sunrise. There was no comparing it with any other he could recall. And one magnifying look through the field-glass was more than enough. Nature's exaggeration of color and loveliness and transparency and vastness, was too great even for the normal gaze of man.

But that superlative grandeur passed, leaving something Jim could accept and gloat over as actual.

From this lofty perch he gazed with narrowed eyes across the shaded hole below, into which no ray of sun had yet penetrated. The black mouth of the gorge yawned hungrily. Above it on all sides spread the gray and red rock ridges, dotted with dwarf cedars, with white washes between, and on to spotted red ragged hummocks that fringed a green level, yellow with sunflowers, which led to an abrupt break into a canyon. The walls showed brown, rust-colored, hard as iron, with dark lines and shadows, beyond which stood up the pyramids and bluffs of the brakes. Here gloomed suggested depths and corrugated slopes, then the infinitely wild, obscure, stratified space terminating in the Henry Mountains, looming colossal in the lilac light of morning, ghostly, black, unscalable, piercing the pale-blue sky.

To their left the lifting sun, losing its gold for red, spread a transparent curtain over the line of level escarpments and mesas, finally to dazzle the canyon country under it to blinding rays. To the right shone many leagues of rock ridges and mounds, broken at intervals by pale gleams of washes and alkali flats and banks of gray clay, ending in the dim, wandering White Bluffs.

Loneliness was paramount. There was no sound—only an immense silence. No life at all! Not a winged creature hovering over that ghastly region! But over this scene of desolation slowly spread the solemn blight of heating, blazing sun, soon to mantle all in illusive copper haze.

Before that hour arrived, Jim Wall took up the field-glass. Below in the camp the men were lazily stirring to a late breakfast. The door of the cabin was open. A glint of gold crossed the dark aperture. Then the tall form of Hays stalked out. He yawned. He stretched wide his long arms. His ruddy face gleamed in the glass to that sight. Wall's whole being leaped.

"By God!" his voice rang out, as if to all which had just enchained him. "Hays, that's your last morning's stretch. . . . Before this day's done you'll stretch forever!"

Let his men have their hour, thought Jim, darkly, but if they did not mete out justice to their chief, the end was nevertheless fixed and unalterable.

Jim settled back and raised the field-glass more from habit than any semblance of the old watchfulness. There was nothing to see but the stark denudation of the brakes.

Suddenly into Jim's magnified circle of vision crept dark objects—a long line of them.

He was so startled that the glass waved out of line. He moved it to and fro, searching. What could that have been? An error of sight, a line of cedars, a conception of idle mind!

"There!" he breathed. He had caught it again. Not cedars—not brush, but moving objects! . . . "By heaven!" he muttered. "Am I dotty?"

Horses! A line of dark horses! His straining eyes

blurred. He lowered the glass with shaking hands to wipe the dimness away. "So help me—it looks like riders!"

A third time Jim caught the objects. He froze the glass on them. Horses and riders—horses with packs! A bursting gush of hot blood ran all over him. The expected pursuit, now long neglected, almost forgotten, had materialized. It looked like Heeseman's outfit, at least three miles away, approaching slowly by a route far to the south of that over which Hays had come.

"About three miles," muttered Jim. "Coming slow. They're lost. . . . But that wash they're in heads into the Hays trail. . . . If they strike that they'll come fast. Not enough rain yet to wash out our tracks. We've not time to pack and ride out. . . . By thunder! they've cornered us! Now, Hank Hays———"

Jim took one more straining look. No hope! It was a big outfit, and not traveling so slowly, either. The leader bestrode a black horse. Jim remembered that horse. Snatching up his rifle, he slung the field-glass over his shoulder and ran down off the bluff to the slope. It occurred to him to locate Hays' horses. He sighted some—six, seven, eight—the others were not visible. Hays would rage like a madman. Then Jim tore down the slope with giant strides. Reaching the valley floor, he ran along the wash, through the entrance into the oval, and once on the grass he fairly flew the remaining distance to camp.

To his profound amaze he espied Hays bound hand and foot, with a stick behind him and through his elbows. The robber sat in an uncomfortable posture against the wood-pile. Moreover, a second glance acquainted Jim with the fact that Hays was gagged and that his visage appeared scarcely human, so malignantly enraged was it.

"What the hell!" cried Jim, breaking out of his bewilderment.

Hays gave vent to an inarticulate sound, but it was expressive. Jim wheeled to stalk under the shack, his hand on his gun, as if he half expected Heeseman to have arrived before him. To his further amaze Miss Herrick was sitting at the rude table, eating breakfast. A big gun, that Jim recognized as Hays' property, lay conspicuously in front of her. Happy Jack, whistling as usual, was serving her.

"What does this mean?" demanded Jim.

"Ask the men," she replied, curtly.

Outside and below the shack sat Smoky on a rock, with the others standing near. They all had the appearance of having been swayed profoundly.

"Mawnin', Jim," drawled Smoky, with a grin. "You see we've got a new chief."

"Who hawg-tied the boss?"

"Reckon I did—with a little help."

"What for?"

"Damn if I know. Our lady prisoner made me do it."

"Miss Herrick forced you to tie Hays up?" queried Jim, trying to conceal his exultation.

"I should shiver she did. Stuck Hays' hair-trigger gun —cocked—right into my belly, an' says: 'Will you tie this villain—an' swear by your honor not to release him or allow any of these other men to do so—or will you have me shoot you?'"

"How'd she get that gun?"

"Wal, she snatched it quicker'n lightnin', thet's how. An' when she cocked it with both hands it went off, *bang!* The bullet went between Hank's legs. Tickled him. You can see the hole in his pants. Scared? My Gawd! you never see a man so scared. Thet gurl cool as a cucumber cocked the gun again, an' held Hays up—then all of us. We was sittin' at table. She made us all stand, hands high, an' then she performed thet little trick with Hank's gun ag'in' my gizzard. Jim, I'd like to die if I didn't go cold an' stiff. But I promised on my word of honor—as a robber—thet I'd tie Hank up an' make the other fellers play square. It was so funny, too, thet I near bust. Hays, soon as he was helpless, got over his scare, an' then was he mad! I reckon no one on this earth ever saw a madder man. He cussed so terrible thet she made me gag him."

"Well, I'll be—blowed!" gasped Jim.

"No wonder. We was wuss. We'd had breakfast, an' Hank was tryin' to face us fellers. I'll say he came clean, Jim. He divided all the money he got from Herrick an' his sister, an' the gold things an' diamonds. 'Fellers,' he said. 'I could lie an' say I meant to give this to you later. But I'm not built thet way. I double-crossed you all— first time in my life. I meant to keep it all, an' the ransom fer the gurl. But now there won't be no ransom, for I'm not goin' to give her up. She's mine, an' I can do as I want, an' if any of you don't like it you can make your kick now.' . . . Wal, we was so plumb flabbergasted thet we didn't see the gurl, who came close on the sun side of Happy's shelter. She heard the whole damn show. . . . Jim, I wish you could have seen her when she stepped up to Hank. I don't know what did it—mebbe her eyes —but he shore wilted. It was then she snatched his gun."

"So that's the deal!" ejaculated Jim. "What are you going to do?"

"Don't ask me. I gave my word an' I'll keep it. Fer thet matter the rest of our outfit air fer the gurl, ransom or no ransom."

Suddenly Jim awoke out of his stupefaction to remember the approach of Heeseman.

"Smoky, I know what you're all going to do, and that's fight," he flashed, curtly. "I was so surprised I forgot.

Heeseman's outfit is coming. I sighted them perhaps three miles. Traveling slow, but sure. We've no time to pack an' get away. We've got to find the best place to stand an' fight, an' pack our stuff into it pronto."

"Heeseman!" cried Smoky, coolly. "So it's come. I reckoned on thet. Git busy, men."

Jim strode under the shelter to face Miss Herrick. She had heard, for she was white.

"We're all but surprised by Heeseman's outfit," he said, abruptly. "We must fight. You will be worse off if you fall into their hands. I'm sorry I must release Hays. We need him."

"Too late!" she exclaimed.

"Pack your things quickly and hurry over to the cave on this side." Then Jim picked up Hays' gun from the table and ran out. First he removed the gag, and then in terse terms he stated the situation. Next he released the robber from his painful fix, and handed him the gun.

"Heeseman, huh! Wal, so be it!" Hays said, facing Jim with an air of finality that intimated relief.

"How far are they away?" Hays then asked.

"Two miles."

"Gawd Almighty!—Where? Which way air they—comin'?"

Facing south, Jim pointed. "Little west—of south. They're in a—wash that'll head—into the trail we made."

"I know thet. But it's rough before it heads in. We've got half an hour—mebbe. Did you think to look fer the hosses?"

"Eight horses in the—valley. Others not in sight."

"You — — —!" cursed Hays, suddenly furious. "Fine scout you air. How come you didn't spy them soon enough fer us to rustle out of hyar?"

"I couldn't have seen them half a mile sooner," snapped Jim. "They came out from behind a bank."

"Hell's fire! Tell thet to *me*? You was sleepin'."

"You're a liar," flashed Jim, leaping clear of the others. "Open your trap to me again like that!"

"Say, it's you who'll shet his trap," replied Hays, stridently. "Or you'll git a dose of medicine I gave Brad Lincoln."

"Not from you—you yellow dog of a woman thief!"

Smoky Slocum ran out in time to get in front of Jim.

"Hyar! Hyar!" he called, piercingly. "Is this a time fer us to fight each other? Cool down, Jim. Make allowance fer Hays. He's wuss'n drunk."

"I don't care a damn if there're ten outfits on our trail. He can't talk to me that way. . . . And, Smoky, I reckon you're presuming on friendship."

"Shore I am," returned Slocum, hurriedly. "I'll not do it again, Jim. Hays is what you called him. But leave your dispute till we settle with Heeseman."

"All right. You're talking sense," replied Jim. He had been quick to grasp the opening made by Hays. "There must be ten riders in Heeseman's outfit."

"Wall, thet suits me," rejoined the robber, harshly.

"Now think fast," snapped Smoky.

Hays pulled himself together. "Mac, you an' Jeff run like hell to fetch what hosses you can find quick. . . . Jack, you an' Smoky an' Wall hustle the grub, cook-kit, packs, an' beds into thet cave across the wash. I'll git up high an' watch. When I yell dig fer cover."

"You aimin' to fight or run?" queried Smoky.

"We might git packed light, if somethin' holds them up. But we can't leave the way we come in. Dirty Devil too high. Heeseman has stumbled on the next best way. If we had plenty of time. . . . But rustle everybody."

Mac and Jeff were already in lumbering flight up the oval. And Happy Jack, not concerned enough to stop his whistling, was sacking his utensils. Hays made for the notch in the bluff west of the cabin. Jim sprang into action, while Smoky dashed off toward the cottonwood grove.

Chapter Fourteen

UPON Jim's first return trip from the cave he encountered the girl, burdened with her effects.

"Helen, I'll carry that. Hurry! We've no time to lose."

At the back of the cave there was a crack deep enough to protect Helen. He directed her to hide inside and await developments.

"*Jim*—promise me you'll shoot me—before letting Hays or any of them—get me."

He considered that a moment, then answered, "I promise."

Her reply was incoherent, though couched in passionate tones. Jim ran on toward the camp, resolving to withhold a shell in his rifle and to keep a sharp watch on Hays.

The next quarter of an hour was filled with strenuous and unceasing action. Their united efforts collected all the supplies, utensils, saddles, and packs, and several of the beds in the three-cornered cave back and to one side of the shack. A huge slab of stone lay across the top of this triangular notch in the cliff. The wall had been hollowed by the action of water. A small stream flowed out from the base of the wall. At the extreme apex of the notch there was an opening, but hidden from above by thick bushes. Also bushes of the same kind screened the west side of this notch. Beyond the shack and in close around the opposite corner a corral had been built under that shelving wall. It was the best place for defense in the oval, and Jim believed Hays' outfit could hold it indefinitely, though not to save the horses. If it came to a siege they could be released.

Smoky came panting in with Hays' pack, and started off again.

"That's enough, Smoky," called Jim.

Slocum returned. "Nothin' left—'cept Hank's bed," he panted. "I—couldn't—locate thet."

"Listen!"

"What do you hear?"

"Horses."

"Sure, I catch it. . . . Which way?"

"Damn if I can tell."

"Grab a rifle. Seems to me if Hays was up on top somewhere he'd hear horses before we could—in that direction."

"Shore. Must be Mac an' Jeff."

Smoky had guessed correctly. Half a dozen horses appeared tearing over rocks and through brush into the oval, with the two men, riding bareback, in close pursuit.

Then above the noise rose Hays' stentorian voice: *"Ride! Ride fer camp! . . . Let the hosses go!"*

The robber chieftain came plunging down the gap. He was warning Mac and Jeff. There must have been more danger for them, on the moment, than for him.

"Jim, keep your eye peeled on thet cliff," said Smoky, and stole forward under cover of the brush.

Presently a white puff of smoke showed above the ragged rim. *Spang!* The fight was on. One of Hays' men —Bridges—let out a hoarse bawl and swayed over, almost losing his balance. Jim looked no more at him, but concentrated his gaze on the rim. Another puff of white! Something dark—a man's slouch hat—bobbed up. Jim's rifle, already raised, swerved a trifle—cracked. The hat went flying.

"Wal, if thet bird didn't have it on a stick he got scalped, I'll gamble," observed Smoky, which remark attested to his keen sight.

The horses came over the bench, frightened, but not stampeding, and Mac drove them into the corral. This was around the corner from the range of the sharpshooter on the rim. Bridges, reeling on the horse, followed Mac, who ran out of the corral to catch him as he fell. Then, as they came along close to the wall, Hays arrived puffing from the other direction.

"Heeseman—with his outfit—nine in all," he heaved. "They're scatterin' to surround the roost. . . . But they can't cross—below us—an' across there it's—out of range. . . . We're all right."

"Yes, we air! Haw! Haw!" ejaculated Smoky, glaring back.

Mac half carried the bulky Bridges into the safety zone, and let him down on the ground with his head on a bed-roll.

"Where's he shot?" demanded Hays. "I seen thet feller who did it jest a little too late."

"Through the belly."

"Hank, I'm done fer," said Bridges, weakly.

"Lemme see." And the leader, kneeling beside Bridges, tore open his bloody shirt. He had been shot in the back, the bullet going clear through. "Wal, I should smile! Say your prayers, Jeff. . . . Somebody take his gun."

"Take it yourself, Hays," rejoined Mac, sullenly.

"Hank, you go hide with your lady prisoner an' we'll do the fightin'," added Slocum, who had crawled back from the edge of the brush.

"Hide!—What'n hell's eatin' you?" roared the chief. "You know what, you — — —!"

"Hays, we'd a damn sight rather die fightin' than owe our lives to one bullet of yours," said Happy Jack, in a cold contempt Jim had not thought possible of the man.

"Wal, I'll take you up," rasped Hays, after a moment of assimilation. He had degenerated to a point where he let passion sway him utterly.

"You stay here, Hays," ordered Jim, hotly. "You got us in this mix. You lied and cheated. You betrayed us.

And you'll fight, by Heaven! unless you're as much of
a coward as you are betrayer."

The chief grew livid where he had been gray. Only
then had he grasped the significance of this fiery scorn
of his comrades.

"You-all double-crossed me!"

"Shore. Same as you did us. If we git through this
deal, which I've a hunch we never will, there'll come a
reckonin' with me, Hank Hays," declared Smoky.

"I meant to make a clean breast of it—divvy all the
money," said Hays, in a strangled voice. "But I got crazy
about the gurl. I couldn't think of nothin' else."

"Haw! Haw! fer thet first crack, an' okay on the
second. . . . *Now!*"

A bullet thudded into the wall and spanged away, followed by the report of a rifle.

"Duck back! Thet was from somewhere else," shouted
Hays.

They dove twenty feet farther back. Here they were
apparently safe, except from the grassy ridge of the oval
in front, which it was unlikely any sharpshooters could
reach in daylight. Smoky peeped around the west corner,
Mac round the one opposite. Hays knelt on one knee,
rifle in hands, peering out. Jim went back to the apex of
the notch, and bracing one foot in each side, clinging with
one free hand, got up to a shelf from which he could
peep out of the hole. He was exceedingly wary. In front
was thick, low brush; on his right a thinner fringe, and
the left was open. The rocky ground ridged away from
the oval and the deep gorge below. A sharp scrutiny in
that direction failed to discover any of the attackers Hays
had affirmed were attempting to surround the oval. But
there might have been some crawling behind the rocks
or down the fissures.

After a careful study Jim crept out into the brush,

stirred by a renewal of firing from the west rim. Wisps of white cloud, thinning on the light wind, located the positions of the shooters. First Jim peered through the growth of brush directly in front. He did not espy any men, but half a mile over the hummocky rocks he saw a little cove full of horses. The packs had not yet been removed from some of them, nor saddles from the others Heeseman had come to make a siege of it.

Jim did not move hastily. A ragged section of cliff, quite high, above and to the left of the south exit, gave him misgivings. That was a likely place for ambush. Farther to the west, however, where the shooting came from, there was some hope of locating an enemy.

Lying flat, Jim wormed his way a few yards to the fringe of brush, and took another survey. Almost at once he caught a movement of a dark object through a crevice in the rim. The distance was far for accurate shooting at so small a target. But with a rest he drew a coarse steady aim and fired.

The object flopped over. A shrill cry, unmistakable to any man used to gunplay, rent the air. Jim knew he had reached one of the Heeseman gang, to disable him if no more. Next instant a raking fire swept the brush on both sides of Jim. Like a crab he scuttled back, almost falling into the hole. Bullets had hissed only a foot above his head. He dropped down into the cave.

Smoky stood there, in the act of climbing.

"Fire in your eye, Jim," he drawled.

"They damn near got me," rang out Jim. "I hit one of them way over where they shot at Bridges. There's a bunch of them hid on that cliff to the right of the outlet, you know, where Jeff went up to scout."

"Ahuh. Thet's way this side of the smoke I seen."

"Yes. It's pretty close. But they can't do us any harm from there, if we keep low bridge."

"Jim, they got us located," replied Slocum, gravely.

"Sure. But so long as they can't line on us in here ——"

"They can move all around. An' pretty soon Heeseman will figger thet men behind the high center in front can shoot straight in hyar."

"Smoky, you're right. One of us ought to be on the far side of the oval."

"I can work round there without bein' seen. Along the cliff wall hyar, 'crost the gorge, round under the cotton-woods, an' up thet draw on the far side."

"You might. But suppose some of Heeseman's outfit are below, as Hays said?"

"Thet'd end history for Smoky Slocum."

"Wait, then. Don't risk it. I believe I can see over that high center."

"Whar from?"

"This hole above. The side towards the oval is a foot lower. It'd be reasonably safe."

"I'll go up with you."

Bridges lay groaning, his big hands clutching his clothes, his face a bluish cast. Mac sat helplessly beside him. Hays knelt out by the corner of wall, with Jack whispering behind him.

"Hold my rifle. I'll go up," said Jim. Without encumbrance he readily climbed to the shelf, finding to his satisfaction that he could stand on it and look out over the oval without being seen from the cliff.

"Hand up both rifles."

Smoky complied, and was soon beside Jim, but owing to his smaller stature he could not see over the rim. However, he found steps for his feet, by which he surmounted the difficulty. Like a general he swept the lay of the land. "Jim, there's only one place we couldn't see, an' thet's straight back of the center. If they savvy it they'll almost shore try to work in from the west."

"You're right, old-timer," replied Jim, grimly, and pointed to the western entrance, where two stealthily moving figures could even then be discerned slipping, like Indians, from bush to bush.

"Jim, you're a right fine fightin's pard," quoth Smoky, delighted. "Now, ain't thet jest a shame? They won't have sense enough to run like hell, givin' us hard shots. They'll sneak it. . . . Shore, look at 'em. I could almost bore one already."

"It's nervy of them at that," admitted Jim, "after I shot from the top of this bank."

"They might not know thet. It takes a good quarter of an hour to grade round thet cliff an' down. . . . Where'd they go, Jim?"

"They're below the ridge now. Look sharp, Smoky, or they might get a couple of shots in first."

"Wal, if they do, I hope both bullets lodge in Hank's gizzard."

"My sentiments exactly. . . . Smoky, I saw something shine. Tip of a rifle. Right—to the right. . . . Ah!"

"Take the first feller, Jim. . . . One—two—three."

The rifles cracked in unison. Jim's mark sprang convulsively up, and plunged down to roll and weave out of sight. The man Smoky had shot at sank flat and lay still. Next moment a volley banged from the cliff and a storm of bullets swept hissing and spanging too uncomfortably close.

"Low bridge, Jim," chuckled Smoky. "Gimme your gun. Drop down. They're shootin' lower."

Jim slid and leaped to the floor of the cave below. Smoky, by lying down, lowered the rifles to him, and then came scrambling after.

Hays had slouched back to them, followed by Happy.
"What'd you shoot at?" he queried, hopefully.

Jim did not deign to notice him. "Smoky, I winged
mine and you hit yours plumb center."

"Two more. Heeseman ain't havin' a walk-over. By
Gawd! if we can *kill* two or three more, an' particularly
Heeseman, we'll have thet outfit licked!"

"Yes. But how, Smoky? We're stuck here. And they'll
take less risks now."

"Wal, luck's with us. An' in a pinch I can work way
round behind them."

"Smoky, I don't want you to try that."

"Wal, Jim, I ain't carin' a lot what you want. The
thing is we can't let night overtake us in hyar."

"Why not? It's as safe for us as for them."

"Safe nothin'. We can't make no light. This green
brush wouldn't burn. An' Heeseman has us located. He'd
be slick enough to station men after dark. Behind the
center an' the rocks. In thet wash, an' shore above us
watchin' our hole. Then when daylight come we'd be
snuffed out. No, if we don't end it before dark we shore
gotta sneak out of hyar after dark."

Hays swaggered closer. "Thet's a good idee, Smoky."

"Air you talkin' to me?" asked Slocum, insolently.

"Shore I am, you spit-cat! What'n hell's got into you
—an' all of you?" shouted the robber, hoarsely.

"You wanta talk, huh?"

"Course I do. I'm boss hyar, an' what I say ——"

"Hey, fellers, the boss wants talk," interrupted Slocum,
fiercely. "You, Happy an' Mac, talk to the skunk who
used to be our boss. An' you, Jeff, air you able to talk to
Hays?"

The dying man raised a haggard, relentless face, which
needed no speech to express his hate for the fallen chief.

"Hays, when I—meet you in hell—I'll stamp your

cheatin'—guts out!" whispered Bridges, in terrible effort
to expand all his last strength and passion in one denun-
ciation. Then he sank back, his head fell on his breast,
and he died.

"Gone! Thet makes three of us," ejaculated Mac,
twisting restless hands round his rifle.

"Talk to Hays, damn you," yelled Smoky. "He wants
talk."

"I wouldn't talk to him if it *was* my last breath, like
Jeff, an' talkin' would save my life."

"Jim, can't you oblige our former chief an' pard?"
asked Smoky, turning to Jim.

"I'm past talking to him, Smoky—that is, with my
mouth."

"Wal, so it's left to me," declared Slocum, bitterly.
"Me who ranged Utah with you fer ten years! Me whose
life you saved an' who cottoned to you as to a brother!
Me who slept with you, fought with you, robbed an'
killed with you!"

How potently significant that rifle barrel of Smoky's
almost aligned with Hays' body! Jim felt a cold thrill of
expectancy—Smoky would kill the chief. Hays might
have held himself proof against words, but not against
bullets.

"Hank Hays, some one of us will live long enough to
tell the Utah border what you sunk to," went on Slocum.
"An' this place, which I bet a million will be your grave,
won't be forgot in history. Robbers' Roost? It oughter
be Robbers' Grave. For many years, outfits like ours used
to be will hole in hyar. An' many a low-down rustler
or common hoss thief will laugh an' say: 'Hank Hays
croaked in hyar, after doin' dirt to the best men who ever
throwed a gun for each other. An' all fer a white-faced
slip of a woman who was sickened near to death at him!'"

"Aw, you go to hell!" shouted Hays, malignantly. "I ain't croaked yet."

"Wal, if Heeseman doesn't do it, I will."

"Man, air you drunk or crazy?" burst out Hays, in dazed incredulity.

"Neither. An' thet's my last talk with you, Hank Hays," concluded Slocum, in cold finality.

Jim, sitting back on a bulge of wall, watched and listened. He could not have asked more, though he had hoped Smoky would finish the chief then and there, despite the pressure of the peril from without. Hays' bravado did not deceive Jim. The foundation of Hays' manhood had been torn asunder, as indeed they had decayed during this last wild enterprise. He realized it, and the effect seemed tremendous. He was in his last ditch. Heeseman, an enemy of years' standing, was there to kill him. And if he and this remnant of his outfit succeeded in beating off the attackers, even then his doom was imminent. Smoky did not make idle threats. And if he failed to kill Hays, then this stranger, this mysterious gunman from Wyoming, would do it. Thus Hays' mind must have worked. Only one chance in a thousand for him! It looked as if he meant to take it in desperate spirit.

"Jack, gimme Jeff's gun an' belt," he said, and receiving them he buckled them over his own. Next he opened his pack to take out a box of rifle shells, which he broke open to drop the contents in his coat pocket on the left side. After that he opened his shirt to strip off a broad, black money-belt. This was what had made him bulge so and give the impression of stoutness, when in fact he was lean. He hung this belt over a projecting point of wall.

"In case I don't git back," he added. "An' there's a bundle of chicken-feed change in my pack."

There was something gloomy and splendid about him then. Fear of God, or man, or death was not in him. Rifle in hand, he crept to the corner on the left and boldly exposed himself, drawing a volley of shots from two quarters.

"Ahuh. I'll upset thet little party," he muttered, and crossing the front of the cave he passed his men and started to glide along the zigzag wall on that side. He had to dodge out around the end of the corral, which move, however, did not draw fire. Then he disappeared.

"Wal, we set the old devil up, didn't we?" said Smoky, his tragic mien softening. "Hangin' thet money-belt there showed Hank with his back to the wall. I seen him so far gone once before. Gawd Almighty! . . . Heeseman is standin' on the verge this minnit, Jim."

"What's Hays' idea?"

"He must know a way to sneak around on them. . . . Jim, if he makes it an' they git to shootin', I'm gonna try my plan."

"You'll cross around on the other side?"

"Shore. One day I figgered out the thing I mean to do now."

"If Hank gets them all shooting, you might risk it, Smoky. But wait. Let's see what ——"

A metallic, spanging sound, accompanied rather than followed by a shot, then a sodden thud right at hand, choked Jim's speech in his throat. Before he wheeled he knew that thud to be a bullet striking flesh. Happy Jack had been cut short in one of his low whistles. He swayed a second, upright, then, uttering an awful groan, he fell.

Smoky leaped to him, bent over.

"Dead! Hit in the temple. Where'd thet bullet come from?"

"It glanced from a rock. I know the sound. Was that an accident?"

"Shore. How else could a bullet reach us in hyar, un-less from straight across behind that mound."

"No. The bullet came ——"

Spoww! The same sound—another shot, and another heavy lead, deflected in its course, struck the stone above Jim's head and whined away to whip at the gravel.

"Thet rock thar," shouted Smoky, pointing. "See the white bullet mark. . . . Jim, some slick sharpshooter has figgered one on us."

Twenty feet out, a little to the left of the center of the cave, lay a huge block of granite with a slanting side facing west. This side inclined slightly toward the cave. On its rusty surface showed two white spots close to-gether.

Another *spang* and shot followed, with a banging of another heavy bullet from wall to wall. It narrowly missed Mac, who was quick to flop down with a surly yelp.

"Come on, Jim, it ain't healthy hyar no more," said Smoky, hugging the wall and working to the extreme left-hand corner. "It do beat hell. Thet's Heeseman. He's a bad feller to fall out with. I remember once hearin' Hank tell when he an' Heeseman was pardners in cattle-raisin'. Funny, ain't it? Wal, some rustlers made a cattle steal. Hank trailed tracks into what's called Black Dragon Canyon. There was a cave high off the bottom, an' Hank told how he an' Heeseman, an' their riders, shot ag'in' the wall of the cave an' shore routed out them rustlers."

"Smoky, if they're loaded with ammunition they can rout us out, too. That infernal rock! We couldn't move it, even if we dared try."

"We gotta kill Heeseman."

"I had somewhat the same hunch myself. . . . *Bing!* There's another."

"I seen the smoke then. Look, Jim. There's a rock sticks up like a owl's head. An' it come from left of thet, out of thet wide crack. He's back in there, the bugger. Let's give him a dose of his own medicine. We got shells more'n we'll ever use."

"Wait till he shoots again. Then you empty your rifle and give way to me."

Soon the little white cloud puffed up, and a crack instantly followed. Smoky, on one knee, fired deliberately, and thereafter worked the lever of his rifle steadily until the magazine was empty. Jim saw the red dust of bullets strike here, there, everywhere in that crack on the rim. And before that dust settled Jim emulated Smoky's feat.

"Mebbe thet'll hold the sucker fer a spell," muttered Smoky, as he reloaded.

But it increased the ricocheting of the bullets, to the growing embarrassment of the besieged.

"I'm goin' up in thet hole," declared Mac, furiously, after another leaden missile had chased him around the cave.

"Mac, it ain't any safer up there," warned Smoky.

"All I'm lookin' fer is to kill one of them cusses."

He laboriously climbed up out of sight, and presently Jim heard him shooting. No volley answered him, only a single shot. Conditions were changing up on top. Mac fired again, then bellowed down the hole:

"Smoky, I crippled one runnin'."

"Don't cripple nobody, Mac. Kill 'em!" yelled Smoky. "Keep your head down."

Other shots pattered out from the cliff. Jim heard a scuffle above, then the clang of metal on stone. Mac had dropped his rifle. A shock of catastrophe affected Jim, and flattening himself against the wall, he stared at the aperture. A sodden crash did not surprise him. Mac had fallen back into the hole to lodge upon the shelf. His shaggy head hove in sight over the edge. It dripped blood. Then he slid heavily off the shelf to fall like a loaded sack into the bottom of the notch.

An instant later, before either Jim or Smoky could comment on this further diminution of their outfit, another spanging, zipping, spatting ounce of lead entered the cave. It actually struck both walls and the ceiling before it droned away into space.

"Jim, the only safe place from thet—is hyar, huggin' this corner," declared Smoky. "An' there ain't room enough for the two of us."

"Keep it, Smoky. I'm not going to get hit. This is my day. I feel something in my bones, but it's not death."

"Huh! I feel somethin' too—clear to my marrow—an' it's sickish an' cold. . . . Jim, let's both sneak out an' crawl back of them. Thet's my idee. I don't have wrong idees at this stage of a fight."

"Leave that girl here alone? Not much."

"Hell! I clean forgot her," declared Smoky, his hand going up. "I'll go an' you stay. . . . Jim, it'd be a pity to let Heeseman's outfit git her. Why, they'd devour her alive, like a pack of bloody wolves!"

"It would, Smoky, by Heaven!"

"Wal—wal! . . . Hank is goin' to raise hell out there, an' if I do the same on this other side, between us we might stave Heeseman off. But if we don't an' there's no chanct fer you to take thet poor gurl back home——"

"Smoky, you forget."

"Aw! . . . But if you see the fight goin' ag'in' us—Jim, you could kill her. Thet'd be merciful."

"Smoky, I promised her I would," returned Jim.

"Wal, thet's all right. . . . Now! . . . Another glancin' hunk of lead. —— thet sharpshooter. I'm gonna snip off the top of his head. . . . Jim, there's only one thing more thet sticks in my craw."

"And what's that?"

"Hays. I'd never be comfortable in hell if he lived on, crucifyin' thet gurl. . . . I had a sister once. Gawd! it seems long ago! She had gold hair, not so gold as this one, though."

"He sticks in my craw, too, Smoky. And in my throat and brain and blood."

"Wal, then, it jest ain't written thet both of us could croak an' Hays be let live. . . . Jim, I reckon we understand each other."

"Yes. . . . Smoky, I'd have liked you as a pard, under happier circumstances."

"Wal, it's too late, 'cause we can't both git out of this mess. But I'm sayin' you shore air a man after my heart."

That was the last he spoke to Jim. Muttering to himself, he laid a huge roll of bills under the belt Hays had deposited on the little shelf of rock. The act needed no explanation. Then he took a swig of whisky from the flask beside Bridges ghastly form. And as he dug into his pack for more shells another spanging, ricocheting compliment from the sharpshooter entered the cave.

Jim wheeled to see if he could return the shot. There was no sign even of smoke. When he glanced back again Smoky had gone. Jim caught one fleeting glimpse of him darting round the corner of the corral, and then he vanished.

Scarcely had he gotten out of sight when Jim thought of the field-glass. Smoky should have taken it. Jim risked going back to his pack to secure it, and had the fun of dodging another bullet.

What had become of Hays? A moment's reflection dissolved Jim's natural return to suspicion of further treachery. No.—When Hays forgot the woman, and under the flaying of Slocum's scorn went out to kill Heeseman, he had swung back to his former self. It was not only a flash back, but a development, perhaps a borrowing from despair. Heeseman's outfit would hear presently from this dethroned chieftain, and to their sorrow.

Jim returned to his safest cover and waited. Sitting against the wall he used the glass to try to locate Smoky across the oval. But birds and rabbits were the only moving objects that fell under his vision. Meanwhile the sharpshooter kept firing regularly, about three shots to the minute. Jim became accustomed to the *whang* of the bullets.

Next he attempted to locate the diligent member of Heeseman's outfit. This man evidently shot from behind the rim, low down, and not even the tip of his rifle could be seen. From his position, however, as calculated by the puffs of smoke, he certainly must be exposed from the west side of that cliff. Jim had a grim feeling that this fighter would not much longer be so comfortable. Before this, Smoky must have passed the danger zone below. He could work up the ravine on the north side, climb a ragged rock slope, go down into the valley beyond the oval, and under cover all the way, get high up somewhere behind those of Heeseman's riders who were still on that west side.

What had become of Hays? Waiting alone amongst these deflecting bullets wore on Jim's mood. He decided to peep out of the hole again, making sure that his impatience would not result in recklessness. To this end he climbed to the shelf, rifle in hand and the glass slung round his neck. There was a great blood patch where Mac had fallen.

He could command every point with the aid of the field-glass, without exposing his head. Through apertures in the brush the glass brought most of that west cliff, at least the highest third of it, clearly and largely under his eye.

The sharpshooter had eased up a bit on wasting ammunition. Jim sought for the owl-shaped piece of rim rock and got it in the center of the circle. Just then, up puffed a wisp of smoke—crack went the rifle, followed by the spanging and pattering in the cave below.

An instant later a far-off shot thrilled Jim. That might be Smoky. Suddenly a dark form staggered up, flinging arms aloft, silhouetted black against the sky. That must be the sharpshooter. Smoky had reached him. Headlong he pitched off the cliff, to plunge sheer into the wash below.

This tragedy heralded war on the cliffs. Dull booms of heavy guns vied with sharper reports, and between, in slow regularity that indicated cool and deadly nerve, cracked the rifle beyond the cliff. Smoky had at least carried out his idea. He was up somewhere, behind cover or in the open, as the exigency of the case afforded, and he was making it hot for the Heeseman gang.

The rattle of rifles fell off, but still what was left was not the scattering, desultory kind. It meant a lessening of man power. One at least for every two shots of Smoky Slocum's! And those on the cliff grew louder, closer, Heeseman's gang, what was left, were backing from that fire out of the west.

Jim swung the glass to the left and swept the cliff, and the rocky approach to it. Suddenly he espied Hays boldly mounting the slope at that end. Bold, yet he lunged from rock to rock, taking advantage of what cover offered. But it appeared that he had not been discovered yet. Those on top were facing the unseen peril to the west.

Jim marveled at the purpose of the robber chief. Certain death, it seemed, awaited him there. But he kept on. Jim, transfixed and thrilling, waited with abated breath. Still another shot from Smoky—the last! But Hays had reached high enough to see over. Leveling the rifle, he took deliberate aim. How menacing and deadly his posture! His shaggy locks stood up. His rigidity was that of resistless and mighty passion. Then he fired.

"Heeseman!" hissed Jim, as sure as if he himself had held that gun.

Hays, working the lever of his rifle, bounded back and aside. Shots boomed. One knocked him to his knees, but he lunged up to fire again. He made for a rock, gained it but it was not high enough to shield him. Again he was hit, or the rifle was, for it broke from his hands. Drawing his two Colts, he leveled them, and as he fired one, then the other, he backed against the last broken section of wall. Jim saw the red dust spatter from the rock above Hays, on each side, and low down. Those opposing him were shooting wild, or from difficult positions, or were retreating. Hays seemingly could not stand there long. He had emptied a gun. One more instant Jim watched, frozen to the glass. What a figure of defiance! From Jim's reluctant heart was wrenched a sullen respect and admiration. At the end, this robber had reverted to the man who had won Smoky and Latimer to extraordinary loyalty. He was grand in his disregard of his life. When he started up that slope he had accepted death. But it had not come.

The shots thinned out, and ceased. Hays was turning to the left, his remaining gun lowered. He was aiming down the slope on the other side. He fired again—then no more. Those who were left of Heeseman's outfit had taken to flight. Hays watched them, strode to the side of the big rock, and kept on watching them.

Soon he turned back with an air of finality and, sheathing one gun, took to reloading the other. It was at this moment that Jim relinquished the field-glass to take up his rifle. With naked eyes through the aperture in the brush he could see Hays finish loading his gun. Then the robber examined the top of his shoulder, where evidently he had been shot. His action, as he folded a scarf to thrust up under his shirt, appeared one of indifference.

This moment, to Jim's avid mind, was the one in which to kill the robber. He drew a bead on Hays' breast. But he could not press the trigger. Lowering the hammer, Jim watched Hays stride up among the rocks to disappear. No doubt he meant to have a look at that enemy whom he had so deliberately shot with the rifle.

A storm was imminent. The sky had darkened, and a rumble of thunder came on the sultry air.

Jim leaped up out of the hole to have a better look. Far beyond the red ridge he discerned men running along the white wash. There were three of them, scattered. A fourth appeared from behind a bank, and he was crippled. He waved frantically to the comrades who had left him to fare for himself. They were headed for the cove where the horses still stood. And their precipitate flight attested to the end of that battle and as surely to the last of Heeseman's outfit.

Jim picked up the field-glass, and slinging it in his elbow, he essayed a descent into the cave. On the shelf he hesitated, and sat a moment locked in thought. A second time he started down, only to halt, straddling the notch. The battle had worked out fatefully and fatally. Would he see Smoky again? Yet nothing had changed the issue. The end was not yet. With his blood surging back to his heart, Jim leaped down to meet the robber chief.

Chapter Fifteen

HAYS was not yet in sight. Thunder was now rolling and booming over the brakes, and gray veils of rain drifted from purple clouds. The storm, black as ink, centered over the peaks of the Henrys. To the west the sun shone from under a gorgeous pageant of white and gold. And over the canyons hung rainbows of vivid and ethereal loveliness.

Between the intervals of mumbling rumble there was an intense quietness, a sultry suspension of air. Even in that moment the beauty of the scene struck Jim as appalling. It seemed unnatural, because death lay about him, bloody and ghastly; and down the arroyo stalked the relentless robber.

Jim strode out. The chief hove in sight. He walked slowly, with an air of intense preoccupation.

Jim deliberated. A survival of the fittest entered into this deliberation, yet there was in Jim a creed born of the frontier. It was what Hank Hays had lived by before he threw everything to the winds for the beauty of a woman. Hays had reverted to it, in the hour of his extremity. He had gone out to bear the brunt of Heeseman's attack and he had expected to die. The fortune of war had favored him. Therefore, it was not Jim's confidence that forbade him to kill Hays at long range. Not even for the girl's sake would Jim force himself to such a deed, however justified by Hays' villainy.

The robber chieftain neared the cave.

"Where's Smoky?" called Jim, his lynx eyes on Hays' right hand.

"Cashed in," boomed Hays, fastening great hollow eyes of pale fire upon Jim. "He had cover. He plugged I don't know how many. But Morley's outfit had throwed in with Heeseman. An' when thet gambler, Stud, broke an' run, Smoky had to head him off. They killed each other."

"Who got away? I saw four men, one crippled."

"Morley an' Montana fer two. I didn't recognize the others. They shore run, throwin' rifles away."

"They were making for their horses, tied half a mile back. Where'll they go, Hays?"

"Fer more men. Morley is most as stubborn as Heeseman. An' once he's seen this roost of ours—he'll want it, an' to wipe out what's left of us."

"Heeseman?"

"Wal, *he* didn't run, Jim. Haw! Haw!—His insides air jest now smokin' in the sun."

The chief strode to the mouth of the cave and stared around. Jim remained at the spot he had selected, to one side, between the robber and Helen's covert.

"Jack an' Mac, too?" he ejaculated, in amaze. "How come? No more of thet outfit sneaked down in hyar."

"Mac stuck his noodle too far out of that hole in the cave. And Happy Jack stopped a glancing bullet. See this rock here. Look at those white spots. Every one made by a bullet. Must have been two dozen or more slugs come hummin' off that rock. They'd hit the walls and glance again."

"I'd know who started thet if I hadn't seen him," said Hays, to himself. "Old Black Dragon Cayon days!"

"Two of us left, Hays," returned Jim, tentatively. The robber had utterly forgotten such a thing as sworn retribution, or else, now that Slocum was not to be reckoned with, he had no fears.

"The storm's travelin' this way," he said, as thunder boomed, and rolled like colossal boulders down the canyons. "Reckon we can hang out hyar one more night."

"Going to bury your dead?" queried Jim, in curt query.

"Wal, we might drag these fellers to the wash thar, an' cave in the bank on them."

"Sand and gravel would wash away."

"What the hell's thet to us? If I do anythin' atall it'll be fer my gurl. Them stiffs airn't a pretty sight."

If Jim Wall needed any galvanizing shock to nerve him to the deed he had resolved upon, that single possessive word was enough.

"I'll bury them later," he said.

"Good. I'm all in. I climbed moren't a mile to get to them fellers." Hays sat down heavily, and ran his right hand inside his shirt to feel of the bulge on his shoulder. Jim saw him wince. Blood had soaked through his shirt.

"You got hit, I see."

"Flesh wound. Nothin' to fuss over this' minnit. An' I've got a crease on my head. Thet hurts like sixty. Half an inch lower an——"

"I'd have been left lord of Robbers' Roost?"

"You shore would, Jim. Lousy with money, an' a gurl to look after. But it jest didn't happen thet way."

"No, it didn't. But it will!"

That cool statement pierced the robber's lethargic mind. Up went his shaggy head and the pale eyes, opaque, like burned-out furnaces, took on a tiny curious gleam. When his hand came slowly down from inside his shirt his fingers were stained red.

"What kind of a crack was thet?" he demanded, puzzled.

"Hays, you forget."

"Oh-ho! Reckon I did. Never thought I'd fergit Smoky's blastin' tongue. May he roast in hell! . . . But, Jim, this wasn't no mix of yours."

"I've made it mine."

"You an' Smoky come to be pards?"

"Yes. But more than that."

"You're sore thet I didn't divvy square?"

"Hays, I take it you double-crossed me same as you did them."

"Uhhuh. Wal, you got me in a corner, I reckon. Thar's only two of us left. I'd be crazy to quarrel. . . . Would a third of my money square me?"

"No."

"It wouldn't? Wal, you air aimin' at a bargain. Say half, then?"

"No."

A tremor ran over the robber's frame. That was a release of swift passion—hot blood that leaped again. But he controlled himself.

"Jim, I don't savvy. What's eatin' you? Half of the money hyar is a fortune fer one man. I did play the hawg. But thet's past."

"I won't make any deals with you."

"Ahuh. Then we've split?"

"Long ago, Hays."

"Air you tryin' to pick a fight with me?"

At this Jim laughed.

" 'Cause if you air, I jest won't fight. I'd be senseless. You an' me can git along. I like you. We'll throw together, hide somewhere awhile, then build up another outfit."

"Hays, you're thick-skulled," retorted Jim, sarcastically. "Must I tell you that you can't bamboozle me."

"Who's tryin' to?" demanded the robber, hotly. "All I'm tryin' is to patch it up."

"It can't be done."

"I'll give you two thirds of the money."

"Hays, I wouldn't take another dollar from you—that you gave willingly."

"No money atall!" ejaculated the chief, bewildered. His mind was groping. Probably his natural keenness had suffered dulling for the hour.

Jim had turned his left side slightly toward Hays, concealing his right hand, which had slipped to his gun butt, with his thumb on the hammer! For Jim then, Hays was as good as dead.

"It'll all be mine, presently," he replied.

"Holdin' me up, huh?" rasped Hays. "Learned to be a shore-enough robber, trainin' with me, huh?"

"Hays, I promised Smoky I'd kill you—which he meant to do if he had lived to come back."

The robber's face grew a dirty white under his thin beard. At last he understood so much, at least. What volumes his stupidity spoke for his absorption! It changed. Jim's posture, his unseen hand, suddenly loomed with tremendous meaning.

"Shore. Thet doesn't surprise me," admitted the robber. "When men's feelin's git raw, as in a time like this, they clash. But I did my share to clear the air. An' if Smoky had come back he'd have seen it different. I could have talked him out of it. . . . Jim, you're shore smart enough to see thet, an' you oughter be honest enough to admit it."

"I dare say you could have won Smoky back. He had a fool worship for you. . . . But you can't talk me out of anything."

"Why, fer Gawd's sake—when I'm givin' you all the best of the deal?"

"Because I want the girl," thundered Jim.

A great astonishment held Hays stricken. Through it realization filtered.

"*Thet!*—Thet was it—all the time!" he gasped.

"All the time, Hank Hays," replied Jim, steadily, and it was the robber's eyes, pale fires no longer, that he watched for thought and will.

Still he saw the violent muscular quivering which slowly diminished to freeze into rigidity. He had struck the right chord. In whatever way possible, Hank Hays loved this woman. However it had begun, the sordid, brutal thing had ended in Hays' worship of the golden-haired sister of Herrick. Jim read this in the extraordinarily betraying eyes; and read more—that it had been Helen the robber had fought for, not his lost caste with his men, not the honor of thieves. It was this that accounted for the infernal blaze of unquenchable hate, of courage that death itself could scarcely have stilled. All this immediately coalesced into the conscious resolve to act and kill!

As the robber sprang up, Jim's first shot took him somewhere in the breast. It whirled him half round. His gun, spouting flame, tore up the gravel at Jim's feet. A terrible wound with its agony, a consciousness of its mortality, added to the overwhelming ferocity of jealous hate, gave the man superhuman physical activity. He whirled bounding the other way so swiftly that Jim's second shot missed him altogether. Hays' gun was booming, but it was also describing the same curves and jerks as his body. Then as passion gave place to desperate need and the gun aligned itself with Jim, Jim's third shot destroyed aim, force, and consciousness.

Hays' demoniac face set woodenly. The gun, with hammer up, dropped to explode. And the robber lodged against the slant of wall, dead, with the awfulness of his mortal passions stamped upon his features.

It was over. Jim breathed. The hand which held his gun was so wet that he thought his blood was flowing. But it was sweat.

"I wish—Smoky could—know," muttered Jim, over a convulsive jaw. He shoved Hays off the wall.

Wiping his face, Jim staggered to the rock and sat down. All the sustained excitement, culminating in such passion as Jim had never known, had weakened him.

Spent and heaving he sat there, his will operating on a whirling mind. It was over—the thing that had had to come. All dead! Loyal and faithless robbers alike. What to do now? The girl! Escape from that hell-hole, soon to be besieged again! He must pack that very hour and ride —ride away with her. His heart swelled. His blood mounted to burn out the cold horrible nausea. To save this woman—this golden-haired, violet-eyed goddess with her wonderful white skin—to ride with her for one day, one hour—Jim Wall would have paid what the robber chief had paid.

"Jim!—Oh, Jim!" came a cry from the back of the cave.

"Helen—it's all—over," he called, hoarsely.

She appeared in the opening. "Gone?" she whispered.

"Yes, gone—and dead."

"I—saw—you. . . . Is *he*—dead?"

"You bet your life," burst out Jim, his breast oppressed.

"Oh, help me out!"

He ran to assist her. She came sliding out, to fall on her knees, clasping Jim with fierce arms. Her head fell against him.

Jim's hands plucked at her arms—caught them. Yet they seemed hands of steel binding his knees to her breast.

"Get up," he ordered, sharply, trying to lift her. But she was more than a dead weight.

"God bless you!—Oh, God bless you!" she cried. The voice was husky, strange, yet carried the richness and contralto melody that had been one of Helen's charms.

"Don't say that!" he exclaimed, aghast.

She loosened her hold and raised her head to look up at him. He saw only her eyes, tearless, strained in overwhelming gratitude.

"Jim! You've saved me," she whispered.

"No—not yet!" he blurted out. "We must hurry out of this."

She arose, still clinging to him. "Forgive me. I am selfish. We can talk some other time. I should have realized you would want to leave here at once. . . . Tell me what to do. I will obey."

Jim stepped back and shook himself.

"You kept me from thinking," he began, ponderingly. "Yes, we must leave here. . . . Put on your riding-clothes. Pack this dress you have on—and all you have. Take your time. We're safe for the present. And don't look out. I've got to bury Hays and the men."

"My spirit wouldn't faint at that," she replied. "I saw you kill the wretch—and I could *help* you bury him."

"I won't need you," replied Jim, constrainedly, and wheeled away, a victim of conflicting tides of emotion. What manner of woman was this? She had blessed him to God! She could not see in him anyone but a savior. Harder to bear—inexplicably sweet and moving—she had clung to him willingly! Madly he rushed to and fro, cursing while he searched the dead robbers, to fling their money and valuables in a pile, cursing while he dragged them to the brink of the wash and toppled them over. He hauled Hays by the hair—gave him a shove into a grave with villains who were better men. Then he carried rocks and rolled them. He performed prodigious feats of strength, and lastly he pushed an avalanche of sand and gravel, a whole section of bank, down to half fill the wash.

He was as wet as a dog coming from the water. And he burned. Yet he felt cold within.

But action had begun to steady Jim, if not compose him. He shoved all the money into his saddle-bag. Next he packed every one of his shells. He might be attacked again, in that hiding-place. Then he selected supplies for two packs and filled them, not forgetting a few utensils. Poor Happy Jack! That fellow would whistle no more. He unrolled his bed, which consisted of three blankets and a tarpaulin.

His next move was to strap blankets and saddles on the two gentlest horses. Those he led back to the cave, and packed them. It was an indication of his state that, though he had always been a poor, slow packer, he now developed into a swift and efficient one. After that he had only to saddle Bay, and the gray horse Helen had ridden there.

Suddenly he thought of Smoky. If he had been alone, or with another man, even a helpless one, he would have taken time to find that strange and faithful robber and have given him decent burial. But he would not leave the girl.

While he stood there, trying to think what else to do, he remembered a sack of grain that Hays had packed from Star Ranch. He found it half full and tied it on the lighter pack. Sight of his rifle started another train of thought. He put it in his saddle sheath.

Huge, scattered raindrops were pattering down on the hot stones and earth. The storm was working toward the northwest, trailing gray veils across the canyons. The tail of it would flood Robbers' Roost and the canyon below would be impassable. Southward sunshine and silver cloud, blue sky and hazed desert, threw the balance on his inclination that way.

He hurried back to the girl, calling, "Are you ready?"

"I've been waiting," she said, and came swiftly out. The rider's costume brought out the rounded grace of her form. She had braided her hair. The sombrero he remembered shaded her face.

"Where is your veil and long coat?" asked Jim, seeing her as on that unforgettable day.

"He burned them," she answered, in a stifled voice.

"Get into this." And he held his slicker for her. It enveloped her, dragged on the ground.

"I'm lost in it."

"We're in for storm. Rainy season due. You must keep dry."

Turning to the gray horse, she mounted. But she nearly fell, owing to the cumbersome coat. Jim saw and sprang quickly to right her. Then his swift hands attacked the too long stirrups.

"How strong you are! I saw you toiling like a giant with those huge stones."

But Jim had no reply for such inconsequential speech. His mind was racing again, yet wild as were his thoughts they could not outstrip his savage joy. She was saved. The endless wait was past. Dependent upon him now! Strong? He could have laughed like a hyena. He could drag down the pillars of the escarpments for her. He could wade through gore. Something vague and new crept into his sense of possession. It edged into his rapture.

His hands, just lately so swift and efficient, fumbled over the task of shortening stirrups, of cinching the saddle. It was because he could not avoid contact with her.

"Ride close beside me where there's room. Just ahead where there's not," he directed her.

Jim tied the halters of the two pack-animals to their packs, and started them off. Then he vaulted upon Bay— the first time for many weeks. The horse pranced, but steadied down under an iron hand and heel.

Helen looked back as one fascinated, but Jim bent stern gaze ahead.

"I would destroy this canyon if that were in my power Come," he said.

They rode up out of the oval, driving the pack-horses ahead. The rain was now falling heavily, great spattering drops that kicked up a smell of dust. Over the low wall the trail led up and down, across the hummocks. On the gravel ridge to the west Jim saw a dead man lying prone. Soon they entered the wide, shallow wash, in the sand of which Jim espied footprints filling with water. Behind, the lightning ripped and the thunder crashed. They rode out of the tail of the storm and into a widening of the wash, where it reached proportions of a small valley. Scrub cedar and brush and cactus began to show, and patches of sunflowers on low, sandy knolls. They passed the cove where the raiders' horses had been left. Broad and deep was the trail to the south.

"Are you all right?" Jim queried.

"Oh, I did not know I could feel rapture again. Yes, I am."

"You're dizzy, just the same. You sway in the saddle. Ride closer to me, while you can. . . . Give me your hand. Don't talk. But look—look! You might see what I do not see."

They rode at length to a canyon head, down which the hoof tracks turned.

"We came this way by night, but I remember," she said. "Do you dare to follow them?"

"We must not."

"But that is the way to Star Ranch!"

"Yes, on the trail of desperate men and across that Dirty Devil River. These summer rains. It will be in flood. I could not get you through."

"You know best. But just to be free. . . . To see my brother Bernie! It is unbelievable."

Jim Wall looked away across the brakes. Presently he said: "I will try to find a way out of this hole. The country is strange. I'll be lost soon. But somewhere up out

of here—we'll find a lonely canyon where there is grass
and water. I must not run into cattlemen. Robbers are
not my only enemies. I don't want to be hanged for—for
saving you."

"Hanged! Oh, you frighten me!"

"I didn't want to tell you. It is no sure thing that I
can safely elude the rest of Heeseman's outfit, if I try to
get out through the brakes. It'd be far safer to hide you
awhile—south of here, out of the way of riders."

"Take me where you think best," she said, tremulously.

"When you get out, you must go home to England."

"I have no home in England. Bernie is my only kin,
except very distant relatives who hate the name of Herrick."

"Then go to a country as different from this naked,
stony wilderness as day from night. . . . Say, Min-
nesota, where it snows in winter, and in spring there are
flowers, birds, apple blossoms. . . ."

"No, I shall not—leave Utah," she replied, positively.

A flash of joy leaped up in Jim at her words, but he
had no answer for her. He led on, away from that broad
fresh trail, into an unknown region. And it seemed that
this point of severance had an inscrutable parallel in the
tumult within his heart.

The sun set in an overshadowed sky and storm threatened all around the horizon. Far north the thunder rolled,
and to the south faint mutterings arose. Jim could not
hold to a straight coarse. He wandered where the lay
of the land permitted. Rising white and red ground,
with the mounds of rock falling, and green swales between, appeared endless and forlorn. He began to look
for a place to camp.

At last, as twilight darkened the distant washes, and
appeared creeping up out of them, Jim came to another
little valley where scant grass grew, and dead cedars

stood up spectral ghosts of drought, and on the west side a low caverned ridge offered shelter. He led over to this, and dismounting, said they would camp there. Her reply was a stifled gasp, and essaying to get out of her saddle she fell into his arms.

Chapter Sixteen

TO JIM WALL it seemed a miracle that he did not snatch Helen to his breast. Like a wind-driven prairie fire his blood raced. But it was her unexpected little laugh, her dependence upon his strength, her relaxing to his clasp, that compelled his restraint. He set her upright on the ground.

"Can you stand?" he inquired.

"I think so. But my legs feel dead."

"Then you'd better walk a little."

She essayed to, and letting go of him, plainly betrayed her spent condition. Jim helped her into the shallow hollow under the rock and sat her down with shoulders and head raised against the slant of wall.

"My spirit is willing but my flesh is weak," she said.

"You did wonderfully. It was a hard ride, after a tough day," he replied. "I'm afraid I did not have thought enough for you. . . . Rest here while I unpack. Then I'll soon make you comfortable."

Jim flew at the task, his rush of physical action a counter-irritant to his agitations. In the quarter-hour before dusk he had unpacked, hobbled and fed the horses, built a fire and put water on to boil. He had brought three canteens full of water and one canvas bag. Rainstorms, he reflected, would be good for the horses and bad for travel. He would take any chance before attempting to cross the Dirty Devil. Through his mind ran recollection of Hays one night telling about a marvelously fertile valley far up this river—a place once cultivated by Mormons, and then deserted. Jim would find that valley if he could.

He carried his bed under the shelf and unrolled it, changed and doubled the blankets and folded the tarpaulin so that it could be pulled up in case rain beat in. That was likely to happen, for the rumble of thunder had grown closer and the cavern was not deep enough for shelter, unless the storm came from behind.

The fire sent a ruddy light into the cavern, and all at once Jim discovered that the girl was watching him with wide, dark, unnaturally bright eyes. In that deceiving light the ravages of the past weeks did not show so plainly in her face. It seemed to have an unearthly beauty.

"Are you able to get up and walk a little?" he asked. "And you must eat and drink, too, or we'll never escape "

"I'll try."

He helped her up, and out of the cumbersome slicker, and led her a few steps, after which she managed it alone.

"Fine! You've got spunk, Helen. Now you walk up and down while I cook supper."

"Are we safe here?"

"God only knows! I think so—I hope so. It's a lonely desert. Our enemies have gone the other way. Don't worry. They're more scared of us than we are of them. But Morley got away with at least one of his men. The others belonged to Heeseman's outfit. They know they nearly wiped out Hays, and they'll try again with reinforcements. They knew Hays had a fortune in cash—and *you*."

"Morley? . . . I remember the name, but not the connection. Hays was always telling me stories of love— what *he* called love—and hate, revenge, death. . . . Would this Morley try to capture me to hold for ransom, too?"

"Helen, that ransom idea of Hays' began in sincerity, but—lonely, hunted men in this hard country are wild dogs," ended Jim, gloomily.

He did not look up from his tasks, and she passed on with her light, dragging step. Rain had begun to fall, sputtering on the hot coals and the iron oven. He did not need to bake biscuits, for he had packed a sackful, a few of which he warmed. With these, and fresh meat, sugar and coffee, and canned fruit he felt that they fared well. Now and again he was aware of her passing, but he never looked around at her. No matter where they camped or what the peril was, she must be free to come and go at will. But he would caution her that because he was a fugitive, so was she. At last he called her, only to discover that she sat behind him, watching.

To his concern and discomfiture, she ate very little. She tried, only to fail. But she did drink her coffee.

"That is more than I've had for long," she said. "Perhaps if I wasn't so excited I'd have more appetite."

"You'll pick up," he replied, hopefully. "Sleep, though, is more necessary than food."

"Sleep!—Oh, when have I really slept? . . . But now it will be different."

Jim stared thoughtfully into the camp fire. Paling, flowing opalescent embers hissed when the raindrops fell upon them. He must remember to collect dry wood and put it under shelter for the night, and see that the horses did not stray.

"Jim, I can't pull off my boots," she said. "Please help me."

"Better sleep in them, as I shall in mine."

"But my feet hurt so. I'm afraid they are swollen."

She was sitting on the bed when Jim took hold of the boot she elevated. It did not come off easily. The other one, however, was not hard to remove.

"There are holes in your stockings," he observed. "Have you another pair?"

"One other. . . . My feet are so sore. They burn. What a luxury a bath would be! The few I've had were stolen. Hays would fetch me hot water, and then sneak around to watch me, so that it was always cold before I could use it."

"Shut up about Hays, please," replied Jim, sharply.

"I'm sorry. But he has so hung over my days and nights, like the weight of a mountain," she murmured in explanation, startled by his abruptness.

"Look to see if you have any blisters," he said. "I'll bathe your feet in a little cold water and salt."

"Cold water? And have ice blocks for feet all night?"

"I have a stone heating for you. I'll wrap it in a sack. That will keep you warm."

Bringing a pan of water, he knelt before her; and to look at her then was to find the past destroying weeks hard to believe.

"I never had any gentlemen bathe my feet," she said, with a flash of humor which Jim was almost too perturbed to notice.

"Don't stand on ceremony, Helen. Stick out your foot. . . . My dear woman, this is purely kindness on my part. I really don't want to do it."

"You've changed somehow since Star Ranch," she mused. "Very well, thank you." And she put out her small feet.

Jim lost no time in pressing them down into the cold, salt water, which made her cry out, and what he lacked in gentleness he made up for in effectiveness. And he had to use his scarf to dry them because he had no towel and hers was in her bundle. Then he rubbed her feet until they were red, during which operation she did not exactly squeal, though she emitted sounds which were similar.

"Put your stockings back on and sleep in your clothes," he said.

"I could scarcely do anything else, Mr. Jim. . . . Tell me, did you ever have a wife?"

"My God, no!" ejaculated Jim, hastily.

"Or sweetheart?"

Jim dropped his head. "Not really—not one I could speak of to you. . . . Long ago, before I became a thief ——"

"Nonsense! You're not a thief. I asked you because you did that in such a—a detached manner. I once had pretty feet, if I remember rightly. But you did not notice them. Oh, how silly of me! . . . Jim, I can't help talking. My tongue appears to be freed!"

"Talk all you want, but no more tonight. We'll have a tough day tomorrow. . . . Wait before you crawl in— I'll bring the stone."

He kicked the round rock out of the fire, and wrapping it in burlap, he laid it under her blankets. "Push that down."

"Ooooo!" She stretched out with a slow, final movement, and pulled the blankets up under her chin. Her eyes were purple pools, unfathomable with emotion and thought.

"Go to sleep," he said, gazing down at her, conscious that these involuntary words were not what he thought he wanted to say. "I can't swear we're safe or that I'll get you out alive. But if we're caught I'll kill you before they do me."

"In any case you are my savior. I grew hopeless back there. I could pray no more. But I shall tonight. God has —not—forsaken—me."

And it appeared that almost instantly she fell asleep with the flickering firelight upon her face, and her white hands clasped over the edge of the blankets.

Much of Jim Wall's life, since he was sixteen, had been spent in the open around camp fires. But there had never been any night comparable to this. He could not understand the oppression upon his heart. His moods changed in a trice.

He walked out to find the horses close to camp and making out fairly well on the grass. Rain was falling steadily now, though not copiously. No stars showed. Far off down the desert fitful flares of lightning ran across the horizon, revealing black, weird buttes and long, level escarpments. In the south thunder still rumbled. Probably tomorrow the storm would set in. The place appeared more desolate than the roost because there rustling leaves and tinkling water seemed to break the solitude, while here there was nothing. Even the rain fell silently.

Jim gathered a quantity of dead cedar wood which he stowed away to keep dry. Then he unrolled the bed he had brought for himself. This one had belonged to Smoky. Jim thought of the implacable little gunman, lionhearted, going out to save his comrades because he felt that he alone could do it. Lying stark and stiff now, out on the naked rock, with the rain beating down upon his face! That was his creed toward men. His creed toward women could not have been very different.

Jim paced to and fro, unmindful of the misty rain. He put another billet upon the fire and some bits of dry brush. The flame licked up through the twigs and brightened the shadow, and appeared to cast a halo round the girl's white face. But that was the gold sheen of her hair. Softly Jim took a step or two closer, to peer down. Deep in slumber as any child! Strangely his mother's face stood out of the dim years—as she had looked when she lay dead. Fugitive from the law, he had risked liberty to see her once more. A sad and heart-broken face it was, yet not as this sleeping girl's, helpless in his power, trusting him as she would have trusted her brother.

He patrolled his beat between the flickering fire and the sleeping girl, up and down from shadow to shadow, bowed, plodding heedless of the rain, sleepless for hours, on guard, almost as ruthless to himself as he would have been to maurauders of the night. And after that when he slept it was with one eye open.

Toward dawn he got up and rolled his bed. The air was raw and cold, blowing a fine rain in his face. It was still too early to begin preparations for breakfast and too dark to look up the horses. So he strode again the beat of the preceding hours, which seemed farther back in the past than one night.

Two days' travel, sixty miles, without delay, ought to take them out of the brakes. Would the girl be able to make it? He had to choose between a serious break-down for her and the possibility of being held up in the brakes by the rainy season. His decision was instant. He would carry her in his arms, if she gave out, but if the floods came, their predicament would be deplorable. All this region, except the rock, when it got thoroughly wet, became what the riders called gumbo mud. And the overdue rains appeared about to burst upon them.

Under the cliff the deep shadows grew gray as dawn approached. As soon as it was light enough to see, Jim looked at Helen. She lay exactly as she had fallen asleep ten hours before; even her hands had not come unclasped. Her face made a pale blotch against the dark blanket. She might be dead. A pang rent him. Bending low, he listened, to be rewarded by the sound of soft breathing. Then he sprang erect, conscious that former emotions stirred. Must he have them to fight every day?

Jim hurried out to find the horses. It was a sodden, wet world, overhung by clouds as gray as the shrouded ridges and dismal flats. The horses had strayed and he felt alarmed. Still, he could track them by daylight. Leaving Helen alone, however, small as the risk was, he hated to consider. As luck would have it, he came upon all four animals grazing in another little valley. Taking off their rope hobbles, he drove them back to camp, an easy task

with horses that had been fed grain the night before
He had four square pieces of canvas upon which he
spilled a quart of grain for each horse. Then he strapped
on the pack-saddles. The riding-saddles, however, he left
for the last task.

By the time breakfast was cooking daylight had broken.
The rain had ceased. There were breaks in the gray
canopy of cloud, but no blue showed. The air seemed to
be pregnant with storm. Finding a thin, flat rock, Jim
placed Helen's breakfast upon it and carried it to her
bedside. Then he called her. No answer! A second call
did not pierce her deep slumber; whereupon he had to
give her a little shake. At that her eyes opened. Jim re-
coiled from the purple depths. She had awakened as on
mornings past. Then as he knelt there came a transformation in her gaze, which, when he realized the absolute
reversal in it, flayed him more bitterly than had the other.
No help for him! He seemed at the mercy of uncontrol-
lable vagaries of feeling.

"You were hard to awaken," he said. "I've brought
some food and strong coffee. You must get it down somehow."

"I heard you call. I felt your hand. I thought—" She
broke off and struggled to sit up. "I'll eat if it tastes like
sawdust."

Jim repaired to his own breakfast, after which he
wrapped up biscuits and meat to take on the day's ride.

"Did you steal my boots, Mr. Robber?" she called.

He made haste to get them from the fire, where he
had placed them to dry.

"I am more of a robber than you think," he replied.

"You've dried them. Thank you. . . . Play your
strange part, Jim Wall, but I know what I know. . . .
Oh, I'm so stiff and sore! My bones! But I'll do or die."

She pulled on her boots, and crawling out and straightening up with slow, painful effort she asked for a little hot water. Jim fetched it, and also the bundle that contained her things.

Free then to pack, Jim applied himself with swift, methodical hands, his mind at once both busy and absent. At length all was ready except her bundle, which he turned to get. He saw her coming along the shelving wall, walking slowly, her hat shading her features.

"I did better this morning," she said, presently, as she reached him.

"Let's see if you can get on your horse," he replied, and led the gray up. "You can put on the slicker after you're up."

She did mount unassisted. Jim helped her into the long slicker, and tucked the ends round her boots.

"It'll be a tough day," he went on. "But we're starting dry and if you don't fall off in a puddle you'll stay dry. Hang on as long as you can. Then I'll pack you, if necessary. We absolutely must get out of these brakes."

With that he tied her canvas bundle back of his saddle, and donning the slicker that had been Smoky's he lined up the pack-animals, and they were off.

Beyond the ridge the country looked the same as it had to the rear—hummocks of rotting shale, ridges of brush and gravel, swales and flats and little valleys on each side, with the difference that they enlarged to the west and to the east they roughened up into the dark red, irregularly streaked brakes. Jim traveled as best he could, keeping to no single direction, though the trend was northerly, and following ground that appeared passable. The pack-horses led, and one of them scented water or knew where he was going, possibilities not lost upon Jim. He followed them, and Helen brought up the rear. Watching her at first, Jim lost something of his anxiety. For the present she would not retard their progress.

It began to rain and that did not cause Jim to spare the girl. They had to travel as fast as the pack-horses could walk on rough ground and trot where possible. Jim could not see more than half a mile to the fore. Dim mounds stood up in that cloud that overhung the whole country. Jim conceived the idea he was swinging to the west, but for the time being could not make sure.

The rain fell all morning, and let up at intervals. Again the clouds broke their solid, dull phalanx, to let light through. Once a rift of blue sky showed far ahead, with sunlight gilding a very tall, strangely tipped butte. Jim marveled at this, and believed it was one he had seen from the high slope under the Henry Mountains, a hundred miles and more to the southward.

Shortly after this, black clouds gathered, and a storm, with thunder and lightning, burst upon them. The thirsty horses soon had opportunity to drink. Water ran in sheets off the rocks, where Jim, without dismounting, filled the empty canteens.

Soon down every gully and wash rushed a muddy torrent. The lead pack-horse knew his business and earned Jim's respect. Jim was sure now that he had traveled this way before. The rain slackened, but the floods increased. At length the fugitives came to a veritable river at which the lead horse balked. Bay, however, did not show any qualms. The flood was fifty yards across, evidently a shallow gully, down which rocks bumped and rumbled in the current. All about was desolation. No shelter or wood or grass could Jim see. So he put Bay to the task. The big horse made it easily, with water coming up to his flanks. Whereupon Jim rode him back, after which, the pack-horses, intelligent and sensible, essayed the ford. The one with the heavier load was all but swept away. Luckily, he kept his feet, and lunged out in a great splash, snorting his terror.

Then Jim returned for Helen.

"I'll carry you while you hang on to your bridle," said Jim, riding close to the gray. "Slip your feet free and come on." He had to lift her sheer off her horse and around in front of him, where he upheld her with his left arm. "Here's your bridle. Hang on. . . . Get up, Bay, you old water-dog."

They made it, with the splendid horse staggering out under his double burden just in the nick of time. A perceptible rise in the flood, like a wave, swelled by them. He let Helen down.

"Look at that!" exclaimed Jim. "See the water come up? If we'd been in the middle then it'd been good-by."

"To what?"

"I don't know. All that's ahead. Hear the water roaring below, where it drops into a gulch? . . . I tell you luck is with us."

"God and luck," she corrected.

"Are you afraid?" asked Jim.

"Not in the least. Under happier circumstances this would be an adventure. . . . I must move about a little. My legs are gone. And I have a terrible pain in my side."

"You are doing fine. We have come eighteen or twenty miles. But I don't like the look ahead. We're climbing all the time. I think I hear the Dirty Devil."

"That dull, distant rumble? . . . If we had gone down the way he—the way we came—we'd surely have been lost. Could those men have made it?"

"No. They might be marooned on some high bank, or they might have turned back. In which case they would see our tracks."

"Would they follow us?"

"I don't know. Not soon. But we can't afford to waste any time."

"We will get out safely. I feel it. Please help me up."

When once more they were on the way Jim gave her a biscuit and a strip of meat. "Eat. The rain will be on us soon."

And it was, a deluge that obliterated objects at a few paces. The lead pack-horse did not show himself at fault. He had indeed been along there. Jim saw evidences of an old trail and this encouraged him. It must lead somewhere. That storm passed, leaving a drizzle in its wake. Wide pools stood on the flats and cataracts leaped off the rocks. But the washes were shallow.

Late in the afternoon there was a momentary brightening of massed clouds in the west. Dull red and purple gloomed over the dun hills.

They rode down out of these low gravel hills that had limited their sight, into a long, green, winding valley from the far side of which came a sullen roar. A red river, surely the Dirty Devil, ran, ridged and frothy under a steep wall of earth. As Jim looked an undermined section went sliding down with hollow crash.

The remnant of a trail hugged the base of the hills. The valley seemed a forbidding portal to even a harsher country.

"I can't hang on—longer," faltered Helen, faintly.

"I'll carry you. Why didn't you tell me sooner?" reproved Jim. He knotted her reins and dropped the loop over the pommel of her saddle. Then he lifted her off her horse onto his. She fitted in the narrow space in front of him, and he supported her with his left arm. "Come on, Gray."

So Jim rode on, aware that her collapse and the terrible nature of the desert, and another storm at hand, were wearing away even his indomitable spirit. It might well be that he was riding into a trap—on and on up this infernal river to where it boxed in a canyon or widened into a morass of quicksand, either of which would be impassable

If he had to turn back where would it be to? There were foes behind, and anyway Robbers' Roost was unthinkable as a refuge. Still he had faith in that lead pack-horse. They plodded on, and the rain beat in his face. He turned Helen on her side so that her back was toward the storm, and though he spoke she did not answer.

When he weathered that storm he had traveled some miles and was approaching the head of the valley. Ragged, red bluffs stood up all along his right, with acres of loose rock ready to slide. The base of these narrowed to a bank of earth, cut straight down on the outside, which fronted on a muddy flat now reduced to a width of scarcely a hundred yards by the river.

The lead pack-horse kept plodding away, apparently not sharing Jim's growing apprehension about the abrupt turn under a huge beetling bluff. The Dirty Devil, however, swung away to the left again and could be seen sliding round a wall miles farther on. Night was not far away, being hastened by a sinister black storm.

They swung in behind the bluff, and then out again to the higher and narrower bank upon which the old trail passed around the corner. But for this lead animal Jim would never have attempted that. He knew when a horse was lost or indifferent. This horse headed for some place with which he was familiar. He disappeared around the corner where the bank was scarcely ten feet wide, slippery and wet, with streams running down from the bluff above and rocks rolling. The second pack-horse, sure of the leader, rounded the point.

"Whoa, Bay," called Jim, hauling up to wait for the gray. "I don't like this place. Don't look, Helen."

As she made no reply, Jim leaned back to get a glimpse of her face. Asleep! If he had marveled at many aspects of this adventure, what did sight of her thus do to him?

For one thing it shot him through and through with a fierce something which excluded further vacillation.

"Come on, Gray," he called to the horse behind, and to Bay: "Steady, old fellow. If that narrows round there you want to step sure."

It did narrow. Eight feet, six feet—less! Bits of the steep bank were crumbling away. But the pack-horses had gone round. A strange wrestling, lashing sound struck Jim's ears. Water running somehow! He did not look up from the trail, but he sensed a fearful prospect ahead. It would not be safe to try to turn now. The drop on his left, over which he hung, was fifty feet or more straight down, and below an oozy flat extended outward from it.

Suddenly Jim encountered a still narrower point, scarcely five feet wide. The edge had freshly crumbled. It was crumbling now. Jim heard it slop, despite the growing hollow sound farther on.

Bay stepped carefully, confidently. He knew horses with wide packs had safely passed there. He went on. Jim felt him sink. One hind foot had crushed out a section of earth, letting him down. But with a snort he plunged ahead to wider trail.

Jim's heart had leaped to his throat. His tongue clove to the roof of his mouth. He heard thud of hoofs behind, a heavy, sliddery rumble. Looking back, he saw the gray horse leap from a section of wall, beginning to gap outwards, to solid ground ahead. Next instant six feet of the trail, close up to the bluff, slid down in an avalanche.

"Close shave for us all!" cried Jim, huskily, and looked up to see what more lay ahead.

Right at his feet a red torrent rushed with a wrestling, clashing sound from out a deep-walled gorge of splintered, rocking walls. And the roar that had confounded

Jim came from the leap of a red waterfall from the high rim-wall. Everywhere red water was pouring off the cliffs. Rocks were bounding down the stepped slope right in front of him, to hustle off the bank and plunge below. Slides of gravel, like the screech of pebbles in a tide, were running down.

This was an intersecting canyon, a tributary, a vicious child of the hideous Dirty Devil. It barred Jim's progress. Thirty paces to the fore, on the widest part of the bank, stood the pack-horses. Jim forced his startled gaze to the rear. No rider would ever come or go that way again.

Chapter Seventeen

THE rain had slackened; otherwise Jim could not have seen far in advance. The girl, stirring in his arms, roused him out of his bewilderment.

He rode on to a huge section of cliff wall which had fallen from above and now leaned at an angle over the trail. It appeared to be a safe retreat unless the whole cliff slipped in avalanche, and as this consisted half of stone and half of red earth and gravel the possibility of such catastrophe was not remote.

Jim dismounted carefully with Helen and, stooping as he moved under the leaning rock, he set her down on dry dust.

"Where are we? What's that awful sound?" she asked, and her voice came to him in a whisper.

"We're held up by the storm. . . . Let me get this wet slicker off."

"Is it the end for us?"

He did not answer. Folding the slicker into a pillow, he laid her head back upon it. She seemed hardly able to sit up without his support. He tried to avoid her eyes, but was not wholly successful. Scrambling up, he removed the saddle from Bay and dropped it under the shelter. Then, leading the horse, he stepped forward to where the gray and the pack-animals had halted. The clatter of rocks, the screech of gravel, the thresh of strange waves in the torrent below, and the roar of the waterfall made an increasing din. If it rained any more this gorge would be a hell-hole compared with which any place on the trail back would seem paradise. But Jim did not waste time to look around.

The instinct of the horses had guided them to halt behind the only safe spot on the unsafe bank, and this was where several immense boulders had lodged at the widest part. The horses were tired, but not appreciably frightened. Jim removed their packs, leaving the saddles on. He had tied the sack holding the pieces of canvas and the grain so that he might get at it quickly. Without hesitation he poured out all of the grain, about two quarts for each horse. Lastly he jammed the packs under the edge of the boulders, and left the horses free to take care of themselves.

Then he took stock of his surroundings and conditions. A sinister red twilight invested the gorge. It was about a hundred yards wide, with the opposite wall low, and consisted of detached blocks and slides of rock on a background of red earth. Innumerable little streams were twisting, meandering, pouring from the walls. About one hundred and fifty yards up, the gorge turned to the left. Here the waterfall leaped off from a crack in the high cliff and shot far out to roar down in the rocks. Already it was appreciably fuller. Most fearful, however, was the gigantic slope to the left, of which Jim now had his first clear view. It was very high and rugged, and sloped so far back that he could not see the top. Streams above were pouring together into a main torrent, the outlet of which he could not place, though he believed he heard it. This slope was veritably a mountain-side, unstable and treacherous as quicksand. Everywhere there was motion, not only of water, but gravel, mud, and small rocks of all sizes. In past storms thousands of tons of rock had piled off that slope, most of which jumble had been covered with earth and which formed the bank upon which he stood. This was fifty feet wide at its widest, and several hundred feet long, and the upper end sloped down to the bed of the gully, where evidently the old trail ran. Lastly, this short gorge opened out into the valley of the Dirty Devil, whence came a roar heavy enough to be heard above the nearer din.

Above this infernal trap a murky sky, partaking of the red hue that dominated the unstable earth, presaged more storm. Low down over the gorge rims, black clouds showed tiny threads of zigzag lightning. But if thunder accompanied them Jim could not hear it. He had a growing thunder near at hand.

"If that storm breaks over the head of this gorge we're lost," soliloquized Jim, in dark solemnity. Had he endured the past weeks, had he made his desperate stand against the raiders and then Hays, had he saved the girl —only to have her drowned or crushed by rock or swallowed by avalanche? But for what had he endured— fought—saved? The very elements had combined to defeat him. Gloomy, weighed down by inscrutable events, he hurried back to the shelving rock.

He dreaded the coming hours—the night—the—he knew not what. But whatever time intervened between now and death or deliverance would be dreadful to live. He felt that.

Jim removed his slicker and folded it into a long pad. He was dry, except for his feet. As he crept closer the girl stirred again and spoke. He thought she asked if he were there. Many weary nights Jim had sat up to watch or wait, and he knew what it meant. He placed the slicker in the best available place and covered that with the drier of the two saddle blankets. He pulled the saddle closer. Then he lifted the girl over his lap so that her legs fitted across the saddle. With the dry blanket he covered her. Then he leaned back against the stone with her head on his shoulder and his arm supporting her. The sombrero he had removed. It was not only that he wanted to keep her dry and warm: he had to have her in his arms while he waited for the nameless terror he anticipated.

In the fast darkening gloom he could see her wide eyes, black as holes in white parchment. Her lips moved.

"I can't hear you," he answered, bending low.

"You are afraid?"

"Yes, I guess it's that."

"For me?"

"Certainly not for myself."

"What really has happened?"

"I followed an old trail. The country is new to me. And so we've gotten stuck in a terrible place. We can't go on or back. You hear the flood—the slides—the rocks . . . And there's a heavy storm about to break."

"You fear we've little hope?"

"One chance in a thousand."

She was silent a moment, then she raised her head so that she could speak close to his ear. He thought he felt a light hand touch his shoulder.

"For myself I'm not afraid. . . . But for you I am. You brave—splendid man! . . . To fight as you did for me—indeed you must have loved me. At Star Ranch I did not believe. . . . God bless you. You did—your best. I'll—pray—for you—with my last—breath."

Suddenly the earth under Jim trembled and a terrific boom momentarily drowned the other sounds. An avalanche or a falling rock! But this he had expected. It added not a tithe to his terror. That was not physical.

Staring out into the gathering darkness, he pondered this thing. It had come from her last words. She had no fear at the prospect of death. A curling flame might have licked at the heart of Jim's manhood. Brave and splendid she had called him. Craven and ignoble he called his past. It was what Helen Herrick had said that had wrought this transformation in his feelings—this swelling, flaying reproach, this hate of that which allied him with the robber who had carried her off. Of course he had loved her, though he had not dwelt often or thoughtfully upon that. Up until now love in his crude opinion had been the hunger, the need of a woman, without regard to her mind, her heart, her spirit. But that was not what she had meant. . . . And again she besought God to bless him—and she would pray for him with her last breath.

A hard pang clutched Jim's breast. It numbed his throat. And for the moment his mind became chaotic. Let that last breath of hers mingle with his last breath, drowned in that thrashing torrent or smothered under tons of crushing rock and earth. . . . It would have been nothing to die for her—that he had risked—but to die with her, to have her locked in his arms—that would be great. . . . What had he ever done with his life that he should want to prolong it? . . . A ne'er-do-well, a failure, a rolling stone, a robber, a killer! Could he pray to save it now, to go on being the same kind of hard, wicked, useless man? No, by the God she whispered of —he could not. He would not. . . . And now that she lay helpless, trusting, dependent upon him, the truth of his monstrous past roared in his inward ear mightier than the storm and flood.

He relaxed his stiff frame against the wall. A shudder-ing spell or a demon of spirit seemed wrenched out of him and flung to the night. This free and wild life had been part of him, and the whole savageness of it seemed to have cumulated in the fury of the elements, to cast his sin out, to change his whole life was yet left to feel, to understand, to grovel in repentance.

The God she called upon and the Nature he knew had conspired to defeat him. The former he could only tremble before as One unfamiliar, never recognized until now when it was too late. But Nature he had lived with and now he welcomed her furies.

Thunder buried all the other earthly sounds and a red

flare of lightning showed the appallingly black sky and the ghastly gorge. The heavens above appeared to burst and a deluge descended upon that place, so that no sound pierced the continuous, beating roar of rain.

Jim Wall gathered Helen up in his arms and drew her breast to his. He felt her warmth. But she was unconscious or so deep in slumber that she could not awaken. Now let the very firmament fall upon them! Two lost humans, inexplicably hounded into this desert, where fire and water and earth were hollowing a grave for them! The terror that Helen's acknowledgment of his heroism and his love had roused, abode within him still, but was losing itself in the defiance he threw into the teeth of this cataclysm.

This was the climax of the storm that had been gathering for days. Out upon the level desert it would have been serious for travelers; here in this gorge it was a maelstrom. Jim did not expect to live to hear it pass away. Yet he did. And then began the aftermath of a flood let loose upon such unstable earth. The waterfall gradually rose to a thundering, continuous crash. It dominated for a while, until the thousand streams from above poured over the rims to deaden all, to completely deafen Jim.

A sheet of water, sliding over the rock, hid the opaque blackness from Jim's eyes. Any moment now a flood would rise over the bank, and when it did Jim meant to climb higher with the girl, to front the hurtling rocks and slipping slides, and fight till the bitter end.

But many changes as the hours brought, that flood did not rise above the bank. Jim saw the sheet of water fail, and the black space of gorge again. He heard the avalanches and the great single boulders come down, and the furious back-lash of the torrent below, and the lessening roar of the waterfall. The time came to Jim, as if he dreamed, when all sounds changed, lessened, faded away, except the peculiar threshing of the stream below. And he got to listening for that sound, which occurred only occasionally. For a while the sliding rush of heavy water swept on, suddenly to change into a furious contention. At length Jim calculated it was a strong current laden with sand, which at times caused billows to rise and lash their twisting tips back upon themselves. Long he heard these slowly diminishing, gradually separating sounds.

The streams ceased flowing, the slides ceased slipping, the rocks ceased rolling, and the waterfall failed from a thundering to a hollow roar and from that to a softening splash. Nature had audited so much for that storm, and still the mountain-side appeared intact with its fugitive atoms of flesh and spirit.

Jim imagined he saw dim stars out in a void that seemed to change from black to gray. Was dawn at hand? Had they been spared? The gurgle of the stream below merged into the distant, low rumble of the Dirty Devil. Jim rested there, staring out at the spectral forms on the opposite wall, thinking thoughts never before inhabitants of his confounded brain.

But the sky was graying, the gorge taking shape in the gloom, and this place which had heard a concatenated din of hideous sounds was silent as a grave.

At last Jim had to accept a marvelous phenomenon— dawn was at hand. Gently he slipped Helen into the hollow of the saddle. She was still asleep. His cramped limbs buckled under him and excruciating pains shot through his bones and muscles.

In the gray light objects were discernible. He could not see to the head of the gorge, where the waterfall had plunged out from the wall. But silence meant that it had been surface water, a product of the storm, and it was gone. Beneath the bank ran a channel of fine-

ribbed sand where not even a puddle showed. On the
bank the horses stood patiently, except Bay, and he was
nosing around for a blade of grass that did not exist on
the sodden earth. The great slope appeared the same
and yet not the same. A mute acceptance of ultimate
destruction hovered over it.

Sunrise found Jim Wall topping a rise of rocky ground
miles beyond the scene of his night vigil. Again he followed the lead pack-horse.

The sky was blue, the sun bright and warm, and on the
moment it crowned with gold the top of the purple butte
Jim had seen twice before. It appeared close now, rearing
a corrugated peak above yellow and brown hills. Jim
was carrying Helen in front of him. Conscious, but too
spent to speak or move, she lay back on his arm and
watched him.

There had been a trail along here once, as was proved
by a depressed line on the gravelly earth. When Jim
surmounted this barren divide he suddenly was confronted by an amazing and marvelous spectacle.

"Blue Valley!" he ejaculated.

Below him opened a narrow, winding valley, green
as emerald with its cottonwoods and willows. Only in the
distance did it shine blue under the hot sun. Through it
the Dirty Devil wound a meandering course, yellow as
a bright ribbon. It was bank full in swirling flood. And
from where it left the valley, which point Jim could not
see, a dull chafing of waters came to his ears.

"Blue Valley! . . . Helen, we're out of the brakes!
. . . Safe! Mormons live here."

She heard him, for she smiled up into his face, glad
for his sake, but in her exhaustion beyond caring for her
own.

There was no sign of habitations, nor any smoke. But

Jim knew this was Blue Valley. It was long, perhaps fifteen miles, and probably the farms were located at the head, where irrigation had been possible. How could even Mormon pioneers utilize that ferocious river?

The startling beauty of this lost valley struck Jim next. It resembled a winding jewel of emerald and amethyst, set down amid barren hills of jasper and porphyry, and variegated mosaics of foothills waving away on the left, and golden racks of carved rocks, and mounds of brown clay and dunes of rusty earth. All these were stark naked, characterized by thousands of little eroded lines from top to bottom. The purple butte to the west dominated this scene, so magnificent in its isolation and its strange conformation, that it dwarfed a yellow mesa looming over the valley.

Jim followed the lead pack-horse down into gumbo mud. The floor of the valley supported a mass of foliage besides the stately cottonwoods. Sunflowers burned a riot of gold against the green. Willows and arrowweed and grass, and star-eyed daisies sprang in luxuriant profusion out of the soil. And at every step a horse hoof sank deep, to come forth with a huge cake of mud.

At midday Jim passed deserted cabins, some on one side of the river, some on the other. They did not appear so old, yet they were not new. Had Blue Valley been abandoned? Jim was convinced it could not be so. But when he espied a deserted church, with vacant eyelike windows, then his heart sank. Helen must have rest, care, food. He was at the end of his resources.

An hour later he toiled past a shack built of logs and stones, and adjoining a dugout, set into the hill. People had lived there once, but long ago. Old boots and children's shoes lying about, the remains of a wagon, a dismantled shovel and a sewing-machine, gave melancholy attestation of the fact that a family had abode there.

Jim's last hope fled. He was still far from the head of the valley, but apparently he had left the zone of habitation behind.

The afternoon waned. The horses plodded on, slower and slower, wearying to exhaustion. Helen was a dead weight. Despair had seized upon him, when he turned a yellow corner between the slope and the cottonwoods, to be confronted by a wide pasture at the end of which a log-cabin nestled among cottonwoods. A column of blue smoke rose lazily against the foliage. And behind this transfiguring sight loomed the purple butte, commanding in its lofty height, somehow vastly more to Jim than a landmark.

The horses labored out of the mud to higher ground. Jim rode up to the cabin. Never in all his life had he been so glad to smell smoke, to see a garden, to hear a dog bark. His ever-quick eye caught sight of a man who had evidently been watching, for he stepped out on the porch, rifle in hand. Jim kept on to the barred gate. There were flowers in the yard and vines on the cabin—proof of feminine hands. And he saw a bed on the porch.

"Hello!" he shouted, as he got off carefully, needing both hands to handle Helen.

"Hullo, yourself!" called the man, who was apparently curious but not unfriendly. Then as Jim let down a bar of the gate with his foot, this resident of Blue Valley leaned his rifle against the wall and called to some one within.

Jim hurried on to the porch and laid Helen on the bed. She was so exhausted that she could not speak, but she smiled at Jim. Her plight was evident. Then Jim straightened up to look at the man. Friend or foe—it made no difference to Jim—because here he would see that Helen received the care and food that she needed. Jim could deal with men. His swift gaze, never so penetrating, fell upon a sturdy individual of middle age—a typical pioneer of the Mormon breed, still-faced and bearded. The instant Jim looked into the blue eyes, mildly curious, he knew that, whoever the man was, he had not heard of the abduction of Herrick's sister.

"Howdy, stranger!"

"My name's Wall," said Jim, in reply, slowly reckoning for words.

"Mine's Tasker. Whar you from?"

"Durango. . . . My—my wife and I got lost. She wasn't strong. She gave out. I'm afraid she's in bad shape."

"She shore looks bad. But the Lord is good. If it's only she's tuckered out."

"What place is this?"

"Blue Valley."

"And where is Blue Valley?"

"Sixty miles from Torrey."

"Torrey? Never heard of it."

"It's a Mormon settlement, friend. Yes, I've stuck it out here, but I'll be givin' up soon. No use tryin' to fight thet Dirty Devil River. Five years ago there was eighty people livin' hyar. Blue Valley has a story, friend ——"

"One I'd be glad to hear," interrupted Jim. "Will you help me? I have money and can pay you."

"Stay an' welcome, friend. An' keep your money. Me an' my womenfolks ask nothin' fer good will toward those in need."

"Thank—you," Jim replied, huskily. "Will you call them to look after my—my wife?"

Helen was staring up at Jim with wondering, troubled eyes.

"Is everything all right?" she asked, faintly.

"Yes, if to find friends an' care is that," replied the Mormon, kindly. Then he stepped to the door to call within. "Mary, this rider was not alone. It was his wife he was carryin'. They got lost in the brakes an' she gave out. We must take them in."

Chapter Eighteen

THAT night, after the good Mormons assured Jim that Helen was just worn out and she had smiled a wistful guaranty of that, Jim went to sleep under the cottonwoods and never moved for seventeen hours.

When he awoke it seemed to be a transfigured world. The Dirty Devil had ceased its rumble. There was a sunset glory crowning the purple butte—a light that seemed not of the earth. Some day soon Jim promised himself the reward of climbing high where he could see this challenging sentinel that had so guided him. It had done more—what, he could not tell, any more than he understood the thing that had come to him in the fury and thunder of the storm. But he felt almost free of terrible fetters, of a past that had gone.

At supper the Mormon bowed his head and prayed: "O Lord, bless this food to our use. Bless this good stranger within our gates. Heal his wife and send them on their journey rejoicin' in Thy name. Amen."

That night Jim heard the sad story of Blue Valley and the brief conquest of the Dirty Devil. Yet, singularly, this settlement had ever been given a wide berth by the rustlers and robbers of Utah. At least, when strange riders went through, as used to happen in former days, they left only pleasant recollection. The Mormon, accustomed to loneliness and loving men, loosed his tongue; and when Jim went to bed that night he knew where and how to go out of the country.

Helen sat up the second day, white and shaky indeed, but recovering with a promise that augured well. Her eyes hung upon Jim with a mute observance. They haunted him in his walks along the river, under the cottonwoods where the sunflowers followed the sun with their faces, and at night when he watched the stars. He never went

far from the cabin. He had never yet climbed to make
his in memory forever that grand purple butte. Factory
Butte the Mormon called it, and there was where he
dug the coal he burned. It was the coal that gave it the
strange, dark colors. No blade of grass or bit of shrub
grew upon this mountain. It would not sustain life. Even
the eagles shunned it.

Next morning while the women were at work in the
fields and Tasker was away somewhere, Jim approached
Helen on the porch. She sat in a home-made rocking-
chair, and she had marvelously improved, considering
the short space of time. Her hair, once again under care,
shone like burnished gold.

"Well, you look wonderful this morning," he said.
"We must begin to think of getting away from this haven
of rest."

"Oh, I'm able to start," she replied, eagerly.

"We mustn't overdo it. Tomorrow, perhaps. And then,
if we're lucky, in three days you'll be back at Star Ranch.
. . . And I——"

His evident depression, as he broke off, checked her
vivid gladness.

"You will never go back to—to your old life?" she
questioned, quickly.

"No, so help me God! This I owe to you alone, Helen.
It will be possible now for me even to be happy. But
enough of myself. . . . You are gaining daily. Oh, you
have such beauty! . . . But—we are still in the wilds
of Utah, with its strange secret, underground channels.
With its Dirty Devils! . . . I have traded two of the
horses for Tasker's light wagon. I will take you to the
stage line and soon you will be at Grand Junction."

Jim ceased. Her hands slipped from her eyes, to expose
them wide, filmed with tears, through which shone that
which made him flee.

"Wait—please wait!" she called after him as he made with giant strides for the gate. But he did not go back. If she pitied him he did not want to see it.

This time he made for the bluff which he had promised himself he would climb. He had to walk far to cross the deep gully out in the level floor of the valley. And he found the bluff farther away and much higher than it had looked from the ranch. And then what had appeared the top was only a rim of a slope, rising gradually to a rock-studded summit.

At last, hot and wet, with his heart thumping audibly against his ribs, and his breath coming in whistling pants, he surmounted the ridge.

Then he stood transfixed and gasping. The wild brakes, the mysterious canyon country, the illimitable, lilac-hued escarpments, the grand, black-sloped, white-peaked Henry Mountains—these lost incomparably to the scene unrolled before his rapt eyes.

Far out there on a plain rose the butte which had influenced him from afar. But he had seen only its crown. This pyramid towered alone and its effect was staggering. Jim had spent days and weeks in the silence and solitude of the brakes; and now he recognized the top of this butte as the one he had so many times watched with longing, as the loftiest and farthest point from his prison in Robbers' Roost. It had typified not only freedom, but for him the unattainable. His idle, dreaming thoughts, gaining a foothold now and then in the interstices of his plans of blood and capture, had made of this rock thing a goal.

And now not only was it a possession of magnifying vision, but something he had attained symbolically.

From the bluff a gulf yawned at his feet leagues wide in every direction, dominated by this phenomenon of nature in the center. It was a naked plain. Beginning

under him the rust-colored rocks, ragged as a stubble-
field, marched in an endless circle round the margin of
that vast plain. Barren threaded soil and stone, deceiving
to the eye, stretched on and on, for miles and miles, to
the first rise of the base of this incredible butte. Ridged
and traced, the slow upheaval of the mountain burned a
flaming saffron, which merged into blue, and that to
violet, and through all the darker shades, up and up
the swelling slopes, with their millions of tiny irregular
lines of cleavage, to the great wall of purple-black that
crowned the peak.

The creation which had built this stupendous edifice
of isolation and grandeur, flaunting its millions of years,
yet melancholy with the evidence of decay and erosion
that would sometime lay it flat on the plain,—the Nature
or the Omniscience that had made it was responsible for
him, for his unwelcomed birth, his wayward boyhood, his
footsteps that partook of evil, and the maturity that had
seen his moral collapse and his victory. He had looked
upon a physical thing that typified his conception of himself. And the future held the same for both.

But inscrutably, though none the less surely, he felt
that he had arisen out of that whorled and traced rock,
alive, with beating heart, with mind and soul and will,
and in that he was incalculably more. He had risen out
of the depths, he had found love, the greatness of which
might be denied better men.

In the moonlit hour that night, late, when the good
Taskers had gone to well-earned rest, Jim heard his name
called. He ran with swift, noiseless feet to Helen's bedside.

"You did not come back," she whispered. "I cannot
sleep. . . . There is something I—want to say."

He sat down upon the bedside and clasped her hand

in his, to look down into the white face, with its un-fathomable, midnight eyes.

"Is your real name Jim Wall?" she asked, with more composure.

"No. I will tell it, if you wish."

"Are you a free man?"

"Free? What do you mean? Yes, free—of course!"

"You called me your—your wife to these kind people."

"I thought that best. They would be less curious."

"I was not offended—and I understood. . . . I want you to go back to Star Ranch with me."

"You ask me—that!" he exclaimed incredulously.

"Yes, I do."

"But you will be perfectly safe. Some one will drive you from Grand Junction."

"Perhaps. Only I'll never *feel* safe in Utah again—unless you are near. I've had too great a shock, Jim. I suppose one of your Western girls could have stood this adventure. But this was my first rough experience. It was a—a little too much."

"I can never go back to Star Ranch," he replied, gravely.

"Why not? Because you are—you *were* a member of a robber gang? I had an ancestor who was a robber baron. To be a robber is not such a degradation—provided he be great—like you."

"That's not the reason," he said.

"What is it—then?"

"If I leave you now—soon as I've placed you in good hands—I can ride off in peace—go to Arizona, or some-where, and be a cowboy—and be happy in the memory of having served you and loved you—and through that having turned my back on the old life. . . . But if I went back to Star Ranch—to see you every day—to—to ——"

"To ride with me," she interfered, softly.

"Yes—to ride with you," he went on, hoarsely. "That'd be like what you called your rough experience—a little too much. It would be terribly too much. I'm only human."

"Faint heart never won fair lady," she whispered, averting her face and withdrawing her hand. "Jim, I believe if I were you, I'd risk it."

Jim gazed down at the clear-cut profile, at the shadowed eyes, hair silvered in the moonlight; then stricken and mute, he rushed away.

Chapter Nineteen

BEFORE dawn Jim had beaten his vain and exalted consciousness into a conviction that the heaven Helen hinted at for him was the generosity of a woman's heart. She could not yet be wholly herself. He must not take advantage of that. But to reassure her he decided he would conduct her to Star Ranch, careful never to reopen that delicate and impossible subject, and after she was safely there and all was well, he would ride away in the night, letting his silence speak his farewell.

At sunrise Jim acquainted Tasker with his desire to leave for Torrey, provided Helen felt recovered sufficiently.

"Reckon I'd better see you through Capital Wash an' as fur as Torrey," replied the Mormon.

That was relief to Jim. A whole day with its endless scenes and incidents, and the companionship of the Mormon, might make it possible for him to stand by his resolve.

At breakfast, and in the bustle of departure he was sure Helen felt something aloof and strange in him, and he dared not meet her thoughtful eyes.

Soon they were on the way, Helen comfortably settled in the back of the two-seated wagon, and Jim riding beside Tasker in front.

Factory Butte furnished a fascinating hour for Jim, and from that on the scenery lost nothing by its vicinity to this grand monument. The Mormon was talkative and told the story of Blue Valley, and other narratives relative to the region. Capital Wash was a rent through a high ridge of red rock and the road was a stream bed, running free with muddy water. Toward the end, this passage grew to be a splendid canyon.

A Mormon rancher, at whose place Tasker stopped,

invited them to pass the night at his house, and next morning take the road from there to Grand Junction, which could be reached in a long day's drive. Jim accepted both invitation and advice. In the morning Tasker bade them good-by and Godspeed.

"Thank you, Mr. Tasker," replied Helen. "I shall remember your kindness. And I'd like to buy back the two horses Jim traded you."

"I'll fetch them, if you'll tell me where," replied the Mormon.

"Star Ranch, north of Grand Junction."

"I've heerd of thet. Wal, you may expect me some day, though I had taken a likin' to your bay hoss."

Jim drove off in the clear cold air of a mountain autumn morning before the sun had come up.

"Helen, you shouldn't have asked him to fetch the horses," said Jim, reprovingly. "He'll find out I lied."

"Lied! What about?"

"I told Tasker you were my wife."

"Oh, that!" laughed Helen, and turned away a scarlet face. "It can be explained easily—if necessary. . . . Look!—This glorious country! . . . No, I don't ever want to leave it."

Somehow Jim got through that long ride of suspense, fear, and thrills, and when they reached Grand Junction just after dark, it was none too soon for him. Fortunately, he got Helen into the little inn before she was recognized, and then returned to put the tired horses in the care of a stable-boy. Jim did not risk entering store or saloon. Hays had secret friends there. Yet Jim was keen to hear the gossip about Star Ranch. He was late for supper, having taken time to shave and change his shirt.

To his surprise, he found Helen radiant.

"What do you think Bernie has done?"

"Bernie!" ejaculated Jim.

"Yes. My brother. This good woman told me. . . . Jim, you are the richer by ten thousand dollars."

"Richer? . . . Me!"

"Indeed. Bernie offered ten thousand dollars for my safe return."

"I won't take it," replied Jim, darkly.

"I certainly wouldn't, either," she retorted. "It is not the half or quarter what your service was worth."

"You know I wouldn't take a dollar!" flashed Jim.

"Well, What *do* you want, Jim?" she inquired, with a woman's sweet tantalizing mystery. "However, never mind that now. Listen. Bernie raised the very devil. He hired all the riders available to hunt for me. Also he found where Hays sold our cattle, and he forced the buyers to sell back every head, at the price they paid. He threatened to take the case to Salt Lake City."

"That's sure good news. It might have a tendency to end rustling, at least in wholesale bunches. Did you hear how badly your brother was hurt?"

"She did not mention that. Anyway, it couldn't have been much, for Bernie has been here. . . . Aren't you going to eat any supper? Oh, I shall not sleep much to-night. . . . And *what* shall I tell Bernie?"

That query was arresting to Jim and he hastened to direct her mind into other channels, trying to make her feel concerned that they had still fifty miles to cover.

"Jim, I'll never pooh-pooh dough again," she replied, her eyes darkening.

"It's you who is not eating," he reproved. "Better eat and drink. And go to bed soon. We will be leaving before daylight."

Every moment of that ride next day was a joy and a pang. It seemed as short as the preceding one had been, long. Helen was gay, sad, thoughtful, and talkative by turns, but she did not infringe on the one subject that crucified Jim.

It chanced that as they surmounted the Pass that led down into Star Ranch Valley, the sun was setting out of a glorious cloud-pageant over Wild Horse Mesa and the canyon brakes of the Dirty Devil. Jim judged of its beauty and profundity by the sudden silence it enjoined upon his companion. She never spoke another word until Jim halted the team in front of the ranch-house porch. "*Home!*" she whispered, as if she had never expected to see it again.

At Jim's halloa Herrick came out on the porch. "By Jove! here you are!" was his greeting, as cool and un- emotional as if they were returning from a day's visit to the village.

"Yes, Bernie, here I am—thanks to my gentleman escort," replied Helen.

Jim helped her out, while some cowboys came running, shouting to others below.

"I'll take the team down," Jim said, hurriedly.

"You come in," returned Herrick, as he gripped Jim's hand and gave him a searching glance. He kissed Helen and led her in, with his arm around her. Jim purposely lingered at the task of collecting Helen's worn and muddy luggage, and carried them in. Brother and sister stood with arms locked, and their gaze was hard to meet.

"Jim, you will have supper with us," she said. "I'll leave you and Bernie. . . . Oh, what will a tub and a change feel like!"

She gathered up her things and ran out of the living- room.

"Jim Wall, you bloody shooting cowboy!" ejaculated Herrick.

"That's not my right name," Jim made haste to reply.

"To hell with that, as you Westerners say. . . . Jim, come have a drink."

Herrick poured out red liquor with a hand that shook. They drank, and the rancher refilled the glasses.

"Helen hadn't time to tell me much," he said. "Hays kidnapped her for ransom. Took her to a hell hole down in the brakes. Robbers' Roost she called it. Held her there captive—and she would have been degraded but for you. They fought among themselves—gambling with my money. Heeseman's crew found them. There was a battle. In the end you killed Hays, and brought Helen back. . . . That's the gist of her story. But I want it in detail."

"I have all the money, almost to a dollar, Herrick," replied Jim.

The Englishman waived that as of little consequence, and urged Jim to a recital of the whole affair. At its conclusion Herrick said, hoarsely:

"Let's have another drink! Let's have two."

"As a rule I don't drink. But this is an exceptional occasion. . . . To your good health, Herrick, and to your sister's happiness and well-being in Utah!"

Presently Herrick spoke with something of gravity. "Helen told me that I was to keep you at Star Ranch. I hope you won't let this Hays *débâcle* drive you away."

"It'll be impossible for me to stay," rejoined Jim, briefly. "But thanks for your kindness."

"I'll have you manage the ranch—give you an interest. Anything ——"

"Please don't embarrass me further. I can't stay. . . . It's hard to confess—but I have had the gall, the absurd luck, to fall in love with your sister. I couldn't help it. . . . I want you to know, however, that it has turned me from that old outlaw life. I'll go away and begin life over again."

"By Jove! So that's your trouble. Does Helen know?"

"Yes, I told her. It was after she asked me to come and stay at Star Ranch. Said she would never feel safe again unless I came. So I had to tell her."

"Declare I don't blame her. I'd feel a little safer myself. That devil Hays left his trade-mark on me. Look here. . . . By thunder! Wall, it's a blooming mix. I understand you, and think you're a man to respect and like. Can't we get around the trouble somehow?"

"There is no way, Herrick."

"Helen has her own sweet will about everything. If she wants you to stay, you'll stay, that I can assure you. Is there any honorable reason why you ought not stay— outside of this unfortunate attachment to Helen?"

"I leave you to be judge of that," replied Jim, and briefly related the story of his life.

"Deuced interesting, by Jove! Let's drink to it."

"One more, then," laughed Jim, with a load off his mind. Somehow he had wanted to stand clear and fair in this Englishman's sight.

"Damn me, I like your West. I like you Westerners!" Herrick exploded. "Whatever Helen wants is quite right with me. . . . I can't conceive of her insisting on your staying here—unless there is hope for you."

"My God! That is wild, Herrick. *I* can't conceive of such a thing. It wouldn't be fair to take her seriously— after the horror she's been through—and her intense gratefulness."

"Beyond me!— Let's have another drink."

Long Jim paced to and fro under the rustling pines that night, favoring the shadow because the stars somehow mocked him. Yet a sense of worthiness, almost happiness, abided with him for the first time in many years. Who was he to have had such an opportunity, not only to do good, but to lift himself out of the depths? His gratitude to chance, to life, to whatever had guided him, was intense.

The ordeal was over. It seemed scarcely likely that the Herricks would be subjected to another such raid. Such things as Hank Hays had evolved never happened twice in the same place. Jim felt it incumbent upon him to give Herrick some strong advice about running a ranch. For a moment Jim allowed himself the pleasure of dreaming over what a wonderful and paying ranch he could make it, had circumstances permitted him to accept Herrick's offer.

As for himself and his future, he had a singular optimism. He felt the meanest of labor could never detract from the glory and the dream of the thing that was his. Some men never lived at all; a few lived well or ill; it was given to one here and there to live some extraordinary experience that sufficed for all the remaining years.

The rangeland and the ranch-house were locked in slumber. Jim listened for the old familiar night sounds, but the only one was the song of the pines. That seemed everlasting. Pine needles, like aspen leaves, were never still. At length Jim repaired to the room assigned him by Herrick, and having extended his powers of mind and body to their limit he dropped into heavy slumber.

When he awakened it was with a sense that during his sleep something vital had been decided for him. Star Ranch would see the last of him that day, if he had to walk away.

As he dressed, his thoughts dwelt upon Helen. Probably he would spend most of his waking hours with her in mind, from this day on. But what a beautiful and incomprehensible woman! At supper she had appeared in a white gown, in which he did not know her, so lovely was she. Not a word, not a sign that the Robbers' Roost incident had ever transpired! How was it possible for any woman to hide emotions that still could not be effaced? But Jim paid mute tribute to the nerve and poise of these English. As soon as they learned the West they would fit into it, and by their character and work make it better.

Helen came in to breakfast attired in the riding-habit she had worn on that never-to-be-forgotten day of their last ride. She was cool, sweet, and her eyes were audacious. The thrill that enveloped Jim's frame seemed equivalent to a collapse of bone and muscle structure.

"By Jove!" exclaimed Herrick. "If I were you, I'd never want to ride again."

After greeting her, Jim could only look his admiration and wonder.

"I am taking up my ranch life where it left off—with reservations from sad experience," replied Helen, as she took her seat. "Bernie, we had to trade Jim's horse, Bay. What can he ride today?"

"He may take his choice. There are any number of good beasts."

"By the way, Jim, I told Tasker to follow us at once with our horses. I shall treasure that horse, Gray. A robber's horse! . . . Tasker ought to be here soon, maybe tomorrow."

Jim felt the solid earth slipping from under his feet.

"I expected to leave today," he said, casually. "But I'll wait till tomorrow. Bay is a horse I hated to part with."

"So soon!" exclaimed Helen, with dark inscrutable eyes on him.

"You are home. All is well with you. . . . I must be on my way." It seemed a forced, cold speech from a man inwardly burning.

"Bernie, could you not induce Jim to stay?" she queried.

Herrick waved a deprecatory hand, and went on with

his breakfast. She smiled at Jim as if in explanation. "Bernie has consented to let me share his ranching enterprise. I'd like to see it pay—a reasonable interest, at least. And I have rather conceived the idea that it'd be difficult, if not impossible, without you."

"Not at all," replied Jim, constrainedly.

Presently she arose. "Come, let us ride. We can discuss it better in the saddle. . . . Bernie, will you come?"

"No, thank you. I want to stow away all that money Wall returned to me," rejoined Herrick, and as Jim followed Helen out, he called after them. "Jim, look out for kidnappers!"

"Whatever did he mean by that?" ejaculated Jim as they went down the steps of the porch.

Helen laughed. "Bernie is clumsy in humor. I rather think he meant I might try Hank Hays' way with you. . . . Jim, entirely aside from my wishes, my brother wants you to stay. He needs a man he can trust—one who can see through these riders—especially one who will be feared by those with reason to fear."

Jim could not find his tongue. He was vastly concerned with this ride. After it, would he be as strong as he was now? To be near her ——

Barnes led the onslaught of ranch-hands upon Helen, and the welcome she received could not have been anything but gratifying. Helen replied to one and all, and ended with the simple statement, subtle as it was strong: "Hays made way with me to Robbers' Roost. Heeseman trailed us. There was a fight, which wiped out all of Hays' gang and most of Heeseman's. Jim killed Hays and brought me home."

Barnes gave Jim such a glance as a man might receive once in his life. "All the time I knowed it! Shore all the time!"

He did not vouchsafe what he knew and perhaps from any point of view that was superfluous.

Soon Helen was mounted. "Barnes, we will not want the hounds or any attendants today. I cannot ride far or long."

Jim got on the horse Barnes saddled for him and followed Helen, who, to his surprise, took the road back up to the ranch-house. Perhaps she had forgotten something. But when he turned the bend she was mounting the trail that led up the ridge. If there had been giants on huge steeds pulling Jim back, he still would have kept on. When they got up to the level ridge, among the pines, he trotted to catch up with her. But she kept a little ahead. Jim's thoughts locked around one astounding fact—this was the trail they had ridden down, after that encounter when he had kissed her. Sight and hearing, his sense of all around him, seemed strangely intensified. The pines whispered, the rocks had a secret voice, the sky burned blue, the white clouds sailed, the black Henrys loomed above, and the purple-gray valley deepened its colors below. There was as much presagement in the air as on the day he plunged down the slope into Robbers' Roost with the news that the enemy was upon them. But how vastly different!

Helen halted her horse under the very pine where they had stopped to listen to the hounds and cowboys racing up the ridge after the deer.

"My sense of direction seems to be all right," said Helen, turning to face him. But her flashing eyes and her pallor rendered her levity null.

"Helen, I fear it's better than your sense—of kindness, let me say. . . . Why did you bring me here?"

"Please look at my cinch," she replied, coolly.

Jim dismounted, more unsure of himself than ever in any of the many crucial moments of his career. He did not understand a woman. He could only take Helen literally.

Her saddle-cinch was all right, and he rather curtly told her so.

"Then—maybe it's my stirrup," she went on, lightly, as she removed her booted and spurred foot.

"Well, I can't *see* anything wrong with that, either. . . . Helen. . . ."

Something thudded on the ground. Her gloves and her sombrero. But they surely had not fallen. She had flung them! A wave as irresistible as the force of the sea burst over him. But he looked up, outwardly cool. And as he did, her ungloved hand went to his shoulder.

"Nothing—the matter with—your stirrup," he said, huskily.

"No. After all, it's not my cinch—nor my stirrup. . . . Jim, could any of your Western girls have done better than this?"

"Than what?"

"Than fetching you here—to this place—where it happened."

"Yes. They would have been more merciful."

"But since I love you ——"

"You are mad," he cried.

"And since I want you—presently—to behave somewhat like you did that day."

He reeled under that. The truth was almost overwhelming. The strong, earnest light of her eyes told more than her words. Her pallor had vanished. She was no longer cool.

"Jim, you might have saved me this—this abandon. But perhaps it is just as well. You are laboring under some delusion that I must dispel. . . . I want you—ask you to stay."

"If you are sure—I will stay. Only, for God's sake, don't let it be anything but—but ——"

"Love," she added. "Jim, I am sure. If I were going back to England, I would want you to go, just the same. . . . It's what you *are* that has made me love you. There need be no leveling. I lived years down in Robbers' Roost. That changed me—blew the cobwebs out of my brain. This hard, wonderful West and you are alike. I want both."

"But I am nobody. . . . I have nothing," he cried, haltingly.

"You have everything a woman needs to make her happy and keep her safe. The fact that I did not know what these things really were until lately should not be held against me."

"But it might be generosity—pity—the necessity of a woman of your kind to—to pay."

"True. It might be. Only it isn't. . . . I brought you *here*!"

Jim wrapped his arms around her, and for the reason that he was ashamed to betray the tears which blinded his eyes he buried his face in her lap, and mumbled that he would worship her to his dying breath and in the life beyond.

She ran soft ungloved hands through his hair and over his temples. "People, cities, my humdrum existence, had palled on me. I wanted romance, adventure, love. . . . Jim, I regard myself just as fortunate as you think you are. . . . Lift me off. We'll sit awhile under our pine tree. . . . Jim, hold me as you did that other time— here!"

THE END